Is America She Gone?

Is America She Gone?

BEVERLEY-ANN SCOTT

authorHOUSE®

AuthorHouse™
1663 Liberty Drive
Bloomington, IN 47403
www.authorhouse.com
Phone: 1-800-839-8640

© 2012 by Beverley-Ann Scott. All rights reserved.

No part of this book may be reproduced, stored in a retrieval system, or transmitted by any means without the written permission of the author.

This is a work of fiction. All of the characters, names, incidents, organizations, and dialogue in this novel are either the products of the author's imagination or are used fictitiously.

Published by AuthorHouse   01/17/2013

ISBN: 978-1-4772-8277-9 (sc)
ISBN: 978-1-4772-8276-2 (e)

Library of Congress Control Number: 2012919775

Any people depicted in stock imagery provided by Thinkstock are models, and such images are being used for illustrative purposes only.
Certain stock imagery © Thinkstock.

This book is printed on acid-free paper.

Because of the dynamic nature of the Internet, any web addresses or links contained in this book may have changed since publication and may no longer be valid. The views expressed in this work are solely those of the author and do not necessarily reflect the views of the publisher, and the publisher hereby disclaims any responsibility for them.

Dedications

To my mother Grace, for choosing life.

Acknowledgements

Without the help of God I cannot write and I acknowledge Him as my first assistant in this project. Producing a second book was a challenge. The expectations of readers and in fact my own expectations were higher. Thankfully however, I had the support of people who encouraged me to excel and prevented me from being too hard on myself. My mother Grace Scott, to whom this book is dedicated, has always been very good at this over the years and I thank her profusely for her invaluable contributions.

My cousin Djenessa Jean-Baptise-Joseph once again rose to the occasion with the cover artwork. For helping me to capture the Brooklyn experience, I wish to thank in particular my Aunts Carol Des Anges, and Gemma Thomas. For editing the manuscript, I thank *Catholic News* Editor June Johnston and Jeremy Johnston. I am eternally indebted to Fr. Michel de Verteuil (former Editor of *Catholic News*) who first gave me the opportunity to explore my writing ability in printed media. Thanks to Earl Lovelace and Willie Chen for their continued support.

I want to express my deepest gratitude to my siblings, Chris, Denise and Karen, my nephews, Jason, Jalen, and Jonah and my niece Princess Kathryn, whose hugs and kisses continue to encourage me. Thank you, Uncle Hugh and Aunty Betty for being the rocks on which I can stand tall and proud. Thank you all my cousins, aunts and uncles in the Scott and Thomas families, for embodying the true meaning of family. I especially wish to thank my friends Gwenneth Graham, Jeray Norman, Cheryl Quamina Baptiste, Kafi Rodney, Lenora De Verteuil, Barbara Thom and the Thom family, Sharon Walker, Christine Searwar and the Searwar family.

Because of NALIS' One Book One Community event in 2012, I was able to travel to libraries throughout Trinidad and meet many readers who enjoyed reading my first novel, *The Stolen Cascadura*. I wish to thank these readers for their support and the NALIS staff, especially the Dramatic Expressionz group for their outstanding work during this project. For giving much needed feedback, I thank Denyse Gonzales, Asha Sooklal and Melissa Ray.

To the avid readers and supporters of West Indian fiction, I wish to say that it is because of you I continue to write. Your feedback encourages me. It inspires me to push myself to new heights. Thank you for choosing to read this book. It is my hope that like its predecessor, it will not only entertain but provoke meaningful dialogue, which can help change values and perspectives throughout our twin island.

This year Trinidad and Tobago celebrates fifty years of independence. I pray that as a nation we will continue to grow and leave a legacy that future generations can be proud of.

Be blessed.

Preface

"Is America She Gone?" portrays the life experiences of a single mother who leaves Trinidad to work in the United States illegally for six months. The novel is set between Trinidad and Brooklyn, New York and debunks the myth that all immigrants are able to live a charmed life and enjoy a better standard of living in the United States.

The social impact of West Indian immigration and some of the long-term consequences for family life are examined. The phenomenon of "barrel children" and their fate in a society that suggests they be more grateful for the contents of a barrel than the presence of their parents is explored. Many West Indians have been able to preserve family and cultural values during the process of immigration but many have also abandoned cultural and family values in an effort to belong. This issue of identity disownment and redefinition continues to be a challenge to immigrants even today.

"Is America She Gone?" forces us as West Indians to examine our Caribbean identity which is as diverse as our cultural heritage. No matter where we find ourselves in the world, we create a new history every day as people of the Caribbean. It is my hope that this book will encourage all Caribbean people, and in particular those of the diaspora, to embrace their unique identities and share them with the world.

Contents

Chapter 1: Arrival in JFK 1

Chapter 2: Basement Living 9

Chapter 3: Brooklyn Summers 17

Chapter 4: Secrets, Lies and Other Half-Truths 25

Chapter 5: Learning How to "Play As If" 31

Chapter 6: The Long Island Railway 43

Chapter 7: On Carnegie Avenue 55

Chapter 8: Parental Guidance 67

Chapter 9: More Than Giving Care 77

Chapter 10: Who is Responsible? 89

Chapter 11: Sacred and Unholy Moments 101

Chapter 12: Brooklyn Party 113

Chapter 13: Antonio's Vacation 127

Chapter 14: Gun Barrel—No Barrel 135

Chapter 15: Land of Opportunity 147

Chapter 16: Something Happened 159

Chapter 17: For The Almighty Dollar 173

Chapter 18: What's Love Got To Do With It? 185
Chapter 19: One is One 197
Chapter 20: Autumn Hijackings 207
Chapter 21: Olivia Passes On 219
Chapter 22: "Just So, Just So" 233
Chapter 23: A Matter of Perspective 245
Chapter 24: Breaking The Cycle 255
Chapter 25: Life-changing Decisions 265
Chapter 26: A Long Way From Home 277
Chapter 27: Not What Was Expected 295
Chapter 28: Along Came Papa Chunks 303
Chapter 29: Home Sweet Home 313
Chapter 30: Is America She Gone? 321

CHAPTER ONE

Arrival in JFK

It was way past 11.30 p.m. and the TravelFast flight which was supposed to have arrived six hours earlier, had finally touched down at the JFK International Airport. The flight had left Trinidad at 7.30 p.m. amidst many steupses and under breath cursing from disgruntled passengers who swore they would never take another TravelFast flight in life again. Sandra was too excited to care that the flight had been delayed. In fact, were it not for the rumbling in her belly and the fact that the roti she had planned to consume on the plane had to be eaten a few hours earlier, it would not have bothered her in the least. As long as she got on the plane she knew she would be alright.

"Sandra? Sandra! We over here, gyul!"

"Oh God, oy! Patsy! Patsy, look me here," Sandra screamed causing heads to turn and eyebrows to raise in the busy arrival section of the airport. Patsy shook her head from side to side as she ran towards her thick-thighed cousin who hobbled forward in a pair of red stiletto heels, trailing a large dusty blue suitcase with a broken wheel behind her.

"Sandra girl, ah didn't make yuh out at all, at all, at all. Girl, yuh put on plenty weight," said Patsy as she placed her arms around Sandra's waist and gave her a big hug which turned into a sway from side to side.

"Well, well, look at Madam Sandra." The two examined each other from head to toe as two sisters who had not seen each other in years would. Sandra wore a pair of denim blue jeans which hugged her hips so tightly, that one was afraid to imagine how she was able to put it on. Her large bosoms seemed to be leaping out of her red, shiny, short-sleeved halter top. Her exposed arms were like huge pillows of chocolate gelatin, soft to the touch. Her gold-capped front teeth sparkled in unison with the large gold earrings and the row of bangles that adorned her arms. Sandra's hair stiffened with gel, was pulled neatly back in one, with a long glossy black extension for a ponytail.

"Gyul, I so glad you reach up here."

"Not more glad than me," Sandra replied.

"Dexter go be so happy to see yuh."

"Dem children must be so big by now. Dey mightn' even recognize me!"

"How they could forget Aunty Sandra? After all the good times down in Marabella? Nah man."

Patsy was doing her best to reassure her cousin. She knew Sandra was afraid and anxious and there was much to be anxious about, but the hardest part was over. She had managed to secure her US visa and she had finally arrived. She had finally come to America, and Patsy knew that it had been a huge step to make for the mother of two who had never traveled outside of Trinidad her whole life. It was hard for Sandra to leave Antonio and Andrea behind. Everything she did was to try to make life better for them. She tried to remind herself of that as Andrea stood crying and holding on to her at Piarco International Airport. She was crying as if she was never going to see her mother again, while Antonio stood silent and aloof. Sandra convinced herself that when she returned to Trinidad, the sacrifice she was making would be worth it.

"They young Sandra. They still in school. Is better yuh go now and sort out yuhself. Besides, the father ain't have nothing more to give yuh. Yuh have to think about them," her mother had advised. Sandra was worried that her mother already seventy would not be able to cope with the demands of raising a ten and sixteen-year-old. But Granny Maye had always been there. She had helped Sandra raise those children and she loved them like her own. Perhaps things would get better for everybody now that she had made it to the States.

"We have to take the subway. I sorry Lenny couldn't pick yuh up with the car but he have to work tonight," said Patsy in an apologetic tone as she helped Sandra with her suitcase.

"Oh gosh is me yuh know. I accustomed taking red band maxi," Sandra joked.

"Like you pack the whole of Sangre Grande in this suitcase ah what! How it so heavy?" Patsy had just noticed that the suitcase was missing a wheel and threatening to topple over.

"It was the only one ah had and ah tell mehself ah will get a better one up here nah."

"Well I hope them high heel shoes you have on hold up better than the suitcase because we have some walking to do." Patsy and Sandra both gripped the handle of the suitcase firmly and followed the red EXIT signs to the train. They looked quite a pair making their way out of the airport; weaves swinging and gold teeth shinning. The train ride to

Brooklyn would not be long and they had a great deal of catching up to do.

Earlier that morning a ten-year-old girl sulked.

"So when she coming back Andrea?"

"I doh know. She say she will send fuh meh if she get she papers sort out to stay longer," the soft-spoken girl replied. Andrea was twirling a piece of wax paper between her dark fingers as she stared down at the black pitch floor that was the courtyard of her primary school.

"So when she getting she papers sort out?"

"Ah doh know? Stop asking me so much ah questions. Ah done tell yuh already that ah doh know."

Andrea was sullen-faced as she discussed her mother's departure with Judith. She tightened the yellow ribbon that held her short corn-rowed hair together. It was recess and they had just finished hustling down hot aloo pies from the school cafeteria. Andrea didn't feel like talking much today, but Judith was excited about the notion that Miss Sandra had gone to America. "So she going and see snow for real?" Judith asked, oblivious to Andrea's mood.

"Ah doh know but now is not snowing time in America. Now is ah think de summering time. When is Christmas time it will snow." It was difficult for Andrea to remain upset with Judith for too long. She always felt sorry for her because of her mole.

"She could send down some snow for you? Ah never see snow before yuh know."

"No Judy. It go melt in the plane. Besides she have more important things to send for me and Tony."

"Andrea, I wish I was going up in America yes."

"Me too Judy. Me too." Andrea whispered softly. In a few minutes the school bell would ring to mark the end of recess and Andrea and Judith would make their way back to class. The day would be a dull one for Andrea because, for the first time in her five years of primary school, there would be no Mommy bouncing through the door around seven o'clock with Caramel wafer bars or pone or currants rolls; no Mommy to share all the little news about what Miss did and said for the day and no Mommy to insist that she took her time and did all her homework. Tonight for the first time there would be no Mommy in the house at all and for the first time Andrea dreaded going home.

Tony, as he was fondly called, shared no similar dread. In fact he was not planning to go home at all. He knew that he had to; that Granny Maye would not allow him to be out all night, but for the first time he felt that he didn't really have to be the older more responsible one. For him it was always "Tony do this, Tony do that." When he had asked permission to pierce his ears like his cousin Martin, he received a long lecture from Granny Maye and Sandra. His father's other son had earrings in his ears, so why couldn't he? He had argued. But Sandra would not have it. Chester could allow his other "chile-mudders" to let their children run wild but her children were going to make something of themselves and ear-piercing was not the kind of birthday gift Sandra would allow her already deviant-prone son to have.

Tony knew he would miss his mother but he was too excited at the prospects of how much the American money she would be sending would allow him to "bling". It was more than that though. Now that she was gone, Tony knew he was going to have to be the man in the house and although he figured that meant a bit more responsibility than he was used to, in his mind he was sure that it also meant more freedom. His mother had always been the only boss in the house, now he could be his own boss. And although he knew that Granny Maye was now the woman in charge, he was confident that she was in no position to prevent him from doing as he pleased.

"Mama Maye. Mama Maye . . . Look a minute is Barbara here." The tall pommerac tree in the front of Granny Maye's home was laden with red, juicy pommeracs which all seemed destined to fall and join the company of the fruit flies on the already pommerac covered earth beneath the tree. The moss-laden barbed wire fence which secured the Denton property was bending away from the rusty, rotting iron poles that had attempted for over eight years to keep the wire taut.

The house itself was not very large. It was part concrete, part wood and part galvanize. Renovations over the years had been arrested at different stages, either because of a lack of funds or because of lazy workmen who somehow seemed to be constantly adjusting the estimates for the cost of materials and labor. Although the roof of the house was unpainted, the outer walls were white on one side, grey on another and tan at another end. Still it had been home for all Granny Maye's children. Those she bore and those who she had to take under her wing because nobody else could or would.

When Granny Maye's husband died, after years of suffering from a debilitating stroke, Granny Maye welcomed widow-hood almost as if it was a breath of fresh air. She was tired, and her wrinkled hands, sagging breasts, and toes curled outward from arthritis, needed her to slow down. She kept going though. She was not one to wallow in self-pity either and as long as she could get up every day and move, there was always something she felt she needed to tend to that nobody else could. With her children all gone from the nest, Granny Maye had envisioned a quiet, lonely sunset after Mr. Denton's death but then Sandra came back. Like the prodigal daughter she returned, running from blows and a controlling man whose only claim to the children she had for him was that they were his.

"Mama Maye..., Mama Maye!" The woman who stood with hands atop the unpainted crumbling wrought iron gate was getting impatient. Her voice was being drowned out by the loud barks of a mangy, flea-infested mongrel who probably imagined himself to be a Doberman in real life.

"Buster, get in the back, get in the back. Mash!" Buster wagged his half-hair and half-skin tail and sniffed the edge of Granny Maye's duster before retreating behind her promptly.

"Dat dog is something else yuh hear. When is time to bark, he ain't barking and when time to shut up he making noise," said Granny Maye as she emerged onto her shaky, wooden front porch.

"I just come to find out if Sandra reach alright," Barbara asked as she shielded her eyes from the morning sunlight so she could look up at Granny Maye. "Yes man. She reach alright. I talk to her last night. The flight was late. Yuh know TravelFast and them how they does operate. It really should name Travel Slow ... but she land good." Granny Maye pulled her duster over her chest. She did not want to give Barbara who her grandchildren had nicknamed "Miss Come to Find out", more information than was necessary.

"And how the children making out since she gone?"

"Is only yesterday she gone, yuh know. She ain't gone long. Them children doesn't study nuttin. Yuh know dese young people nowadays is a different breed ah young people." Granny Maye wanted to go back inside. She was in the middle of saying her morning prayers when Buster started the unholy barking notifying her of Barbara's presence at the gate and she desperately wanted to get back to it.

"Anyway, ah have to go yes. Ah have a pot on the fire."

"Alright then. We go pick up later."

"Right oh. You have a blessed day."

Granny Maye turned and slowly returned to her bedroom, slipping back under the sheets. For a split second she dallied with the idea of staying in bed and nursing her aches and pains, but it was only for a second. Her grandchildren needed her now more than ever. Sandra needed her too; to keep them going in the right direction or at least prevent them from going too far in the wrong direction. She sat up on her bed and looked down at her bending toes. "We have real work to do today," she said to her feet. "Real work."

Half an hour later, she eased herself off her spring mattress and planted her feet firmly in her pink, fluffy bedroom slippers. She did not know where to start to clean as she looked around her cobwebbed room, but the whistle of the kettle she had on the stove suddenly made her jump. She had forgotten all about the hot water for her morning tea.

CHAPTER TWO

Basement Living

By the time Sandra and Patsy made their way to the place Patsy called home it was after midnight. Sandra's exposed arms were unprepared for the chilly night air. Fortunately Patsy had a windbreaker which she was able to lend her cousin, even though it was too small to be buttoned up in the front. After emerging from the subway they trekked two blocks to East 23rd Street, turned left and walked past four houses before stopping.

"But gyul yuh didn't tell me yuh have a nice big house up here in Brooklyn," remarked Sandra as she marveled at the red brick attached two-storey home with well-trimmed lawn and potted pink petunias in bloom on the front stairs. The surrounding brick homes had neatly painted awnings above their front staircases. Some yards had an array of potted flowering plants with green, healthy lawns. Sandra was impressed.

"No gyul, we not upstairs yuh know, we downstairs on the side," Patsy responded with an embarrassed giggle as she pushed open a tiny wrought iron side gate and pointed the way down a short flight of narrow steps. Sandra had never seen a basement before.

"But like is a underground thing gyul?" asked an apprehensive Sandra

"Yes, is a underground thing."

"It doesn't flood and thing?" asked Sandra who was surprised and a bit disappointed that she would be living underground and not in the impressive structure above what she viewed as a hole in the ground.

"No, gyul this is not like living in Tarouba Road yuh know. Is America. They does do things properly out here." Patsy reassured her.

After struggling with the front door lock for a few seconds, Patsy finally managed to open it. Light and warm air smelling of pizza greeted them. "Good night! Finally! Hey Aunty Sandra! Welcome. Welcome," said a young man who Sandra only vaguely recognized as Patsy's son Dexter. Dexter was tall with dark, smooth skin. The six foot five almost college graduate was well built with a washboard abdomen he loved to boast of and use to his advantage when pursuing the ladies. Patsy had not seen him in almost eight years.

"Dexter, I thought you were working tonight. What happened?" asked an alarmed Patsy with an accent that sounded slightly American. Sandra had noticed that Patsy's accent would change intermittently. Sometimes she sounded American and other times she sounded Trini. She assumed that it was because she had been living in the US for almost ten years and had no choice but to adopt the American accent in order to be understood.

"Yeah Ma. I was supposed to work but then I decided to call in sick. I just don't wanna deal with my boss. He is so messed up. I just didn't feel like having to deal with him tonight," said Dexter calmly. Patsy steupsed and shook her head as she helped her cousin push her bags through the doorway.

"Well Jesus Christ of Nazareth . . . Look at my crosses! Is Dexter get so big! Boy come here and give yuh auntie a hug up!" Dexter dutifully arose from where he was seated in front the TV, set aside the pizza he was eating and walked slowly over to his Aunty Sandra in order to give her an embrace and a greasy kiss on her cheek.

"Look how dis boy get like a muscle man . . . but what trouble is dis?" She questioned with genuine disbelief.

"Girl, is all them girls what have him so with his head big like a water melon," said Patsy in a disapproving tone of voice.

"Pa-Pa, leh me watch yuh nah . . . . earring in yuh ear and . . . . wait . . . where yuh get all them tattoos boy?"

"Ask me this thing!" a frustrated Patsy responded.

"I tired telling this boy that tattoo wasn't make fuh we kinda skin. Yuh can't even make out what the thing saying on the boy skin. That is white people thing. I tired telling him that but like he want to mash up his whole skin with this stupidness name tattoo."

Dexter shook his head in the direction of his irate mother as he strode back to where he was sitting. Sandra smiled at the sight of her well-toned muscular nephew. He oozed confidence as he walked, like a male super model.

"Aunty Sandra, Ma hasn't changed one bit, always working up herself for nothing. Never mind her. Sit down and tell me how sweet T&T going," he asked as he took a large bite of the slice of pizza he was holding.

"Yuh see he, Sandra. He ain't sorry fuh his mother. He see we here with this big suitcase. You think he studying to help us?" Patsy steupsed and grumbled under her breath. She was right though. Dexter had seen his mother struggling with the faulty suitcase and had comfortably returned to the kitchen table to finish his pizza.

He eventually got up and helped his mother squeeze Sandra's suitcase through the narrow bedroom door. Sandra looked all around the tiny basement. She couldn't help but notice that despite the lack of furniture, the whole apartment seemed pretty cluttered. Two big barrels stood in one corner of the living room packed to the top with clothes, shoes and cereal. A love seat and coffee table made up the living room and there was a small television perched on a blue plastic stand. On the living room coffee table stood a dusty artificial poinsettia plant in a wicker pot. On either side of the plant were two brass-looking figurines of the Statue of Liberty. A pile of old newspapers lay under the table. Sandra pulled one out and saw that it had been folded on the classifieds section. There were several job listings circled with blue ink. She was taking it all in when Dexter returned from helping his mother and asked her again about Trinidad.

"Boy, same ole thing. Nuttin ain't changing. Prices going up. Everything more expensive. That is why ah tell mehself ah have to come up here and try and do a little work and make some change. Ah had to try something. Things too hard home and poor people ketching dey tail as always," she replied.

"Listen, girl, this here America ain't easy yuh know. Yuh does have to work damn hard. That is why I tell this boy here that he have to stop playing de arse. But he too harden. He doh listen to nuttin I tell him," said Patsy as she brought down a pair of cocktail glasses from her glass cabinet.

"Yuh want a drink? Something to eat? I have sorrel, ginger beer, Sprite, apple juice, whatever yuh feeling for." Sandra wasn't that hungry but she decided to wet her lips with the Sprite.

Dexter disappeared into the other room and emerged a few minutes later smelling of cologne with a cap on his head facing backwards. His jeans were hanging well below his waist revealing his plaid cotton boxer shorts. He wore a white vest, Tommy Hilfiger boots and had changed the earrings in both his ears.

When Patsy saw him, a heated exchanged ensued.

"Where yuh think yuh going boy?"

"I'm just going to chill out with a friend."

"How the hell yuh goin an chill out. Ah thought yuh was sick. You go ahead. When yuh see they fire yuh arse yuh go know something. Steups!"

"Why you working up yourself Ma? It's my job not yours!" Dexter shouted back. Patsy mumbled something under her breath while Dexter grabbed his windbreaker and headed for the door.

"Aunty Sandra I will see you later," he snapped as he slammed the door on his way out. Patsy set the two glasses of bubbling soda on coasters and placed them on the coffee table with a tin of salted cashew nuts. "Girl I tired talk to that boy yuh know." She released a heavy sigh. "I tired talk."

"How old he is now, twenty-one?" Sandra asked concerned.

"No, girl, he reach twenty-four already and harden as hell. He doh listen to nobody," she replied.

"Yuh know ah did think when he reach up here that that chile will make something of himself. He not stupid yuh know. Ah try to show him that in America opportunity doesn find yuh home lying down in yuh bed; that yuh have to get up and look for it. It have plenty things for him to do. I was glad he finish high school but ah tell him he coulda go further than that if he want. He had got into college but girls is what have his head tie up. He fail out his first year and we didn't have the money to send him back. I try my best with him. Here he woulda get so much help from government to finish college if he wanted. They have all kinda scholarships for fellas like him. Ah show him, ah tell him. The boy just wouldn't listen. Only studying his friends. Last year he was working in Burger King, he ain't like his boss there. He and the boss fallout and he walk off the job. Now he working Mc Donald's, is the same damn thing. He ain't like no boss, no where, no time at all. And yuh see how he playing up in he arse so, just now he gonna lose that work too."

Patsy grabbed another handful of cashew nuts and popped it in her mouth. Sandra did not know what to say. She knew how stressful it was to be a single mom and even though Patsy had her husband Lenny, Sandra knew that in reality, having a husband like Lenny was just as good as having nobody at all. She thought of her son Antonio and felt a pang of guilt. She had left him at a time when he most needed to be guided and disciplined. She wondered how Granny Maye would cope with him. She knew her mother could not deal with the teenage rebellion that she sensed he was getting ready to unleash, but what could she do.

She had to think about Andrea too. She wanted them both to go to university but she was realistic. Tony might not make it but Andrea had the potential. She wanted to give her children the best and she would receive much better pay in America for doing the same thing she was doing in Trinidad anyway. Patsy was still talking but Sandra was not listening to a single word. She had drifted on to other thoughts. The sound of an ambulance siren whirring past brought her back to what her cousin was saying.

"The work not hard. Is two old white men I taking care of and they nice, they ain't miserable. I does just feed them, bathe them, change they pamper and make sure they take their medication. That is all more or less. Dey shit does be sorf and watery but I ain't mind, because they sweet an is ah easy work and best thing of all it does pay good money. Is something so yuh want. No setta back-breaking slavery work like other places." Patsy explained.

"Well girl, yuh know me. I come up here to work so I could do whatever. I just want to get a good change so ah could send some money home and some things fuh dem children an dem," Sandra responded. The women were getting sleepy but they stayed up for another hour and a half, chatting about the good old days, their kids, Trinidad and a whole lot of things.

Patsy's daughter Diane was estranged from the family. She was living with an Italian mafia man known in the Brooklyn underworld. She was not his only woman. He had many, and she was simply one of many. All attempts to get Diane to leave him and return to the family had been futile. She was living a life of opulence as a result of illegal activities and Patsy and Lenny did not wish to be any part of that. Her gifts to the family had been returned and for the most part contact with her had been limited. Only Dexter tried to keep in touch and it was the money she gave him from time to time that allowed him the liberty to not feel like working on any given day.

By the time Sandra and Patsy got into bed it was already 3.00 a.m. Patsy slept soundly and snored loudly as always but Sandra had trouble falling asleep. She had so many questions; so many anxieties about getting a job. She had six months to make her time in America count and she did not want to waste a single day.

CHAPTER THREE

Brooklyn Summers

Brooklyn was a beautiful place to be in the summer time. The weather was warm and inviting, the air was humid and ever so often, a breeze would blow around that hot summer air to dry the sweat from bodies that had been kept indoors for too long. Flatbush and Church Avenues were alive with the bustle of the summer bargain hunters. Summer sales, lemonade with crushed ice to cool the heat, hot, sweet-smelling, honey-roasted peanuts and children who could finally play jump rope outdoors, without the need to bundle up, were everywhere. It was as if the flood gates had been opened signaling the end of many months of the cold, harsh winter, several inches of snow and ice, bulky unflattering clothes and rainy, wet springtime. Summer shouted to every man, woman and child: "Here I am. Shed your clothes. Feel my sun on your bare skin. Run, laugh, dance, sweat, for I am Summer and I love to play outside with you".

In Brooklyn, the young, the old, the obese, the skinny, the single mothers, the teenagers with taut and well-toned bodies, the seasonal joggers, the models whose belly buttons had been covered since the fall, all answered the call of Summer. Legs of every size, shape and hue, cellulite or not, donned short pants of every dimension and cut. Belly buttons peeked out from under every manner of tank top, revealing bellies of varying contours and levels of definition or lack thereof. Some belly buttons did not have to peek at all. Sweat ran down foreheads and in between breasts, on arms and legs, on tummies. Women and kids on rollerblades, boys on bicycles, old folks in wheelchairs all welcomed the summer with a collective sigh. There was definitely an excitement in the air and it was the kind of excitement that beckoned the housebound to come out on their porches and look out their windows so that they would not miss anything.

Sandra awoke the following morning to the sound of a kettle whistling. The sound reminded her of home. Patsy was up and about making a breakfast of bake and saltfish buljol. She had already made arrangements for Sandra to visit the home of a job placement agent later that day. Patsy had met the woman at a Caribbean party on at least two occasions and had been told by a friend that she specialized in getting jobs for people who came up to the US to do 'six months' work. She wanted Sandra to make the most of the time she had in the US. After freshening up, a yampie-free Sandra emerged for breakfast.

"Morning, morning, gyul."

Patsy was already sitting down with her coffee having her breakfast.

"Yes, so what is the plan for today?" she asked, almost knowing, hoping that she would hear the answer she desperately wanted to hear.

"Well, today you have an appointment with a lady name Ms. Goodridge. She is very good. She does get jobs for plenty West Indians coming up here. Just whatever she ask you, if you could do it just say 'Yes', no matter what it is. That is the key. She don't like it if yuh sound like yuh ain't know what yuh doing," Patsy explained.

"Alright, no problem. Ah think ah could manage that one."

"Yuh sure?" Patsy was not so convinced.

"Doh worry bout me," a confident Sandra responded. "Is me yuh know. I could handle anything."

"And you have to dress professional," Patsy added. She was so hopeful that Sandra would be able to work. She knew that Antonio and Andrea really needed her help. They were getting older and they needed things as all growing children do.

Around ten o'clock that morning, Patsy and Sandra headed out to meet Ms. Goodridge. She lived on Rockaway Parkway, two bus rides away from where Patsy lived. They walked on to Flatbush Avenue to catch a bus. Sandra was now able to see Brooklyn in the day time. The weather was beautiful. It was hot, not too humid and there was a sea of activity all around. Sandra was like a child, eyes moving left and right observing it all. She only imagined being in this place they call America. At last she was finally there.

"Now pay attention to where ah showing yuh because it easy to get lost out here. It not like Trinidad, yuh know. Is a big place," Patsy warned. Sandra nodded but she had no idea of exactly where she was and was terrible with directions. She could not get over how clean the place seemed and how fresh the air was. Everything somehow looked better, brighter and cleaner. There was a variety of sounds and smells all around her—Latin music, Haitian music, the smell of curry coming from a nearby roti shop. West Indian accents were everywhere. She was in awe. She followed Patsy blindly without really listening to the instructions she was receiving. She hoped she would get a job with decent people and would be able to make at least a good seven hundred dollars a week; that would be the most amount of money she had ever worked for in her life. She was busy multiplying that money by six in her head when Sandra interrupted her thoughts.

"Yuh listening to me at all!"

"Oh gosh sorry . . . Yes . . . ah was jus thinking about something," she replied.

"Listen here, it have enough time to think later . . . right now yuh have to pay attention to which way we going."

They crossed the busy intersection and walked a few yards before arriving at the bus stop. "Now yuh see the bus coming up there?" Patsy pointed in the direction of a large white bus flanked with blue stripes. "That bus is a Limited bus. That mean that it doh stop on all the stops. So doh take dat bus no time till yuh sure yuh know which part yuh going. Yuh see how de orange sign on de top say Limited?" Sandra nodded her head. She was looking at the bus as though she had never seen a bus before. Although she didn't fully understand what a Limited bus was or why it did not stop at all the stops, she registered in her head that she should never take a Limited bus. With a loud screech and a small puff of smoke, the bus that did not seem that far away came to a stop in front of Sandra and Patsy. Suddenly out of nowhere it seemed, many people were coming forward to get this Limited bus. A tall, skinny white man ran hurriedly across the street towards the bus in a pair of jeans that seemed ready to fall right off his waist and a white vest that exposed his long black under arm hairs. A little old lady who looked like seventy-something gingerly put one foot in front of the next at a labored pace as she held on firmly to a silver walker and made her way to the side of the bus. Sandra saw the blue stripes on the side of the bus, the letters MTA and the words "New York City Bus" with a number behind it. She marveled at the way the bus door opened automatically and gazed at the female bus driver whose belly folds seemed to be in combat with the restriction of the starched blue shirt she was wearing. She liked the way the bus driver said "Good morning" to each person that entered the bus and the friendly exchange of banter that occasionally ensued.

Patsy tugged on Sandra's arm and pulled her aside so the passengers leaving and entering the bus could go through. Everything seemed to happen pretty fast. Passengers got off, passengers got on, the doors closed. A young Hispanic-looking woman came running toward the bus with a small child in tow just as the bus doors closed. Sandra assumed that the bus driver would reopen the doors and allow the woman and her child on the bus but the driver simply shook her head as if to say "Too late!" and began to drive off while the woman knocked angrily on the bus door with her fists screaming "Abre la puerta! Abre la puerta!"

"Oh gorm! Yuh mean to say she couldn't open the door? She see the woman have a chile an she still gone? Oh gorm that is real wickedness!" exclaimed Sandra. She looked at Patsy in shock and disbelief.

"That is rule number one. Doh feel that if the bus driver see you running down the road that he go wait fuh you yes. Dem doesn't wait on nobody, excepting if is ah nice driver. Yuh could be banging down the door it doh matter. Once dem doors close, tell yuhself that is it. I tired get set up with that. I doesn't even bother to run down bus now. Cause dem bus driver an dem doh have you to study at all."

The disheveled Hispanic woman was visibly upset and began to mumble and curse to herself in Spanish. She yanked the little girl roughly by the arm, which led to the spontaneous onset of mouth-opened crying by the child who looked a little less than five years old. Sandra could hear the screeching brakes of another bus and soon enough, peeping around the corner of Flatbush Avenue was another blue and white MTA bus. By the time the bus came to a halt at the bus stand, Sandra and Patsy were at the head of the line, positioned for entry. "Now this is a Metro Cyard. This is what yuh have to use to get on the bus. If yuh doh have this yuh must have coins because the machine doh take no dollars." Patsy was waving the yellow and blue card in her hand while explaining everything to Sandra, who did not really appreciate the very public tutorial session. Sandra knew she had a lot to learn and it was not that she was not willing to learn, she just didn't need everybody to know that she had just arrived in America. Those passengers who were stopping off alighted from the bus and when they were through, Sandra and Patsy stepped up on to the bus adding a collective three hundred and ninety pounds to the weight on board. Patsy swiped her card twice in the slot and said 'good morning' to the driver. The ladies made their way to the first available two-seater. The pair sat sandwiched together on the bus with their fleshy, sweaty arms touching. Sandra looked out the bus window into the hair shop she had just been standing in front of. A pink neon light above the store read, "*Hair We Are*". She knew what was going to be first on her list of things to buy when she got paid. She had to change her weave.

Flatbush Avenue was like the Frederick Street of Port-of-Spain, the Regent Street of Georgetown, Guyana or the Ocean Boulevard of Kingston, Jamaica. There were stores of every imaginable size selling every possible commodity. Whatever was needed could be found on Flatbush Avenue, which Sandra soon discovered was one of the longest commercial avenues in downtown Brooklyn. Shoes, toys, clothes, hair, books, cell phones, food from every culture could be found on Flatbush Avenue. There were big name stores like T-mobile, Staples and CVS pharmacy as well on Flatbush. As the bus continued on its way, Sandra was happy to see the diversity of the people on the streets. They were not all white or black or Indian or Hispanic. There were people of every color, shape and size. She had expected to see more white people in Brooklyn. That is just how she had always imagined it in America. But Brooklyn was not all of America, just the part that she had always heard about from Patsy. Somehow seeing the diversity of people moving about, going to work, rollerblading in the streets, shopping, made her feel at home. She smiled to herself.

The Flatbush community of Brooklyn during the 1970s and early 1980s had seen an influx of immigrants from the Caribbean. Most of the immigrants were from Haiti but there were many from the islands of Trinidad and Tobago, Jamaica, Grenada, Guyana, Barbados, St. Lucia and Belize. Immigrants from India and African countries such as Ghana, Zimbabwe, Nigeria, and Kenya made their presence felt in this part of Brooklyn too. The 1990s had witnessed an increase in the size of the Hispanic population and this only added greater richness to the cultural collage. The once predominantly white, Irish, Italian and Jewish area had become an immigrant one dominated by Hispanics and West Indians, most of whom were Haitians. Many of the older Jewish and Italian families that remained in Brooklyn owned homes that had been passed on to children and grandchildren. Many of the original land and homeowners from the early 1920s and 30s had either died, or had sold their homes and moved away by the time the demographics of the Brooklyn population had begun to change, but some had remained because for them Brooklyn was home.

There were still many Orthodox Jews in Brooklyn who went to the synagogues on Fridays and wore their peyots proudly. The Italian community, though still present and well represented in business, especially in the food and restaurant industry, had dwindled in the numbers that existed in the 1980s. The last wave of Italian immigrants who came to Brooklyn in the 1960s, some unable to speak any English were much older now. They had witnessed a significant change of the area's demographics, whether they liked it or not. The older wave of immigrants had to accept that the new immigrants had added a hue to the Brooklyn community that was very different from their predecessors. Kwéyol and Spanish were the new foreign languages that dominated street corners and it was not uncommon to find Masses in the Catholic Church being said in Kwéyol or Spanish.

This was the new Brooklyn; a real melting pot. It was because of this diverse nature that many West Indians sought refuge in Brooklyn, even illegally. You see in Brooklyn it didn't matter whether you had an American accent or not. Whatever your accent was, in Brooklyn you could feel right at home.

Chapter Four

Secrets, Lies and Other Half-Truths

"Oh gosh, de way dat dog does be barking so, you would swear he ain't know who I is!" Buster it seemed simply did not like the sight of Barbara standing in front the Denton's front gate.

"Ah coming! Buster! Stop it! Stop it, Buster! Get in de back!" Granny Maye shouted as she hobbled down the unpainted front stairs.

"Dis dog ah tell yuh, like he haunted girl." Buster with tail wagging fast, was jumping excitedly at the bottom of the front step as Granny Maye approached. She opened the latch on the small wrought iron gate that kept Buster off the front steps and signaled for him to go to the back of the house. He cowed his head slightly, tail still wagging, as if hoping that Granny Maye would change her mind about vanquishing him to the backyard. "Mash ah say!" The flea-infested mongrel ran off with his tail between his legs.

"Ah bring some green pawpaw fuh yuh from de tree. Ah know how yuh like to make pawpaw ball and thing. Ah say yuh could make some fuh dem children and dem."

"Thanks, Barbs. So when yuh say Sandra coming back, Maye?"

"Next month."

She was lying. She did not want Barbara to know that Sandra had gone for more than a few weeks. Barbara was the village gossip. She was like a fly collecting food in its proboscis; gathering some news here, dropping off another set of news there and contaminating every news item with additions or subtractions from her mouth.

"So she only gone for a short time then?"

"Yes. So she say. She gone to look fuh she cousin Patsy."

"So she gone on a vacation then?"

"Well kinda. She gone to give she cousin Patsy a help out nah."

Granny Maye was eager to change the subject.

"So how yuh husband feeling dese days?" Barbara's husband was twenty years her senior and had recently been diagnosed with prostate cancer. Barbara had not shared that information with Granny Maye. It was thanks to another friendly neighbourhood 'fly' called Mrs. Brewster that Granny Maye had that information. All that Barbara had told Granny Maye and anyone who asked, was that her husband was sick with kidney problems. Perhaps it was her pride or her refusal to accept that her husband was dying but it could have easily been that her husband had forbade her to discuss his problems with anyone. Mr. Perkins, her husband was a tall, strong, virile looking seventy year old who in a matter of months had practically whittled away to a thin frame of flesh barely covering bones. No longer could he be seen striding down Evans Street, with that steady gait that belied his age. He was now confined to bed and had requested no visitors. After a three-week stay at the Sangre Grande Hospital, he had emerged a mere shadow of his former self. According to Mrs. Brewster, who had peeped out of her window to see him being carried into his home the morning of his discharge from the hospital, "he had death written all over him."

"Yes I see him good. Dey come early, early like six o'clock and thing when light now coming up. Like Barbs didn't want nobody see he nah. But when ah see how de man looking, ah shock. Ah tell mehself is only two things does bring down people small small small, fast fast fast, like that. He either get de Big C or de AIDS. One ah dem two." Mrs. Brewster had reported the news to Granny Maye almost as if it was her solemn duty to do so. Granny Maye suspected that it was cancer and this was confirmed by later reports from Mrs. Brewster.

She had liked Mr. Perkins. He was a pleasant old chap, very polite. He would never pass the Denton gate without stopping to say hello or asking after Sandra and the children. He was tall with broad shoulders, a pleasant smile and a good set of dentures. He was brown-skinned and lean with handsome features. Granny Maye imagined that he was quite a ladies' man in his youthful days. Even with aging his gentlemanliness, class and good manners shone forth. How he had managed to end up with a lady like Barbara and stay with her had baffled many women in the village who would have done many more things than Barbara had done to get some of Mr. Perkins Petrotrin pension money. The thought of Mr. Perkins laying at home in bed sick, saddened Granny Maye. She would have liked to visit him but Barbara insisted that he wanted no visitors and was always giving the impression that he was doing well and would soon be out and about once more. It had already been two months and no one had seen Mr. Perkins leave the house. Granny Maye knew that was a bad sign but as much as Barbara annoyed her, she could not bear to crush the hope Barbara bore that

Perky as he was fondly called, would somehow beat a cancer that had already metastasized to bone and lungs.

"So how Perky doing? He alright?" Granny Maye asked again.

"Yes man, he going good. Ah jus leave him home there. He was coming out yuh know but he say he want to stay inside and read de papers. Ah never see a man like papers so. Steups."

"So he eating and thing alright? Ah wanted to send a mango from de yard fuh him yuh know. Mango season finish and dry so, dry so ah see one lonely Julie mango come out on de tree in de back. Ah say but like dis mango didn't wake up in time or what! Season done finish and gone and he now come out."

Barbara and Granny Maye shared a brief laugh. It was a good laugh just enough to ease the heaviness of the conversation.

"Anyway ah keep de mango fuh Perky. Leh me give yuh before it get too ripe." Granny Maye walked slowly towards a small wooden shed in the back yard that housed yard tools, plant seeds, old cans of paint and other miscellaneous junk that was too good to throw away but not good enough to use.

"Ah keep it in de cool in de shed. So it ain't too ripe but ah don't want de owner to come and take it or bird to pick it nah. Yuh know how them birds done greedy already."

She handed the firm mango with its pretty green and dark pink speckled skin unspoilt and unbruised through the gate to Barbara. "Thanks Miss Maye. Anyway leh me make a turn eh. Jus now is lunch time and ah have to cook and all dem kinda thing. Ah go tell Perky yuh say hello."

Barbara wasn't hurrying home to do anything actually. She just did not want Granny Maye to see that her eyes were welling up with tears. She shielded her eyes from the sun as she bid her farewell. Looking down sadly at the mango, she wondered if she could make it into a purée drink for old Perky. She doubted he would be able to tolerate it. He drank clear soups for breakfast, lunch and dinner and on a good day would eat a little porridge. She would eat the mango for breakfast tomorrow morning she thought to herself. There was no point in letting a good Julie go to waste.

Chapter Five

Learning How to "Play As If"

"Now whatever she ask yuh, jus say yes. Doh do like yuh ain't know what she talking bout. Just say yuh know how, whatever it is. Is a wuk yuh looking for, right." Patsy had said the same thing at least ten times to Sandra during the half hour bus ride to Rockaway Parkway. They were going to meet Ms. Goodridge, who was the lady who got jobs for Trinis coming to Brooklyn to work for six months. While on the bus Patsy had pointed out different streets, stores, and told a few stories but everything she said had been punctuated by one constant interjection "Whatever she ask yuh jus say yes." It was like a drum roll in Sandra's head now and she was feeling a bit nervous.

They had been on the bus for almost half an hour before they arrived at their stop on Rockaway Parkway. Sandra had been observing the rhythm of the bus, the routine of the stopping, the people getting off, the passengers getting on, the beep of the metro cards and the occasional clanking of coins thrown into the coin collector. There was an order to it. There was no rushing and pushing the way she was accustomed to at City Gate in Port-of-Spain, where grown men sometimes could be seen climbing through windows in order to get into a red band maxi on a rainy day. No, it was not like that at all. The people were orderly. Those waiting to get on let those who were coming off get off before making their way on to the bus. Sandra liked that. It was so different from what she had grown used to in Trinidad. "Now when we reach dere eh, whatever she ask yuh just say 'yes' yuh know how. And fix yuh face, put on some powder. Yuh have to smile and look excited like you really want de work. Walk brisk and talk fast. Look energetic. Yuh know how some people does feel as yuh big yuh lazy so try to look lively," Patsy insisted. Sandra did not know who Patsy was calling big since they were about the same size. She wanted to comment on that but decided not to. She was too nervous. She just agreed with her and nodded her head. "Doh jus shake yuh head when yuh reach eh. Yuh have to open yuh mouth and talk." Sandra had forgotten just how bossy Patsy was. Her continued instruction was starting to get on Sandra's nerves, however she thought it best to hold her tongue at least until the interview with Ms. Goodridge was over.

Sweat trickled down Sandra's back and had started to make a wet patch on her red, sleeveless blouse. Her makeup had begun to run off her face. She pulled a pink washrag out of her handbag and began to wipe off the sweat from her forehead and with it some of the makeup.

"And we doesn't use too much ah wash rag and thing up here in America eh. Dem kinda thing doesn't look so good. Too ghetto-ish. Doh do dat when we reach by Ms. Goodridge, eh. Here take a handkerchief it more ladylike."

Patsy gave Sandra a navy blue handkerchief with a white embroidered border. Sandra could no longer hold her tongue. She knew Patsy meant well but she felt that she was going overboard with the advice. She opened her mouth to respond to the ridiculousness of what Patsy had just said but before she could say a word the bus screeched to a noisy stop. Patsy tapped her on the shoulder and began making her way to the front of the bus. A frowning Sandra followed and consoled herself with the notion that the ordeal would soon be over.

A gentle breeze kissed Sandra's face for only a few seconds as she set foot on the sidewalk. The sun had not yet reached its zenith in the sky so it was not too hot. The streets were clean and although the buildings were tall, they were still short enough to let the sun's rays find their way through. Patsy was talking a-mile-a-minute now but Sandra had zoned out. She closed her eyes for a second and enjoyed the tingle of the sun's warmth on her face. She began to daydream of Andrea and Tony. She wondered how they were doing and how they were coping. It would be different with Granny Maye now. True they were used to living with their grandmother but Granny Maye was not like her and not likely to spoil them the way she used to. She was not as worried about Andrea as she was about Tony. He had been so indifferent to her leaving. Andrea was the more sensitive child. She remembered how excited she would be to see her in the afternoon. Sandra would always bring something for them on her way home from work; whether it was custard cream cookies, sweetbread, cake or a KFC chicken meal, she liked surprising them. She enjoyed being a mother. She knew she was not always the best mother she could be and felt guilty about having to leave them for six months. She had never been away from them for so long since they were born but she believed everything would work out in the end.

"Is for their betterment and yours, Sandra." She remembered how Granny Maye had encouraged her, even though she knew it would be an additional strain on the old lady. Sandra could not let her down. She couldn't let any of them down.

"And even if is a living-in work yuh get, they must give yuh a break. They cannot have yuh working Sunday to Sunday. Yuh must get a chance away from them even if they nice but if they miserable they had better be giving yuh a chance to get the hell away from them." Patsy had not stopped talking for the entire duration of Sandra's summer reverie. Sandra was simply putting one foot in front the next as her thighs rubbed one against the other in her tight, light blue denim jeans. She was slightly knock-kneed so it seemed as though her feet were kicking outward as she walked.

"This is the place," an out-of-breath Patsy declared as she came to an abrupt halt before the stoop of what seemed to be a two-storey apartment building. The building's facade was made of red brick, neatly bordered by white painted trim in the traditional Georgian style. There were two flower-beds on either side of the stoop filled with blue asters and pink carnations. Orange, red and white gladioli stood tall beside yellow daisies and blue hydrangea. On the glass door facing them, the numbers 414 could be clearly seen in gold. Sandra liked how fancy the place looked. She looked around. Most of the area seemed pretty upscale. There were neat yards fenced in low with gardens that were even more elaborate than the one she had just seen. As they entered the building, Patsy began digging in her handbag.

"Oh gosh, doh tell me ah lose the number."

"What number?"

"Nice, look it here." Patsy said with a tone of relief.

"Now dis here is ah intercom system whey yuh does have to use to call people. Is fuh security so nobody cyah just barge in yuh place so, right. Yuh have to look fuh the apartment number on this thing here," Patsy pointed to what seemed like a dashboard with a list of numbers.

"Yuh press the number. Yuh pick up the phone and yuh talk. Ah going and show yuh now." They were standing in the foyer of the building. Another glass door which appeared locked, prevented them going in through the door.

"Look a man coming out we could go inside," said Sandra excitedly just as Patsy was about to press the apartment number on the dashboard.

"No, no, no . . . it have a proper way to do everything, Sandra. Dis is America. It have a proper way to do things. The sooner yuh know that, the better. Step aside. Let the man pass."

The elderly white gentleman made his way slowly through the door and said good morning as he did so. He was hunched over and seemed to rely heavily on his cane with every step.

"Good morning, sir."

After the man had exited the foyer Patsy resumed her lesson.

"Right, yuh press the number which is 4H and yuh wait till yuh hear de person answer . . . right."

Patsy waited till she heard the familiar voice.

"Hello," Patsy quickly reached for the handset.

"Is me, Patsy. Ah bring meh cousin fuh yuh."

"Yes, Patsy girl ah opening up fuh allyuh now."

There was a loud buzz and the glass door clicked open so that it was only slightly ajar. Sandra pushed the door open and smiled. When the two were alone in the elevator Patsy took the opportunity to give a final pep talk.

"Put on some powder, yuh face looking greasy. And smile eh; look energetic like yuh is a good worker. And whatever she ask, if yuh could do it, just say yes, even if yuh can't do it, cause yuh really want the work."

Sandra had decided that she would not complain about Patsy's tone or the never ending pedagogical sessions on what seemed to be the basics of getting around in Brooklyn. Although she knew she needed to be taught many things, she did not like the way Patsy bossed her around as though she were a little child. However she reminded herself that she was, as the old people say, "begging a lodging" and that reality meant that it would be wiser to hold her tongue until better could be done.

"Oh gosh gyul, is ah long time ah ain't see yuh." A moderately obese woman smelling of butter with fleshly arms gave Patsy a big squeeze.

"Lorna, this is meh cousin Sandra."

"Hello, Ms. Lorna. Pleasure to meet you."

"Oh gosh! What is this wid the hand shaking? Look come here gyul. Yuh is ah Trini like mehself."

Before Sandra had a chance to say much more of anything she was overwhelmed by the smell of lard and Lorna's sticky arms and soft, mammoth-size breasts.

"Right. Come and sit down here. Doh mind the place little messy and thing."

Ms. Goodridge's apartment seemed to be the exact opposite of the outer structure Sandra had just viewed. In the narrow corridor that led to the living room were magazines piled up high on wooden shelves, teetering as if they would fall over at any minute. A dust-laden bookshelf with books on art, law, interior design and numerous other hobbyist subjects stood guard outside the living room and seemed almost out of place. "Take off yuh shoes," Patsy whispered to Sandra under her breath. Sandra didn't want to remove her shoes. The living room carpet was grey and dirty-looking, matted in some areas, probably with lard, Sandra thought. Still she obliged.

"Ah coming eh. Just give me a minute. Ah have a pot on the stove here. Ah making some souse for dem boys and dem." As Ms. Goodridge entered the kitchen, Sandra could now see her full form. She wore a long, pink cotton dress that looked like a nightgown. Through it Sandra could see the outline of her white underwear. Her blue bedroom slippers were worn and as she looked at Ms. Goodridge's feet she could see that they were actually the largest part of her. Elephantiasis. She had seen it before only a few times back home. It would explain the hobbling and the unsteady gait of her soon-to-be employer. "Leh me get meh diary."

Ms. Goodridge returned with diary in hand and entered the living room. As she passed between the two ladies seated quietly on the couch Sandra got a whiff of a different odour she could not quite identify. All she knew was that the smell made her feel sick. Ms. Goodridge sat with a heave on the living room love seat and pulled her red and brown head-tie off her head revealing significant alopecia and interspersed tufts of black curly hair no longer than an inch.

"Whew! It making hot in here today," she started, as she began to flip through the pages of her diary.

"So allyuh alright? No trouble finding the place, right?"

"Not at all," they chanted in chorus.

"So Sandra, what you could do gyul?" Lorna stopped on a page in her diary and looked up from beneath her spectacles.

"Well she could do anything and everything. She could cook, clean, wash wares, iron, mind baby an . . . ."

"Ah was asking Sandra. Ent she could talk for she self?" Ms. Goodridge said with a voice that sounded almost stern.

"Well jus like Patsy say," said Sandra nervously.

"Ah could cook and clean, wash wares, iron clothes. Ah very good wid children. Ah very good wid ole people. As a matter of fact ah was taking care of meh mudder back in Trinidad. Ah is a very hard worker and if is one thing ah know to do is to wuk an ah really need a wuk." Sandra knew Granny Maye was not the kind of elderly person who needed taking care of but she would say whatever she needed to if it would ensure that she would leave Ms. Goodridge's apartment with a job that morning.

"Hmm . . . . Nice."

Ms. Goodridge studied Sandra's face. Sandra sat upright on the pale yellow sofa, with her legs crossed and her hands clasped firmly. She was trying to look as enthusiastic as she possibly could. She didn't know if to smile or if to keep a straight face but opted instead to raise her eyebrows and look directly at Ms. Goodridge with a sort of half smile.

"Yuh have children?"

"Yes, two. A boy and a gyul."

"Hmmm . . . ." Ms. Goodridge began flipping through her diary then stopped after a couple of pages. There was a deafening silence in the living room, which made Patsy uncomfortable.

"Listen, this gyul could do basically anything," said Patsy with a nervous laugh. She slapped her hand on Sandra's thigh. "Ah know Sandra from small so," she gesticulated with her other hand marking the air about two feet off the ground. "She honest, she does work hard, she doesn't lie nor tief. If she get a work, is like I get a work. Ah could close meh eyes and promise yuh that."

Patsy did not like the silence. She was hoping Sandra would have kept talking, extolling her good qualities, selling herself. Instead she just sat there smiling.

Patsy felt she needed to intervene.

"Hmm . . . . Ah have something. Ah not sure yuh will like it."

"Whatever it is she will like it. Ah promise yuh that."

"Well let her be the judge of that."

"Ah will like it." Sandra promptly responded.

"Everybody does say that at first. Then one month down the road is one setta story bout the work too hard and the people not nice and all kinda thing."

"Nah, nah, nah! We not so at all. We is people of we word. Lorna, ent yuh know how I is?" Patsy did not like the fact that she had to do so much speaking. She wanted Lorna to get to the damn point instead of all this pussyfooting.

"Well, is some ole women up in Long Island. Two sisters. One have sugar the next one have pressure. Is something so. The one that have sugar going blind in one eye but the next eye good as ever and both ah dem mouth not easy but they is nice people and the pay good. Five hundred dollars a week." Sandra could not believe her ears.

"Is living-in of course. Working Monday to Friday with weekends off. The last gyul ah send up there she work two days and she fire the wuk. But is a young gyul that lazy since she small. Ah was just trying to give she and the mother a help out but it ain't work out and I ain't take her for no other work. That is one thing wid me. If yuh do bad on a wuk it ain't have no more wuk for yuh to get wid me. So that gyul lose out bad, bad, bad. Imagine, five hundred dollars a week. Hmmm." Lorna shook her head in disappointment.

"But these sisters is nice people. They ole but they sweet."

Lorna let out a loud sigh and removed her spectacles.

"So how that sounding to you, Sandra?" Lorna asked.

"Sounding good to me."

"And me too," Patsy chirped in.

"Alright ah like that attitude. That is the problem wid the young people today. They have too much of bad attitude. Anyway, so yuh think yuh could take on a work like that?"

"But of course. Ah could start from today self."

"Well nice. Today is Tuesday. Sort out yuhself fuh Monday. Not this Monday coming, the next one. Yuh have to sign some papers and thing today and ah will give yuh the address and directions wid the phone number. The place not hard to find at all. Good. So yuh will start Monday right?" Ms. Goodridge seemed to be asking as if she were not quite sure that Sandra had said yes.

"Of course!"

"Alright, well come by so and sign up some papers then yuh will tell me what going on in sweet T&T."

Sandra would have signed away her life that day so happy was she at the thought of working for US $500 a week. That was TT$3,000 a week if you multiplied by six and TT $12,000 dollars a month if you multiplied the weekly figure by four. She was so excited that she didn't bother to read the documents Ms. Goodridge gave her to sign in the narrow corridor that day. She simply thought she was signing a job contract. All she remembered was that she had signed in three places and that Patsy could not contain her jubilation on their way home.

Ms. Goodridge breathed a sigh of relief after the pair left her home. She was tired of Trinis coming to America trying to get things for free and tired of doing favours for a friend of a friend from Trinidad. There were many significant details that taking care of the two sisters involved, which Ms. Goodridge had not verbalized but she didn't care. She knew Sandra would never last one month with those two witches. She could tell this from the look of excitedness on her face and the way she signed the papers without reading a single line or asking a single question. Yes, in her twenty years in Brooklyn Ms. Goodridge had seen it all. She loved money and she hated fools, especially Trinis who felt they could get something for nothing from her just because she was a Trini. She was tired of it.

"This is America and yuh believe people still coming up here stupid, stupid yuh know!" she would tell her husband later that night.

"Like they doh know this is America ah what. Nothing is fuh free."

CHAPTER SIX

The Long Island Railway

Patsy had hoped for somewhere closer than Long Island. It was not that she wasn't happy that Sandra had got a job, it was just that working in Long Island meant taking the Long Island Railway. It also meant that Sandra would not be a bus ride away from home. Still she was grateful. Times were hard. Something, no matter how small, was still better than nothing at all and it was certainly a hell of a lot better than anything she could ever get in Trinidad for sure.

Joan and Olivia Englefield lived in an apartment complex on Carnegie Avenue, Huntington, Long Island. Most of the inhabitants of the complex were old, wealthy and ill. Some were Irish, some Jewish, some Polish. The Englefield sisters were from a large family of British ancestry. They had outlived their five brothers and were the only two left. They had never married or had children just as their aunts before them. Their nieces and nephews were all grown and for the most part did not keep in touch. All they had were each other.

Olivia was eighty-five. She had diabetes and hypertension and was blind in one eye. Olivia also had Alzheimer's disease, a most pertinent fact Ms. Goodridge had failed to mention. She had no teeth in her mouth and ate soft foods like porridge and pudding; anything that could bump between her two gums and slither down her feeble throat. Joan was healthier and older by one year. She became bed-ridden after suffering a broken hip two years prior. Her caretaker said she fell but Ms. Goodridge suspected that she had been pushed. The hip had healed but she would not use it. She was no quiet one though. She chattered incessantly and was always going on about the thieves that kept taking her money and the men that kept coming in her room at night to touch her. Her last caregiver was from Guyana. Ms. Goodridge said the woman called her out of the blue one day and said she quit. It sounded highly suspicious to Patsy.

"People lazy. They come up here looking for work. When you get something for them, they never satisfy. Always want things easy. This is America! Yuh ain't see how everybody always hustling and running around on the train going here, going there. Is money they trying to make! Yuh can't live in this America without money and you don't get money just so, just so," Ms. Goodridge had told them.

On a sweaty summer morning that was too selfish to let a breeze blow long enough to cool the heat, Sandra and Patsy made their way to Penn Station.

"Now you following the directions so far, right?"

"Yes." Sandra lied.

"I could only go with yuh up to Penn Station. After that yuh on yuh own. Call me when yuh reach so I know yuh reach alright and yuh ain't lose, alright?"

"I will reach doh frighten."

"After that don't call me on that phone unless is an emergency. Turn it off yuh hear me. Here in America they always looking to find a way to get money outta unsuspecting people who don't know. That is ah emergency phone. Don't call nobody but me wid that phone yuh hear me?"

Patsy was happy and afraid at the same time for Sandra. She reached into her bag and gave her the crumpled piece of paper with the directions and the address scribbled on it.

They were standing on the pavement outside Penn Station. It was rush hour. New Yorkers on left and right, stone faced, walked briskly in every direction. Two white men in suits tried to run through the pedestrian gridlock on their way to catch a train perhaps and bounced into a young woman almost knocking her over.

"Hey watch where you're going you jerk!" she yelled, but they had already disappeared into the maze of bodies moving as fast and as frenzied as ants trying to move a parcel of food back to the anthill.

Sirens blared while yellow cabs moved up and down the street. The traffic light changed, allowing pedestrians to cross and Sandra watched as an entire army of people seemed to cross the street leaving behind a second batch that had not been able to cross in time.

"And hold on to yuh purse. Don't trust nobody. It have a lot of crooks out here. Trust me, I know. And treat the people nice, even if they have little bad ways and thing eh .... Don't show no bad face. Even though yuh might be grinding inside put on a sweet smile so they wouldn't have nothing bad to say and ...."

Suddenly Patsy realized that Sandra really wasn't listening to her at all. Although she was nodding in agreement, her eyes were roving all about.

"Sandra! Watch me. Watch me in meh eye."

Patsy's change of tone somehow re-focused her.

"Just do yuh best, alright. I know yuh wouldn make me shame."

Patsy hugged her tight for all of two seconds.

"Ah have to go. Ah will be late for work, alright. Call me when yuh reach, alright, but turn off the phone after that, alright."

Patsy knew that there was not much more she could say to Sandra. She knew that she would learn many things on her own. She knew that it would be a while before she wised up to the ways of life in America. She could not shield her from everything. Patsy joined the march of workers on their way to work and soon disappeared in the crowd. Sandra turned and made her way into the chaos and noise that was Penn Station. It was eight o'clock.

That morning Andrea woke up sick and Granny Maye was forced to keep her home from school.

"What's the matter darling? Yuh belly hurting?"

The ten year-old just moaned and groaned and rolled in her bed. The night before she had said she was feeling weak but Granny Maye thought nothing off it. She touched the child's forehead with the back of her hand and quickly pulled it back. "Roasting fever! Good Lord. What is this?"

She didn't expect an answer really. It was just her way of bemoaning the fact that the girl was indeed sick with something. With some haste she put the kettle on the fire and looked to the clothesline in the back of the kitchen where, prominently displayed were several orange peels long and gnarly looking, brown and dried. She dragged off one of the rinds about one foot long and placed it in a pot. Still in her nightgown, she opened the wooden back door and looked in the direction of her vegetable garden. She was trying to remember if she still had carpenter grass somewhere in that patch of bush.

"Of all the days for this girl to get sick," she mumbled to herself.

"Maybe she missing the mother too much," was the explanation Barbara had offered her later that morning when she came by her usual news gathering route.

"And what about Sandra? She call yuh?"

"No. Not since the first call when she reach up."

"But why that girl cyah call you yet? Is two weeks now not so? Phone card cheap in America. I find she could damn well get a phone card and let you know she alright or something."

"Well you know no news is good news, as they say. Maybe she just busy."

"Busy my eye!" Barbara said under her breath.

"Well, anyway, let me check on this child. I gone, Barbs."

Granny Maye was simply tired of the nettling hen that was her friend Barbara. Granny Maye needed Barbara as much as she despised her. Because of her, Granny Maye was able to keep abreast of all the goings-ons in the small Evans Street community. Besides, Barbara was a good person to know if you wanted to get a drain cleaned or a burst water line repaired, or a fire truck to pump water out your house when it was rainy season and your house got flooded out. Mr. Perkins had strong connections in the Regional Corporation and although he was now ailing, Barbara made sure to remind those connections of the many ways they owed her husband.

As she walked up the back step Granny Maye pondered Barbara's words. Why hadn't Sandra called? It was two weeks already. She knew she had got there safe but what if she was in trouble? She would have called if she was in trouble. She would have said so. But what if it was the kind of trouble that you couldn't get a call home? Hmmm... Granny Maye's mind was racing with possibilities. She would get a phone card and call Patsy today. That would be the only way to curb her anxiety. She hoped Sandra was all right but most of all she hoped she had got a job. Money was tight and her little pension was not enough to take care of Andrea and Antonio.

Sandra had managed to join a line for ticket purchases and get a ticket to Huntington Station on the Long Island Railway. She had forgotten to ask the attendant in the vending booth where she could board the train and her attempt at stopping people to ask for directions was a real eye-opener. She had first tapped an elderly, white gentleman on the arm and didn't get a chance to get a word out because by the time he turned and looked at her, his face, full of fear, was transformed to an even ghastlier white. It was as if she had done something dreadfully wrong by touching him. He pouted and walked off without saying a word.

In the melée that was Penn Station on a Monday morning during rush hour, Patsy eventually made it to the ticket barriers below the sign that read: "Long Island Railway", with an arrow pointing right. She paused and observed what other people were doing with their tickets in order to get through the barriers. She tried not to stare or appear confused so that it wouldn't be obvious to anyone that she had never taken a train before. She pulled her train ticket from her jeans pocket and approached the ticket barrier with confidence and did as she had seen everyone else doing. She looked for the slot and placed her ticket inside it but the silver barrier like a three-pronged sword did not move and she heard a funny beeping noise. A tiny, red light appeared where others before had seen green.

"Jesus!" A man behind her fumed and moved to another ticket barrier. Sandra panicked. What if something was wrong with the ticket? She pulled it out the slot quickly and looked at it puzzled as if she were expecting to find something out of place on it.

"Just turn it over."

The voice did not have an American accent. A light, brown hand with polished nails reached forward, held Sandra's hand and placed the ticket in the slot. Sandra turned to see the smile of a young East Indian woman.

"Doh watch me. Go through!"

Sandra held the silver bar that met her at her hips and pushed it down. It was cold but it moved under her hand allowing her through the barrier.

She waited for the kind stranger to come through.

"Oh gosh, thanks so much."

"Is no problem. Where yuh going?"

"Huntington Station. Is my first time taking . . . . going to Long Island and I not from here I from . . . ."

"Shhh. Follow me. I am heading that way," the woman said softly as if they were about to embark on a top-secret military operation. Sandra followed the sweet-smelling woman as she moved stealthily and quickly. She struggled to keep up. There was a sea of commuters; walking, running, talking loudly on cell phones. Everyone seemed busy and in a hurry to go somewhere to do something. Over a loud speaker which Sandra did not see, a man's voice made the announcement.

"Attention all passengers. The Long Island Railway heading to Port Jefferson will depart in approximately five minutes."

The woman's footsteps quickened and so did Sandra's who could feel the sweat running down her inner thighs as they rubbed together. Like a snake in the jungle, the angel she had met moved swiftly and adeptly through the crowd and finally stepped up on to the cool air-conditioned train. The woman paused as her eyes moved in search of two empty seats. Sandra was panting by the time they sat down. The woman turned to her as if it was finally safe to speak.

"Yuh alright. We almost didn't catch the train."

"Whew. I . . . alright yuh know . . . . just sometimes ah does get a little short breath . . . ."

Sandra was speaking in short phrases as she wiped her forehead and neck with a handkerchief and caught her breath.

"Where you from? St. Lucia?"

"No. I from Trinidad. Is meh first time up here. Ah going to a work in Huntington for some people. Where you from?"

"I from Gee-yanna. My name is Lindy." She stretched out her hand for a proper handshake.

"What kinda work you going to do?"

"Ah have to take care of some old ladies. Is meh first day going there. Ah have the address here." Fumbling through her handbag Sandra pulled out the crumpled piece of paper and showed it to Lindy.

"Nice area."

"Yuh know where it is? Yuh ever work there?"

"No," she said coldly. "But I know the area."

"So how long you in New York?"

"Well is meh first time up here. I jus here for six months then ah going back home."

"So yuh don't have papers?"

"No. You?"

"Domestic work is hard work. I did it before but now I don't have to work as hard," said Lindy looking out the window as the train began to move.

"So you do this kind of work before? How it is? Up here ah mean? Ah mean I take care of my mother when she was sick but that was home in Trinidad. Ah doh know how it is up here in America nah."

"Pretty much the same. You have to have your wits about you. You have to know how to say yes when you really want to say no. You have kids?"

"Yes, two. A boy and a girl but they back home in Trinidad. You up here a long time?"

"Long enough. What's your phone number?"

"Ah have it here." Sandra dug through her big, brown handbag once more for an ever-important piece of paper.

Lindy pulled out her cell phone and with a few swift finger movements saved the number.

"So you have family from Trinidad up here?"

"Yes. Meh cousin. Her whole family living in Brooklyn," said Sandra proudly.

"Nice." Lindy didn't seem impressed.

They continued in silence for a few minutes. Lindy looked out at rooftops going past, trees, graffiti painted walls, electricity poles, and the bodegas of Jamaica, Queens. Sandra looked out too, over the jet-black strands of hair of this Guyanese woman seated beside her. She was a fellow West Indian like herself trying to make a living in New York City. With each stop of the train Lindy seemed to be paying attention to the people getting on and those getting off, almost as if she were making mental notes. Sandra could smell her. She smelt like lavender or one of Granny Maye's old Fabergé colognes. She wore a face powder that was one shade too light for her brown complexion with bright red lipstick. It made her look older than she actually was. The brief silence was too deafening for Sandra.

"So where yuh working? In Huntington too?"

"Thereabouts."

"I so nervous eh. Today is meh first day on the job. Ah supposed to meet the lady who had the job before me for her to tell me what ah need to know. Ah never look after white people before."

"Are they Jewish?"

"No. Well ah doh think so."

"Good. Then you won't have to worry about kosher and cutlery."

"Kosha? What is that?"

Lindy turned to her with a look of annoyance.

"Let me tell you something, Sandra. You in America now. I don't know what yuh cousin tell you but out here you have to be smart. You can't ask too many questions otherwise people will think you don't know. You can't trust people too easily either. This is the land of schemers and schemes and dreamers and dreams. If you not careful a good schemer could work a scheme on you and then its goodbye to you and all your dreams. You have to pay attention all the time and always have your wits about you. Never let down your guard."

Sandra didn't like Lindy's tone. It reminded her too much of Patsy. She was sick and tired of hearing people talk about America as if it was this dreadfully terrible place. If it was so terrible, how come everybody seemed to want to come here?

"I'm a big woman you know. I know how to handle myself."

"Oh really. I took one look at you this morning and I knew you were fresh off the boat. Now, how do you think I knew that?"

"I doh know but I ain't stupid. Nobody could pull any wool over my eye jus so jus so."

"I'm just saying don't trust people so easy. You came with me because I helped you get through the ticket barrier but I could have been setting a trap for you."

"Well ah realize you is a West Indian like me so ah know you wouldn't do that."

"Don't be so sure. You don't know me, or what I would and wouldn't do. West Indians ripping off each other up here all the time."

There was a moment of silence as Sandra thought on what Lindy had just said.

"Anyway, my stop coming up just now. Yours is the one after. I hope you get through with your job."

"Thanks and you too. Where did you say you worked again?"

"I didn't say."

The train came to a screeching stop at Cold Spring Harbor.

"Oh and here's your phone. Don't ever come on the train with an unzipped handbag."

Lindy reached in her jacket pocket and returned to Sandra the new Nokia cell phone that Patsy had given her just that morning.

"How you? . . . . When you?" Sandra was perplexed.

"I'll call you. And next time, don't talk so much to people you meet in the train station. It's not safe."

The skinny woman, like a wisp of hair was bounding out the train doors before Sandra could say much more. The doors slammed shut as Sandra waved goodbye. Lindy did not look back. Soon the train began to move again and Sandra looked out the window to see if she would catch a glimpse of the mysterious woman. She was grateful that she had made a friend but was alarmed by the fact that Lindy's advice sounded pretty much like Patsy's. America was the land of milk and honey after all.

Both Patsy and Lindy made it seem as though she was in the middle of some sort of war zone instead, like Afghanistan, with predators lurking at every turn. She would tell Patsy about Lindy. She didn't know much about her. In fact Sandra didn't realize that Lindy hadn't shared much about herself at all. She knew that Lindy was from Guyana and that she had got off at Cold Spring Harbor. She knew she used to do domestic work before but not much else. Still she liked Lindy. She had met a good person in New York, she thought to herself. She just hoped that the Englefields' were as kind as Lindy had been.

CHAPTER SEVEN

On Carnegie Avenue

By the time Sandra arrived at the Carnegie Avenue apartment complex it was almost ten o' clock. She had taken a cab just as Patsy had told her to. It cost her fifteen dollars. The next time, she vowed, she would find a way to take the bus. That was just too much to pay to get to work and she hadn't even collected her first pay cheque.

"Two forty-one, two forty-three, two forty-five ... This must be it."

Sandra looked up at the fifteen-storey red, brick building to her right. There were four buildings actually, cordoned off with continuous black wrought iron fencing interrupted by red brick posts. The fences were lined with neatly landscaped troughs, filled with flowering plants and other perennials. There were purple asters, yellow zinnias, white hydrangeas and pink bearded irises shooting up like arrows. Beneath a huge Southern Magnolia tree was a crisp carpet of vinca vine, hemmed in by a border of grey-brown fieldstones stacked one on top the other about ten inches high.

"Good morning ma'am. May I help you?"

"Yes, I am here to the Englefield residence."

"Are they expecting you?" the security guard asked.

"Yes. I'm a bit late," she said looking nervously at her watch.

"Hold a moment please."

Lindy was right Sandra thought, the area did look posh.

"Yes, ma'am. Go right on through to the lobby. You can take the elevator. They are on the eighth floor."

"Alright. Thanks."

"Not a problem. You have a good day."

A young white couple entered the elevator with her. They were laughing and chatting arm in arm. They were also heading to the eighth floor. The woman was blonde, early twenties. She wore a blue silk blouse and a grey flannel pants. Sandra examined her, head to toe, and felt somewhat inappropriately dressed in her faded jeans and long green tee-shirt. She looked at the pair of sneakers she was wearing. They could use a good cleaning. On the eighth floor the elevator doors opened. The couple stepped out and turned left. Sandra decided to turn right. She could feel her heart pounding in her chest as she pressed the Englefield buzzer. She listened anxiously to footsteps growing louder as they came towards the door and stood with bated breath as the chain then the lock, clanked open.

"Morning. You is Sandra?"

"Yes."

"Steups!" the much shorter, heavy-set woman turned her back and walked briskly inside. Her name was Janet Winters. She had a short Afro, low and neat.

"Come. Yuh know how blasted long I waiting for you. What time they tell you to come for not six o'clock?"

"No they said . . ."

"Anyway, come quick. I jus glad to get outta dis blasted wuk. Thank God it was jus a temp thing." The woman made a beeline for the bedroom, moving swiftly past the spacious living room area, down a wide corridor. She opened a bedroom door without knocking. Sandra got a blast of the scent of pee as they entered the room.

"Ms. Joan. Ms. Olivia. This is Sandra. She come to take care of you from now on alright."

"What?"

"I say. This is Ms. Sandra she going to take care of you from now on."

"What did you say? Speak up now."

"Look. All their medication to take on that dresser right there," the exasperated woman whispered to Sandra.

"The medication in the fridge is for diabetes for Olivia and she have eye drops there too that you will give her in the night."

"I don't like the way you speak to me, Janet. I don't like your tone. And I think its time I get a bath because I have to go out this afternoon and I need to be ready," said the grey-haired lady seated in her nightgown at the end of the bed.

"Alright, Ms. Joan. Not to worry. Ms. Sandra here will get you ready. Alright."

"What? What did you say?"

"Come, Sandra."

Ms. Winters left the room and closed the door behind her.

"This is your room here. It's right next door to theirs so you can listen out for when they calling. And trust me, they always calling."

Sandra looked at the large queen size bed and was grateful the room had a television.

"Now in the day you could keep their door closed, but in the night keep it open. Because night time is your busiest time, especially with Olivia. Well sometimes both of them."

"Alright. So what about meals."

"Right. Let me show you in the kitchen."

Ms. Winters hurried back down the corridor, past the living room into the kitchen.

She gripped the shiny, silver door handles of the stainless steel refrigerator and opened it.

"So Olivia ain't have no teeth so everything she getting must be sorf. And she on a special diet because of the sugar and the pressure and so on. So everything for her have to be sorf sorf sorf cause she ain't got no teeth in she mouth. I have containers here with her food for the week. You see. Everything marked." She pulled a container off the shelf.

"O is for Olivia and J is for Joan. They don't eat much but Joan could eat meat and things like that. Sometimes you have to feed Joan but sometimes she will eat for herself but you always have to feed Olivia cause she can't see with one eye. It easy you know. Everything straightforward. The hardest part is dealing with them witches when they start to act up."

"That's alright I accustomed with old people."

Ms. Winters chuckled. "Not these kinda old people."

"Anyway this cupboard here has all the groceries and the adult briefs. Always wear gloves when you changing them and do it fast because Olivia likes to act up whenever you take off her panty and she will bawl and scream like a cow . . . like you killing her. Just stay calm."

"Okay."

"This is my number. Call me if you have a question," said Ms. Winters as she gathered a few bags she had on the floor in the foyer.

"Ronaldo comes by once a week to take them for some fresh air. Nice fellow. You will like him. You will give him the list of groceries and things you need and he will get everything for you but make sure you make a thorough list because he only goes once a week. Don't worry you will be just fine."

"Yes I think so . . . . What was your name again?"

"Janet. Listen I hate to leave like this but I have to go. I hope you have a good time with them. Better than mine."

"I'll try."

"This is the key. Don't open the door for anybody except Ronaldo and well Mr. Bell. I'll tell him on the way out that you are the new lady."

"Mr. Bell?"

"Yes. The porter, tall, dark, handsome fellow? You didn't see him on the way up?"

"No."

"Well, not to worry, you will meet him eventually."

"Ms. Winters. What about weekends?"

"Oh I forgot. Well you leave Friday night when the temp comes and come back by Monday morning or Sunday night according to how you want to work it out."

"So it have somebody who does come on weekends then. That is good. What is her name?"

"Oh its different people all the time. By the time you get used to one face there's another new face. It's a well-run service. Ms. Goodridge didn't tell you?"

"Tell me what?"

Ms.Winters chuckled again.

"Ah, that Lorna," Ms. Winters said as she held on to the brass doorknob.

"Well, Sandra. Good luck. I'm sure you will do fine." The woman smiled as she turned to go. Sandra locked the door behind her and hooked the security chain to its track. She felt a sense of relief. She had made it.

Slowly she surveyed the Englefield apartment. It was nothing like Patsy's basement home. Air and light filled the living room which was clearly demarcated by a three-piece black leather sofa set, love seat and lazy-boy with ottoman. To the right of the sofa was a wide fireplace and above it a mantle with pictures; one of a blue-eyed smiling baby, another family of five, then a young couple, then an older couple. Above the mantle, placed right into the wall was a large forty-inch flat screen TV. On the living room floor, a delicate multi-coloured rug formed an intricate tapestry. It was partially hidden by the Victorian-style oak coffee table, adorned with a large ceramic bowl of fruit. A glass sliding door led onto a small porch where two wicker rocking chairs stood like a pair of old guards keeping watch.

The drawn curtains seemed to welcome the light into the room. They were a pale yellow with a brown floral pattern. Sandra ran her fingers along them. They were heavy, laden with dust. In fact the whole place had a musty, dusty feel to it. Even the bowl of fruit was dusty. Sandra was eager to set her things down in her bedroom and make herself at home. In her Macy's shopping bag, she had packed everything she thought she would need for the week; toothbrush, toothpaste, underwear, painkillers, Bay Rum for if she got sick, soap, towel, washrag and a nightie. She unpacked her things in the wooden chest of drawers. The drawers had the smell of mould. Her room was not big but it was air-conditioned and there was a television. She changed her clothes and hit her bed a few slaps to see just how strong it was. When she sat on it, it made a squeaking noise. Then she crawled up to the pillows and let them caress her cheeks. She closed her eyes and inhaled the smell of hair grease, probably from Ms.

Winters. Sandra didn't care. She held the grease-stained pillow to her chest and thought of home.

She wondered how Antonio and Andrea were doing and how Granny Maye was coping in her absence. She transported herself home to Evans Street and in her mind listened for the bark of that mongrel Buster, tail wagging and mouth slobbering with saliva as he came down the back step. She felt Andrea's corn-rowed head resting gently on her belly; the way she would rest it when she sneaked into her bedroom in the morning to wake her up for work. She remembered the sound of Granny Maye's footsteps in the kitchen as she put the kettle of water to boil on the stove. She recalled the anger in Antonio's voice, the time she told him that he could not pierce his ears.

He had shouted at her. He had raised his voice as if he wanted to let her know that he was no longer a boy. That he was becoming a man. He shouted at her as if she did not understand that there comes a time when a boy looks at his mother and wonders where his father is and why a woman must teach him the things that a man ought to. A time when a boy becomes angry that there isn't a man to show him how to be a man in the world or help him understand that he cannot always yield to the surging of his loins. There is no father to show him how to treat a lady, how to care for her. Instead, there is this woman that is his mother, who cannot understand what it is like to be young and to feel all the emotions that young men feel. A woman who cannot understand what it means to have the respect of other men, or what it takes to earn that, or how it feels to be accepted or to belong. And so the boy is angry, at God, at the world and at his father who lives with another woman—not his mother. And even though he does not know that that father is not a father to his children by that woman either, the boy is jealous and angry. Who to blame for that? Only the woman who loves him, who has tried so hard to be both mother and father and to show him the right way in life. You see, in his juvenile mind, still undeveloped, his mother lacks what that other woman has. He doesn't know what it is she lacks, all he knows is that she lacks that which his father needs, because if she had it, his father would be there. Sandra lay on her soft spring mattress and held that feather pillow tight and thought of Antonio and all the things she wished she could have done for him if only she had the money. She missed him. She missed her family.

Her thoughts were interrupted by a loud thud. A shrill cry followed. She jumped off the bed and headed to her charges.

"Eh horse. Whaz de scene?"

"I good. Jus cool."

Antonio and Martin greeted each other with a friendly bounce of closed fists as they sat down on a concrete bench on the Brian Lara Promenade. The promenade was alive and bustling. It was a fortnight payday and it was a Friday. The banks were crowded and there were people everywhere; old men playing checkers or dominoes sat around the concrete tables on the promenade, while teenage boys "breaking biche" in school uniform could be seen getting snow-cones and hotdogs for lunch in preparation for an evening of mischief. It was not uncommon to see men walking on the promenade with cold beers in hand on any day of the week, but today was fortnight Friday and men with money needed to spend some of it on alcohol of some sort.

There were lots of women on the promenade too. There were the older women who sat alongside the men liming or playing dominoes. They watched their men like hawks in order to prevent them from gambling or drinking away whatever little income their fortnightly work had yielded. Then there were those women who were not so bashful. Unprepared to wait for money to be graciously given to them, they found their men and took their pound of flesh. Whether it was at the exit to the bank after cheques were cashed, at the entrance to the rum shop, or at the gambling spots, they found their men; some even skillfully carrying along the small children that had been fathered by said men as a potent reminder about where their fortnightly salaries should be directed. Men who were not willing to yield to the bullying demands of their dependants were sometimes subjected to a good cussing out. One such cuss out was in progress on the promenade and Tony and his cousin Martin had ring side seats to the unfolding drama.

"De boy need books, he need tings fuh school. Why you playing up in yuh arse so boy?" A buxom woman with a large gold nose ring, tight-fitting jeans and a yellow vest which revealed much more than cleavage could account for, stood centre stage on the eastern end of the Brian Lara Promenade. A bewildered four year-old boy stood beside her in a green plaid shirt which was halfway in and halfway out of his brown khaki pants. She held the boy in one hand and gesticulated with the next to a bearded man who seemed almost sixty.

"All yuh men wicked yuh know. Yuh too blasted stupid. What all dat rum and gyamblin doing fuh yuh eh? Stinkin dutty ole man like you. Ah should ah never put mehself wid yuh. Yuh know how much ah man I could ah get? Better man dan you and I gone an pick up wid yuh ole ass!....Steups!... I wasting my time yes. Come boy leh we go." She turned away from the man who had said nary a word to her and walked cursing and ranting in the direction of Frederick Street.

As she walked away passing directly in front of the boys, Tony and Martin got an eyeful of her well shaped body that seemed to be bursting out of the clothes she wore. "Yuh think you could handle that?" Martin poked Tony jokingly.

"Ah could handle anything. Ah taking anything," he said as he thumped his chest a couple times. Martin laughed. He liked Tony. Now with his Aunty Sandra gone, Martin who had no brothers could spend more time with the closest person he had to a brother; his cousin Tony. Martin was two years older than Tony, ten times faster on his feet and one hundred times more likely to get into trouble than Tony on any given day.

Sandra did not like her nephew hanging around the house too much. He was really her ex-husband's nephew and she could see from the time he had hit secondary school that it would not be long before he got into trouble. She didn't have to wait long to be right. Martin had been suspended from school on average three times each term from Form One right up to Form Five. In fact a recommendation had been submitted to the Ministry of Education by the school Guidance Counselor requesting that Martin be placed in a school where remedial work could be done with him on an individual basis, so that he would not be a disruption to his classmates, teachers and in fact the entire school. His mother, who was always ready to come to his defense, had petitioned against it. If Martin was in trouble, no one would ever guess it. He was the coolest, most relaxed young man you could find on Brian Lara Promenade. He was cutting class and his demeanour was no different than if he had been drinking coconut water under a tree at Maracas Bay.

"Ah have to meet a pardner by City Gate to get some things and den ah have to reach down Tunapuna. We goin an take some girls in the cinema." He said with a chuckle that didn't need to be explained. Although the boys attended different schools, Tony was slowly being introduced to Martin's clique as someone who was not to be interfered with. Being Martin's cousin gave him a certain degree of immunity from assault and general interference.

With Sandra gone, Tony had been able to successfully miss school for several days already. Nobody was checking and from all appearances, no one in his school seemed to notice or to care. "Dis gyul ah getting fuh yuh she sweet, nice boobs and ting. She sixteen and yuh could try anything yuh want on she when yuh reach in de cinema. Yuh wouldn have no trouble." Tony nodded his head and smiled. He was a little surprised, even a bit nervous but he could not let his cousin take him fuh a wuss. "Dat sounding sweet." He smiled and gave Martin a bounce. He never knew when he broke biche to meet Martin what the lime would entail. The last time they met, they went to a video games arcade and played games all afternoon, till late. Another time they had gone with some of Martin's clique to a pool hall in Curepe and played pool. After that he had tried to smoke a cigarette but had choked so much from coughing, that his eyes turned red and watery. Martin had laughed and his friends along with him. Tony was embarrassed, but if there was one thing he knew, it was that no matter what happened, Martin was the boss. His minions knew it. They laughed when Martin laughed, they did as they were told and would be ready to beat any man, woman or child in defense of Martin, so strong was their loyalty. Tony knew that on the totem pole of the group he was untouchable as Martin's cousin and so it made embarrassment though painful a little more tolerable.

"Yuh ever smoke weed, horse?

Martin looked at Tony with intent as he stood in line to get a corn soup from the corn soup van. He knew the answer to the question he had asked; he just wanted to see the look on Antonio's face.

"Nah horse. Yuh know how my moms dred. Steups. Dat lady does get on like a mad woman for real horse."

"Well, here what horse. We goin an fix dat situation tonight."

"Come leh we eat quick. We ha to meet dem girls jus now."

Tony had never smoked weed, neither did he want to actually, but he knew that were it not for Martin he would not have been exposed to all he had been in the last month. Martin was the leprechaun leading him into a treacherous lair but unlike Irish folklore, once captured, there would be no three wishes granted in exchange for release.

Chapter Eight

Parental Guidance

"Good morning students!" The teacher shouted for the second time after getting no response to her first "Good morning". The giggles and chatter didn't come to a complete halt but a few students began to push their desks and get in their seats.

"Steups!"

"Wait a minute. Is that Antonio Denton I see?"

One student let out a loud cackle followed by a girlish giggle.

"Like yuh geh ketch horse," another student muttered under his breath.

"Well Mr. Denton. We have not seen you here in quite some time. How nice of you to come back," she said with a hint of sarcasm.

Antonio sat slouched on his chair. He rolled his eyes upward in disgust and annoyance but said nothing. A black Afro comb stuck out from the front of his head while in the back a field of neatly twisted squares of small plaits, each about a half inch thick, stood up straight as arrows.

"Well Mr. Denton, its always nice to see you. But the thing is it doesn't work that way. We need to make a trip to the principal's office. Come on. Now!"

Antonio let out another steups as he grudgingly put the Afro comb in his brown back pack.

"I'll finish the hair later," mumbled his classmate turned stylist.

The other students watched and made other grunting noises as they watched Antonio leave the class. Soon they would be back to their noise-making, ignoring the assignment that Ms. Ramadhar had scribbled with chalk on the blackboard.

Moments later, after making Antonio sit in the secretary's reception area, the sultry Ms. Ramadhar would knock and enter Mr. Guerra's office with childish glee, as though she had caught a rare bird or some exotic delicacy which gave her a legitimate reason to enter the office of the brawny principal.

"And you are looking quite lovely, Ms. Ramadhar."

"Oh thanks Mr. Guerra. I am just trying to take care of myself. You know how it is," a blushing Ms. Ramadhar responded.

"But of course."

After the brief moment of flirting for which she had hoped, the Form Four teacher would get right to the business at hand.

"Yes, and he hasn't been in class for two weeks, Mr. Guerra."

"For two weeks eh?"

"Yes. With no excuse letter, no note, nothing. And imagine he just shows up to class today as normal. Or as the young people say 'normel, normel.'"

Mr. Guerra let loose a hearty laugh like someone who had not laughed in a long time. Antonio could hear him laughing from the reception area where he sat listening to the click, click clank, clank of the secretary's typewriter. He knew he was going to get in trouble. He knew it but he didn't care. Because of his cousin Martin he was having a lot of sex with a lot of girls and he had had the opportunity to smoke weed. He liked the way he felt after smoking the weed. Martin would give him some to smoke after he had had sex with a girl. He had advised that it was always better to smoke the weed after sex instead of before. In fourteen days he had had sex with five different girls from Martin's school. Martin had told him to pace himself, that they were his girls and they would do anything for him. There was one that Antonio liked. The first girl. She was not exceptionally pretty and he was not her first but she was not afraid of Martin. She had put him in his place when he tried to be cheeky with her and Antonio liked that. Perhaps it was because somewhere in his head he was afraid of Martin; afraid of what he was capable of doing. Her name was Cindy. He remembered that. He was not sure about the others.

The principal's door opened and Antonio could see every tooth in Ms. Ramadhar's mouth as she smiled on her way out his office. Her belly and her bottom seemed to form one mass as they struggled against the green linen skirt suit that tried to reign in her assets.

"Young man, come this way," an almost laughing Mr. Guerra summoned him.

It was no laughing matter but Antonio was glad that Mr. Guerra was smiling. That would make it easier.

"Sit down. So I hear you are not in school for two weeks. What have you been doing?"

Silence filled the room.

"Nothing to say eh."

Antonio looked around at the posters on the wall of the principal's room. His eyes fixed on one that read, "Attitude is Everything."

"Well listen, boy. You ain't wasting my time today you know. I get my education already. I have a nice house, a nice car. Don't you want those things?"

Antonio kept looking at the poster. He wished he could be anywhere but sitting across a desk from Mr. Guerra. He tried to recall the feel of Cindy's soft skin and the excitement he felt when she unhooked her bra and pressed her breasts against his chest.

"I don't have time for this headache, nah. You ain't see what going on boy? Trinidad don't have place for little black boys like you who want to waste the government free education you know. In my days it didn't have no free education you know, boy. You getting free school, free food from the government, free university eh. You could be anything you want to be and what you choosing to do, eh? Steups! Boy if you only know how I don't have time for fellas like you."

Antonio let out a soft steups under his breath to counter Mr. Guerra's steups. His eyes were still fixed on the poster. The six foot four man stood up from his soft armchair and opened the door to his office.

"Geraldine!"

The click, click, clack of the typewriter came to a halt.

"Just call the Guidance Officer for me please. What's her name again?"

"Mrs. Mohammed."

Mr. Guerra knew what her name was but he disliked the fact that he had to see her in his office so early in the day.

"Let her know I have an issue with a student here. Ask her to come to my office."

"Boy, come and sit outside. I don't want you raising my blood pressure this hour of the day. Steups!"

He slammed the door shut as Antonio sauntered out and sat slouched again in another chair.

It wasn't long before Mrs. Mohammed arrived in the principal's office, with her usual brisk saunter; spectacles perched on the tip of her nose. She was as fond of Mr. Guerra as he was of her but remained undaunted in the face of his criticism. Mr. Guerra had accused her of fighting a losing battle, and grudgingly supported her school initiatives to improve the school's dropout rate. She had fought many a battle with him and was convinced that he did not really care about the young people in the school.

"Good morning, Mrs. Mohammed."

"Good morning, Mr. Guerra."

"So this Denton boy. Antonio Denton. He's in Form Four I think?" he shuffled some papers on his desk nervously.

"Yes."

"He's missed school for two weeks, no excuse letter, no note from the parent, nothing. So I think that is your area. You would enjoy this one," he smirked.

"Did he tell you anything or say why he was absent?"

"No, the boy ain't saying anything."

"Well did you ask him?"

"But of course!" he shouted indignantly, upset that she even dared to question him.

"What about the parents? Did you try to reach them?"

"Well, I know that is your area, that's why I called you."

"Well, its your area too, you know."

"You think I have time with these fellas. Is some fellas just like him who hold me up and thief my car. I don't have time to waste on them boys. Only thing left to do is open they brain and put the education in there. They too lazy!"

"Well all the more reason you need to be concerned about what happens to them don't you think? Otherwise this school will just become a bandit making factory."

"That's ridiculous. Don't blame me you know, Mizz Mohammed. That have nothing to do with me. These parents send their children here with their bad ways and their bad attitude and expect us to work miracles. Well it don't work so. They getting everything free and still you have to force them, eh. Free school, free food, everything, eh! In my day you know how hard my father had to work for me to get a blazer to go to Presentation College? I used to be eating bake and butter when the day come eh . . . . flour porridge and them kinda thing. I had to walk to school and when I reach home, I couldn't get a chance to study. I had to go in the hog pen and help meh father clean out dem stinking hog pen and feed them hogs and dem. These boys ain't know bout that. They getting everything free and instead of studying they book they only looking to get into all kinda bad company and make all kinda trouble."

The veins in Mr. Guerra's neck were bulging and a few drops of sweat appeared on his forehead.

"I know you will disagree with me, Mizz Mohammed. I know you will disagree because you had a different training and your training believe in giving boys like that a chance and understanding them and all kinda things like that but that is not the answer. Those kinda boys need hard cuffs. That is all they will understand. We can't give them hard cuffs and their parents not doing it, so it only have one place for them boys. Steups! I fed up, yes. But you go ahead and try what they teach you with your psychology business and whatsoever and so forths and so fifths. That is not my area."

Mrs. Mohammed sighed inwardly. She had heard that tirade on so many occasions, more than she wanted to recall.

She could almost recite it—all about the blazer, the walking to school, the bake and butter, the hog pen. It was as if he was stuck in a time warp and angry with the world; angry that he had not been born at a different time, when education was free and there was a school feeding program. A time when he didn't need a stuffy blazer. He seemed almost jealous of the boys who made their way to his office charged with different offences. To him they were ingrates, lazy good-for-nothings. To Mrs. Mohammed they were misguided youth, needing care. With their views so far apart on the spectrum of opinion, it was no wonder they couldn't see eye to eye and no surprise that his ability to recall Mrs. Mohammed's name so variable.

"Well you know, like I always say, we ALL have a responsibility too, Mr. Guerra." She shook her head disappointedly and looked down on the floor as she held the doorknob to his office signalling that she was on her way out and not about to engage him in a battle that could go on ad infinitum.

"Of course. That's why I called you right away. That's my responsibility."

"I'll get the file from Geraldine."

"Yes," he mumbled as he leaned back in his chair and reached for the daily newspaper. The veins on his neck were returning to their normal size. He let out a loud sigh as Mrs. Mohammed closed the door behind her and flipped through the pages of the newspaper looking for the horoscope section.

By the time the telephone rang, Granny Maye had just nestled her grey head onto her pillow and was beginning to doze off. She didn't like hustling to answer the phone and she didn't like the phone ringing when she was trying to take her afternoon nap.

"What yuh say?" she paused in disbelief.

"Oh gorm! But what trouble is this! You know that boy leaving here every day to go to school. I seeing him in his uniform every day!"

Granny Maye sat down and propped up her face with one hand and held the phone in the other.

"Well his mother not here right now you know. She went away for a little while."

"Well the father doesn't really be around too much, you know. I mean he around. I could call him but I ain't sure he would want to come. But I will call him and see if he could come."

"What time you say? Tomorrow. Nine o'clock. Okay then, alright."

"No, I don't know where he does be going. All this time I thinking he in school."

"Coming home late? No not really. He does come home same time every day around six o'clock, seven o'clock so."

"Morning shift? Yes, but I know he will take a little lime with his friends and them."

"No. I don't know his friends too good but I know he will lime with his cousin Martin. But he in a different school."

"Yes. Yes. I understand."

"Well, tomorrow please God. Okay. Yes. Alright. Bye."

Granny Maye turned her eyes upward as she pondered the conversation she had just ended.

"But what trouble is this! The boy mother now leave!"

The one thing Granny Maye didn't like was feeling that she had been hoodwinked. Antonio had been skipping school for two weeks.

"Two weeks!" she exclaimed in disbelief. It was not something that he had done before. She would call Sandra today and the boy's father. She would need transport to get down to the school for nine o'clock and the least his father could do was give her a ride to the school. Now more than ever Antonio needed a father and since Chester had abandoned that role long ago, she hoped she could get him to play the role of father figure, if only for a morning.

Chapter Nine

More Than Giving Care

It had been two hours since Sandra started cleaning up after Joan. Two long hours. When she fell off the bed, she had knocked over a bowl of porridge on a nearby side table.

"You alright, Ma'am? Ah so sorry?"

"Who are you?"

"I am Sandra."

The woman sat on the floor and stared wildly around the room like a crazed animal enraged.

"Where did Janet go?"

"I am her replacement. Let me help you up," said Sandra as she stooped with arms outstretched to lift the woman up. She did not anticipate the stinging slap, hot and wet that Joan delivered to her cheek. "That's for taking so long. I'm an old lady. I could have died." A dumbfounded Sandra had been taken totally by surprise. She bent her head to wipe off the wetness on her cheek and smelt the ammonic smell of urine.

"Sorry Ma'am. I'm so sorry."

"Well help me up then!"

She reached her hands under Joan's armpits and slowly pulled her up on to the bed. Joan's skin was wrinkly and thin. Softened by age, the blue veins of her hands gave colour to the pale freckled skin. She passed her bony hands over her dishevelled hair and looked at the clock above the bedroom door.

"It's late and I need to go out and I need to be cleaned! Do you hear me!" she shouted.

"Of course, just let me get a few things so ah could tidy up, alright?" she smiled at Joan hoping she would smile in return.

Joan stared at her angrily, her pink lips tightly pursed with eyes wide open and arms folded.

"Look at the mess. Just look at it! I'll never make it on time," she mumbled in despair looking down at the beige carpet under her feet. A bowl of oatmeal porridge that had probably tipped over with the fall, had splattered in a long arch between the two beds. Sandra looked over at Olivia, who seemed unperturbed by all the commotion, to find her rocking rhythmically back and forth, arms curled up on her chest as if she were shielding herself from something. She looked straight ahead at nothing. Her face was expressionless. Sandra wondered how long she had been that way.

"I'll never make it to the dance," Joan began to sob. She covered her face with her pillow and began to cry.

"What dance? No. You go make it to the dance," said Sandra almost instinctively.

"No I won't. Look at this mess." Her sobs grew louder and louder.

"Not to worry, Ms. Joan. I will get you ready in time."

"You can?" the teary eyed woman whispered softly with the most childlike voice.

"Of course. You just wait right here. Don't move a muscle, okay."

Sandra took another glance at Olivia. There was no change.

"I'll be right back."

Sandra was trying to speak better English as Patsy had advised. Patsy had told her she should try to say 'I' instead of 'ah' and 'you' instead of 'yuh' if she wanted to be understood by the Englefields. It was awkward for her but she was trying.

Between the store cupboard and the bathroom, Sandra found every imaginable thing that she could use to clean an old lady. There were washrags, a wash-basin, soap, adult briefs and towels. Under the kitchen sink she found carpet cleaner and disposable kitchen cloths. However, by the time she returned to the room armed with all that she would need in the wash basin and with the towel thrown over her shoulder, she found Olivia kneeling in a corner, naked as she was born. Olivia had her pampers at her side and was using her faeces to make a mural on the bedroom wall, the carpet and the white cotton bed sheets. She looked at Joan in shock and disbelief. The brown-eyed woman looked at her sister making her art and turned to Sandra with a wistful smile.

"Where's Janet?"

"No, No, No, Ms. Olivia."

Sandra set everything down and snatched the open faeces filled brief. She folded it up tightly and put it in a nearby bin.

"Come, come."

She held Olivia by the shoulders. Olivia pulled away making groaning sounds.

She grabbed her again. This time, a little harder, and pulled her up off the floor. Olivia was stronger than she thought. Joan followed Sandra's every move with her beady eyes. Olivia fought Sandra hard but as strong as she was, she was no match. Sandra pulled her back to the bed.

"Stay. You stay right there," she threatened. She could see Olivia getting ready to make a dash for the wall again.

"No! No!" Sandra shouted.

Joan giggled.

"She's not going to stay you know. You're going to have to tie her. She doesn't like going to dances. She's the prettier one and she doesn't like going to the dance." Joan scoffed as she looked at her unpolished finger nails.

Sandra was still standing guard, arms outstretched, in an effort to keep Olivia on the bed.

"Just tie up the wench, you fool."

"Tie her up, Goddamn it!" You're going to make me late!" she screamed.

Joan's face was flushed. Sandra stood there, not knowing what to do, trying not to inhale too much of the scent of Olivia's waste. She couldn't tie her. That wouldn't be right. Olivia stared, not at Sandra, rocking back and forth, hands crumpled up on her naked breasts. Sandra, still with arms outstretched, waited. After a few seconds, her arms came down and relaxed at her side. Olivia was still rocking, rocking, staring.

"Good girl. Nice girl."

She smoothed the silvery strands of thinning hair with the back of her palms. She knew she had faeces on her somewhere. The whole room smelt stink of it. Her hands were sticky.

"Very good girl. Very nice girl."

Sandra stepped back with one foot, then another, slowly, all the while with eyes on Olivia. She glanced across at Joan to see her looking in a handheld mirror, inspecting her lips and mouth.

What kind of women were these? Sandra thought to herself. What had she got herself into? She wondered how Ms. Winters had managed to deal with them. She thought about calling her but then decided against it. It was a tough situation but she could handle it. She had to. She needed to get through one week then another, then another. She needed to make that money so she could send home a barrel for Andrea and Tony.

"Put her in the tub and give her a bath. She's always smelling stink of shit." A much calmer Joan advised.

"She's the pretty one, pretty one, pretty one. She is the pretty one and always stinking, stinking, stinking, la-la-la-la stinking, stinking up the plaaaace . . . ." Joan sang softly as she looked at herself in the mirror.

Sandra walked over to the bathroom door. It was made of frosted glass. She pushed it open, all the while glancing at Olivia who was still transfixed, silently, rocking, rocking. A white tiled shower with tempered glass sliding doors and aluminum frames greeted her on the left. She slid the doors open with one hand. They were light and glided open easily. The shower looked as though it had not been used in a while. She could see the dried, white soap scum spots on the inside of the door and the tiles at the base of the shower. Greenish black lines lay between the grout of adjacent tiles on the small shower bench. The bench looked out of place. Probably a late addition, perhaps as the women got older she thought. The toilet seat was wide, white and clean as was the wash-basin adorned with stainless steel faucet heads. She flicked the light switch on. It gave the room a yellowish hue. In a corner at the end of the room was an open window about one foot wide. The bathroom area smelt sweet of air refresher but Sandra couldn't help but notice that there were no signs of recent use; no drops of water in the wash basin, or on the floor. There was no toilet paper on the toilet paper rack.

A dusty mirrored medicine cabinet beckoned above the toilet tank. She opened it to find a tube of toothpaste, a small transparent bag of tiny pink pills shaped like hexagons. Scribbled in blue ink were the words "Emergency Sleep". She wondered what that meant. Sandra passed her fingers on the cabinet shelves. They returned dust laden and sticky. She suddenly remembered that she needed to wash her hands. She did and dried them quickly in a nearby towel. She returned to the bedroom to find Olivia still rocking and Joan still humming to herself in the mirror. Sandra decided she would tackle Olivia first.

By midday Sandra was exhausted. She had managed to drag a belligerent Olivia to the shower and give her a good old-fashioned scrub down with a wash rag. Olivia bawled and screamed in anguish throughout the ordeal just as Ms. Winters had said she would. The woman was frail and wiry but strong. Sandra was surprised to find dried faeces stuck to Olivia's gluteal folds. She wondered when last water had touched her skin. She tried not to rub her down too hard. The woman's skin felt as fragile as petals that if touched too hard would easily come off in her fingers. She washed Olivia's hair with shampoo she discovered in a cupboard under the sink and by the time she had finished with her, the woman looked almost sane until she started with her rocking again. Sandra was dripping wet from head to toe when she emerged from the shower. She removed her clothes, towelled herself dry and remained in her bra and panty to continue with Olivia. She dressed Olivia in the bathroom, taking great care to powder her neck, back and between her legs. Carefully she put on her briefs and nightgown and when she had finished,

Sandra put the toilet seat down and left Olivia sitting there looking like an angel.

"Stay now, darling. Stay." she warned as she pulled the bathroom door shut and came out to assess the condition of the bedroom.

"My, My, My! You can't possibly be going to the dance like that," Joan laughed with mouth covered as she ogled Sandra's plump frame and loose flesh hanging on her back, belly and thighs.

"Oh I know, I will be looking prettier than you. I may not be the prettiest one but I am not the fattest one," said Joan.

Sandra tiptoed to her bedroom to change her clothes and made her way back to Joan and Olivia's lair in less than five minutes. She found a pair of yellow rubber gloves and tried to use the carpet cleaner to remove the porridge that had spilled.

She successfully used bleach to clean the faeces off the wall but in the process damaged the carpet when some of the bleach accidentally fell on it. She tried to get as many of the smears off the carpet fibres and while doing so couldn't help but observe that there were other patches of worn carpet that seemed soiled with fibres clumped together. Perhaps Olivia was a regular with this kind of behaviour. Sandra hoped not. She couldn't imagine going through this every day. Periodically she opened the bathroom door to check on Olivia who sat like an obedient child, traumatized by the bath she had received and still rocking. Joan was busy retrieving things from the nightstand at the side of her bed and laying them out across her bed in a straight line. Sandra was thankful that Joan didn't move much from her place on the bed. She knew she could not manage two Olivias.

After sheets were changed and some semblance of order restored to the bedroom, Sandra asked Joan if she was ready to get dressed for the dance.

"Of course, but where's Olivia? I keep telling her that I cannot go without her and she will not listen. And don't you know she's the prettier one and she still won't be on time."

"I know," Sandra responded.

"You know!" said Joan in disbelief.

"You think she's prettier than me, don't you."

"No, Ms. Joan. You are both pretty."

"But you just said it! You just said it!"

"No, Ms. Joan. No . . . you are pretty too, even prettier. In fact . . ."

"You lie. You know. You just said you know," she began to sob.

"No Joan. No."

"It's Ms. Joan to you," she snapped, lifting her head from her hands.

"Ms. Joan how about we get ready for the dance. I know you will feel better." Sandra whispered in her ear as she gently placed her hand on the old woman's shoulder.

She could feel Joan's body shaking as she cried.

"Shhh . . . is okay . . . is okay . . ." Sandra sat on the bed, her arm still around Joan's shoulder. She felt sorry for her, for both of them. She imagined how she would feel if she got old and ended up like them. The thought made her cringe.

"Let's get ready for the dance, okay."

"Okay."

It took Sandra another two hours to get Joan ready for the dance. Since she had been advised that Joan's hygiene needs were to be taken care of on the bed, she had to position her cleaning materials and do a whole lot of manoeuvering.

It was a real balancing act trying to get Joan to co-operate with her.

"I need to wipe under your arm."

"Why? I can do it."

"Okay, well do it then," a frustrated Sandra responded.

Joan took the washcloth and dashed it on the ground. Sandra picked it up rinsed it out in the bowl of clean water on the nightstand and started again.

"And you are moving too slow. I am missing the best parts of the dance right now."

Sandra wished Joan would really go to the dance and stay there.

"Oh you're a chubby one, Ms. Winters."

"It's Sandra."

"Yes, whatever."

"I wonder what you will get at the dance looking all juicy like that."

Sandra's smooth dark skin contrasted against Joan's as her hands glided down each of Joan's vertebrae with the slippery bar of soap. Joan was definitely a bit bigger than Olivia and certainly more vocal. She couldn't remember who was older between the two but she imagined that it must be Joan. And why was she going on about this dance so much and about Olivia being the prettier one? Sandra wondered. Ms. Goodridge had not made any mention of mental illness when she spoke about these ladies. Sandra guessed that Olivia had Alzheimer's Disease, but what on earth was wrong with Joan? Sandra had never seen one person go through such a wide range of emotions in such a short period of time. Now sad, now angry, now crying, now mean and shouting; one minute sane the next insane. There must be a name for that disease she thought.

After she had finished with Joan, changed bed sheets, combed hair and made the room smell acceptable, Sandra felt a sense of accomplishment. Confident now that she could return Olivia to the bedroom, she placed her hand on the bathroom doorknob to find it locked. Panic ensued. Where were the keys? She tried to peer through a small area of the frosted glass door that was not frosted. She did not see Olivia on the toilet seat where she had left her. She opened her eyes and nose as wide as she could, pressing them against the glass to see where the woman had moved to. She knocked hard on the glass door.

"Ms. Olivia! Ms. Olivia! Open the door."

"Ms. Joan, do you know where the key for this door is?"

"I don't know anything about any key, Ms. Winters. Besides it's already lunchtime. Shouldn't I be getting something to eat?"

"What to do, Sandra? What to do? What to do? Think. Think, think," Sandra mumbled to herself. She couldn't pick a lock and she didn't want to break the glass door. "What if she doesn't open the door? What if she stays in there all day, all night! What if she was smearing down the bathroom walls with faeces? What if . . . . Oh God!" Sandra began to feel sick.

"Ms. Olivia! Ms. Olivia! Open the door please!"

"Why did you put her in there, Ms. Winters. I told you not to and you still did it! Why? You knew she would make me late for the dance. You knew and you still did it. Now I have to get her out because she's the prettier one." Joan pouted.

"It isn't fair. And she's always telling lies on me and always stinking up the place with her shit and why? Because she's the prettier one."

"Well, can't you ask her to come out, Ms. Joan . . . . Please . . ."

"Well maybe. But you must tie the wench. You must tie her because she's always stinking up the place with her shit and making me late for the dance."

"Maybe this had happened before. Maybe Joan knew what to do. Maybe I should call Ms. Winters. Yes. I'll call her." Sandra thought.

"Olivia! Olivia! Walter is here," said Joan softly.

For a moment silence. Then a click.

The bathroom door opened slightly. Olivia white as a ghost sat in a corner naked on the ground. Sandra breathed a sigh of relief, grateful that a near catastrophe had been averted.

Later that day after soft pudding-like meals had been fed and medication forcefully given, Sandra would take Joan's advice and tie Olivia's feet to the bed post. She could not have another morning like the one she had just had. Somehow, she would have to find a way to cope.

Chapter Ten

Who is Responsible?

Antonio would spend the day in Mrs. Mohammed's office. He liked her. She seemed to care. She didn't scold him, she tried to listen but he wasn't in the mood for talking. In any case it was not as though he could tell her all that he had been doing for the past few days with Martin and his friends.

When the school army bell rang at 12:15 p.m. like a drill hammer, signalling the end of the morning shift, Mrs. Mohammed would keep Antonio in her office for one more hour before setting him free from the prison of his chair. She had done her best to talk to him.

"Miss, my mother gone away yuh know. You doh understand she yuh know. Hmm."

"Well you tell me then."

"Miss you wouldn't understand," he said covering his mouth with the black washrag he was holding.

"Well, help me to understand then. I want to." Her eyes were big and brown like deep pools.

"Nah Miss yuh wouldn't . . . is like . . . nah Miss."

That was all she would be able to get out of him for the day. She knew when to push and when to let be. He was a first time offender. She could wait.

Later than night when a red-eyed looking Antonio pushed open Granny Maye's rust-ridden gate he would be surprised by the look of vexation and hurt on her face.

"Tony boy, what it is with you, boy? What wrong with you, boy?" she pleaded, arms akimbo.

"Like you ain't realize what going on out here, boy. Your mother slaving away for you in America for you to get a chance and is this stupidness you looking to do? Boy, what kinda man you going to be? Open your eye, boy. Open your eye. You think Mr. Singh son doing the stupidness you doing? Every day you see how that boy going to school in Hillview College, eh. You see how every day Mr. Singh going out on the road with he goats taking them to graze and planting up pumpkin on that empty lot of government land! You think that boy studying to break biche. No, not he, but you who going senior sec what you doing eh? ... Boy ... boy .... You want to work security like yuh father? Well yes. It look so but even that ah think you need some subjects for now. So what you going to do? Your mother ain't expecting you to be no doctor or no lawyer, you know. But oh gorm, if you get a few subjects self, even if is a little English a little Maths it will have something you go be able to do. You hearing me, boy? Antonio?"

He stood there oily-faced, sweating and as high as a kite from the joint he had smoked before heading home.

"Well answer me, boy! You understand what I saying?"

"Yes, Granny."

"Look around you and see. If you don't get a education boy is hell for you to ketch down the road, you know. Hell, I tell you ... real hell. Why you think your mother reach where she reach? She gone up to work, because you know why? Not because she stupid you know but because she didn't study her book when she had the chance and end up getting fool up by your father."

Antonio didn't like hearing about his father in that way. It made his hair stand on end. Chester had done very little for him but he had acknowledged him and would bring a bag of groceries for Christmas or if he had won some money playing whé. But it didn't help that he had other children and another woman to mind. Still, Antonio resented any negative comments regarding his father and whenever Chester would come around he would feel a sense of longing and excitement. It was enough to see his father's sheepish grin and the way he nervously scratched his almost bald head while he spoke to Granny Maye. It was as if he was trying to apologize to Granny Maye without saying the words, because he knew deep down that words would never be enough.

"Well, the school call me today, you know. Yes. They call," she said as if she had dropped the biggest bombshell.

"Two weeks, boy. Two whole weeks and I here like a jackass watching you walk up the road feeling good to know that even though you ain't going Hillview College like Mr. Singh boy that at least you getting a chance to get some subjects.

Where you went boy? What you was doing boy? Ah hope you wasn't liming with Martin you know. Your mother tired tell you that boy only going one place. She tired tell you and I tired tell you. Friend does carry you but they doh bring you back, you know. Alright. You have your mother like a jackass breaking she back in America for you, boy! Nah. You ain't have no heart, boy. You ain't studying yuh poor mother, yuh granny, yuh sister eh? You ain't thinking bout we?"

At that very moment he imagined that this was what his father had fled from—the constant nagging of a mother-in-law who had felt her daughter was too good for him. Or was it the disappointment he felt when he looked at his grossly overweight wife who was no longer the shapely young woman he had married. Antonio believed that he understood why Chester had to go. Antonio knew the secret. It was because of this . . . . this nagging, the demands, and now with Chester gone he was the new victim, because he was the only man in the house, him and Buster.

"Well I call your father. He working PH tonight but he say he will try to pick us up and drop us off in the school tomorrow. And he will come in the school because like you need a man to talk to you, because all me and your mother saying ain't making no dent. It ain't making no dent at all, at all, at all. Head too hard . . . too hard." she wiped her brow. She had worked up a sweat with all her talking and could feel the salty liquid running down under her drooping breasts.

"How you think your mother feel when I tell her this thing, eh boy? How you think she feel? Tony boy, like you ain't have no heart, boy. We try but like you growing up like you ain't have no parents, like it don't have people to show you the right thing. We showing you the right thing and you going and do the wrong thing and the first thing people will say is that is we who ain't bring you up right. But they don't know is not so. They wouldn't know how yuh mother try and how I try. Anyway go in your bed and think about what you going an say tomorrow. I ain't going to be raising my pressure in my old age."

That night Antonio rejoiced inwardly at the thought of seeing his father in the morning. He viewed him as a fellow sufferer. His father had escaped the prison of the household leaving him behind as a prisoner. Ironically he didn't resent

Chester for leaving him behind but sometimes he wished with all his heart that he had grown up with him instead. The last time he saw Chester it was Christmas time. He had pulled up in the little white Nissan March smelling of alcohol with glassy eyes and two brown grocery bags bursting at the seams under his arms.

"Merry Christmas. Merry Christmas Ms. Maye."

"Tony boy, how you going," he patted him on the head and then on the back.

"Daddy, Daddy!" Andrea screamed excitedly as she wrapped her little hands around his waist and pressed her face into his jersey to inhale the smell of cigarette smoke that had overtaken the fibres of the fabric.

"Where your mother? She inside?"

"Yes. She resting."

He had asked only as a matter of course. Sandra was always inside whenever he came. He knew she didn't want to have to be civil to him after the way he had treated her and was grateful that she allowed him to see his children and had not taken him to court for child support money the way some of the other 'chile-mudders' of his friends had.

Antonio remembered that he gave him a cap with the letters NY on it and also a pair of Clarks that were too big and looked slightly worn but that didn't matter. He gave Andrea a doll with long, yellow hair and blue eyes that rolled up and down. Andrea liked those kinds of dolls and sat for hours the following day combing its hair in different styles and introducing it to her other dolls with all the usual girly dollhouse talk. Those times his father didn't seem so bad, not as bad as Sandra had made him out to be. Perhaps Chester was just like him, misunderstood, he thought. But Chester had got out, he would have to wait till he was eighteen or maybe he could find a way to get out before that. Maybe he could find a way if he was smart. With thoughts such as these he drifted off to sleep.

The following morning Antonio awoke to the sounds of Granny Maye puttering around in the kitchen as she made breakfast. The smell of scrambled eggs tickled his nose as the rays of light like sharpened pencils peeked under his bedroom curtains. He heard the chirping of birds on the mango tree outside and heard the front gate shake and rattle as Buster jumped on it to protest the passing by of a stray dog. Grudgingly he got ready for school and prepared to face whatever would happen. Andrea was up early too, wanting to stay home sick another day from school, but her fever had gone and complaints of belly hurting were not enough to convince Granny Maye that she needed another day at home.

"Peep, Peep." A car horn blared.

"Alright, Andrea. Don't forget your book bag."

The usually obedient child tied her shoelace before placing the heavy load that was her school bag on her back. She ran out front to the waiting car and greeted the two other girls similarly dressed. The driver, waved up to Granny Maye as she looked out the living room window. She waved back.

"Well Tony boy we just have to wait for your father now. Is almost nine o'clock so better be ready."

Her even mask on her heavily powdered face had already begun to disintegrate as the morning heat drew out a few drops of sweat. She wore a navy blue top with a high neck collar and a long black gathered skirt that exposed her bony ankles. She only wore that top on solemn occasions and Antonio missing school for two weeks certainly qualified as one of those.

It was almost ten o'clock by the time they heard the weak beep of Chester's car horn at the front gate.

"Well finally he reach. Tonnnyyyy! Tonnnyyyy! Your father reach. Time to go."

"Sorry Ms. Maye. Ah work late last night and I get up late this morning."

"Is alright."

"Tony, Good morning."

"Morning."

"So I hear you giving your granny trouble, boy?"

There was silence in the back seat.

Chester didn't press him. He had said that only because it was what he felt he was expected to say. The truth is that he had little knowledge of what took place on a daily basis in the Denton household. He had problems of his own in his own household and even though Granny Maye had asked him to come to the school with them he had a sense of diffidence regarding his own ability to guide his son in any direction at all.

"So you understand why we've called you in today?" asked Mrs. Mohammed after exchanging pleasantries with Granny Maye and Chester.

"Well yes."

"Two weeks is a lot of time to be away from school without a note from a parent or guardian. Naturally if he was not sick, we would be concerned, as should you, about what he has been doing all this time. Sometimes young men end up getting into bad company and end up in all kinds of trouble and I mean this is the first time I have had to deal with Antonio in my office. So what we want to do this morning is just talk about what is going on with him. You know . . . and try to find out why he's doing what he's doing."

They all sat around a round table. Granny Maye with legs crossed, Antonio slouched and Chester wiping furiously the beads of perspiration from under his chin. He didn't like being around people with too much education. They always made him nervous. He didn't like feeling conscious about how he spoke or having to make the effort to make sentences where subject and verb agreed. It was precisely because he usually failed in that endeavour, that he looked at Granny Maye in the hope that she would be the one to speak first.

"Mrs. Mohammed, I really don't know this boy to be behaving so you know. Normally he is a good boy. He mightn' be bright, bright but is only since his mother gone away he doing this. I could tell you that for a fact. If she was here he wasn't going to be behaving so."

"Yes, you told me she went abroad."

"Yes, she in New York working."

Mrs. Mohammed knew what to make of that statement.

"So you are taking care of the children in the meantime?"

"Yes."

"And what about you Mr. Parks?"

"Well me and the mother not together nah so I ain't really know what going on too much every day an thing nah but I does help out regular an thing with groceries and thing nah."

Granny Maye fumed inwardly at the thought that he had deceitfully and knowingly portrayed the bringing of groceries once a year at Christmas as regular assistance.

"I have other children too nah but I does try to help out nah. Try to be a father nah."

Granny Maye was boiling.

"Well, I think it has been very hard on him his mother going away and all and I think he is just acting out because of that."

"Isn't she coming back in a few months?"

"Ah-hem. Well yes. Yes."

"So perhaps it is something more than that then. It is not as if she isn't coming back and usually when children behave this way they are doing so in response to something, some hurt, perhaps something they are upset about that they cannot even verbalize."

Chester was beginning to feel overwhelmed. The talk seemed to be getting too high for him.

"Antonio, is there anything you want to say?"

Silence filled the room as three pairs of eyes looked squarely at him. "Are they for real?" he thought to himself. Mrs. Mohammed was a lot dumber than he thought. If he had not said anything to her when they were alone the day before, why would she think that he would have something to say now with his grandmother and Chester present?

"Well Antonio?" said Mrs. Mohammed expectantly.

The pause was long and uncomfortable and bore no fruit. Granny Maye sought to speculate about what it could be.

"Well I will say this. He have a cousin who he does lime with who is older than him and I think he may be getting influence by him as he's an older boy, nah."

"Who, Martin?" Chester inquired.

"Nah, Martin is a good fella. Not Martin. Yuh cyah blame Martin for Tony staying away from school."

"Well, I sure if you ask Martin he go be able to tell you where Tony was going these last few days because I sure some one of them days he was with Martin."

Antonio's heart began to race. What if they knew about him and Martin? What if they had found out?

"Tony, you was liming with Martin, boy?" an irritated Chester asked.

Antonio looked at him like a trapped animal wanting to say something but not knowing what to say.

"Answer me, boy!" Chester shouted. He sat upright in his chair his eyes opened wide, nostrils flaring, biceps taut under his washed out green jersey.

"Boy, I talking to you! Boy, I . . . ."

In an instant Chester was on his feet. The metal legs of the folding chair scraped against the tiled floor as he pushed it back. He lunged forward over Granny Maye and grabbed Tony by the collar of his shirt, hitting her jaw hard in the process with his elbow.

"Mr. Parks! Mr. Parks! Please."

"Boy, I is yuh father. I talking to you, boy!"

Granny Maye stood up quickly, inadvertently making way for Chester to get a better grip on the teenager.

"Chester! Chester!"

"Boy you making a ass out ah me in front dese people boy!" He twisted his fists around Antonio's shirt by the collar and the flank. A button had already popped off.

"Security! Security!" Mrs. Mohammed was trembling at the doorway, calling for security. The situation was volatile.

"Chester! Chester! Let go the boy!"

Antonio's eyes were swollen with tears as his scrawny frame lay victim under his father's fists. His belly was exposed as his shirt had been pulled up high. He looked up at Chester unable to move.

"Boy, open yuh mouth and talk before I buss open yuh mouth and yuh lose some teeth eh."

A tear ran down Antonio's cheek as if it knew too that it needed to escape Chester's wrath.

"Boy, ah tired . . . . (cuff) . . . tell you . . . (cuff) to show . . . . (cuff) respect . . . ."

"Sir! Sir! Sir!"

Chester's last cuff was arrested by two security guards in moss green uniforms who held his arms tightly as he prepared to deliver one last blow. They wrestled his fists from off the boy's shirt and freed Tony from his captor. Chester had not heard Granny Maye's bawling.

"Oh God! Doh kill him! You go kill him! Oh God, Chester! Stop!"

A visibly shaken Mrs. Mohammed sought to gain control of the situation by having Chester removed from her office. Antonio had winced with each blow. His father's hand was heavy. Standing erect now he wiped the tears from his eyes and pulled his shirt straight. Granny Maye was panting. She had not screamed like that in a long time. She needed to sit down to compose herself, catch her breath, allow her heart to return to its regular rhythm.

"Would you like a glass of water, Mrs. Denton?"

"Yes . . . please . . . thanks."

Antonio could hear his father cursing the security guards in the corridor.

"Is my f—king son. Is my child. Don't f—king touch me. I have a right to be in there. I is the father."

"Sir you need to control yourself this is a school. There are . . ."

"Don't f—king tell me my rights. I is he father. I, Chester Parks . . . I is he father."

The voices faded as the guards escorted Chester further down the corridor then finally off the school premises. Chester all the while, making a scene, hurling abuses, embarrassing himself.

A dazed Antonio stood at Granny Maye's side, feeling bad that he had caused her to have to shout and become so upset. He had never seen Chester so angry. Never. The outburst had surprised and hurt him not just physically. He pondered over Chester's words. "I is the boy father" and wondered why Chester had made such a point of repeating that as if he wanted to convince himself of the fact. And what did he mean by "he tired tell me". "He ain't tell me nothing in six whole months," Antonio thought. That day Antonio decided that he didn't ever want to be a father. Whatever being a father meant, he was never going to be one. For the first time since Sandra had gone Antonio missed his mother.

Chapter Eleven

Sacred and Unholy Moments

Her first night of sleep was the worst. Sandra stayed awake in bed tossing and turning. It was not that the bed was uncomfortable. It was the strangeness of sleeping in a strange place knowing that she was the only sane person. It was about the same as being in a house all alone. If anything happened she would have to call 911. "I'll have to defend myself if there is an intruder," she thought that first night.

Twice that night she was awakened by Olivia's screaming and bawling. Twice she ran into the room to find Olivia curled up in a corner with a wild-eyed look on her face as though she was running from something.... someone. With all Olivia's screaming and carrying on, Joan lay in bed awake completely unperturbed. It was as if she knew exactly why Olivia seemed so afraid and knew that there was nothing that could be done.

Sandra tried to console Olivia. She put her arms around her and tried to drag her up to the bed but it was clear that Olivia was inconsolable.

"Leave her be, Sandra," said Joan softly

Finally she had called Sandra by name.

"There's nothing you can do. There's nothing to be done. It has to be like this all the time."

"All the time? Every night?"

"Not all the time. Most nights."

"Tonight is not too bad. She will be fine in a little while."

Sandra didn't like the sound of that. If that was a good night, she most certainly didn't want to see what a bad night looked like.

On Tuesday morning Sandra awoke with a stiff neck. Her bedroom pillow was soft but perhaps a bit too high. She had been accustomed to a flattened sponge filled pillow back in Trinidad. This pillow was too full and too firm. She got dressed for the day and checked on her charges only to find them both asleep. They were not snoring so she tiptoed into the room to be sure they were still breathing. She observed them silently for a while. What was their story? She wondered to herself. There was something eerie about the two. Who was Walter? The mention of his name had been enough to get Olivia to free herself from the prison of the bathroom the day before. Satisfied that they were very much alive, she headed to the kitchen to prepare breakfast for herself.

There wasn't much food for her. There were several boxes of oatmeal, bottles of pudding, and other milk drinks for diabetics in the pantry. There was no bread at all, a few rotting strawberries and blueberries in the refrigerator; some mouldy cheese, a box of crackers, not even a single egg she could boil. She had cut off the blue mouldy parts of the cheese and had managed so far eating crackers and cheese for breakfast and dinner. She helped herself to some of Olivia's oatmeal and searched through the freezer to find it empty. No meat, no sausages, no chicken. Sandra believed that she would surely lose weight and wondered what Ms. Winters had been eating. She remembered that one Ronaldo was supposed to stop by to get her grocery list and wondered when he would come. She had had her fill of oatmeal, crackers and cheese. Thankfully there was instant coffee. She drank it black and hot. She heard a shuffling noise at the front door and opened it to find a newspaper hanging in a blue plastic bag—*The New York Times*. She opened the glass sliding door that led on to the small verandah. The air was fresh and she could see the other buildings that made up the apartment complex. She stepped onto the verandah, closed her eyes and took a deep breath in. There was salt in the air. She could smell the sea. She opened her eyes and listened. Yes. The sea. She heard the gentle crash of waves lapping against something, perhaps a shore, perhaps a jetty ... somewhere close by there was water. She walked to the end of the narrow porch and listened. Yes there was definitely water somewhere close. The nearby buildings were blocking her view but the thought that there could be a view of the sea thrilled her and made her eager to get out of the apartment where she had already begun to feel like a prisoner. She wished Ronaldo would come soon to take the ladies out for some fresh air. Perhaps that would help to calm them down. God knew she was tired of smelling their shit.

It was only on Wednesday morning when she heard the doorbell ring and the rap, rap, rap of the door-knocker that she began to feel some sense of relief.

"Hello. Hello," the male's voice bellowed in the corridor.

"Yes," Sandra answered as she stood still in the narrow foyer.

"It's Mr. Bell from downstairs."

"I don't know no Mr. Bell."

"I'm the doorman. I have mail for you."

There was silence behind the wooden door.

"Ms. Winters . . . Janet . . . she told me you're the new caregiver?"

Suddenly Sandra remembered.

"Oh yes, of course. Of course."

Sandra opened the door just a peep.

"Good morning, ma'am," Mr. Bell said in a Southern American accent.

The tall gentleman smiled down at Sandra revealing a perfect set of polished teeth.

He wore a dark blue uniform and cap with golden tassels which fell from the sharp contours of his shoulders. His face was smooth and his dark skin didn't appear too wrinkled. He smelt of cologne, sweet and musky, mixed with the smell of cigarette smoke.

"There's no need to be afraid, ma'am. I work here," he grinned as he showed her the picture on his staff I.D. hanging around the long chain on his neck.

Sandra relaxed a bit when she saw the I.D. She relaxed her grip on the door and opened it a little wider but not too much.

"Wow. Ms. Winters told me you were from Trinidad but she didn't tell me you were nearly this pretty."

Sandra smiled.

"Well, ma'am. I hope you enjoy your stay here. My name's Damian Bell. I'm the doorman for this community. If you need anything or have any questions you can call the front desk and ask for me. Just dial zero on the phone and ask for Mr. Bell. I'll be happy to help you."

"Are you the one who gets the groceries?"

"No, ma'am. I wish I were because I'd get a chance to spend a moment with you but I'm not so lucky." He smiled again.

"The person you want is Ronaldo. He usually stops by on a Thursday."

"Oh I see," said a disappointed Sandra, knowing that she would be consigned to another day of oatmeal and crackers.

"I'm sure you'll be fine till then. In the meantime, here's your mail."

"For me?"

"That's right. Just for you."

He handed her a bundle of envelopes bound tightly in a rubber band.

"Okay. Thanks."

She took the bundle feeling a bit perplexed.

"Damn. Are all the women in your country this beautiful or are you the only one?"

Mr. Bell had dimples that made him pleasant to look at. Sandra giggled and blushed.

"I didn't get your name, ma'am."

"Sandra . . . Sandra Denton."

"Well, Ms. Denton. You can call me Damian or anything you like for that matter. I would answer to a pretty voice like yours by whatever name you called."

Sandra had not received a compliment from a man in ages, at least not from a man as dashing as Mr. Bell. He could see that he had hit a mark when she blushed.

"Well I had better be getting on my way. You have a beautiful day now."

"And you too, Mr. Bell."

"You can call me Damian you know. I don't bite unless asked," he said with a wink of his eye.

"Okay."

"Well goodbye."

"Goodbye."

Sandra pushed in the door but only slightly. She wanted to see the back of Mr. Bell. She watched him stride confidently down the red-carpeted hallway to the elevator. She didn't notice a wedding ring but figured that he must be married. She knew that some married men didn't wear wedding rings. Her ex-husband was a case in point. Mr. Bell was like a tall mug of hot chocolate on a cold day; easy on the eyes, with a voice like Luther Vandross. It was kind of him to come by she thought, after she shut the door. He would be a refreshing change from having to deal with Olivia and Joan all the time.

The apartment was humid now and there was no breeze coming through the living room door. It was almost midday. She began to prepare the containers of soft foods labelled J and O in the refrigerator. There were only a few containers left. She would have to call Ms. Winters today to find out about making some more of those containers. She seemed to be getting the hang of taking care of the women's hygiene needs. She decided that she would bathe Olivia every other day. All the mess and the crying associated with giving her a bath was simply too much to go through every day. It was easier to set a basin of warm water on her side table and clean her off with gentle strokes of a soapy washrag. Olivia responded better to it as well. There was no bawling, although occasionally she would let out a moan and a groan. She wondered if Olivia ever got tired of rocking. She seemed to be rocking all the time. Sandra had managed to clean her on the bed without creating too much of a mess. By the time she changed the bed sheets and set Olivia back on the bed, Joan would be fussing and fretting about being late for the dance and about Olivia being the prettier one.

That Wednesday morning she gave Olivia another bedside bath but Olivia was not in a good mood it seemed.

Sandra began with gentle strokes of the soapy washrag. Olivia in an instant grabbed the washrag and began to hit Sandra with it, raining a sea of swift blows to Sandra's head and face. The move took Sandra by surprise. Soap got into her eyes, temporarily blinding her. Olivia was enraged and kept pounding, pounding, pounding her.

Joan laughed all the while during the assault.

"Oh no, Olivia. Not so much." Joan giggled.

Sandra caught her balance and grabbed the woman's arms so tightly that she would later find blue black marks where she held her. Olivia began to rock again looking about almost as if she had done nothing at all. Sandra, still with eyes burning from the soap, wiped her face in her sleeve and let out a loud steups.

Joan mocked her, imitating the sound she had just heard Sandra make.

"You go ahead. You are next missy," said Sandra. Her eyes hurt and her head throbbed in pain.

"You should have done me first but you go there because she's the prettier one. I'm pretty too, you know. Walter liked me first you know and he would have been much better off with me too."

There was that name again. Walter.

"Well I'm sure Walter didn't know how much hell you could give," said Sandra.

She tied Olivia's feet to the bed posts, one to each post. Before she could tie her hands, Olivia knocked the basin of warm soapy water over onto the carpet, creating a new mess for Sandra to clean. The next day Sandra dragged Olivia to the shower and gave her a bath. Olivia did all her usual, crying and screaming and bawling but Sandra didn't mind. It had taken her two hours to clean up the mess Olivia had made in the bedroom the day before. No wonder the bedroom carpet couldn't remain clean she thought to herself.

On Thursday morning while she was still giving Olivia her breakfast, the telephone rang.

"Hello."

"Hola, Señorita. Buenos dias. Hoy is Jueves. Me llamo Ronaldo. Cómo estás?" a male voice with a Spanish accent rattled off.

"Hello. I think you have the wrong number."

"You mean you don't speaka Spanish? Oh my God!"

"Hello?"

"You are Ms. Denton yes?"

"Yes."

"New lady taking care of the old ladies of the Englefields?"

"Yes."

"I am Ronaldo Guiterrez. I'm the gentleman who provides the groceries and takes the ladies out for the fresh air once a week."

"Oh, yes right. I know."

"So may I come now and collect your list of groceries?"

"My list of groceries? I didn't make a list. I'll have to make one now."

"That's alright I will come on up and wait. No problema."

"Okay, alright."

"See you in a bit."

"Okay. Bye."

Sandra's mind raced as she began to think about what the grocery list should look like. She was clear about one thing though. She needed meat.

"Sausages, chicken, peanut butter, eggs, milk, cheese.... What else?"

Sandra was still scribbling on a piece of paper when the doorbell rang. She looked through the peep-hole to see a full head of black, wavy hair and bushy eyebrows.

"Ma'am, I am Ronaldo Gutierrez."

When she opened the door, Ronaldo shook her hand and walked right into the apartment as if he were the rightful owner.

"You shouldn't need too many things we made a lot of groceries last week because we knew you were coming so we . . . ."

He paused as he opened the pantry door.

"Ay dios mio!" he mumbled under his breath as he let out a sigh. His back was facing Sandra.

"I haven't seen too many groceries in the cupboard or the fridge. Mostly oatmeal and crackers and things like that."

The man who was slightly shorter than Sandra had a puzzled look on his face. He opened the refrigerator doors and gasped.

"Is this all you found here?"

"No there were some strawberries and some blueberries but they were rotting so I threw them out."

Ronaldo began to curse in his native tongue under his breath. He was cursing Ms. Winters for stealing last week's groceries. Sandra could not understand a word that he was saying but she could tell by the way his eyebrows met in the centre of his forehead and the way his mouth and black moustache moved, that he was not happy at all. He was not a bad looking man. He had a slim build and his skin was a pale tan. He wore a pair of jeans and a light blue shirt neatly tucked in at the waist. He smelt of cigars and cheap cologne. Still mumbling in Spanish, he walked down the corridor with Sandra behind him and entered the ladies' bedroom.

"Buenos dias, señoritas," he said with a smile.

"Buenos dias, señor," Joan replied

Sandra was surprised that Joan knew Spanish.

"Señorita Olivia, how are you?"

"Come." said Olivia in a weak, frail voice.

Sandra was aghast. She could not believe that Olivia was capable of intelligible speech. The short man stepped forward and leaned his face close to hers. Sandra, afraid that Olivia was getting ready to assault Ronaldo, dashed forward in time to witness Olivia plant a wet, sloppy kiss on Ronaldo's cheek.

"What! She really like you boy."

He turned to Joan who was now red-faced and blushing and planted a kiss on her cheek.

"To the most beautiful señorita in the ball."

Joan blushed a little more and smiled.

"This afternoon we will go on the most beautiful adventure. The weather is perfecto. The sun is shining in the sky. The water is calling for you."

He sounded like a used car salesman selling the day that way.

Sandra stood bewildered. Clearly this Ronaldo had a thing going with the ladies. Olivia had spoken and given him a kiss. Perhaps she really was sane. Perhaps she knew what she was doing when she was hitting her in the head. The thought of this began to make Sandra's blood boil.

Ronaldo seemed eager to be on his way.

"Is the list ready?"

"Well, I wrote down some things that I think we need, and that I think that they need. I know you accustomed getting their things so you would know better than me . . . ."

"May I see?" he said almost snatching the list from her hand.

He checked each item with his finger.

"Uh hum .... Uh hum ...."

"I will get you some of the briefs because I am sure you will be needing those and then later this afternoon I will take them out for the walk on the pier."

"Is the water close to here?"

"Yes, a most beautiful sight to see. Maybe when we go you can come along and see."

"I would like that."

"No problema, señorita."

"I didn't know Olivia could talk. She didn't say nothing since I reach."

"She can speak. Very much."

"They like you a lot." Sandra remarked.

"I have known them many years. They are good women," he said almost admiringly.

Sandra wondered what he would think of Olivia if he had seen her on Monday morning smearing her shit on the wall. She wondered if he would think she was so good.

"Well, I will be back around three o'clock with the groceries and then we can go for a walk." He was in a hurry. That evening after the groceries had been bought and the women saddled up in a fancy two-seater battery-powered scooter that looked almost like an adult pram, Sandra and Ronaldo left the apartment bound for the pier.

It was her first time out of the apartment since Monday and she was glad to have the opportunity to get some fresh air. On the ground floor she paid close attention to all she had not noticed before—the lobby chairs, the plants, the décor, the water cooler, the marble coffee table. She had hoped to see Mr. Bell again but he was nowhere in sight and an obese round-faced white man sat in his place at the front desk. Ronaldo took what looked like a service elevator down to the basement and when the doors opened, Sandra could smell the salt in the air. There it was, the huge expanse of blue water that was Huntington Harbor. She could hear the lapping of the waves against the moss laden wooden jetty. A shoal of white sailboats seemed motionless in the distance. She could see green land. The skyline was hazy and grey from the clouds of airborne pollutants. The lawn grass carpet under her feet smelt freshly cut. A warm breeze touched her skin. There was silence as Ronaldo pushed the scooter along the paved walkway. She strolled next to him on the grass.

"So where are you from you said? Jamaica?"

"No. I'm from Trinidad."

"Oh Trrrrinidad . . . ." he said rolling his tongue almost mockingly.

"I know a few people from Trrrinidad."

Sandra realized the tongue rolling was not intentional.

"Nice people the people of Trinidad and Tobaaaaaago."

"Tobago." she corrected.

"Yes. Nice people."

They walked on in silence.

When they got to the jetty, he pushed the sisters half way out and stood there on the strong wooden structure. Sandra stood beside him quietly, listening to the water crash against the wooden legs of the jetty. The moment seemed almost sacred. It was the kind of moment that demanded silence; that words could spoil. She watched the sun setting in the sky spreading its fiery tongues across the blue canopy. She wondered what her mother was doing. Granny Maye had never been to America. How Sandra wished she could share that moment with her.

CHAPTER TWELVE
Brooklyn Party

It was Friday evening and Sandra was looking forward to returning to Brooklyn. She hated not being able to go and come as she pleased. Staying in that apartment day in, day out, made her feel cut off from the outside world. Now that she had seen the blue serene waters of Huntington Harbor, she resented the fact that she could not run away to the jetty as often as she pleased. Still, she had managed to survive one entire week of Joan and Olivia and in light of all that she had experienced she considered that an accomplishment. Tired of looking at American television, she longed to hear Patsy's sweet Trini accent that had only been slightly corrupted by many years of living in Brooklyn.

Sandra had called Patsy on Monday night.

"Yes, I reach good but them ladies and them not easy Patsy."

"Oh gosh .... well I so glad you reach good, but don't talk long on this phone cause you don't want to run up the bill."

"Okay. But wait, you hear anything from Trinidad."

"Yes. Mama Maye call yes. Something with Tony and school and Chester and something."

"What she say?"

"Girl, I cyan't give you all that story now. We using up good minutes. When you come on the weekend nah."

"Alright no problem."

"Okay, well bye. And remember to just treat the people and them good, you hear. Even if it hard just smile and bear it."

Sandra believed that Patsy would not have said that if she had any idea what the women were like. She was anxious to hear what trouble Tony had got himself into but more than that she wanted to get her US$500 for that first week.

Her weekend relief came around five o'clock; a Spanish-looking woman named Suzie with a Bajan accent, hazel coloured eyes and light brown, wavy hair.

"They alright?"

"Yes. You know them?"

"Yes. I beeeen here befaar. I know what them bitches does give. Go on ahead and come back on time. Monday maarnin seven o'clock."

Sandra was glad to take her leave with her little Macy's bag packed with dirty clothes. Suzie had told her how to catch a bus to Huntington Station so that she wouldn't have to call a cab. On her way out the building she looked at the front desk to see if there was any sign of Mr. Bell. Her heart sank when she saw again the overweight white gentleman sitting like an overstuffed egg, on a chair that would probably be crying out for mercy, if chairs could speak. Maybe next week she would see him, she hoped. For now her first order of business was getting home and getting her first week's pay.

By the time she got to East 23rd Street it was almost seven o'clock but the sun was still in the sky as if it was still early in the afternoon. An excited Patsy and a sombre looking Lenny greeted her.

"So how it went?"

"Girl, if you know. It wasn't easy. Dem women and dem not easy."

"Eh heh.... How you mean?"

"Well, one I don't know what she have. One minute she good, good, good, talking normal, next minute she crying and bawling and carrying on."

"I think it have a name for that you know. What they call that again?... Oh gosh... I think is bi-something.... bi.... bi... bi-colon.... yes bi-colon... ain't Lenny?"

Lenny was washing dishes trying not to listen to what the women were saying.

"Yes. But I think the word is bipolar."

"Ain't that is where yuh does get depress and then get back happy?"

"Something like that."

"Well Ms. Joan definitely bi-colon," said Sandra, not making the correction.

"And well as for Ms. Olivia I don't know what is she problem. I think she have Alzheimer's, because she doesn't look like she know what going on no time. I have to spend a lot of time making sure she don't wipe her shit all over the place."

"Oh gosh! That Alzheimer's does be something else you know. I know a lady that get that. It not nice at all."

"Girl, I so glad you reach back this hour. It having a back in time basement party down by Johnny and I was hoping you could come."

"Party Patsy! Girl I so tired. I ain't get no good night of sleep yet for the whole week. Plus I want to get my pay so I was hoping to pass and check Ms. Goodridge."

"Oh gosh come nah girl. Them parties by Johnny does be so nice. You will like it. And we could still pass by Ms.Goodridge on the way to the party. Lenny here so we could get a drop to go and come back. Oh gosh, come nah!" Patsy pleaded.

"You will have a nice time. I promise."

Sandra was exhausted and in no mood for a party but she did not wish to disappoint her host.

"Well alright but let's call Ms. Goodridge about my pay first, after that we could go."

Two hours later the women were dressed to the hilt and smelling up the small living room with their perfumes. A call to Ms. Goodridge would bring disappointing news.

"Good night, Ms.Goodridge, is Sandra here."

"Sandra?"

"Denton . . . . Patsy Wallace cousin."

"Right, from Trinidad, the one in the Long Island job. How you going?"

"Good. Good."

"How is the job going?"

"Good. Good. It's going very good."

"That's what I like to hear."

"Well as meh first week finish I was wondering if I could come by for meh pay nah."

There was a moment of silence.

"No, well you see, you have to wait until month end you know. You don't get paid till month end. I don't have any control over that," she said non-apologetically.

"That is the agency arrangement. That is a special agency job." Sandra was confused. She thought Ms. Goodridge ran the agency.

"Yes, so all the arrangements for that job is by another agency. I am just the facilitator. So I have to wait until they give me the money for the month and then I can pay you and the other workers, like all who filling in on the weekend and so on and so on."

"Ohh . . . ho . . . . So I have to wait till month end then. You is just the facility then."

"Facilitator . . . Yes dear."

"Alright."

"Yes so call me month end, nah. I will have your money for you by then."

"Okay. Alright. Bye."

When Sandra explained the situation to Patsy she was not happy at all. Not being able to get her five hundred dollars after putting up with a whole week of Olivia's wailing and of eating crackers and oatmeal put a damper on the evening plans.

"But I don't understand that, Lenny. What you think about that? So you mean you have to work a whole month before you get pay? But people have to live! How you could tell the people that! But what happen to Lorna, boy?"

Lenny didn't like the sound of it either. The sight of the women sitting there, with worried looks on their faces was disconcerting. If they opted to spend the night indoors, that would most certainly cramp his style. This prompted Lenny to say more words than he normally would under the circumstances.

"Look, there's nothing to be done about it right now. Why don't you ladies go on to the party, have a drink, dance a little bit and relax. No point in staying here to worry about it," said Lenny.

"Is true, Sandra. Best we go. Not to worry, month end is just now. Most important thing at least you have a work and you don't have to worry about paying no rent or bills or nothing like that."

Sandra forced a smile. She wasn't sure they understood how she felt. Lenny had a stable job working as a toll-booth operator with the New York-New Jersey Port Authority. Patsy, after working for many years as a live-in caregiver was now working the day shift as a nursing assistant in a retirement home. Their son Dexter had a job, even if it was one he didn't want. Their estranged daughter lived out in New Jersey with her boyfriend. But she, what did she have? No husband to rely on; an elderly mother, no money in the bank and two growing children with needs . . . real needs. No, they couldn't understand and she realized just then that it would be foolish of her to expect them to.

"Yuh right. Let's go, yes. I just have to pass some water. And I hope they have Guinness yes. I could really use one." After Lenny dropped them off he headed straight for the I95. His mistress was waiting for him in Queens and because of the delay he would have to cut short the length of his visit.

The music was blasting. A string of cars lined the streets and Sandra could hear the laughter and the sounds of people having a good time.

"Patsy! Patsy!" a tall, red-skinned woman called as they entered Johnny's backyard through a side gate.

"Lystra you here?" The women hugged.

"Oh gosh so long I ain't see you. How you going? Where's Lenny?"

"You know, Lenny. Boring as ever. He don't like crowd. You know how he stop."

"And who's this?"

"Oh this is my cousin from Trinidad, Sandra. Sandra, this is Lystra, a very good friend."

Before Sandra could start to say hello the woman gave Sandra a huge embrace. She smelt of rum and held a cigarette gingerly between the fingers of her right hand.

"Well Sandra. Welcome to Brooklyn. How long you visiting for?"

"She just here for a short time. Not long," Patsy offered before Sandra had the opportunity to tell the truth in her customary naive way.

"Well come on downstairs and get something to eat. You know how we party up here in Brooklyn. Patsy make sure your cousin have a good time you hear?" She puffed on her cigarette and turned her head away, blowing grey smoke up into the sky.

"We'll talk later, Patsy, okay." And with that she was off.

There were about fifteen people in the backyard on chairs around round tables, mostly men and a few women. A bottle of Johnny Walker Black was the centrepiece, flagged by a still taller half full bottle of Vodka and another shorter bottle of Scotch Whiskey. Short cocktail glasses filled with ice and liquor were everywhere. The men were talking loudly, laughing, slapping their legs as they discoursed. The women sat on garden chairs chatting, smoking, and enjoying the night air.

The music in the basement was booming and as the Marvin Gaye classic began to play, the crowd began to scream in delight.

> *"I've been really tryin', baby*
> *Tryin' to hold back this feelin' for so long*
> *And if you feel like I feel, baby*
> *Then come on, oh, come on*
> *Whoo, let's get it on*
> *Ah, babe, let's get it on*

Let's love, baby
Let's get it on, sugar
Let's get it on
Whoo-ooh-ooh"

Sandra and Patsy had descended the basement stairs and could now see the crowd. There were at least one hundred people there, jamming, dancing, wining. They seemed mostly in their late forties and early fifties but there were some older ones. Men held their women tightly as they swayed to the rhythm of the music. Some people were eating. A few women seated on chairs were drinking and laughing. On the food table there was every imaginable West Indian food—souse, pelau, oil down, pepper pot, ackee and saltfish, coo-coo and flying fish, rice and black-eyed peas, roti with curried channa and potatoes, aloo pies, green fig pie, mountain chicken, jerk chicken, Jamaican patties and every other imaginable delicacy.

After they had over-filled their plates with every possible food, they made their way to a corner of the room where they sat side by side.

"So who is Lystra?"

"Lystra? She's a good friend of mine. I met her some years ago. She came up just like you to do a six months and ended up marrying her cousin in order to stay up here."

"Her cousin?"

"Yes, people do that you know. Is plenty lying and plenty hard work to convince the immigration people but people does marry strangers all the time for a green card to be up here, you know. Pay four thousand US dollars and all kinda thing. Sometimes the people does run off with the money and leave them in one setta problems because they ain't go through with all the paper work. Lawyers too, a next set of money hounds. So she decide might as well marry the cousin and stay and her cousin ain't look nothing like her. His hair straight, straight, straight. Fella looking one hundred percent Indian but he mother black like you and me. So they pull it off and she get to stay up here."

"Hmm! They still married?" Sandra asked in disbelief.

"Of course not. That was just for the papers. You self."

They continued to have their fill of the food and listened to the sweet sounds of soca by Shadow, Sparrow, Kitchener, Baron and the like.

"Music sweeeeeeeet," said a woman who had just come to sit beside them with a plate of food. Patsy girl, how are you going?"

Sandra could tell by Patsy's body language that she did not care to talk to the woman who had come to sit beside her.

"Good. I'm good."

"Wait. This is your relative, Sandra? How she resemble you so?" the meddling woman asked.

"Yes, is my cousin. She from Trinidad."

"Nice. I didn't know you still had cousins in Trinidad I thought all your family were up here already."

Patsy, not wanting the woman to pry further, grudgingly opted to ask her a question that she knew would keep her babbling incessantly for a little while.

"So Amanda how is everything with you?" That was the magic question the woman seemed to be wanting to hear. She fell into Patsy's trap like a fish to bait.

"Oh the children are doing great. Lester just finished his thesis for his Master's degree at Colombia University and Celeste is graduating next year from Yale. You know that Yale is one of the best universities in the country. Actually it's ranked number one and it's very difficult to get in there.

Anyway she and her husband say they want to move to Pennsylvannia. I don't really like there but you know. You should see him, Patsy. He is like something out of a magazine, with blue eyes and curly blonde hair. You should see him. I can't wait for them to make my grandchildren. And of course, well Joanna is doing simply marvellous. We just got her placed into a school for children with above average intelligence and do you know we found out that it's the same school that a famous US High Court judge used to go to? I mean it is just amazing how wonderful the children are all doing and of course my husband Peter . . . . Patsy, you met Peter already, not so?"

"Yes."

"Well, he just got promoted at the company. He works for a Fortune 500 company, you know. Procter and Gamble and he's doing very well, very well. So we are even thinking of moving out and buying a place up in Long Island, you know. Just to get out of the city. The properties there are so expensive but Peter's doing so well now I think we can afford it. And well me I'm so busy with . . . ."

Sandra tried to pretend that she was listening attentively to what the woman was saying, to compensate for Patsy's obvious lack of interest. Thankfully the monologue was interrupted by the loud laughter of a short brown-skinned man who approached Patsy with arms outstretched. Patsy who had by now finished eating, greeted the gentleman, who looked about sixty, with a warm embrace.

"You know how long I looking for you baby?"

"Don't talk stupidness," said Patsy with a smile.

"Ladies, goodnight. I don't know why you all sitting down allowing sweet soca music and nice rockers to waste but I am stealing this lady from you if you don't mind."

The woman smiled as did Sandra who dreaded the idea of being left alone with the monologue queen. Her fears were alleviated as she soon realized that all that boasting and bragging had really been for Patsy's benefit and not hers. The woman couldn't find too many words to say to Sandra and left shortly after Patsy made it to the dance floor with the sweet smelling gentleman. Later that night Patsy would explain to her.

"That wretch name Amanda. Always boasting, always talking about what the husband do and what the children do and what they get and what they buy. She like to show off too damn much. She come up in America eight years now and the husband get a lucky break and now she feel that she have to tell everybody how good she doing in life. I can't stand her. She too damn arrogant. And I hear she father sick back home in Trinidad and she wouldn't even send a red cent for him. Imagine . . . . with all the money the husband making. Imagine that. And she works noooooowhere. She only talking so but the woman have no education at all . . . . smart as a rock that one. Grow up in the bush in Mayaro you know, now pretending like she don't know nothing bout Trinidad."

On the dance floor the charming gentleman who had whisked Patsy away seemed to be dancing a bit too close. Patsy whispered in his ear in a way that was a little too familiar. Sandra sat alone enjoying the music. The DJ was working the crowd; playing one sweet melody after another. Soca, reggae, rockers. She was feeling too sleepy to get up and dance. Her muscles were sore and her body ached. Then she heard a most familiar voice beside her.

"Well tonight must be my lucky night. I have set my eyes on the prettiest sight."

Mr. Bell. There he was in a white silk shirt and black pants, smelling like Old Spice sitting beside her. The buttons of his shirt were slightly open and in the dim basement lights she could see his hairy, muscular chest.

"What you doing here?" she asked trying her best to hide how excited she was to see him.

"I got invited by a friend of a friend," he answered

"You looking so lovely sitting down here all alone."

"I'm with my cousin. That's her there on the dance floor," she pointed in Patsy's direction.

"So you live in Brooklyn?"

"Sure do. No other place I'd rather be especially when there are queens like you around."

Sandra blushed.

"I looked for you at the front desk today when I was leaving but I didn't see you."

"Today's my day off."

"Oh. Okay."

"But listen I don't want to spend the night talking about work when we could be grooving on the dance floor. So what do you say?"

Just then the music changed and Keith Reid's song began to play.

> *"We skipped the light fandango turned cartwheels 'cross the floor*
> *I was feeling kinda seasick but the crowd called out for more*
> *The room was humming harder as the ceiling flew away*
> *When we called out for another drink the waiter brought a tray*

And so it waaaas that laaaater as the miller told his tale that her face, at first just ghostly, turned a whiter shade of pale"

Mr. Bell stretched out his hand, palm facing upward. Sandra put her hand in his and allowed him to lead her into the crowd.

CHAPTER THIRTEEN

Antonio's Vacation

After Chester's violent outburst in the Guidance Counsellor's office, Granny Maye had tried her best to put Antonio on lock down but it was holiday time and school was out and there were endless possibilities for mischief. With threats and warnings she tried to forbid him from seeing Martin. She begged him to try to get a job with the nearby S & S grocery store as a packer. Antonio scoffed at the idea. He felt he was too intelligent for that kind of menial labour and had found more profitable opportunities for income earning with his cousin. One night when he returned from a day of nefarious activities or doing the God-alone-knows-what-things Granny Maye assumed he was doing, she threatened to take him to the police station and give him to the police to mind. She begged and pleaded with him for the sake of his mother, to stop coming home late and to stop keeping bad company. She didn't know where he was getting his money from but wherever it was, she knew it most certainly did not involve gainful employment.

"Boy, is a bullet I trying to save you from yuh know boy. Is only so long yuh could go on doing whatever the hell you doing before the law ketch up with yuh. And when that happen I ain't going to pretend like you is no good boy you know. I ain't going to be bawling and crying and saying you never do dis and you never do dat . . . . Is only yuh poor mother who go be bawling and crying cause she bussing she ass in America for you and what you doing eh . . . what you doing? Where you getting the money for them brands shoe yuh buying, eh Tony boy? Yuh works nowhere but yuh drawing pay . . . . tell me nah Tony boy. Which man does be doing dat, eh?"

Antonio steupsed. He was tired of the nagging and the constant harassment.

"You ain't bound to tell me yuh know but one day it will ketch up with you. One day you will have to tell the police or the judge but that is if yuh live to tell. Otherwise yuh will jus be another little black boy that get kill and all yuh mother do, eh . . . . all yuh mother doing now for you just going and be a big waste." She wanted to be hard on him. She hoped somehow something she said was making a dent. Maybe it was. She hoped it was. But when at ten o'clock in the night he hadn't returned home, she knew that wherever he was it was no place good. And when he would bounce in at almost midnight smelling of cigarette smoke or sometimes marijuana she knew that her fears were confirmed.

Every night Granny Maye went to sleep worrying about Sandra and Antonio and Andrea. She wondered why Antonio couldn't just behave and study his books like Mr. Singh's son; why Sandra couldn't have married a better man than Chester; a man who wasn't a womanizer and a wife beater; a man who would take care of his children and be a father to them.

She would argue with a God who had seen it fit to inflict her in her old age with the challenge of parenting two young children. She had done her fair share in her days of child-rearing. Now she wanted to relax and spend her days reading and planting her vegetable garden, not packing lunch kits and staying up late to see what hour Antonio would come home.

"You tell Sandra anything?"

"No. I don't want to worry her."

"But you will send up yuh pressure Ms. Maye. What sense that make? Tony and Andrea is Sandra cattle horn. That is she cattle horn. Remember cattle horn never too heavy for he head to carry. You carry your cattle horn already!"

Barbara was sorry for her. She had a sick husband but that was her husband, her worry. Poor Granny Maye couldn't rest with Antonio being out those late hours doing as he pleased.

"Gyul, I know. I know. And the father ain't business at all. That boy need he father. He need a man to show him things about life that a woman can't, to show him how to be a man. He need a father to show him that man does have to work hard for what he have if he want to have anything in the world. But the father not studying him and now the mother gone up. Who is me the grandmother to tell him what to do?"

"Is true. But I worried for you, Ms. Maye. When Sandra coming back?"

"Maybe in a few months."

"Well ah hope he ain't get into no trouble because it go be hell to pay, I tell you real hell. That boy ain't see that police shooting first and asking questions later ah what.

You ain't see dem boys down in Point who get shoot up sitting down in a car. The police saying how they fire on them but up to now dey can't find no gun what dey say dem boys use."

"Is true."

"One hundred bullets you know Maye . . . . not ten not twenty . . . . One whole hundred bullets for two people. Steups! Tony better study he head before he collect one ah dem bullets and dead."

"Barbara, gyul I ain't know what to say again. Dat boy head hard as nails. Hard like stone. Anyway, let me go and see bout meh garden eh. I have a pumpkin growing nice, nice. When it get big I will cut a piece for you."

The women ended their conversation but Granny Maye went inside with a heavy heart. The thought of law enforcement catching up with her grandson deeply saddened her. However, it was almost inevitable.

Later that day when Granny Maye went to her vegetable garden and saw the patch of fresh dirt out of place under her pumpkin vine she didn't have a clue. There was the dirt, brown and freshly dug, patted down. Some broken leaves told the tale. Someone had been there. Who? There was nothing missing. The pumpkin was still there. It was not yet ready. The ochroes, tomatoes, limes, they were all there. Odd. Someone had been digging there. Looking for something? Hiding something. Buster had not barked or raised an alarm. She wondered. Tony. She waited up for him that night. But that night he did not come home. It was the first night that he did that. It would be one of many such nights.

In a few short weeks, Martin had found significant use for Antonio in the criminal world. Martin whose alias was "Tall Man" because he was an impressive six footer at such a young age and Antonio whose new alias was "Smart Man", because his English was so good, had become essential to a bandit by the name of Psycho.

Psycho was one of the small fish in the underworld of a drug baron who ran a foreign used car dealership in Chaguanas. The car dealership was the legitimate business through which monies could be laundered. Full container loads of used vehicles with cocaine hidden in welded, spray painted compartments, behind gauge clusters, went unnoticed by customs officers on the port of Pt. Lisas. It was a money-making business and the cost of keeping the eyes and mouths of custom officials closed was well worth the profit raked in by the multibillion dollar industry which flourished throughout the island. This entrepreneur, known in the business world as Mr. Fung Ki Chi, was simply referred to as "El Jefe" by those who would do the less honourable work that was involved in running a drug cartel. Psycho was one of those lower down on the food chain who would be called to make key evidence disappear or a witness have a sudden bout of amnesia or, on occasion, permanently close the mouth of a customs officer who, after several years of dishonest dealings, had suddenly found Jesus and wanted to confess his sins, not only to God but to the police. You see there was no turning back unscathed once you put your hand in the pot of criminality; especially when it involved doing business with Mr. Fung Ki Chi.

Psycho and Martin were acquaintances long before Antonio met him. Martin aka Tall Man was doing so well for himself that Psycho had promoted him, in a sense, changing his responsibilities to more serious ones. With the promotion came a vehicle. And after two driving lessons together with a few bribes at the licensing office, a driver's permit followed. Therein lay the opportunity for Martin to bring his cousin Antonio into the business and assume the responsibilities that would no longer be his, that of becoming the mongoose. It was not hard for Antonio to assume the role of being the mongoose. He was the perfect candidate for the job and Granny Maye's vegetable garden the perfect mongoose hole. Psycho did not look anything like Antonio imagined he would. He wasn't unkempt or poorly dressed. He didn't look mentally unstable. He was the essence of suave and civility; a brown-skinned man of medium build, bald, well-shaven and well-dressed. Psycho seemed an inappropriate name. It simply did not fit. He had only seen him from a distance when he came to talk to Martin. It was as if Martin was trying to shield him from Antonio. Now with Martin moving up in rank he would have a chance to meet Psycho up close.

It happened one night at Matura Bay. It was dark and a fierce wind stirred the angry waves as they crashed violently against the shore. A pale crescent moon, with stars like subjects in attendance waiting on a king, lit up the night sky. A soft glow of light floated on the water and the damp, cold sand. Except for the noise of the waves the bay was quiet and lonely, not the way it usually was when turtle watchers would come to see the massive leatherback turtles dig their holes and procreate, thick mucus dripping from their eyes. Martin looked nervously at his watch. The last car had passed ten minutes ago. He knew better than to call Psycho. Psycho didn't like being called, among other things.

"Da is him coming there."

"How you know?" Antonio asked.

"Ah jus know .... Wait."

The lights of the oncoming vehicle blinded them somewhat as it pulled up alongside them.

"Tall man."

"Psycho."

"Come for a drive nah."

Antonio and Martin almost instinctively got into Psycho's car. It was cool and sweet smelling. The seats were leather. The car continued on the long winding road.

"So Smart Man, is real easy. As Tall Man tell yuh."

"Two thousand dollars a month. All yuh have to do is hide whatever yuh get. Don't ask no f—king question. Don't say nuttin to no f—king body. Once yuh get it yuh hide it. Don't care where yuh f—king hide it. Yuh could hide it in yuh woman c-nt. Ah doh care. Just be sure dat when I ask for it yuh could give it to me."

"Ah could do dat."

"Yuh sure boy? Yuh f—king sure boy?"

"Is serious f—king business, yuh know. If yuh know yuh cyah make, say so now."

Saying no would not have cost him his life that night, perhaps only some respect. But Antonio wanted the job. He wanted that money. Two thousand dollars for hiding guns and drugs for Psycho, he thought. It couldn't be that bad. He knew just the place. Nobody would look there. Nobody would know.

"Men does get day f—king neck pop easy out here yuh know Smart Man. So ah hope yuh is a Smart Man, otherwise yuh go be a dead man and Psycho don't leave any trace. He like de wind. Time yuh feel it on yuh face it done f—king pass," said the man referring to himself in the third person. Antonio swallowed. His throat suddenly felt dry. He knew he was getting into something far bigger than himself.

"Cell phone." Psycho pitched a small neat black cell phone on to the back seat.

"When I call yuh. Ah don't care if yuh in de middle of de hottest shit or de sweetest f—k yuh will answer dat phone eh. Right, Smart Man?"

"Yeah boss."

"Tall Man, just make sure dis man doh f—k me up, eh."

"Dat will never happen," said Martin convincingly.

Psycho said all this without changing his tone or raising his voice or moving his right hand off the steering wheel. His face was emotionless, as cold as his heart. He was the kind of man who could cut off a man's penis just for the fun of it and eat a doubles in the same minute. Rumour had it that he had earned the name Psycho more than ten years prior, when at the age of twenty he had, in a fit of rage, killed his girlfriend by bludgeoning her to death. That had not been enough for him though. He had sodomized her repeatedly with a mop stick, cut off her breasts, gouged out her eyes and rammed a broken bottle up her vagina all post mortem. The girl's mother found him sitting on top of her, clothes bloodied getting ready to do something even more gruesome. The poor girl was only seventeen. It was supposed to be a pretty straightforward case. Then the girl's mother died mysteriously of a heart attack. An autopsy was not done since the woman was in her fifties and her body bore no marks of violence. If they had looked just a wee bit closer, investigators would have found the needle prick on the vein of her right foot where the fatal dose of morphine had been given. But she had on socks and shoes when they found her and neighbours said she had gone to the market that day. And so the case fell apart and Elijah Rubio got away with murder and many more murders after that. Because in Trinidad everybody had a price and Mr. Fung Ki Chi had enough money to name everyone's price. And, if the price was too high or someone was being considered to be too unreasonable, there were always men like Psycho and others who could take care of that.

CHAPTER FOURTEEN

Gun Barrel—No Barrel

It was one month since Sandra had started working in Huntington. She had been almost two months in America and was looking forward to getting paid. Slowly but surely she had adjusted to the rhythm of the week. She had mastered the art of keeping the women clean without cleaning them every day. She knew when Olivia was prone to acting up and when to solicit Joan's help. She had made friends with Ronaldo and looked forward to seeing Mr. Bell at work. He in turn was only too happy to drop by the apartment to exchange little niceties and sweet talk her with his smooth Southern accent. Sandra had danced with him all night at Johnny's basement party. She slept all day that Sunday and had barely recovered from the weekend when it was time to resume her duties with the Englefields.

Her weekends were short but when she was at home she made the most of them. Mr. Bell had helped her with many things too. He showed her how to use the laundry in the basement of the apartment complex; how to load the coin tray and add the fabric softener that came in a pack like bubble gum. He even showed her how to use the vending machine and taught her how to straighten out the dollar bills before having them gobbled up. He called her often too, sometimes from the front desk, other times on her cell phone. One Saturday night when he was off, he took her out to the cineplex at King's Plaza to catch a movie. They walked arm in arm that night and when they sat next to each other in the cinema, he held her hand and stroked her thigh. He held her hand for the entire movie and rested it between his legs so that she could feel his manhood. That night when he dropped her home he kissed her, not on the mouth as she had hoped, but on the cheek. She found it odd that he would be a gentleman just then, when she had spent most of the time in the cinema with her hand on his crotch. Perhaps he was just a gentleman, she thought. She wasn't sure and made little mention of him to Patsy lest nothing should come of the budding romance.

Granny Maye had called her more than once but from what she could gather, all was well and her children were having a good summer vacation. Andrea was in camp and Antonio wasn't doing anything but Granny Maye had assured her that he was going to get a job at the S & S grocery store. Sandra was glad that school was out and Antonio was no longer breaking biche. She didn't like that Granny Maye had got Chester involved in their family affairs. For the most part he was an absent father and Antonio had provided him with an opportunity to pretend that he genuinely cared. But Sandra was doing alright. She was used to taking the Long Island Railway now and Joan and Olivia, though challenging to care for, were getting used to her and had become more pliable. She had made her month of work and would get her pay from Ms. Goodridge. She had even investigated the cost of sending a barrel home to Trinidad. One hundred and twenty US dollars. That was more than enough. With two thousand US dollars in hand she could full three barrels with clothes, shoes and food and send it home to Granny Maye. She knew that her mother's pension was barely enough to cover expenses associated with running a home and caring for two children. But her disappointment that Saturday night would be great when she called Ms. Goodridge to collect her pay.

"Ms. Goodridge?"

"Yes. Goodnight. Is Sandra . . . . Sandra Denton."

"Right. The one with the Long Island job. How is it going?"

"Good, I making out alright."

"Nice. I glad to hear that."

"So I was wondering about getting pay, nah."

"Getting pay?"

"Yes, well you know is a month now, nah and I know you said last time that when the month end is time for pay."

"Oh . . . . yes . . . that's right."

"So, well I wanted to pass for it this evening, nah."

"Right, right."

"Well, listen Sandra is not much you know."

"Well you know with the contract agreement you don't get much from the first month of pay."

"What? How you mean?" Sandra asked, her heart now pounding in her chest.

"Well is just about five percent with the contract. So is not much."

"What? Five percent of what?"

"Five percent of your salary is what you get for the first month, but the next set of months you get the full salary."

"What? But how come you never tell me that?"

"Is in the contract. The contract you signed. Most contracts like that. Anywhere you go they will do the same thing. I ain't doing nothing different from the rest of people."

"Why you didn' tell me?"

"Well I thought Patsy woulda tell you. She know bout these things. She know how it is."

"She didn't tell me."

There was a moment of silence. Sandra was trying to compose herself, trying not to cry and not to curse out Ms. Goodridge at the same time.

"So how much ah have to get?"

"Just about one hundred dollars. Is so small better you leave it till next month and collect it with next month pay. It ain't make no sense you come all the way out here this hour for one hundred dollars."

"Right."

Sandra didn't agree. She wanted her hundred dollars that very instant. It was her money. She had worked for it. Worked hard.

"Besides, I going out in a little while so you not going to meet me home."

"Right."

"So next month, nah?"

Sandra was so filled with rage that she became almost mute. She could barely form the words to come out of her mouth. She wanted to scream. She wanted to curse and threaten to kill Ms. Goodridge if she did not give her her money. Her head was hurting.

"Yes, alright," she whispered into the telephone.

Her eyes were full of tears. She could not hold back the flow. They left their watery trail down the sides of her cheeks and made two distinct puddles on her pants legs as she sat at the dining table in Patsy's basement home and wept. Sandra was glad to be at home alone that day. It allowed her the freedom to cry and cry and not have to hide or hold back.

She wondered what her life was all about and why it seemed that no matter how hard she tried, things never seemed to work out. Every step forward ended up being twenty steps back. It had been like this her whole life. It wasn't that she hadn't tried to do better for herself. She had tried so hard, perhaps too hard. When she married Chester at the age of twenty-five, she had hopes that together they could have a good life. Times were hard for her and she already had a son by him. It made sense to marry him, even though she didn't like the way he would get when he had too much to drink. It made sense to marry him. Everybody said so. She couldn't have known that his drinking would get worse and worse and that he would hit harder and harder, using whatever was at his disposal to do so; sometimes a bilna, other times the mop, a pan, one day even the fan. It just got worse. But he was her husband, the father of her child and a second one was on the way and she hoped things would get better. It was the night she went into labour that she knew that all her hopes of having a happy family went out the door. That night she knew she had to leave. She remembered it as clear as day. She was thirty weeks along, with ten more to go. Her feet were swollen and her hips and back hurt every day. Her belly was big and although she walked with a slow waddle, she still went to work at S& S grocery every day where she worked as a cashier. The hours were long but she needed the money since most of Chester's went in rum. She was watching TV that night he came home drunk and smelling of rum and cigarette smoke. He cursed her because there were dishes in the sink and because she didn't bother to get up from the chair in which she was sitting. He picked up the empty plastic mop bucket she had used earlier that evening to mop the kitchen floor and hit her with full force on the back of her head with it. She remembered getting a headache that instant and she remembered cursing him back, but he just kept on hitting and hitting and hitting, over and over again. She remembered screaming and bawling. She remembered the baby moving. She remembered something wet gushing down her leg. The baby! The baby! She remembered trying to call someone from her cell phone.

She remembered when he snatched it from her and grabbed her by the neck. She remembered waking up in the hospital thinking the baby had died. She remembered that every part of her hurt when she woke up and that her tongue was so heavy she could not speak. She remembered seeing Granny Maye's face and the look that a mother gives when she feels sad because she cannot do anything for her child. She remembered that look and she knew then that she had to leave the monster that was her husband. And that is what she did. With a premature baby, not much bigger than the size of her hand at hospital on ventilatory support, and a five year old, she returned to her mother's house. For many years she hoped she would meet a good man. She was still young and still attractive. But instead she met men with silvery tongues, full of lies and bad ways, whose only interest was getting a chance to use her and boast of it afterward. She had given up on finding true love. It was just a dream and men were all the same.

She kept focusing on her children. They would do better. They would have better. But her money was never enough. Now, here she was in America, trying to get something for her children and this woman was taking advantage of her; taking away her bread and butter. She had worked one whole month and only one hundred US dollars to show for it. That was less than what she would get if she had worked one month in S & S. Overwhelmed with disappoint and hurt Sandra couldn't stop crying. She cried herself to sleep in the middle of the evening.

When Patsy returned later that night to get the story from her about her month's pay she was much more subdued but Patsy would have none of it.

"What! What de arse is dis I hearing here! What yuh tell her?"

"She ain't have no right. She ain't have no blasted right to do that. Lenny! Lenny! Best we go down there and talk to her."

"She say it in the contract, Pat. She say I sign to that."

"Did you get a copy of the contract?" asked Lenny.

"Yes. Why?"

"Well did you read it?"

Sandra hadn't thought to do that. It simply hadn't crossed her mind, not even after she had heard what Lorna had to say. So Lenny got his spectacles and sat in the living room reading Sandra's contract—line by line, page by page. He traced each line with his finger, occasionally piercing the silence with an "Hmmm . . . . Uh hummm." When he had finished he took off his spectacles and released a deep sigh.

"What? What is it?"

"Well Ms. Goodridge is right it seems. It's here in the fine print. You only get five percent of your first month's salary and she considers that her agency fee. You also have to refund her one month's salary if you decide to terminate the contract prior to the contract end date."

"What?"

"So, when does the contract end?"

"Well it's a four month contract and ends October 10th. When do you have to go back?"

"November. November 20th."

"So that means you have one month of no work. But why she do that? And she know you staying the full six months!" said an irate Patsy.

"Well there's more too," said Lenny still holding the contract in his hand.

"This contract states that if any of the persons for whom you are giving care dies, that your salary will be cut in half."

"What?"

"Can she do that? Leh me see where that is."

Patsy leaned over Lenny's shoulders to see the fine print of the contract.

"But how she could do that? Sandra ain't no citizen so she can't do no real legal thing like this with her."

"That's exactly why she can. What she is doing is illegal but what you are doing is also illegal. So you really have no recourse," said Lenny trying to keep an even tone.

"But people doing six months for years. Everybody know that. She making money on people head!"

"That may be so, but I don't think there is a whole lot that you can do other than continue in the job and hope to get next month's pay and the rest after that or leave the job and try to look for another one which you have no guarantee you will actually get."

It was not that Lenny didn't understand why Sandra and Patsy were upset. He was simply irritated by Sandra's ignorance and the fact that she had signed a contract she had never bothered to read.

"You always have to read the fine print here, you know. That may save you your life."

"So what you mean, it have nothing she could do?" asked Patsy.

"There really isn't much. Its sort of a catch twenty-two situation."

"Catch how much?"

"A situation where your hands are really tied."

"So it have nothing she could do? Nothing at all?"

Lenny shook his head.

"Sandra, I so sorry." Patsy could see the tears in Sandra's eyes welling up like a dam getting ready to burst.

"Is alright. Ah mean I will get pay next month. Ah just wanted to be able to send a barrel this month for them nah. I was looking forward to getting pay. Ah don't know how Granny Maye coping wid the expense and thing nah," she said in a shaky voice as she wiped away her tears with her hands and then into her pants.

Patsy sat beside her and gave her a big hug. Don't worry gyul, next month, next month. At least yuh have a job. Next month we go send a barrel."

Granny Maye would be disappointed to hear about the situation with Sandra not getting paid but she was glad to hear from her and to learn that she was coping with the demands of the job. She didn't want to tell her about Antonio. She felt Sandra had enough on her plate to worry about. Granny Maye was looking forward to getting some money from Sandra and had hoped to get a barrel. Things were expensive and funds were low. Even though Antonio seemed to be securing funds on his own, it was not for buying groceries or paying bills but for new clothes, shoes, a big gold chain on his neck and for fake diamond earrings for his now pierced ears. So yes, Granny Maye wanted to see a barrel. What she was not prepared for was the barrel she would be looking down that fateful summer morning when she went into her garden shed and found that a crocus bag of manure she had recently purchased had been moved.

She was hoping to use the manure to fertilize the soil around some dying ochro plants in her vegetable garden. The bag of manure was not where she had left it. Someone had been there. Her heart raced. A thief in the area? A manure thief? She had been noticing little things in her backyard. Things were moving, shifting. She thought she was forgetting at first but then there was the digging and the patting down in different places. It was not Buster. He was too dumb. Now this bag of manure. Walking through the shed she looked for signs. Something, anything that would give her a clue as to who had been entering her yard. Where was the bag of manure? The shed was truly a colossal mess. There were paintbrushes and leftover paint, hardened in tins. There were seeds, seedlings, green plastic pots alongside ceramic ones, broken tiles, a garden hose, fertilizer, a brush cutlass, a gallon of diesel, a wheelbarrow, a pitchfork and other garden tools. Shelves haphazardly built housed a dirt-filled basin, garden boots, containers of putty, screws, bolts and a saw. Wood shavings, dirt and dust were everywhere. If she had not hit her big toe against one of the bags of cement, she would not have noticed the bag of manure leaning beside it. There was the bag. It was open and not where she had left it. Someone was stealing manure. But why not take the whole bag? Why take just a little? She got one of her plastic pots and got ready to scoop up a few clumps of the dried dung, when she saw a black plastic bag sticking out from underneath the bag of manure. She reached for it and had to pull forcefully as it was jammed against the post and partially under the bag of cement. There was something solid in there; round; no straight; no wait . . . . Could it be? No she thought. Beads of perspiration began to run relays down her face and chest. With a little manure for its shield there it was; a silver grey Smith and Wesson 9mm semi-automatic. She didn't know that was what it was, all she knew was that it was a gun. A gun that someone had tried to hide in a plastic bag of manure in her shed and she didn't need anyone to tell her that Antonio was involved. Whether he was the one that hid it or the one who allowed the person into her yard to hide it, when she looked down that gun barrel that morning she somehow knew that Antonio had already sealed his fate.

Chapter Fifteen

Land of Opportunity

It was a Thursday afternoon when Sandra's telephone rang. She was about to get some dessert from the refrigerator for Ms. Joan.

"Hello."

"Yes, I'm calling after Sandra."

"Yes, this is Sandra."

"Is Lindy. The lady you met on the train from Geeyanna?"

"Yes, Lindy. I remember you. How you going?"

"I'm good. How you going with the job and everything?"

"I alright. The job okay. It a little hard but I managing."

"The ladies not giving you too much trouble I hope."

"At first, but I getting the hang of it."

"Every job does be a little hard at first but eventually you goin get the hang of it. Anyway I call you to invite you to a business opportunity."

"Business you say? How you mean?"

"Well ent you trying to make money for yourself, right?"

"Yes."

"And you here for a six months right?"

"Yes but . . ."

"Well if I tell you, you could make twice as much money as you making now in addition to what you making now how you think you goin feel bout that?"

Sandra didn't know what Lindy was talking about but the idea of making money appealed to her, especially when she considered that she had not made any real money as yet. It would be at least another two weeks before she would be due to get her pay from Ms. Goodridge, so she was very open to whatever Lindy had to say.

"Well what day you getting off Friday or Saturday?"

"Friday."

"Perfect. There's a meeting you have to come to. You really must come Sandra. It will help you achieve your goals and make money fast. It's a real good thing."

"What it is?"

"Is hard to explain over the phone. You have to come in person."

"I have to sell something?"

"Have you ever heard of network marketing?"

"No. What is that?"

"You have to come to the meeting Friday. They will explain everything to you. You will come?"

"Well I not sure. Where it is?"

"Right on Flatbush Avenue. Right in Brooklyn. You don't have to go far."

"Well alright. I guess I can make it once I get my relief on time."

"Good. You will not regret it Sandra. Trust me. You will make money."

"You sure I don't need papers to do this netting thing you talking about."

"Network marketing. No and it's a lot of fun."

"Alright well I glad to make money. So I in that."

"I'll call you Friday with directions and we'll hook up then, okay."

Sandra did not have that much education. She knew many things but she had not made it past her Form Three class and for the most part her secondary school education was a huge blur. She had been too busy trying to fit in and keep up with the girls in her class. So the day Ms. Maye discovered a huge hickey on her neck, which she had tried to cover by turning the collar up on her school shirt, was the day her mother decided that she needed to learn a skill. She remembered peeping out her bedroom door to eavesdrop on the conversation her parents were having.

"It ain't make no sense, Daddy," said Ms. Maye referring to her husband in the way her children would.

"She not learning nothing in school. One big bruise on she neck. Her skin dark so you know how hard that boy had to be sucking on she neck to leave that mark there, eh." She turned away from the dishes in the kitchen sink and wiped her hands in her apron.

"And imagine when I asking her what is that, she telling me bout how she hit she neck on a wall. Like I is some blasted fool."

Mr. Denton sat stone-faced. You couldn't tell he was upset except for the meeting of his eyebrows that occurred when he frowned his forehead.

"She need an education. We can't just stop her getting an education. She will need that in life. What she going to do without that? She will have to get a man," he said deeply troubled.

"You ain't see, Daddy. She done taking man already right there in school. And if she ain't careful she belly going to rise while she still in school uniform. It have a school she could go to. A vocational school. She could go there and learn something like cooking, sewing, hairdressing, dem kinda thing. She might like that better. She ain't no bright spark but she could do something."

"Daddy" didn't agree. He didn't like the idea at all. But the day she got suspended for skipping class, he realized the seriousness of what his wife was saying.

In the Venus Vocational School, Sandra was exposed to many skills. She learned how to type a bit and how to sew and cook. She liked it there. Two years later when she finished her programme, she started working at S & S grocery store. It wasn't that she wasn't ambitious, she had simply never been encouraged to dream bigger than what she had seen around her. Her mother was a housewife, her father worked at the nearby post-office as a loader. Most of the people in her community had low-end jobs. Of course there were exceptions like Mr. Persad who owned the hardware and Mr. Lee who had the Chinese restaurant that his nine children helped him run. The truth was that Sandra had no idea what she wanted to do with her life, and was clueless about what she wanted to be. She enjoyed many of the activities in the vocational school but she had no career plans outside of getting married and having a baby, not necessarily in that order.

Chester came around one day at S & S wearing a blue coverall and with the confident stride of a man employed. She was the perfect candidate for his next conquest. He didn't plan on marrying her then. He was young with a penchant for gambling, womanizing and rum drinking but there was something about her. He was not sure what. She was different from other girls he had been with before. She had loved him despite the advice of her parents. Her mother had warned her, her father too. "Is wine, woman, and song yuh know. When it have one, must have the other two," her mother had told her when she would find her home many Friday nights. She would find out only too late the kind of man Chester was. The kind of man who could hit her again and again one night and jump on top of her the next for sex; the kind of man who would not come to see his newborn baby in the hospital ICU for weeks. That was Chester her husband. It was because of him she had to move back home to live with her mother. It was his fault she had to be in America wiping the shit from Ms. Olivia's bottom and having Ms. Goodridge make her work for free. Still, Sandra was resolute. She would make some money in these six months and maybe if she were lucky she would do another six months. She would go to the meeting and find out about network marketing even though she didn't know what it was. Chester was a bad decision but now her future was in her hands.

That Friday evening her relief was late. A short Chinese woman who couldn't speak much English. Sandra wondered if the woman knew what she had to do or what her responsibilities were. She tried to tell her the basics but she could tell from the many nods of her head and the darting of her black marble eyes, barely visible between slits for eyelids, that she didn't understand a word Sandra had said.

This was confirmed when in her heavy Mandarin accent the woman asked "Wha chi no wa? Ole lady na?" When she left for Huntington station she hoped the women would be alright and that at least when she returned on Monday they would be none the worse. Lindy called her soon after she had boarded the train for Penn station.

"You coming?"

"Of course. But the relief was late. I now on the train. Where to meet you?"

"I'm already in Brooklyn but I have some networking to do and the meeting is starting a bit late. Call me when you get on Flatbush, okay. I have to go. See you soon."

Sandra was looking forward to seeing Lindy again. She had not seen her since they first met on the train and outside of the phone call to invite her to the meeting, had not communicated with her. She remembered how Lindy had helped her get through the ticket barrier that first day of work but she also recalled that she had managed somehow to steal her cell phone from her on the train. She was nice enough to return it though, Sandra thought. She couldn't possibly be that bad a person. After all she was a West Indian like herself. A Guyanese, no doubt and Sandra knew the reputation Guyanese had even back home in Trinidad. But here in America they were all the same and the average white American would be hard pressed to distinguish between the sprinkling of islands that was God's most beautiful handiwork. Barbados, Grenada, Trinidad and Tobago for most Americans were all the same.

All except for Jamaica. An island which had somehow managed to become the flagship island for the Caribbean region worldwide. Whether it was because of the music of the great Bob Marley, or because of the food or the athletes that won medals at the Olympic Games consistently raising the yellow and green flag higher than all the others in track and field, white Americans for the most part somehow knew Jamaica. Perhaps it was this distinction, this towering above the others that made Caribbean unity so difficult. Trinidad, although smaller in population and size than Jamaica, was the real economic superpower of the region. How dare

Jamaica stand so tall! While Caribbean unity remained illusive, the Europeans formed their economic union and currency, laughing at the legacy they had left behind in their former colonies. And as the doors of the Caribbean Court of Justice gathered dust and mildew, England rejoiced at the notion that after decades of Independence and hundreds of British trained lawyers and graduates of the University of the West Indies, islands such as Trinidad and Tobago viciously clung to the coat tails of the Privy Council, afraid to let go. Perhaps that is why, even in Brooklyn, West Indians still tried to separate themselves from each other. Perhaps like their leaders, they needed to let America know that they were not Jamaican or Bajan or Trini or Guyanese or Haitian. No. Grenadians were not like any other group of Caribbean people. Neither were St. Lucians and so on and so on. Sandra had no greater experience of this than the night she walked into the small air-conditioned meeting room to learn about how she was going to become rich from selling herbal supplements.

"Is Jamaicans that have the franchise and yuh know how they could be. But it have plenty people from plenty other places here," said Lindy as she and Sandra slipped into two chairs at the back of the room. There wasn't much of a crowd and Sandra was wondering why Lindy had insisted that she come on time. She counted twenty people other than herself and Lindy. A tall man with a Jamaican accent was speaking into a microphone and flashing pictures of cars and luxurious mansions with swimming pools across the wall behind him with the help of a projector. On a table right beside him she could see an array of what looked like medicine bottles of different sizes. Sandra could not see the connection between selling herbal supplements and the pictures on the wall.

"How, you must be wondering, can I become rich by becoming a member of Healthy Way Marketing? How can I go from living an ordinary life to living an extraordinary life?" asked the man on the microphone, whose thick lips broadened as he smiled.

"Well you've got to INVEST in your future, my friend!" he shouted.

"You've got to SAY-HA. I will NOT be POOR-HA. You've got to SAY-HA, I will shake off the yoke of POVERTY-HA!"

"Amen!" shouted a woman in the crowd.

"You've got to SAY-HA, wealth is my DESTINY-HA, and it will not be taken away from ME—HA!"

With each statement he stamped his foot hard into the carpeted floor and shook his head from side to side. He was sweating but dabbed his forehead dry with a white handkerchief he retrieved occasionally from his back pocket. Sandra imagined she was sitting in a Full Gospel church listening to a pastor. The man stretched the end of the last word of each sentence giving it a life all its own.

"AMEN! HALLELUJAH!" another woman shouted.

"You've got to SAY-HA, I will live the HEALTHY WAY—HA. You've got to BELIEVE-HA, that you are supposed to drive these CARS-HA, and live in these HOUSES-HA. Because that is your DESTINY—HA!"

The small crowd erupted into clapping and Sandra almost instinctively did the same. It was not that she was so impressed by what he had to say but it was the way in which he said it. He had managed to energise a small group of twenty people, mostly women, on a Friday afternoon when they could be a number of other places. That certainly deserved a round of applause. His eyes closed so tightly, Sandra swore his butt cheeks were closed just as tightly. His spit and sweat went flying up in the air to left and right as he swung his arms widely around, pointing to the listening crowd. When he had finished speaking, he reached for a nearby glass of water and took his seat exhausted. A short, stocky woman with tree stumps for legs, stepped up to the podium and began making announcements about top performers.

"Sean Tomkins—two thousand dollars!"

"Sheila Patterson—four thousand dollars!"

With each name and amount called there were "ooooos" and "aaaaaahs" and rounds of applause.

"But, I have to say, Lindy Jeeteram has proven herself to be the leader at the head of the pack with a whopping twenty thousand dollars!"

Lindy blushed and nodded quietly as the gasps and clapping came to a climax.

"So if there are new members we welcome you and we will be passing out the sign up sheet for you and your sponsor."

Sandra could not imagine that selling herbal supplements could make that much money. She was speechless when she heard the amounts of money that were being made, especially when she heard Lindy's figure. Twenty thousand dollars! That was more than enough money to buy a piece of land up in Las Lomas. Sandra had not been swayed by the pictures of Mercedes Benzes and Jaguars, luxury homes and boats that Mr. Wiffle had been flashing across the wall. She didn't think she would or could ever own any of those things. What would she do with a boat or a swimming pool? But a piece of land in Las Lomas! Yes. She could use that. She could move out from the Denton home and build something. It wouldn't have to be big. Two bedrooms, maybe three. Just enough for Andrea and Antonio. Las Lomas was quiet, serene. A place "behind God's back," the people she met there had said. She liked that. In her own mind she was already behind God's back. It was only fitting that He allow her to live in a place that was so described. If she could make half as much as Lindy had, she would be able to make her dream a reality. So when Lindy introduced her to Mr. Wiffle and the other network marketeers, Sandra pretended to understand what they meant when they spoke of emerging markets and networking prospects. She nodded when they told her that empires were built on people meeting people and advertising by word of mouth. She smiled when they told her that she needed to create her own advertising budget even though she didn't know what a budget was. Her eyes opened wide when Lindy told her she would have her own business. She let her fingers caress the glossy, colourful brochure and overlooked the words, multilevel marketing, compression, breakage, because she wasn't sure what they meant. But she knew what the word contract meant and she shouldn't have ignored it; not after what Ms. Goodridge had done. She should have paid attention to that word. She should have tried to read the fine print under Terms and Agreement. She should have seen the *no* in italics and bold before the word buy-back policy. She should have, but she didn't. She couldn't really. As lipstick stained lips moved and white and yellow teeth were revealed, Sandra was all the while visualizing the house in Las Lomas. She would paint the walls green. It was her favourite colour. She would have a lawn with green grass too and a dog; not a mongrel like Buster. A proper dog, a pedigree dog. A Rottweiler maybe or a German shepherd. Lindy loaned her the four hundred dollars for the start up kit and the three hundred dollars for some of the top selling herbal products. She would owe Lindy eight hundred dollars. One hundred dollars was the cost of borrowing. But Sandra didn't mind. She really believed that she would make it back and quickly too. After all she was in America; the land of opportunity, where paupers became millionaires in a heartbeat.

CHAPTER SIXTEEN
Something Happened

A cold wind was tickling the mango tree outside Granny Maye's window. As the leaves swayed and danced with the breeze, Granny Maye could see the silhouettes on her bedroom floor of the chickens asleep on the tree branches. Every evening around six o'clock they would squawk and beat their wings as they flew no further than a few feet up to the fruit laden boughs for the night. Eventually the squawking and feathers flying would come to an end and with their heads bent into their breasts, they would yield to the goddess of slumber. How Granny Maye wished she could sleep. She looked enviously at the silhouettes on her bedroom floor and longed to be one of them. But sleep would not come.

She was worried about Sandra and Antonio and Andrea; not in that order really. Antonio was the one who was keeping her up. It was almost midnight and he had not yet come home. It was not the only night. There were many nights like these in the last month. Sometimes he came home in the wee hours of the morning, trying to tiptoe as lightly as a boy his height and weight could, on the squeaky floorboards in the corridor that led to his bedroom. She would hear each creak he made as he stepped on the floorboards, but more than that she would smell the weed and cigarette smoke wafting through her bedroom door. Sometimes when he came in the yard, Buster would start barking loudly, but a few nights before, the barking was followed by the painful yelping a dog gives after being pelted with a stone. Since then the barking stopped. But the floorboards were old and frail and like Granny Maye, they could not bear the weight of a teenage boy pressing on them at two and three o'clock in the morning without letting out their own inanimate yelps of pain.

Granny Maye didn't know what else to do about Antonio. What really was to be done about a boy like that who grew up with an excuse for a father? There was only so much a mother could do and teach. She knew that there were things that only a father could teach a boy. Sandra knew it too. She had done her best. It was not easy to be a single mother but somehow she had managed to keep Antonio in check. He wasn't a bright spark but he was in school. She had hoped at the end of it he would learn some trade; plumbing, masonry, some skill so that he could make his way through life as a man. Sandra was the disciplinarian. The only one who would make him think twice about trying to stay out all night. Granny Maye was afraid that she was too old, too frail to discipline Antonio. But it was not only that. Antonio had changed and truth be told Granny Maye was afraid of what he was becoming. She did not know what to do after seeing that gun lying there hidden under her bag of manure like a scorpion hiding under a plant pot. She thought about moving it, taking it to the police. But what if it was Antonio's gun? What if he had used it? If it was someone else's and Antonio was holding it for them, turning it into the police would surely get him into trouble. She had stood there looking at it for a long time, almost as if by staring at it her questions would be answered. With a heavy heart she had set it back in its place; a place where it did not belong; the place where she had found it; in her shed; in a bag of her manure. Antonio would never know the pain he had caused her that morning. Her shed was a place of joy; a sacred place, a place where she could putter around and feel useful. It was where she set her plants, cared for the sick ones, mixed chicken feed with corn and kept all the things that were too good to discard—bent curtain rods, broken mop handles, empty paint cans, the broken wicker rocking chair Mr. Denton used to sit in. The shed was the place she kept all her treasures. In a flash it had become a place violated, no longer her own. She would never return to the shed after that. She had peeped through the kitchen window later that night when Antonio was leaving, to see him go stealthily into the shed to retrieve what he had hidden. That night, before he left he had shouted at her in a way he never had before.

"What yuh doing, boy? What yuh really doing? Yuh ain't thinking bout nobody. Yuh ain't giving me a hand self. When yuh come home dem hours, what yuh really coming home to do! As soon as yuh get up yuh going in de fridge, yuh ain't asking how food reach there. Then yuh gone same speed again. Ah know yuh not doing nuttin good yuh know. Ah not stupid yuh know. Yuh done on the wrong side ah de law already. Police not holding people again yuh know? Ah hope yuh know dat. Dey shooting on sight and asking questions later, yuh know. Ah hope yuh could take a bullet yuh know and ah hope dem men yuh walking with now know how to take bullet. Cause yuh ain't sure to be lucky to end up in hospital with a bullet, Tony. Bullet does lick yuh up one time. How yuh think yuh mother going to feel? How yuh think yuh father going to feel?"

Antonio stopped fingering through the clothes in his wardrobe and looked down at his feet. She had hit a nerve. He glared at her and slammed the closet door shut.

"Doh tell me nuttin bout dat f—cking man. He ain't do nuttin for me. How he will feel? How he will feel! He ever care bout how I feel! He don't care bout me. I could live or die. He don't care bout me! Doh tell me nuttin bout dat f—cking man!"

His shouting and his cursing had startled Granny Maye. He steupsed and snatched up an off-white vest that lay on his bed and stormed out the house shaking all the floorboards and the glasses in the glass cabinet with each step. It was as though like Granny Maye they too had become startled and suddenly afraid.

As she lay in her bed looking at the silhouettes of chickens on the mango tree, waiting for the sounds of Antonio to come home, Granny Maye could not help but feel weary. She let the breeze blow through her bedroom window and gently pull the curtains apart. Rain was coming. She could smell it in the air. She wanted to get up to close the window but she was so tired. The patter of raindrops on the rusty galvanize began. Light at first then heavier and heavier. The rain came as suddenly as the heaviness of her arm and her tongue. Something was happening to her. She began to cold sweat. A knife-like pain seared through her chest, gripping her throat, silencing her scream, suffocating her, choking her, pinning her to her bed. She opened her mouth. She wanted to scream but no words came. She turned to her open window. The rain was coming in full blast, wetting the curtains, wetting the floor, wetting her. She could hear the galvanize sheets being beaten by the rain. As the pain in her chest squeezed the life out of her. Granny Maye closed her eyes and called the name of Jesus.

This was the way Andrea found her the next morning. With eyes closed and mouth open, her bed wet and damp from the soaking of the night rain. Clad in her green floral printed nightgown, her frozen head was turned to the open window as if looking for something. When Andrea did not hear the shuffle of her feet in bedroom slippers or the sound of the kettle whistling or the six o'clock death announcements on 610 A.M. radio which Granny Maye listened to faithfully, she thought Granny Maye had overslept. She opened her bedroom door and imagined her to be still asleep covered up as she was. Andrea lifted the polyester sheets and slid under but something was not right. The warmth she expected, the softness of the skin with which she had grown familiar was replaced instead by a coldness and a stiffness she had never known.

"Granny? Granny?"

She touched her shoulder, stiff and lifeless. Something had happened but she did not for a moment imagine death. She placed her hand on the damp cold cheeks and stared at the open mouthed woman she loved.

"Granny! Granny! Wake up Granny!"

Her little hands shook the lifeless body in panic.

"Granny! Granny!" She was shouting now. Andrea had never seen death before. She had never been to a funeral. Death was something that happened in movies. It had never happened to anyone that she knew. In her childlike mind Granny Maye was just some kind of sick she had never seen before, but not dead. She ran to Tony's room and banged hard on the locked door.

"Tony! Tony! Something happen to Granny! Something happen! Something happen!"

It was Antonio who would recognize what the something was that had happened to Granny Maye. He recognized it because he had seen it a few nights ago. What he had witnessed was not as peaceful as the sight of Granny Maye lying there in her green floral nightgown. He had seen a man beg Psycho for his life deep in the Guanapo forest. He had held the man down while Psycho chopped off each of his fingers on a boulder, staining it forever with the man's blood. He had watched Psycho shoot the man in his chest and head. He had smelt the gunpowder, the freshness of the blood. He had smoked cigarettes with Psycho and a man they called Choker, while waiting for Martin aka Tall Man to strap the body to a mattress of dried leaves and wood and set it ablaze. "Sticky fingers." That's all Psycho had said about the man after he had died. Martin had told him later that the dead man had stolen money from Mr. Fung Ki Chi. It was the first time Antonio had seen anything so gruesome in real life. He had never seen a man beg for his life the way that man had. He had a look in his eyes; the look of true repentance and of fear. Death was not as clean as it looked in the movies, neither was it as glamorous. When he saw Granny Maye that morning lying there, cold, lifeless, mouth opened, eyes closed, head turned toward the open window, he wondered what her last moments were like. He wondered if she begged God for life the way the man he had watched Psycho kill had begged. It was odd seeing her like that, knowing that she would never nag him again; knowing that he would never hear her voice or hear the shuffle of her feet in the kitchen, or hear her cough the way she did purposely when he came home in the wee hours of the morning, to let him know that she knew he had just come in.

"Granny! Granny!" Andrea's screams were more piercing than the pain he felt in his stomach when he saw Granny Maye that morning.

"Tony! Do something! What happen to Granny! Do something!"

Antonio stood there stone-faced. He touched her icy face and hands. He knew that she was dead. He knew the absolute stillness of it, the coldness that signalled the absence of life. Gently he touched her face and pushed her lower jaw upwards closing her mouth.

"She dead, Andrea. Doh cry. Doh cry."

Antonio pulled Andrea away from the room bawling and screaming.

"Doh cry. Doh cry."

He was trying to convince himself as well.

"Doh cry, Andrea. Is alright. It will be alright."

It was not long before Barbara and many others appeared by the front gate. Andrea's piercing screams had awakened half the street.

Barbara burst into tears on seeing Granny Maye.

"Somebody have to call Sandra and tell her. Oh Lord! And to think, she just gone up in America a few months ago," said a neighbour whose name Antonio did not know. In an instant, his world had changed. His life had changed. Granny Maye was gone. There would be no more nagging, no more footsteps in the kitchen, no one to dig in the yard, or feed the chickens or wash away the stink of Buster's pee with bleach. The news of Granny Maye's death spread like a dry season bush fire through the community. She was the last alive of seven older siblings so there was no sister or brother to call. She had had six children, three boys, three girls and had raised three of her siblings' children as her own. Five of her children were scattered throughout Trinidad and Tobago and seldom kept in touch. Getting the news to them was no small feat but thanks to Barbara, who had taken on the role of official coordinator and information disseminator, word would reach as far as Cedros and Black Rock in Tobago.

Sandra was in Long Island when Granny Maye died. While Granny Maye looked for the last time at the silhouettes of chickens on the mango tree, Sandra was busy trying to place Olivia in homemade cloth restraints on her bed. She had been agitated all day long; tossing things, screaming at Sandra, taking off her clothes after Sandra had painstakingly dressed her.

"Something not right. What happen Ms. Olivia? Walter coming you know. He coming."

But no promises of Walter coming would soothe the old woman who had become permanently flushed in the face from all the screaming and hollering and carrying on. Sandra did not want to grab her arms too tightly. The last time she did she had left a mark on the woman's skin and she didn't want the relief staff to make a complaint to Ms. Goodridge. However something had to be done if she was to have any sleep and she could barely restrain Olivia to give her any of the tablets in the medicine cabinet that would have made her sleep all night.

"What happening to her, Ms. Joan? I never see her so bad before."

"Is around the time of year you know. It was this time," said Joan calmly.

"What time? What happened?"

"Walter. Everybody found out about Walter around this time."

"What was wrong with Walter?" Sandra was intrigued. She had always assumed that Walter was a lover lost, although she was not sure how. She had never assumed that his disappearance was tragic. His name was the magic word that stilled the voices in Olivia's head. In her more lucid moments Ms. Joan had told Sandra about what life was like growing up during the war, the hope that blossomed in the hearts of Americans when Harry Truman became president and the coming home of the brave, embattled men after the war ended in 1945. She recalled events with a mental sharpness that would often make Sandra wonder whether her erratic behaviour was simply a pretense.

"What happened to Walter, Ms. Joan?", an impatient Sandra asked as she double tied the cloth restraints on Ms. Olivia's wrists to the bed frame. She knew that he had never married Ms. Olivia but had imagined that he had died bravely in the war. She didn't know why she had made that assumption. Perhaps it was because she believed that if somewhere in the recesses of Ms. Olivia's brain she could still recall him, it must have been with fondness. Only Walter's name was strong enough to reign in the terrors that made her want to smear her faeces over every available clean surface that had been bleached and wiped for what seemed like more than a hundred times.

"It wasn't his fault you know. Nobody could tell. Nobody knew."

"Knew what?"

"That he had a touch of the blood." Ms. Joan's voice dropped and she looked down at her hands with some measure of guilt.

"You couldn't tell. His cheek bones were high, his eyes deep and blue as the sea, his lips thin and as red as mine . . ."

She ran her hand gently over her lips and held it there for a moment as she gazed at the bedroom wall.

"His mother couldn't have any babies so she took him from that coloured woman. That's what the men from Bluefield had told my papa. Walter wasn't from Bluefield he was from Northampton. Papa said there was too much mixing of the blood going on up there. But how were we to know?" She raised her eyebrows and looked straight at Sandra with eyes begging for forgiveness.

"Walter was a Negro?"

"His mother was high yellow. His grandmother was black. But Walter was as white as Olivia and I. Nobody in Bluefield could have known. His parents came with him to Bluefield as a baby. He grew up with us." Ms. Joan sighed and looked down at her hands again. Sandra could see something wet and glistening on her freckled face.

"We played with him. We loved him. I loved him, but he loved Olivia more. She was the prettier one." Ms. Joan chuckled.

"I loved Walter and John Foster loved me. It made John mad just to see we were such good friends, all three of us, me, Olivia and Walter. He killed Walter."

"Who killed him John Foster?"

"Well, it was just as if he had tied the rope around his neck himself. Poor Walter. He never knew he had a touch of the Negro blood. His mother never told him. His father should have. His father had been going up to Northampton after that high yellow woman. They said she was the prettiest yellow girl in Northampton Virginia. When the black and white mix they make them like that. I heard she had golden brown, curly hair like copper springs. Lots of white folk wanted her, my papa said, but I don't know. That could all be stories the men in Bluefield made up. Maybe she loved Mr. Hayworth. Maybe she didn't know he was a married man."

"Who is Mr. Hayworth?"

"Walter's father. His real father. He was always with his real father but never his real mother."

"So who killed Walter?"

"He killed himself." Ms. Joan let out a long deep sigh, the kind after which no words could follow.

"I'm sorry to hear that."

"He couldn't take it. He had grown up white, with white friends and white parents. He wanted to marry Olivia. He loved her and she loved him. But once the truth came out, once the men in the town found out about him having a touch of the blood, things went badly for him. His father had already died in the war and his mother was sick. He was only twenty-three when he came back from the war. He went when he was just a boy and came back a man. The men in Bluefield gave him a hero's welcome they were so proud of him. He could have had his pick of any girl in Bluefield but he always wanted Olivia. She was the prettier one."

"How did he find out he was mixed?"

"That summer was the Bluefield Dance. We all wanted to go. Every girl in Bluefield got dressed up for it. That was when John Foster punched Walter in the face and told him to leave the dance because he was a Negro. But he didn't say it quite so nicely, if you know what I mean," Ms. Joan whispered under her breath.

"Walter just laughed and told John to go to hell. He told him he was just jealous that he was not a hero of the war. But later on everything came out. I don't know how the men in Bluefield found out but when he confronted his mother she told him the truth. She said she was tired of lying to him and to herself and that he deserved to know the truth. I think she was trying to make peace with God for taking that woman's baby. If she knew Walter was going to kill himself she would never have told him. She loved that boy like he had come from her very own womb."

"So after the dance he killed himself, because he found out he was part black?"

"Oh no. Not right after. Only when he found out the truth for sure from his mother. My father forbade us keep his company and he couldn't see Olivia. I think he could have got over having a touch of the blood in him. It was not being able to see Olivia again that sent him over the edge. The men in Bluefield were pretty mean too and they had known him since he was a baby. Funny how people could be one way today and change the next. I think he knew it wasn't going to turn out any good way for him and Olivia after that. That's what made him do it. They found him on Tucker Hill hanging from an apple tree. Such a waste of a life." Tears were rolling freely down Ms. Joan's cheeks as she spoke and she made no effort to restrain herself.

"That really is sad, Ms. Joan. I really am sorry to hear that. Ms. Olivia must have been heart broken."

"She was. Every year around this time, she goes crazy for a few days well. She remembers. I don't know how, but she remembers. You will have to give her something later to keep her sleeping. She will get out of those restraints in no time."

"These?" asked Sandra in disbelief. She knew how tightly she had tied the knots to the bed and couldn't imagine Ms. Olivia being able to undo them.

"Yes. You think you are the only one that got the bright idea to tie her down to the bed? You will have to give her something because she gets very bad."

Sandra could see that Ms. Joan was regaining her composure and usual miserable temperament.

"Anyway I've said enough. I need to get ready for the dance. Because of you I am always late and I never have a chance to waltz so hurry up!" Ms. Joan shouted.

"Of course Ms. Joan. I will get you ready in no time," Sandra replied.

Later that night she would lie in bed thinking over the story of Walter. While she drifted off to sleep, Granny Maye opened her mouth and breathed her last.

CHAPTER SEVENTEEN

For The Almighty Dollar

"Blessed Assurance, Jesus is mine
Oh what a foretaste of glory divine
Watching and waiting, looking above
Filled with his goodness, lost in his love
This is my story, this is my song
Praising my Saviour, all the day long"

The words of the well-known Christian hymn bellowed through the packed Sangre Grande Roman Catholic Church. It was hot and the ceiling fans in the church seemed only to be circulating the hot air commingled with the fragrance of perfumes, colognes and perspiration scents that were bound to be high, with everyone wearing black jackets and dresses and sweating up a storm.

There was no cool breeze or wind or rain to soften the humidity or remove that malodorous scent that hung between the ceiling and the congregation. The wake had been short — four days. All Granny Maye's children lived on the island. Sandra was the only one abroad and the only one missing in the front row line up of Granny Maye's children. Seated also in the front row were Antonio and Andrea, sombre looking and sad. Andrea rested her head on Ms. Barbara's shoulder and let her tears soak into the black jacket she was wearing. Antonio appeared manly in the black suit Ms. Barbara had bought for him. He had never owned a suit before and had never had the opportunity to wear one. Sullen faced and sweating with all his aunts and uncles around him and his cousins in the row behind, Antonio longed for his mother. He looked occasionally in the direction of the church's back door, wondering if perhaps he would see his mother hustling through it wearing a black dress. He missed her and could not understand her absence at a time like this. He knew he would be alright. He imagined himself to be a grown man capable of taking care of himself but when he looked at Andrea holding on to Ms. Barbara, a woman he knew his mother barely liked, he wondered how Sandra could entrust her to Ms. Barbara's care.

"I can't believe she not coming to her own mother funeral, Barbs," a well-wishing neighbour had whispered to Barbara on one of the nights of the wake.

"She say she need to work or else she will lose the job."

"You knew is work she gone up to work?"

"No. I didn't know. Maye had said it was some vacation but I knew it was more than that."

"What a thing? So she need so much money she can't come and put her own mother to rest? But what really wrong with Sandra, girl?"

"Shhh . . . . not so loud."

Ms. Barbara did not care too much for the gossip. She too could not understand Sandra's logic and reason for staying. She had urged Sandra to trust God for her financial situation and had reminded her that no matter how hard things had been with Ms. Maye, she had never gone hungry or been homeless. But there was no evangelizing for Sandra, who seemed to have processed Granny Maye's death in a way no one could understand.

She received the news with disbelief at first.

"Sandra, I don't know how to tell you this but I have to tell you somehow," Patsy had said, shaking her head as she struggled to get the words out. Patsy had decided to wait until Sandra came off from work so as not to upset her while on the job.

"Is Aunty Maye...." Her voice softened as she continued shaking her head, looking down at the rug on the living room floor of her basement home.

"What happen, Patsy? Something happen to Mammy?"

Patsy shook her head, she could see the look of panic on Sandra's face. She knew there was no easy way to say what she was about to say. She knew no matter how she said it, Sandra was about to have a head on collision with pain; the pain of losing a loved one without having had a chance to say goodbye; the kind of pain that is filled with regret; the kind of pain that does not leave in a day or a month or a year.

"Tell me, Patsy. What happen to Mammy?"

"She dead Sandra. She dead." Patsy had said it and the moment she had she felt a sense of relief. It was as if she had been carrying a load too heavy in her hands and was finally given the opportunity to set it down.

"What!"

"Aunty Maye dead Thursday night, Sandra. Ah so sorry."

"NO! NO! What yuh telling me here!"

Sandra felt her heart racing and her stomach began to ache.

"It was sudden, Sandra. They not sure, but they think is a heart attack she get."

"No! No! No! That cyah be so I leave Mammy good, Patsy. I leave Mammy good, good!" Sandra's body began to tremble and she felt faint. She could feel her heart and head pounding as a sudden coldness swept through her.

"Oh God meh mudder! MAMMYYYY! NO! MAAAMMMY!"

Sandra dropped to her knees on the living room floor with a thud and began to bawl and scream with arms stretched upward, shaking her head from side to side in disbelief.

"Oh God.... What ah do! What ah do! What sin I do so Lord? What it is? Oh God, meh mudder! Meh Mammy! Meh Mammy! MAAAAAMY! MAAAMMMY! WHY?"

She continued like this for almost an hour, on her knees bawling, screaming crying, shaking. Patsy could not console her despite her efforts to do so. Sandra took to her bed and did not leave it the following day. She refused food and drink and would not speak to Patsy.

"Ah feel she studying the job yuh know. She will have to go down to the funeral and she ain't got no money." Patsy whispered to Lenny that night as they lay together in bed.

"How yuh mean she ain't got no money? Where she get all them herbal tablets to buy and trying to sell so. You know last week she try to sell me some thing call Macastamina. She say it make from some Maca root from Peru and it good for sexual stamina. Imagine! A man like me! That is what she try to sell me! I was feeling so insulted. What I wanted to tell her.... Steups!"

"I think she borrow that money you know. She make some Guyanese friend who lend her that money. That is what she tell me. She ain't have no money, Lenny. We will have to help her out with that ticket."

"She ain't have money but she borrowing money up and down the place. She borrowing from you. She borrowing from me. Next thing she will be borrowing from Dexter. But I know he ain't so stupid as to part with his money. He is Mr. Money Kong."

"When she get her pay, Lenny she will pay us back. Remember she up here only two and a half months now. The first two weeks the job hadn't start yet. Then the first month remember Goodridge take all she pay. Now she into the second month. She will get pay this month end."

"But how she going to keep the job if she go down to Trinidad. She wouldn't be in Trinidad just one day you know. Remember she have the children to see bout. Is Aunty Maye was seeing about them. Who going to take care of them now?"

"She will have to call Goodridge first thing in the morning. Maybe she could work out something for her."

"Whatever it is I hope she keep that job cause she owing people money and she can't make one cent yet." Lenny grumbled.

"Is not her fault, Lenny. She trying her best. It not easy out here you know."

Patsy did not want to pick a fight with Lenny but she disliked his attitude towards Sandra's predicament. Patsy knew that Granny Maye's death had only made things worse for her.

"I will buy the ticket for her," said Patsy with quiet resolution.

"What?"

"Yes. I will buy it. She need to go home and put her mother to rest. I will buy the ticket."

"Patsy, you know how things hard with us already. Why you ain't let her ask some other family. She have sisters and brothers you know," said Lenny, irate.

"Yes . . . is true . . . . and all ah dem ketching tail just like Sandra or worse. If you don't want to help her is alright but is my family. I will help her."

Lenny steupsed and pulled some of the bed sheets closer to him.

"When you taking your money to spend it on all them blasted race horse. I don't tell you nuttin. All ah that is why things so tight with us now. All your money going in horse, better you did lie down and sleep with horse one time."

A silence filled the room that signalled the end of the conversation. There would be nothing more to say for the night on that subject or any other. Patsy had not shouted but she would not allow Lenny to chastise her for being generous with Sandra when most of his hard earned money slipped quietly into the hands of the cashier at the off-track betting hole around the corner. Patsy knew there were other beneficiaries of his income; beneficiaries that were not horses either. But she knew the man she had married. He was an addict of familiarity and a master of routine. Their marriage was a routine that he would never have the courage to totally abandon. So she suffered his horses and his women who were never allowed to become significant enough to enter her world. As long as it remained that way they could continue the happy dysfunction that was their marriage.

When Sandra awoke that Sunday morning, Patsy urged her to call Ms. Goodridge and explain the situation to her in order to see what considerations she could get in terms of time to go home and bury her mother.

"Sandra, I sorry to hear about your mother. But at least she in a better place now." Ms. Goodridge offered her condolences with as much genuineness as she could.

"It real hard, Ms. Goodridge and you know ah have two small children home and is me alone now as they father doesn't really cater for them, nah."

"Yes, I understand."

"And the children still young. Don't mind they feel they big."

"Yes, of course."

"So I was thinking I could run home quick and come back up. Cause they want to put the funeral for this week Tuesday or Wednesday. I was thinking I could go down for the week, nah. Leave on Monday and come back up by Saturday, nah."

"Um hmmm."

"So how that sounding to you Ms. Goodridge? I don't know if you will able to get somebody to hold on for me for the week and thing."

"Well, I really am sorry for your loss and everything Sandra but the problem is that right now I have a girl come up from Barbados who want a work bad. Is a family friend nah. And she have a lot of experience and so on. So if I put her in that job you might not have a job when you come back you see . . . you understand what I'm saying?"

"Oh ho."

"Yes. That is the problem you see. Once you come out of a job, it always have somebody to fall in your shoes. Is plenty competition. And I mean I could probably get another job for you but it may not be right away and I know your time is short so by the time I get something else it might be time for you to go back to Trinidad . . . you understand?"

There was silence on the other end of the phone.

Sandra could not understand how Ms. Goodridge could be so unfeeling.... so uncaring. She could not imagine that a Caribbean woman like herself could not appreciate the dynamics associated with a death in the family. She knew at that instant that she needed to get out from under Ms. Goodridge's claws. Whatever was in the contract, she didn't care.

"So, if I go back to Trinidad yuh saying I wouldn't have no job when I come back up."

"Well yes, ... that is the problem. I really sorry about that but is first come first serve in this business."

"But I will still get pay for this two weeks that I work right?"

"Well, no ... cause you see you will be breaking the contract before time. So you wouldn't have anything to get really."

"Nothing at all?"

"No ... Sandra. I really sorry. If I were you, I would try to stay and finish out the contract. You don't have sisters and brothers in Trinidad?"

"Yes, but I have children too. Is different when you have children, Ms. Goodridge."

She thought somehow that that little reminder would have been the prick to the conscience Ms. Goodridge appeared to lack. She did not know that Ms. Goodridge had no conscience when it came to her workers and that at the end of the day it was all about the money.

"I don't know what to tell you. You will have to decide but I telling you now, whatever you do, if you go home you wouldn't have no job when you come back."

Sandra could not imagine that in a country like America where Caribbean people needed to stick together that a woman as cold and as heartless as Ms. Goodridge could exist.

"Not even a two days self?"

"I wish I could tell you different."

"And you calling yourself a Christian woman Ms. Goodridge? . . . Nah."

"Listen, Sandra" Ms. Goodridge's tone changed. "Like you don't understand how it is out here and like Patsy never tell you. Every goddamn day it have people coming up here from the islands—Jamaica, St. Lucia, Guyana, Barbados, St. Vincent, Grenada—all of them hungry for work, willing to do whatever for a little US dollar. Now it have Mexicans and Latinos every where and what you will do for one US dollar they will do for fifty cents, some even for ten cents. It not easy out here. It competitive. It hard. You have to sacrifice plenty before you make it in this place. You doesn't just come up and get rich quick like people feel. It not so easy, I telling you now so make up yuh mind what you want to do, but make it up fast because if you not in work tomorrow, I have my girl from Barbados waiting and ready and she willing to work for plenty less than what you getting."

The conversation did not end well but Sandra knew where she stood and what her predicament was. Although Patsy had offered to pay for her ticket and even help with some of the funeral expenses, Sandra knew that too much was at stake. Her very purpose for going to America in the first place would be totally jeopardized if she returned home. She was already in more debt than she could handle, owing Lindy, Patsy and Lenny. The ticket from JFK to Port-of-Spain was almost US four hundred dollars and she had not even received that amount of money in her hands as yet despite having worked so hard.

"I will stay."

"What!" shouted Patsy in disbelief.

"I will stay," said Sandra even more resolutely.

"You going to miss your own mother funeral because of Goodridge and she nonsense. No Sandra don't do that. Go and bury your mother."

"Patsy, you don't understand. If I go I will owe you more money and I ain't make a cent yet. Now I have all these herbal products to sell. I owing the woman for that too. Plus I ain't even send down a barrel to Trinidad as yet. You ain't see like I just going backward instead of forward."

"Sandra . . . . is your mother. It will always have another work. It wouldn't have no other funeral for your mother, you know . . . . only one. And who going and make all the arrangements and so on, Ms. Barbara?"

"Yes. Is not like the others not there you know. I will send that money you lending me for the ticket for the funeral and I will pay her whatever balance later on. Ms. Barbara have money. Her husband is a Petrotrin pensioner."

"So, you would leave her to bury your own mother Sandra? And what about Antonio and Andrea? Who going to care for them?"

"Not to worry. I will sort that out."

Sandra could see that nothing she proposed would be acceptable to Patsy outside of going back to Trinidad and she was not about to do that. She believed that Ms. Goodridge was looking for an opportunity to get two and a half months of free labour off her and was not prepared to allow that to happen. She could not go back to Trinidad without having accomplished what she had come to Brooklyn for. She had not even sent home a barrel yet. "Why couldn't Patsy understand why she had to stay?" she thought.

When Sandra left for work on Monday morning, she could see the look of disappointment on Patsy's face. That disappointment would turn to disdain and eventually to disgust. In Patsy's eyes, it was bad enough that she had decided to put the job over attending her own mother's funeral but, if love of her own mother could not persuade her, Patsy believed that love of her children would somehow.

She would never see Sandra in the same way again after that. Sandra had done the unthinkable and in Patsy's eyes there was no redemption for her.

Chapter Eighteen

What's Love Got To Do With It?

If there was anyone who seemed to understand the pain Sandra felt because of the decision she had made it was Mr. Bell. For her, he had become a balm in the Gilead that was the apartment in Long Island. When she would become overwhelmed by feelings of despair and entrapment associated with constantly having to supervise her charges, she would call downstairs to the front desk and ask for Mr. Bell. Her reasons for needing him to come up to the apartment were many. There was always some imaginary problem in the apartment that needed to be reported to him so that maintenance could be made aware of it. Whether it was a broken faucet or an electrical problem, there was always a reason to call him up to the apartment. Mr. Bell played the game well too. He would answer the front desk phone with an air of seriousness whenever she called, especially if someone was around and would be quick to grumble to his colleagues about how often things were breaking down in Apt 1A before he left the front desk to go up to visit Sandra.

At least twice a week, he would come up to the apartment and keep her company for roughly an hour. They would sit and chat about any number of topics, while she prepared him a meal or a cup of tea, depending on what time of the day it was. She told him about Trinidad, Andrea and Antonio and he listened intently to her stories. He never shared too much about himself or his past but he was a good listener and Sandra loved that about him. Their conversations were always too short, their time too sprinkled with anxieties about the possibility of being discovered. Before he left the apartment he would always hold her close and press himself against her. Then he would gently caress her face and kiss her on the mouth. It was always a light and gentle kiss, never deep, or probing. Enough to whet the appetite, but never enough to satisfy it. Visits from Mr. Bell had become essential to her emotional and psychological well being and had kept her disposition pleasant, despite the many challenges she faced in caring for the Englefield sisters.

It was Mr. Bell who Sandra turned to in her darkest hours, when it seemed as though even Patsy and Lenny had begun to turn their backs on her. The morning of Granny Maye's funeral found Sandra at Ms. Olivia's bedside wiping faeces off the wall for yet another day. The tears flowed freely down her face and Ms. Joan could not help but notice that there was a change in Sandra's mood.

"What's the matter, Sandra? You seem out of sorts today," Ms. Joan asked.

"I alright, Ms. Joan."

"No you're not. You can't seem to do anything right this morning. What's the matter?"

"Is my mother. Ms. Joan . . . she . . . . she . . ."

Sandra could not form the words. It was as if forming the words would make what was already a reality even more real to her. The words stuck in her throat and would not come forth.

"Good Lord, Sandra. If I didn't know better I would swear your mother had died or something the way you are carrying on!"

When Ms. Joan used the word died, it was as if she had freed Sandra from the responsibility of having to say it. The hearing of the word only served to make the situation more real to Sandra. She burst into tears and loud sobs, slowly dropping the cloth she had been using back into the bucket of murky brown water.

"Oh please now, Sandra. I was just kidding. I didn't mean anything. What is the matter?"

Sandra was crying so much that she was unable to speak. She removed the yellow rubber gloves from her hands, dropped them at the side of the bucket and retired to her bedroom shutting the door behind her. Ms. Joan screamed after her for at least half an hour, scolding her for leaving the bedroom in that state. Sandra could hear her shouting angrily behind her closed bedroom door but she didn't care. She lay there on her bed frozen as if in a dream; a bad dream, a nightmare even; the kind of nightmare that takes place while a person is awake wishing that they were asleep instead. Sandra looked up at the perfect white paneled ceiling, that didn't have a watermark, that wasn't like looking up at the ceiling in her bedroom on Evans Street where she could see the tiny rust-encrusted holes of the galvanize roof where light and rain would come through.

There she was, in a soft, comfortable bed with six hundred thread count sheets, lying on a feather pillow in an air-conditioned room that had the smell of roses from the auto sense air refresher, wishing with every fibre of her being to be looking up at the rusty galvanize roof, smelling the putrid scents of the chicken pen, hearing the annoying sounds of Buster barking at stray dogs on the street. She would have given anything to be home again to see her mother just one last time. The mother she so loved and hated at the same time for always being right about everything she had done wrong in her life, from Chester come down the line. Sandra had wanted to do something right by her mother finally. She had had her blessing to come up to America. She had hoped that her mother would have been able to live to see her finally make some good money. She wanted to be able to send things for her from America. Granny Maye liked the Bouncy brand of paper towels and toilet paper. They were too expensive to buy in Trinidad but she had used them once before.

"It don't have no toilet paper to wipe yuh bottom soft like Bouncy," she had said.

"Sandra, when you reach up, only one thing I asking you for. Just some Bouncy toilet paper and paper towels. Cause they doh make it sorf like that down here."

Sandra had not even had a chance to buy her mother some Bouncy before she died; and now here she was, still ketching her tail like she did in Trinidad, only now she had a little more comfortable place to sleep in at night. It was little comfort however, especially when she realized that she would never see her mother alive again. Several hours later, after she had composed herself and tidied her charges, she opened the door for Mr. Bell. He had not seen her in two days since he had been off.

"I missed you," he whispered, not wanting to make too much noise.

"I missed you too. Why you didn't call me back?"

"I was so tired, Sandra."

She was not convinced but she needed him too much to be upset.

"Come here."

He held her in a long embrace, wrapping his arms around her.

"Is so hard, baby. It so hard."

He kissed her lips softly. He knew she was vulnerable and in pain. He knew she was needy and that he could have his way with her. In fact he could have had his way with her two days ago but he had wanted her to wait, to be sufficiently needy, sufficiently longing and sufficiently vulnerable. He had not answered his phone when she had called because he had been busy and when he stopped being busy he did not return her call. It was deliberate. He had her exactly where he wanted her to be. He kissed her again longer this time.

"Let's go in your room."

"What about the ladies?"

"Let's go in your room." He said again slow and firm.

He did not need to say it again. She was like clay in a potter's hand. And not just any potter, an experienced one. That day Mr. Bell closed the door to Sandra's bedroom and made love to her. She had not been with a man in two years and she had wanted to be with Mr. Bell very much. She tried to be as quiet as she could be under the circumstances, even though the bedroom door was shut tight. She didn't want Ms. Joan to ask her any questions. After they had sex, she watched him get dressed. He was very well built for a man his age. He had tone and definition in his arms and his belly was not that big.

"That was wonderful," he smiled broadly showing off his set of cosmetically whitened teeth.

"Yes."

"You are a beautiful woman, Sandra."

She smiled not knowing what to say. He leaned down and kissed her on the forehead.

"I should leave now. I know they will be wondering where I am." He tucked his shirt in his pants and looked just as he did when he had come through the door, not like a man whose heart had been racing or who had been sweating in ecstasy.

Sandra had hoped that Ms. Joan would not have noticed her absence or Mr. Bell's presence. She did not want Ms. Joan to be privy to her affairs with Mr. Bell. However Ms. Joan said nothing when Sandra returned to her after Mr. Bell's departure. In fact she seemed unusually quiet and that suited Sandra just fine. That night when she called downstairs for Damian at the front desk it was not his familiar Southern accent she heard but that of his white counterpart. She was a little disappointed. She somehow had hoped that after sharing such an intimate evening with him he would have wanted to say goodbye to her before leaving for home. She wasn't hoping for much; a call or a text, maybe just something to make her feel like what they had shared was special for him, if only because for her it was. But Mr. Bell did not call, neither did he text. She called him later that night, twice, or was it four times. She could not recall. He didn't return her calls and a sadness new and different from the sorrow she had felt earlier in the day, came over her.

Later that night, while serving oatmeal porridge to her charges, Ms. Joan whispered something from under her breath.

"He done gone and got you good."

"What you say there Ms. Joan?"

"It's not 'what you say', it's I beg your pardon or pardon me, Sandra."

"Well, begging your pardon, Ms. Joan . . . what is that you say?"

"He's got you good Sandra, just like the rest."

"What you talking about?"

"Bell. He got in your panties just like all the others."

If Sandra were pale she would have turned red with embarrassment. For a moment she paused not knowing how to respond, or more importantly, if responding would have been wise.

"I don't know what you talking about, Ms. Joan. I think you need to just eat your porridge," she replied as she scooped up a spoon of the thick, gooey meal and put it in Ms. Olivia's mouth.

Ms. Joan chuckled. "He is a good looking black man Sandra; tall, strong, muscular. If he were back in the days of slavery, they would have had him breed all the women."

Sandra didn't appreciate that last comment and was sure that it was loaded with prejudice.

"Mr. Bell is a fine man Ms. Joan. He is very helpful and smart."

"Oh he is smart, Sandra. I will give him that. He's smarter than you. You'll see what I mean."

Sandra steupsed and there was silence for a moment. It was a silence that she appreciated. Her secret had been discovered. Ms. Joan obviously knew about her relationship with Damian. She couldn't help but wonder though about what Ms. Joan had said. Who were the others? Other women who had worked there? He had said he was divorced and that he had one grown child living in Atlanta. She knew he was a handsome man who would surely be able to get a woman in Brooklyn. The impression he had given her though was that Brooklyn women were too high maintenance, always wanting money and expensive things he couldn't afford. He had preferred instead the single life, the life of a bachelor, unhindered, unencumbered. What if that had all been a lie? She couldn't have imagined it. He was too sincere in his expressions she had thought. Perhaps it was because he was an American man and so different to Chester and the other men in Trinidad she had known; perhaps it was because of the way in which he spoke to her gently without shouting, never making demands. He was the man she had been hoping to meet. The kind of man she could settle down with. She called him relentlessly in the days after they had made love. He returned none of her calls; neither did he acknowledge them by text. A few days later when he called up at the apartment, she was not sure whether to be excited or upset that he had called. She summoned him up either way.

"Oh darling, I'm so happy to see you," he said smiling as he entered the apartment.

"Why didn't you call me back?"

"My phone is malfunctioning, Sandra. I need a new phone. By the time I saw your calls it was too late to call you and I knew you would be sleeping."

"I was worried when I didn't hear from you."

"Oh sweet thang. You were worried about me? I was alright. You shouldn't worry about a brotha like me."

"Hmm," Sandra wasn't appeased by his explanations.

"I've got good news, baby." He said excitedly. "I'm investing."

"Investing in what?"

"A property."

"You mean like a house?"

"The land beneath the house actually and you can have a share if you put some money together with me."

"Who me?"

"Yes Sandra, baby. I've been thinking that it's time to settle down in a house of my own. All this renting has just been a waste of good money for me."

"Well I know about that. But a house is a big thing to invest in, Damian. You could afford it?"

"By myself? Hell no, but with you and me together . . . ."

Sandra could tell by the look of excitement on his face, the direction in which the conversation was heading and she was not too pleased. He wanted a loan and he wanted it from her and there was no way she could accommodate him with that. She owed Lindy for all those herbal products she had purchased. She had not sent a barrel home or assisted with her mother's funeral arrangements. As lovely as it sounded, her children were a priority and the first thing she had in her mind to do, was to send home a barrel and some money for Ms. Barbara.

She turned to face the patio and could feel Mr. Bell's strong arms reach around her waist from behind.

"What do you say?" He whispered.

"Say about what?"

"About investing in a house with me?"

She didn't know any other way to be with him but frank, even though she anticipated that he would probably be hurt.

"Well I cyan't see how that will happen, you know. I have so much debt. I ain't really start to ketch mehself up here. Plus how I will invest in a house up here when I cyan't even live in America for more than six months?"

"We can get married, Sandra?"

"WHAT?"

"Yes. Not right now, of course, maybe in about a year or so but we can get married, Sandra."

"What you saying Damian? How we will marry and yuh ain't even tell me that yuh love me yet?"

"I love you, Sandra. You didn't know?"

"Steups." She wanted to push him off her but she twisted uncomfortably instead. She didn't believe him.

"So why you ain't return my calls?"

"I was probably sleeping."

"Okay, but when you get up and you see I call, you didn't study to call me back?"

Sandra wasn't convinced of Damian's genuineness and things seemed to be progressing too quickly for her liking. True, she cared for Damian but love was a whole other story altogether. Now he was talking about investing in a house, getting married and he hadn't even met Andrea and Antonio.

Mr. Bell kissed her on her neck gently.

"Oh Sandra. Nobody has made me feel this way before, woman. Do you know what you do to a brotha like me?"

"Look," she smiled and gently pried herself away from his arms.

"Is not like I doh have feelings for you, Damian. I got feelings too. Plenty feelings, but we have time. We don't got to be rushing nothing. Plus I have children back home. I can't just leave them there. They still small and they need me. I ain't get no chance to even send a barrel for them yet. I need to give them something, especially now where you see Ma gone. I is all they have in the world. I got to do right by them first."

Mr. Bell sighed and looked in the direction of the patio and for a moment there was an uneasy silence.

"I'm not saying you have to leave them behind. But if we get this house together we could start to build a home for them. When they come up here, they will have a place to call their own."

"Look, I getting pay in a few days time. I have to send some things in a barrel for them and then I have to put some money towards the funeral. Let me see how my funds looking after that and then we could talk about investing okay?" Sandra was trying to appease him as best she could.

"So when you gonna get your salary?" he asked.

"This Friday."

"Well how about I meet you in Brooklyn when you get off. There's a really nice restaurant I want to take you to. They've got some good Caribbean food and there's music and dancing. I'm sure you would like that."

Sandra was grateful that he seemed unwilling to push the limits of the conversation any further.

"I not so sure yuh know. Ma just dead and . . . ."

"And you still have to eat. Come on Sandra you need to relax. All this stress isn't good for you."

"I guess so . . . ."

"Well it's set then. I will meet you in Brooklyn, seven o'clock."

Sandra saw Mr. Bell out that day and for the first time, felt an uneasy feeling in her stomach. She liked him. She had sex with him, but they had only known each other a short time. The feelings he seemed to have for her were much deeper and stronger than the ones she had for him. This made her uncomfortable; especially the marriage talk, not to mention the talk of money for a house. As fond as she was of him, she truly did not love him enough to want to marry him. When she told Patsy of what he had proposed, she was sure to leave out the part about investing in a house. Deep down she knew there was a gnawing discomfort about that idea. Patsy was excited.

"Gyul, people does pay how much US money, all kinda five thousand dollars to marry for green card and you saying the man want to marry you just so. Gyul, look how you lucky, lucky. Just so. That real nice."

"But Patsy, I doh really love him so. Plus I never get no proper divorce or nothing yet from Chester."

"Gyul, hear the stupidness you studying. Chester. Steups. He who never do nuttin for you. Gyul, marry the blasted man and get your green card you hear. You studying too much ah movie thing. It ain't bound to have love in green card business. In fact, love ain't got a damn thing to do with it."

CHAPTER NINETEEN

One is One

After Granny Maye's death, a silence strange and new enveloped the Denton home. The house became as still as Granny Maye was on the morning she died with her mouth open and her eyes closed. All the noises she used to make had died with her and a blanket of sorrow, thick and heavy descended upon the half-board, half-concrete house. There was no more kettle whistling or feet shuffling or radio playing in the morning. Even Buster seemed to miss her presence. In the mornings he would sit at the top of the unpainted concrete stairway at the back of the house and wait expectantly for the door to open. Sometimes he would scratch the base of the termite-ridden door, permanently swollen and warped by water, and whimper or bark. Whenever Andrea or Antonio emerged, depending on who got up earlier, he would try to stick his nose inside the house, as if he were still waiting for Granny Maye, still sniffing for the scent of her, a scent that faded with each passing day.

It had been one month since the funeral and the forty-day mark was coming up. Barbara, who had played a key role in organizing the wake and liaising with family and friends of Granny Maye, was doing her best to ensure that for the most part Sandra's children were taken care of, and for Barbara that meant making sure that the refrigerator was full of food. She cooked every imaginable thing she thought Andrea and Antonio would like and almost daily, brought food for them—macaroni pie, callaloo, stew chicken, potato salad, fried plantain, pumpkin, ochro and rice. Every day there was some new offering that usually came early in the morning. The refrigerator was full of food that was not being eaten as quickly as it was arriving. Barbara juggled between her ailing husband and the Denton home. In the first few days following Granny Maye's death and burial, she practically lived there and would often spend the night sleeping on the couch since she was afraid to sleep in Granny Maye's bedroom. But once the funeral was over and life returned to normal, she resumed her wifely duties, still checking in on the children on a daily basis. Antonio was often not at home. Barbara was never sure where but she was certain that he was up to no good wherever he was. It was Andrea she was most concerned about. She had no children of her own and took Andrea under her wing, paying special attention to her in Sandra's absence.

The holidays were coming to a close and school would start in less than a week. With no word from Sandra about when she would return, Barbara was becoming worried. Andrea had taken on new roles of cleaning house and feeding Buster and the chickens, even checking the mail. Very often however she was home alone. Andrea didn't mind. She did not enjoy being alone but it was not simply the physical absence of Granny Maye; she could not understand why her mother had not come home. Didn't she know they needed her? Didn't she know that Granny Maye had died? Andrea agonized over these questions and the answers to them. She could not understand how or why her mother was not there; why she had not abandoned everything and come home straight away.

"Things different in America, chile." Barbara had told her. "She will come in time. She just cyah come now." This answer made absolutely no sense to Andrea and only served to fuel her fears and anxieties.

"Why she cyah come now?" she would ask Barbara puzzled, wanting with every fibre of her being to understand that which she could not. Barbara, realizing that no answer would be enough for a mind so young, so fragile, eventually stopped giving answers, explanations and reasons to Andrea and opted instead to divert her mind to other things. Things like school and getting an education. At least she could talk to Andrea. At least Andrea would listen to her. It was quite the opposite for Antonio, whose bed sheets were cold most nights. The first morning Barbara discovered that Andrea had been left to sleep in the house alone was the beginning of Andrea spending nights at Barbara's home.

"It not safe for a girl so young to be sleeping by herself alone in the night. Those children need guidance. Their mother need to come home and mind she children," she had told a neighbour. None of Granny Maye's children, not those that were hers biologically or those who she had taken care of wanted to live in the Denton house. It was not that there was anything wrong with the house. It was old and full of memories of love, good times and hard times. It was just that everyone was busy with their own lives and making their way in the world. Besides, living there would have meant some measure of responsibility for Andrea and Antonio, a responsibility that no aunt or uncle was willing to take on. Many of them could not understand Sandra's absence and naturally disapproved of it, especially after the version of events they heard through the grapevine from her cousin Patsy.

Chester, who had had a golden opportunity in light of the events that had transpired after Granny Maye's death to play a key role in the lives of his children, was noticeably absent. He made an appearance only briefly on the day of the funeral at the gravesite with a visibly pregnant young Indian girl who looked half his age. In the forty days following her death, there was no phone call from him, no visit, no asking Barbara how the children were. It was this lack of concern on Chester's part that hurt Antonio deeply. He had somehow imagined that Chester would want to take him and Andrea to live with him, or at least come to live in the house with them. He had hoped his father would do something, anything to show him and the world that these were his children and that he would take care of them. But Chester was busy with his new madam and other things, so Antonio would have to tolerate Barbara's annoying voice and presence, ordering Andrea around and telling her what to do.

She knew better than to give Antonio instructions. Her tones with him were always soft and apologetic, but with Andrea it was different and Antonio could see and sense this. But he did not care for Barbara's attention. He was going to be his own man. He was making his own money and he was glad that none of his aunts or uncles had decided to take up residence in the house. He had already decided that he was not going back to school in September and would instead work full time with Psycho. He was sixteen, independent and charting his own course in the underworld, where the pay was good and the work endless. He enjoyed being one of Psycho's apprentices and Psycho had taken a liking to him. Antonio was quick and smart, and didn't need that much instruction. He did what he had to do without drawing much attention to himself, but what Psycho liked best of all was that he did exactly as he was told; no improvisations or varying from the script, with all the attention to detail an apprentice should have.

His cousin Martin was not like him in that regard. Martin was loud, boisterous and boastful. It was inevitable that Antonio would find favour with his employers and this favour made Martin jealous. Their friendship had begun to grow cold. They were no longer cousins but competitors in a game of Russian roulette; trying to outdo each other with every exercise. It was a game that would lead to death. And it came for Martin one Saturday night when Antonio was on his way to a mongoose hole to hide a stash of ammunition for Psycho. Martin was in Arima a short distance from the cemetery, sitting in one of Mr. Fung Ki Chi's cars doing business with a young man called Slinky, one of his big distributors of weed in the La Horquetta area. They had concluded their business but something was different. Slinky seemed edgy, nervous. It was dark in the car but Martin could see the white of his eyes darting back and forth as he spoke.

"Like yuh doh like cemetery ah what?"

"Dred, is not dat yuh know. Ah hearing tings."

"What kinda tings?" Martin looked in his rearview mirror and could see the white sea of gravestones behind him dimly in the darkness, as if keeping watch over the night's activities. He thought he saw a shadow move quickly. He wasn't sure. He wanted to be on his way but he wanted to know what things Slinky was hearing.

Then without warning, without a horn or a siren or a shout, it came. A spray of bullets, noise, heat, warmth, pain, flashes of light, glass shattering, the smell of something burning, from in front; no from behind; from every side. There was no end to it. Martin could feel heat searing through his chest and warmth reaching up to his neck. Through the noise and the glass he saw Slinky slumped over in the passenger seat, blood was coming out of his ear. He tried to cover his head with his arms but the onslaught continued. The heat in his chest was getting worse, he couldn't breathe. His heart was racing, something warm was running down his neck. He heard men's voices coming closer and closer. The spray of bullets did not stop. He knew this was it for him. He could feel his chest tighten as he struggled to breathe. Then it was all over.

News of Tall Man and Slinky's death reached Psycho that night. It was a planned execution by a rival camp. Although ten thousand dollars in cash had changed hands between Slinky and Tall Man that night by the cemetery, none of it had been found. And nothing angered Psycho more than being robbed.

"In other news. The bullet-ridden bodies of two men Jamal Thomas, age twenty-six and Martin Rogers, age eighteen, were found on Dere Street next to the Arima Cemetery early this morning. Residents say around midnight they heard loud gunfire in the area of the cemetery but were afraid to come out of their homes. Police reportedly found the bodies of the men in the vehicle already dead at three this morning. Police are still investigating the motive for the shootings."

Antonio was in Sangre Grande when Martin was gunned down. It was Psycho who broke the news to him on his return to the upscale Tacarigua townhouse that was Psycho's home. This was where Antonio would sleep most nights when he was not at home. Martin's death hit Antonio hard. It was not just that he had been killed, but the way in which it had happened, unexpectedly, violently. He imagined that Martin who always carried a homemade hand-gun on these exercises did not have the opportunity to even use it to defend himself. It was too soon after Granny Maye's death. That day Antonio went home. He had not been in days. There was no one there, except of course for Buster. He assumed that Andrea would be where he expected she would be; home with Ms. Barbara. He pushed open Granny Maye's bedroom door. It was the first time he had been in her bedroom since the District Medical Officer had come and examined her body. The room was immaculate, untouched. Everything was neat and in its place. There was a yellow floral bedspread on her bed. It felt out of place in a room where death had been. Antonio could smell the faint odour of lavender. Granny Maye had liked that. He stood at the doorway wanting to step further in. He felt like a thief trespassing on property that was not his. On the floor at the side of her bed he could see the bedroom slippers she loved, neatly placed as if they were waiting for her swollen feet to be put in them once more. He glanced over at the dresser mirror and looked at his reflection. He knew he had let her down and that wherever she was she would not be happy with what he had been doing. But now Martin, his cousin was dead. And Psycho had said that whoever had done it would have to pay with his life—blood for blood. He could see no way to avenge Martin's death without further disappointing his grandmother and a pang of guilt came over him.

He remembered how he had shouted at her the last time he saw her alive and wished he could say sorry. But that was the past and now he was about to embark upon a road from which there could be no return. He felt a knot in his throat as the tears welled up. He wished Granny Maye or his mother was around to shout at him; to stop him, to warn him about the company he was keeping. He wanted somebody to stop him. He needed somebody to put his or her foot down and tell him that if he continued as he was going he would end up just as Martin had. He wanted to believe he could pull back, that he could continue to be the mongoose without having new more deadly responsibilities. With Martin gone his promotion was inevitable and it was not a promotion he wanted. If Martin's killing was a hit, then he could possibly be next and as big and as tall as he was, Antonio became deathly afraid. The day after Martin's death, Antonio began spending more nights on Evans Street. Although Psycho had encouraged him to move into the Tacarigua apartment for his own safety, Antonio believed that he would become more of a target if he were so close to Psycho. "One is One" Psycho had said. "They touch one they touch all." Antonio didn't want to be touched at all but he knew it was far too late for that.

The men of Mr. Fung Ki Chi's organization were placed on high alert. The reprisal killings began and bodies began to surface weekly. Antonio wanted to keep as low a profile as possible. Doing business for Psycho had increased risk. He had been given his own gun, a real gun, not a homemade one. A silver Smith Wesson hand-gun. It was small and sleek and could fit in his jeans pocket. It gave him a new boldness and confidence and helped to reduce some of the anxiety he had after Martin's death. He did not attend Martin's funeral, neither did Psycho or any of the other men. The rumour was that there would be bloodshed if any of Mr. Fung Ki Chi's men showed up at the funeral. Antonio did not mind. He did not want to remember Martin in a coffin anyway. It had been enough for him to see Granny Maye looking stiff and icy, all caked with powder in that long box. He refused to remember Martin like that.

The September term resumed minus Antonio. He had seen too much and grown too much in a few short months to imagine returning to the mundane life of putting on a uniform and going to school. On occasion he would hang around outside the school gates to show off on his old friends and flirt with a few girls from his old class. At those times he missed being in school but he had determined that unless his mother came home and made him go to school, Ms. Barbara would not be able to make him set foot willingly into the establishment. Once or twice he was smuggled on to the compound and had sex in the male toilet with a girl or two. Now that he was no longer a student he had become very attractive to girls. He liked that. He didn't let Psycho know that he was frequenting his old school. He thought it would make him seem childish in his eyes, as if he wanted to go back to school. The truth was that deep down he did want to go back to school. There was simply no one around he respected enough to make him do it. Sandra was the only one who could make him set foot in a classroom again and she was in America. He had not spoken to her in weeks and he missed her. He imagined that she would come back in a few months time and rake him over the coals for dropping out of school and march him back to the principal's office and get Andrea back from under Ms. Barbara's thumb. He hoped she would bring a barrel of shoes, clothes and Captain Crunch Cereal for them and some of that soft toilet paper that Granny Maye liked. But Sandra did not come and with each passing week he grew more and more resentful of her and the America she had gone to work in.

CHAPTER TWENTY

Autumn Hijackings

Autumn in Brooklyn was no ordinary event. True it was autumn in every northern state but Brooklyn autumn was heralded by last minute summer sales. Even before the leaves began to fall and make golden orange and brown soft carpets of magic in Prospect Park, the weather began to change. The evenings were cooler and night came sooner and with it a breeze that chased away the heat of humid summer nights. Slowly and almost reluctantly, the exposed bellies of summer sought refuge under windbreakers; the water hoses that sprayed jets of cool water on barebacked Brooklyn children disappeared, as did the rollerblades the popsicles and the ice-cream cones. Now everywhere instead, was the flamboyant display of oak and cherry trees vying it seemed to be the most majestic of the trees that could claim autumn as their own; sprinkling at their roots and the feet of passersby their leafy offspring. The season brought with it a mood as well. The smiles were less, the frowns were more, the hustle and the bustle of feet on Church and Flatbush Avenues continued. Sandals and slippers disappeared and were replaced by feet in sensible shoes. Exposed skin went into hiding in anticipation of the on-coming winter. Only the trees with their silent but colourful array were reminders of all the summer heat, laughter, and festivity. Everywhere else the festivities were over and a new season had come.

Sandra had been in Brooklyn almost four months already by the time autumn rolled around. She had arrived on May 20th and started work in June. Her June salary was the "thank you" to Ms. Goodridge and her cousin Patsy had hijacked her July salary inadvertently. Patsy didn't mean to take Sandra's money really. She knew Sandra had been working hard but Sandra was costing her. With no money of her own, Patsy had been supplementing Sandra weekly with money for the Long Island Railway, phone card money and pocket money. She had not been happy that Sandra had taken so many of the herbal products on consignment from Lindy. She was disappointed that Sandra had refused to go back home for her mother's funeral. In Patsy's mind, it seemed that Sandra was making a series of bad decisions or rather missteps, with far reaching consequences. So when Sandra called her on the last weekend of July to let her know that she was going to work that weekend since her relief had called in sick, Patsy was pleased.

"Girl, that is the attitude you have to have up here yuh know. The time will finish before you know it and yuh will have to go back home."

"Well, Patsy gyul, Goodridge ask me if ah could fill in and ah tell her yes. She say she have my money waiting for me and I could get it next weekend but I doh like the idea of she keeping that money for one second longer than she need to keep it. I tell her I rather she give it to you. Next thing yuh know she come up with a reason why she have to keep it!"

"Is that. Well, what yuh want me to do?"

"Yuh could pick up that money for me, Patsy? Just hold it for me till ah come off. I have real things to do with that money. Ah need to fix this head of mine and get a nice weave and thing."

"No problem. I will get it for you. Better that money in my hand than Goodridge hand."

That Saturday, Patsy collected the money from Ms. Goodridge and signed the receipt, after reading cautiously every word on every line. She could not help but find herself feeling somewhat irritated and annoyed by Sandra's announcements of her plans for her first salary.

"Imagine, after all this time and all what going on, first thing she planning to get is weave! Steups!" She had told an obviously uninterested Lenny that night.

"Well it just goes to show where her head is. No pun intended," he chuckled.

"What is a pun?"

"Never mind. You were saying?"

"Yes. All I am saying Lenny, is that imagine after all that we doing for her since she come up here eh, giving her money for the train, spending money in phone card and all she studying when she get pay is to get a new weave. Imagine that. Steups! My mother did always say that Maye children didn't have no head for sums and like is true. Cause how she go be thinking so, Lenny? People minding she here, people minding she children home. Minding children does take money yuh know. But like she forget that."

Lenny who was tired of Patsy's diatribe looked up from the Sudoku puzzle he was trying to finish in the *New York Times*.

"Listen. Don't get all worked up about it now, Patsy. I am sure that is just one of the things she plans to do with the money. Remember she keep talking about wanting to send a barrel home. She will probably do that too."

"Yes, but what about us? What about all the money we give her? Is a seven or eight hundred dollars at least."

"Well, I am sure she will give it back in due course but I don't think it makes sense to try to get that from her on this first salary."

"You alright, yes. People like that come like soucouyant. Dey does suck and suck till dey suck yuh dry. But not me! She ain't ketching me in dat. I know what to do."

Lenny didn't like Patsy's tone. He wasn't sure what she had planned but he knew it wasn't anything good. Had he known that Patsy had been asked to collect Sandra's salary that weekend, he might have offered to collect it for her instead, but he didn't know. Neither could he have imagined that Patsy would have decided to deduct from Sandra's salary what she determined was monies owed to her and Lenny.

When Sandra returned to Brooklyn the following weekend, she was eager to get her two thousand dollars. She had worked hard for it and taking care of those sisters was no small feat, but when Patsy gave her the envelope it was much lighter than she had expected and the discovery of twelve hundred dollars therein made Sandra instantly irate.

"What! Is only twelve hundred dollars in here yuh know, Patsy."

"I know."

"Oh gosh doh tell me is Goodridge again? Oh Lord, what now!" Sandra dropped down onto the living room couch with a sigh.

"No, is not Goodridge. Is me."

"How yuh mean is you?"

"Sandra, remember yuh didn't have no work for almost two weeks. Then from June till now you taking Long Island

Railroad, you need money for phone card to call Trinidad, plus on this phone plan we join you up on, you using the phone and we have to pay for that. Everything have a cost you know ... food, phone card, snacks ... is not free."

"Wait, so what you trying to tell me? In the short space ah time I here I use up eight hundred dollars in phone card and travelling money!"

"Well, not only that Sandra is all the up and down too. I end up sending home some money to Ms. Barbara too to help with the funeral too as yuh didn't have money. So is all of that."

"Oh ho. So wait, you send money home for the funeral and you taking it back out of my money? I never tell you send money to Trinidad for me! I tell you that? If I wanted to send money home I woulda send money but I didn't TELL you send money for me. But what de jail is this I hearing?"

"Look, Sandra, is not like you not going to get pay next month. You will get pay in August and that will be yours."

"This is mine too. This money what you take is my money, Patsy."

"Sandra, listen. Don't take it in any bad way but you can't just live off of people up here you know. Everything have a cost. When you go in the grocery and we tell you get what you like and you pulling down big expensive gourmet dinner and all kinda expensive snacks, we ain't say nothing cause we want you to be comfortable. But when you get pay we expect that you will give something back. The phone plan you on is me and Lenny phone plan. We add you to that and you run up the bill. Is we to pay for that. You say yuh want to buy weave. You could still buy yuh weave but we have to get something back and well I just take it upfront. Remember is beg yuh begging a lodging."

More shocking to Sandra than the words Patsy spoke that day, was the brazen faced act of theft she had committed. Sandra could not conceive that her own cousin, her flesh and blood would behave as coldly and as insensitively as Ms. Goodridge. If she wanted to get back some money why not ask first? Why take it without her permission. And eight hundred dollars? That far exceeded what Sandra believed she had cost Patsy and Lenny since her arrival. Not wishing to create a conflict, Sandra had no choice but to accept Patsy's actions. She was not in agreement with them but at least she was still going to be able to send home a barrel. She went to Cosco and bought things in bulk, things she knew the children would need for school—copybooks, pens, socks, underwear, new school bags and the like. What she did not anticipate, was that Patsy would have had things to send to Trinidad in the barrel too.

"Is just a few things for Maria and the kids. It not going to take up plenty space," she had told Sandra. Maria was Patsy's younger sister. She had three teenage children. If Patsy had been considerate enough to only send a few items for Maria, Sandra would not have minded, but by the time word got around to Patsy's friends about a barrel going to Trinidad, some of everybody had something to send home. Soon enough, Sandra was unpacking the barrel and repacking it in order to be sure that Maria got a packet of oatmeal and somebody else got some brand of hair relaxer and this neighbour got a bag of pitted prunes and another one, a container of petunia seeds. The list went on and on. Some of the items had to be carefully wrapped in plastic several times before being put in the barrel. In the end only half of the first barrel contained items for Andrea and Antonio. The rest of the barrel was full of things belonging to persons waiting in Trinidad to receive them.

"Yuh mustn let people know when yuh sending a barrel home. Yuh have to keep it quiet. Otherwise yuh will get ketch with sending all kinda stupidness home for other people. And some of them doesn't even say thanks," Lindy had told her when she saw her next. Sandra's salary finished quickly that month. She barely had enough to get herself to the hairdresser, but she went anyway. She wanted to change her weave and since hair extensions were cheap, it made sense to do so. She made sure however, to save enough money for her train rides to Long Island and to pay for her phone cards because after that incident with Patsy, Sandra was determined to never have to ask her for another red cent.

With the remnants of her July income, Sandra pressed on. She began to try to supplement her income by filling in as often as she could on a weekend as needed. She earned an extra hundred dollars working on the weekend and every dollar mattered. She knew November would roll around much faster than she expected and so she was determined to make the most of every day spent on American soil. She looked forward to her August salary with much anticipation. There would be a little extra from the extra weekends worked. She wanted to send some money home to Barbara. She had not assisted with the funeral costs in anyway and knew that Barbara had played a significant role in organizing things and taking care of her children. Whenever she called home nobody would answer the phone. Whenever she called Barbara, Andrea was always there. Sandra didn't like that much but she knew that with Barbara, Andrea would be safe. Antonio was never reachable by phone.

"He have a cell phone you know. But ah doh know the number, girl." Barbara had said.

"He doh be home so, Sandra gyul. He does be out I dunno where."

"What about Chester? He coming around at all?"

"No gyul. De new woman making baby. He ain't business wid these children at all at all at all. I doesn't know why some men does be so nah."

"Anyway Ms. Barbara we will get cut off just now. I buy a five dollars phone card but the money finish down already."

"Alright, Sandra gyul. But when yuh think yuh will come home so, gyul? Andrea does only be asking me right through."

"I hoping soon. My time go be up just now. I want to send a barr ...."

The call was ended abruptly before Sandra had the chance to finish her sentence. She hated the five dollar phone cards. She always felt that she never had enough time to say all the things she needed to say. She was worried about Antonio. Before Granny Maye died she had expressed her concerns too. She knew that he was up to no good purpose with all those late nights and she knew that she was the only one he would listen to, but she was not there. How she wished she could be. Instead, Sandra chose to focus on the thought of going home with clothes and shoes and books. She wanted Andrea to do better in school than Antonio did. Very soon she would be taking the Common Entrance exam and she did not want Andrea to go to any government secondary school. But what was she to do about Antonio? The only thing she felt she could do was pray. Pray that his misdeeds whatever they were would not catch up with him and that if they did, his guardian angel would protect him from any bullet or knife or harm of any kind.

On the weekend she was due to receive her August salary, Mr. Bell had promised to take her out for dinner and dancing. She was hungry with anticipation. After receiving her money from Ms. Goodridge, she tucked the twenty green hundred dollar bills into an envelope and placed it neatly in her handbag. When she came out of Ms. Goodridge's apartment, Damian was there waiting for her just where she had left him. He placed her arm on his and in that instant Sandra felt like the happiest woman in Brooklyn.

The Cesar's Palace was the equivalent to a restaurant and bar with brothel facilities. It was a West Indian establishment no doubt, one could easily tell by the multiple flags of the Caribbean that adorned every table in the restaurant. The D.J. was blasting some sweet Zouk music and even though neither she nor Mr. Bell understood what was being said, they danced and laughed and swayed to the beat. After a meal of ackee and saltfish served with ground provisions and ochro rice, they were both full and ready to retire.

"Let's go upstairs."

"Upstairs? What it have upstairs?" an innocent Sandra inquired.

"A quiet place where we can be private." Damian whispered.

Sandra was not too keen. She could tell by the way he whispered that there was only one thing on his mind. He had been so kind to bring her to the Cesar's Palace, she thought. Reluctantly she obliged.

The décor of the Cesar Palace bedrooms was nothing like the dining area. The faucet for the bathroom sink was broken, the dirty yellow walls were in need of painting and the bed sheets smelt of cigarette smoke. She didn't particularly like the room at all but Damian, she noticed, seemed to know his way around and she could tell that it was not the first time he had been there. This time the love-making was different. There was no tender kissing or caressing. No foreplay. He seemed rushed and impatient, almost as if he had somewhere else to go and it was still early by evening standards. It was only eight o'clock.

When he dropped her off at Lenny and Patsy's place she invited him to come inside but he insisted that he couldn't.

"Like yuh fraid meh family ah what? They don't bite you know." She smiled.

"No is not that. I just want to meet them when the time is right," he said nervously. Sandra took this to mean when he was ready to marry her but that was not what he meant at all. He kissed her gently on the forehead and with a swift turn on his heels walked briskly away, looking right and left as he went; like a man being followed.

Sandra thought it odd but was too happy to care. She had been paid and this pay was finally hers—all hers.

That night before going to bed, she checked her handbag to make sure those hundred dollar bills were still there. She looked for the white envelope that she had folded neatly but it was not there.

"What!"

"How you mean it gone, Sandra?"

"It not in meh handbag. You see anything fall down anywhere. Oh Lord, my God! Where meh money gone, boy?" Sandra was close to tears.

"You sure nobody ent bounce you on the train or anything?"

"No. Nobody ent bounce me. Ah telling you. The whole time my eye was on my bag. The whole time."

"Oh Lord, Sandra. Yuh just get pay. Money doesn disappear just so. You sure how he name ain't take that money somehow? You sure you didn't give it to him to hold?"

"Why I will do a stupid thing like that, Patsy. Is stupid you think I stupid ah what? After I work so hard I go give all my pay to somebody to hold!"

"Alright calm down, Sandra. Calm down we will find it."

"Oh gosh Patsy I cyah lose that money. I have a barrel to send for dem children."

"Doh worry, we will find it. When Lenny come home he will help us look for it." But Lenny didn't come home early that night and after turning the entire apartment upside down, the money could still not be found. She did not want to suspect Mr. Bell but she wondered if some time during their Cesar's Palace dalliance he had stolen from her. Sandra was puzzled as to where the money could have gone. Exhausted and sad, she cried herself to sleep. That night, Mr. Bell went home, put on his best suit and took his woman to the Ritz Carlton in Manhattan. He had promised he would take her there and he was determined to keep all his promises when it came to her.

Chapter Twenty-One

Olivia Passes On

When Mr. Bell heard of the mishap with Sandra's salary, he appeared to be genuinely concerned. He even gave her two hundred dollars to help her get through September. Patsy was not so understanding. She felt Sandra had been careless, even irresponsible. How her salary had been taken from her, was none of Patsy's concern and even though she felt sorry for her, she was not about to put any more money in Sandra's hands. Sandra tried to see if she could get an advance on her salary from Ms. Goodridge but trying to get money from a lady like Ms. Goodridge, was like trying to get a finger out of a crab's gundy. So in September, a financially impoverished Sandra continued her task of caring for the Englefield sisters as best she could, in the hope that September would end quickly and she would be paid.

Back on Evans Street, life continued in a jerky sort of way. Antonio was sometimes at home, sometimes not. Andrea had her own bedroom established in Barbara's home and had moved most of her belongings there.

"My mommy coming back jus now you know, Ms. Barbara."

"Yes ah know."

"Is only for a short while, Andrea," Barbara had told her that day when she helped her carry across her toys and books.

"She coming back this year self, Ms. Barbara and then Antonio will HAVE to go back to school."

"Yes I know. But for the meantime is best if you stay with me like she said."

"Ah really hope she come back just now, Ms. Barbara. Ah really missing her."

As happy as Barbara was to have a child, a girl in her home to take care of, she too wished that Sandra would come back soon. She had not received a cent from Sandra for all her efforts and in her last conversation with her, she could not tell whether Sandra was trying to outsmart her or not.

"How you mean yuh lose yuh salary, Sandra? Yuh mean somebody tief it. People doesn't lose dey salary just so, just so!"

"Ms. Barbara if you know how that thing still hurting me to think about it. Like I doesn't even like to talk bout it. It does just make me feel sick to my stomach. Yuh get the barrel?"

"Yes but it had plenty thing in it for other people."

"I know. But next time it will only have more things for the children. I ain't telling nobody next time I sending a barrel."

"So yuh really cyah send nothing for these children this month?"

"Next month for sure Ms. Barbara. Month end for sure."

"How is Tony?"

"Sandra gyul, ah worried bout dat boy. He ain't up to no good. He not going back to school for nuttin. And if he keep up at dis rate is just a matter ah time before he get in some kind of big trouble."

"Ms. Barbara gyul, ah don't know what to say. I want to come down bad, bad, bad. I need to talk to dis boy. Yuh cyan't get his cell phone number for me?"

"Girl, is to see him. I cyah see him no time at all. One minute he in the house. Next minute he gone. Sometimes he does even bring fellas there and thing. A time ah see some fellas down in the shed an I thinking is tief but den ah see Antonio wid dem."

"Ms. Barbara ah hoping to send some money next month end for sure. Ah promise yuh that. Ah don't have long again up here in any case. I supposed to come back by middle of November. The time will fly. We done in September already and . . ."

"You have one minute left" a voice on the phone said.

"Sandra, yuh there?"

"Yes. I have one minute. The phone going an cut off jus now."

"Give Andrea a kiss for me eh. I really missing she plenty. She doing alright in she new class?"

Sandra never heard the answer to her question. Her minute was up. "These phone cards does jus rob yuh yes."

What Ms. Barbara did not say that day, was that although the barrel had arrived, she had helped herself to some of its contents. Since no actual US dollars would be coming her way, Ms. Barbara determined that she needed to receive payment for her services in some form or fashion. She sold some of the copybooks to Ms. Gyatri, a woman who owned a nearby parlour. Antonio was not going to school, he would not need copybooks.

That week Sandra noticed that Ms. Olivia was not her usual self. She was not passing stool and she seemed uncomfortable. She would not get off her bed once unrestrained and would pick the cotton from the inside of her pampers, roll them between her fingers and drop little balls of cotton on the ground. Sandra tried to ask her what the matter was but that was as useful as trying to have intelligent conversation with a stone. Ms. Joan did not help out either.

"She can't seem to have a bowel movement. You will have to pull that shit out of her yourself you know. That's what they do."

"What?" The idea seemed violent to Sandra. Even if that was the solution to the problem she was not about to put her hand up there. She had memorized the smell of Ms. Olivia's watery stool. It was bad enough to deal with it on a daily basis but to go looking for it was anathema to her.

"Yes. Or you can give her an enema. Why don't you call your boss? I'm sure she will know what to do." Ms. Joan had advised.

Sandra didn't want to call Ms. Goodridge and she had not become very friendly with the relief staff either. She was of the opinion that they would jump at the chance to take her place on the job and did not trust them one bit. She and Patsy had not been relating as well as before since Patsy helped herself to that eight hundred dollars from her salary.

Sandra opted instead to call Lindy. She had not seen Lindy for at least a month and wanted to discuss with her the possibility of returning the herbal products she had agreed to sell. Apart from one bottle of Macastamina, Sandra had found neither the time to sell the herbs, nor the clientele to sell to. Lindy had called her a few times to enquire how sales were going. She was not happy to hear Sandra's responses. But when Sandra called Lindy that day wanting advice on what to do about Ms. Olivia's faecal problems, she did not expect Lindy to be upset with her at all. So when Lindy dispensed to her the cuss out of a lifetime, Sandra was genuinely surprised.

"Before you be calling me to tell me bout when I goin get my money for all dem products yuh take on credit you calling me to ask me bout ole lady shit! All yuh Trinis feel we Guyanese stupid. Well not me. Yuh goin sell me blasted herbs or yuh goin give me back me money before yuh go back to Trinidad yuh hear. Otherwise I goin report yuh to immigration and yuh ain't never goin to be able to work in America again." With these words and many other expletives in between, the kind stranger who had saved her from embarrassment on the train on Sandra's first day of work, hung up the telephone. Sandra did not know whether or not Lindy had the power to do what she had threatened to, or whether it was simply an idle threat. Whatever the case, she decided she would have to make sure that Lindy got her money by the end of the month, even if it meant giving over more than half her salary. She owed Lindy eight hundred dollars. Now, with interest, Lindy said she owed her one thousand dollars. Once she got her salary, she would give Lindy back her money and use the balance to send a barrel home.

Still, with no solution to Ms. Olivia's constipation problem, after having given her prune juice, whole milk and hot water, Sandra donned a pair of yellow rubber gloves, and taking a kitchen knife, cut off a small piece of bath soap. Plying it between her fingers to make it as soft and as slippery as she could, she then attempted to push the soap up Ms. Olivia's behind.

This was no small feat. The old lady, though frail was quite strong. In the end, restraints were needed but the soap found its way high up in the rectum.

"Why don't you just pull out a bit of it while you're at it! No point putting your finger all the way up there and not trying to pull something down at the same time," said Ms. Joan who had been a diligent spectator to the procedure.

"This is what I learn when I was home in Trinidad. As children they used to do this and give us all kinds of things to drink like cod liver oil, Epsom salts and senna pods to flush you out and get rid of the worms."

"Worms? Senna? It all sounds like mumbo jumbo, Sandra. I am telling you, you need to evacuate her, otherwise she will be very uncomfortable. That soap will not do anything."

"You don't worry about me and my soap. Yuh will see something just now," a confident Sandra had assured.

Sandra believed the soap would work and that pretty soon a spray of fecal pellets, would be heard coming out of Ms. Olivia. She took off her gloves and waited but the pellets never came. In fact Ms. Olivia seemed more listless than before, more agitated and more distressed. By nine o'clock that night however, she had drifted off into a deep sleep and Sandra had become even more worried. She stood by her bedside watching the pale skin covering ribs move up and down under her yellow chiffon nightgown. Ms. Olivia's face was paler than usual and her finger tips not as pink.

"I told you that soap was a waste of time. Now she's got soap up inside her ass and no chance of it coming out any time soon," Ms. Joan scolded

"You going to have to call the doctor first thing in the morning. I don't have a good feeling about this at all, Sandra. That soap could be poisoning her. I have never heard of such utter rubbish in my life. What other barbaric things do you do on that island you come from?"

Sandra did not pay Ms. Joan any mind. As worried as she was, she knew when not to listen to Ms. Joan and when to take her seriously. She decided that she would call Ms. Goodridge in the morning and find out who was the doctor to call. Since she had begun working there, she had never had the need to call a doctor. She did not foresee any major medical problems or hospitalization. Ms. Olivia just needed a good old-fashioned purge. Sandra was just sorry that she didn't have the ingredients to facilitate that all the way out in Long Island.

The following morning Sandra awoke to the sound of thunder. It was raining, which was not uncommon for autumn but it was the first time she had experienced autumn rain. It was not like rain falling back home on Evans Street. That was a noisy kind of rain that would beat on the galvanize like a steel pan and make rust laden holes, through which successive showers could gain entry. It was the kind of rain that made Granny Maye run for buckets to place them strategically throughout the house where the ceiling was prone to leak. Trinidad rain was no respecter of time or persons especially during the rainy season. It did not make allowances for clothes hanging on the line in the backyard or drains not yet cleaned which made the yard prone to flooding. It did not allow time for windows to be closed before the wooden floorboards became water soaked and swollen. Trinidad rain was a rude kind of rain. Sometimes starting off as a drizzle, gentle and mild, then breaking suddenly into a violent downpour beating up the roof, causing the galvanize to jump up and down. American rain was not like that, Sandra thought. It was a well-behaved rain, a mannerly rain. Perhaps she felt that way because she could not hear the sound of galvanize jumping up beneath its force, or see a flood left in its aftermath. She turned to see the time on her alarm clock. It was 7.30a.m. She left her room and checked on her charges. They both lay in bed fast asleep. The thunder boomed again and Sandra wondered how they were able to sleep through all that noise. She pulled the living room blinds and looked out at the balcony. Brown and red leaves, probably blown in from the rain, twirled around in circles in the water on the mezzanine balcony floor, going nowhere. It was a consoling sight. As she fixed her eyes on the leaves she could not help but feel as though she too were being tossed about and going nowhere. She had not done any of the things she had hoped to do since her arrival in Brooklyn, except get a new weave for her hair and send what was really a half of a barrel home to her children. And what good was that for Andrea and Antonio? The sky was overcast and she imagined it would probably remain that way for the rest of the day. She was determined not to let the weather make her sad but she could not help but miss home.

She began to prepare breakfast for the ladies and put on the television, as she usually did, to listen to the morning news. Weather was always a big part of American news not like in Trinidad where the weather news was over in one minute because the waves were always "two metres in open waters and less than one metre in sheltered areas." Just as she anticipated, the weatherman announced that it would be raining all week long. She prepared two bowls of oatmeal porridge and ground Ms. Olivia's pills to a fine powder, mixing it carefully in one spoon of oatmeal porridge. She always gave Ms. Olivia her medication with the first spoon, since there was no telling how many spoons she would take and how much of the oatmeal would end up dashed on the carpet.

"Good morning, ladies. Ms. Olivia, Ms. Joan. How was the night?" she asked as she entered the Englefields' bedroom.

Ms. Joan took a while before sitting up and mumbling what sounded like good morning under her breath. She grabbed the breakfast tray from Sandra with both arms and hung her legs off the bed. That was the furthest her legs would ever reach every day. Sandra did not expect Ms. Olivia to respond to what she had said. But after serving Ms. Joan as she usually did, she turned to touch Ms. Olivia's arm and was greeted not by warmth and softness but a cold rigidity which made her recoil instantly in shock. She stood motionless not wishing to alarm Ms. Joan and looked to see if Ms. Olivia's chest was moving up and down the way she had left her the night before. Her mouth was open as it usually was when she slept and her eyes were closed. Her face was expressionless as if she were asleep but there was no snoring and her chest did not move up or down, or in any direction for that matter. She surveyed Ms. Olivia's frail body and touched her face. It was cold and pale. Her once velvety skin was now stiff and unyielding. Sandra's heart raced.

"Ms. Olivia, like you don't want to get up this morning?" She said that more for Ms. Joan's benefit. She could feel Ms. Joan's eyes piercing through her back. Sandra knew the feel of death. She knew Ms. Olivia was dead. She began to cold sweat. She knew Ms. Joan would think it was because of the soap she had pushed up inside her the day before. She could not let Ms. Olivia die yet. She was not supposed to die under her care. What would Ms. Goodridge say? Panic ensued and Sandra began her own attempts at resuscitation. She jumped on top the narrow bed and bending over, pounded on Ms. Olivia's chest while breathing into her mouth. She was quite a sight bent over that way. A startled Ms. Joan began screaming and shouting.

"What are you doing?"

"She not breathing, Ms. Joan. She not breathing." Sandra could see the look in Ms. Joan's eyes. It was a look of terror. Ms. Joan turned a ghostly pale at once.

"Call 911, Sandra! Call 911!"

Sandra had not thought about that. She rushed to the phone and called 911. She was breathless as she explained the situation to the 911 first responder, who at first had trouble understanding her accent.

"Ah say she not breathing."

"Ma'am I want you to stay calm and tell me exactly what happened."

"Ah find her in her bed not breathing. She skin cold, cold, cold and stiff, stiff, stiff. What to do?"

"Ma'am, are you getting a pulse?"

"No, ah tell you she not breathing at all!"

"Ma'am, do you know CPR?"

"Lady, I don't know who you talking about but ah telling you the woman not breathing and you telling me about CPR. I not calling you about CPR. I don't know who the hell is that. If I had known I was to call him ah would ah call him instead of wasting time on the phone with you. All this time we wasting yuh coulda done give me CPR number to contact. The lady not breathing!"

An infuriated Sandra hung up the phone and returned to the women's bedroom only to find Ms. Joan standing on her two legs holding her sister in a tight embrace. The sight of Ms. Joan standing was one Sandra had never seen before. Ms. Joan had never got out of bed unaided.

Tears rolled down Ms. Joan's cheeks and soaked her sister's silvery hair.

"Ms. Joan. Let her go. Let me help," said Sandra as she tried to pry her arms off Ms. Olivia.

"No. No. No! She's dead already. Leave her be. She's my sister, leave her be!"

Ms. Joan held on to Ms. Olivia and wept and wailed and would not let Sandra touch her. She stood there and held her sister and rocked her gently, whispering in her ears. Sandra could barely hear but she thought she heard her say, "Walter is waiting for you, darling". Moved to tears at the sight and worried about what Ms. Olivia's death would mean for her, Sandra frantically called Ms. Goodridge to give her the news.

"What yuh say?"

"Ms. Olivia dead," she blurted out between sobs.

"When? How?"

"This morning. I don't know how. I jus find her stiff and dead on the bed."

"Yuh call anybody?"

"Yes, I call 911 but like they didn't understand is dead she dead. Like I was supposed to call somebody else or some other office .... CPR or so but I didn't know what she mean so I hang up."

"Oh Lord! That mean EMS coming just now and then police. Listen Sandra, I will get Mrs. Foo Ming Choo to come over there. Let her do all the talking. Don't say anything to the police or the EMS. You not legal. You have no papers to show. Whatever the EMS ask, let Foo Ming Choo talk. You were just visiting for the weekend and Mrs. Foo Ming Choo is the one taking care of them. If they ask you anything tell them you too emotional to talk and tell them the Englefields are like family to you. And cry plenty too. Ah don't care how you do it. Not too much to raise suspicion but just enough for them to leave you alone. I will send her there now and when she come let her do all the talking. Don't say anything at all."

It wasn't too long after that, there was a knock on the door and Mrs. Foo Ming Choo, the short Chinese lady who often relieved her on weekends, came through the door with an air of knowing, as if she had come to save the day. She went straight to the bathroom and shut the door. A few minutes later she emerged with a flushed face, red, swollen eyes and tears streaming down her cheeks.

"You no cry enough Ms. Sandra? Old lady die now. You must cry. Rub this underneath your eye."

She handed Sandra a short stick that smelt of menthol which Sandra applied generously beneath her eyes. A few seconds later, Sandra felt her eyes were on fire. It was as if she had rubbed raw onions in her eyes. The tears sprung forth but what was worse, she could not properly open her eyes so intense was the burning.

"Oh gosh, boy. Meh eye burning."

Mrs. Foo Ming Choo led Sandra by the hand to the kitchen table and handed her a piece of tissue paper.

"You cry now, Ms. Sandra and stay here now."

Before nine o'clock, screaming sirens with flashing red lights could be heard coming down Carnegie Avenue. The Emergency Medical Services team arrived and pried a screaming and kicking Ms. Joan away from her sister. Sandra did not know that Ms. Joan had that much strength in those legs. Mrs. Foo Ming Choo did all the talking while a distraught looking Sandra fought off the effects of the menthol stick Mrs. Foo Ming Choo had given her. She wished she had not put so much of it in her eyes and thought to herself that both Ms. Goodridge and Mrs. Foo Ming Choo were pretty smart. Ms. Goodridge for making sure that she had another one of her workers in the building and Mrs. Foo Ming Choo for making her believe that she spoke very little English. She could see that not only could Mrs. Foo Ming Choo speak very good American English but that she also had a very strong American accent. Perhaps it was her short stature or her simple unassuming appearance or the way she offered the police officers green tea. Whatever it was, Mrs. Foo Ming Choo was in full control and had successfully removed all suspicion that may have arisen in anyone's mind that Ms. Olivia had died from any cause other than natural.

By lunchtime both the EMS and the police officers had gone and a tired Mrs. Foo Ming Choo reclined gracefully on the living room couch. Her feet gloved in white socks touched the sofa handle. She closed her eyes as if asleep. Sandra decided to check in on Ms. Joan. She had had a difficult morning. She had been handled roughly and had been given medication to put her to sleep. The sister with whom she had lived for the last ten years of her life in an instant had been taken away from her and with it all the familiarity she had known. But for Sandra more importantly than all those events was the fact that Ms. Joan had stood. She had stood up on her own two legs. She had not used a cane, or a walker, neither had she asked for help. Ms. Joan had stood and walked and Sandra was convinced that if she had done it before she could do it again.

Sandra could not help but wonder about the piece of soap she had forced up Ms. Olivia's bottom. She had been careful not to mention it to Ms. Goodridge and thought it best to leave that bit of information untold. However she wondered if it had in anyway contributed to her death. Either way she was not about to make it a point of discussion. "Dead men tell no tales," she remembered Granny Maye saying to her as a child. She would miss Ms. Olivia. She had been difficult to care for but when she heard of the story about her and Walter she had been moved with compassion for her. Perhaps her life would have been different if she had married Walter.

Maybe she would have had children and grandchildren and not been so sick. Sandra hoped Ms. Olivia was in a happier place and worried now about how Ms. Joan would do now that her last surviving sibling had died.

After one hour of laying perfectly still on the living room couch, Mrs. Foo Ming Choo got up, put on her shoes and made ready to leave.

"Thanks so much, Mrs. Foo Ming Choo. I really didn't know what to do. I was so scared."

"It okay now. I am sorry for Ms. Joan. She cry now. She cry every night now." She retorted in her familiar Chinese accent.

"True, but I think she in a better place. Better than here anyway. She wasn't easy to take care of nah but she was nice."

"I am sorry for you too, Ms. Sandra. Ms. Goodridge say your mother die too," she said as she made her way to the door.

"Is alright I will be okay."

"I know but now Ms. Olivia die. So now less money. I sorry for that too."

"How you mean?"

"Well only one ole lady now. Less work. Less dollars."

Mrs. Foo Ming Choo was on the other side of the doorway now and before Sandra could press her further she bade farewell and was on her way.

Sandra could not help but think on Mrs. Foo Ming Choo's words. Now that Ms. Olivia was dead, it would mean less work but she could not imagine that Ms. Goodridge would reduce her pay because of that. Ms. Olivia had died of natural causes. It was not her fault and she was not going to allow herself to be held to ransom for that.

Chapter Twenty-Two

"Just So, Just So"

"In life things does happen just so, just so, sometimes, you know. It doesn't give you no warning shot; no messenger does come to bring news before hand. Sometimes just so, just so, is baddam bam baddam bam and yuh whole life change up braps! Just so."

Barbara was standing in her yard by her wrought iron front gate shielding her eyes from the morning sunlight as she spoke to her neighbour and friend Ms. Janice. Ms. Janice was a market vendor who had moved into the community only two years prior with a string band of young children and no husband.

"Gyul, you doh have to tell me bout dem tings yuh know. Look at me. Jus so, jus so I lose my land up in Santa Cruz, eh. Nice land, fertile land, good land. Because some man wid a piece a paper say he own de land. Talking bout he is family of the first man that had the land. I never see nuttin so. Then jus so, jus so Jesse my nice girl chile get pregnant and jus so, jus so she gone off. Steups! Barbara you don't bound to tell me bout life nah. I know it."

Ms. Janice shook her head for a while.

"Janice gyul, if anybody did tell me I woulda be minding Ms. Maye grandchild I woulda tell them no yuh know. Look at how Maye come and die jus so, jus so. She wasn't even so sick as all that."

"But is when Sandra going an come back and see bout she children, Barbara?"

"I doh know. I didn't even know is a six months she gone to do. Maye never tell me that yuh know. She say the girl gone on a short holiday. Now the son drop out ah school and like she cyah come back because of the work she doing. I doh mind that yuh know but send down some money for who minding yuh children. Yuh believe she ain't send a dime for me up to now! Like I have a money tree in my backyard! Steups!"

"Doh worry she might send a little something just now."

"I ain't think so you know. Is four months going on five and she ain't send a cent for me yet."

"Anyway let me go and mind dem children and dem yes. Plenty work to do today."

As Ms. Janice walked away, her hips swayed from side to side, as if they were too heavy for her body to carry. Ms. Barbara retired to the kitchen to start to prepare some food for her ailing husband. As she crushed the potatoes she had boiled and mixed them with a bottle of Ensure supplement, she wondered to herself how Ms. Maye had managed to die before her husband. It was not that she wanted him to die, but with each passing day he became more and more frail and she wondered just how long he would be able to hold out before he would need to be back in the hospital again on "drips". She wasn't sure how she would cope if that happened. Intent on that event not happening, she put a little more zeal into preparing his meal. As long as she could help it, he was not going back to Sangre Grande hospital; at least not anytime soon.

In a flash, Sandra's daily reality with the Englefields' had changed. Just like that, there was no more Olivia. There would be no more tying down with restraints made from cloth and diapers to prevent Ms. Olivia from smearing up the wall with her daily excrement. There would be no more wailing or screaming or outbursts; no more cleaning up of shit on the wall or scraping of porridge from the carpet. Ms. Olivia was gone and just like that, the workload became lighter, the days became longer and Sandra became a little bit sadder.

There were many reasons for her sadness. It was autumn and the days were not as bright as summer days. As the weather changed, she would no longer look forward to her excursions to the grocery with Ronaldo and the visits from Mr. Bell became fewer and fewer. The falling brown, red, fiery leaves were no longer magical to her. They fell instead like the tears that fell daily from Ms. Joan's face—their decay a reminder of death that comes to all. Sandra waited with bated breath for month end to see what Ms. Goodridge would do. Mrs. Foo Ming Choo's parting words hung like a heavy necklace around her neck. "Less work, less dollars," she had said. Sandra knew what less dollars would mean for her. Less dollars meant no barrel for Antonio and Andrea, no money for her. She had promised to pay Lindy back the money she had borrowed from her. She felt she had been tricked and was angry at herself for not realizing that given her hours of work, she would hardly have found the time to sell anything at all. Why hadn't Lindy told her? Now she owed her all this money and all that had been said about living the healthy way and driving the fancy cars and living in a fancy house seemed like a cruel joke. Sandra knew she would never be driving any of those cars or living in any house. She had barely been able to do anything for herself. The American dream she had been told of was not the reality she was now living.

Mr. Bell's behaviour was telling as well. There was no more talk of marriage or buying a house. He would not come up to the apartment even when she called the front desk. She left numerous voice messages on his phone but these did not solicit a response from him. He had said that he was busy but Sandra had been around long enough to recognize when a man was losing interest in her. As much as she hated to admit it, Ms. Joan had been right about him. Perhaps he slept with all the women that worked there. She could not have imagined though, that he would have had any luck getting Mrs. Foo Ming Choo to take off her socks and shoes and open up her legs for him. She was too smart for that, too calculating. Besides Sandra imagined that even if she was not really married, a big, black man like Mr. Bell would not have been her type. She missed him at first but then longing turned to hurt and hurt to resentment. Now, like the falling autumn leaves, Sandra felt discarded and betrayed by a man who she thought loved her but who really did not love her at all.

Back home in Trinidad Antonio's life was about to change "just so, just so". He had taken over the Evans Street property for the most part. Although initially after his cousin's death he shuffled back and forth between Psycho's place and Evans Street, he decided that Psycho was too much of a neatness freak for him. There were too many rules about cleanliness in Psycho's place, which Antonio found surprising considering that Pscyho was nothing but a gangster and a thief. So the day when Psycho scolded him for leaving an empty glass on the oak kitchen table instead of placing it in the dishwasher, Antonio decided that he would rather be in his own place where he could do as he pleased. He enjoyed the camaraderie of Psycho's apartment but he grew now to enjoy the solitude of Evans Street even more. Sometimes, he would invite some of Psycho's fellas over to lime but Evans Street was far removed from the action of Tacarigua and the East-West corridor. Liming in Evans Street was boring for them and soon Antonio found himself alone at nights, having to drive back and forth from Psycho's place more often than he would have liked. Psycho was the one dispensing the work and the payment for jobs completed. He had sensed Antonio's distancing from him but was glad when his fellas stopped liming at Evans Street. He was concerned that Antonio might have been trying to usurp his authority and that was not something he could afford to treat lightly. Jobs were varied for Antonio. The killings that ensued following Martin's death seemed to have subsided. A temporary truce had been made between Fung Ki Chi's men and the Arima Bloods gang, a gang from upper Dere Street that had been responsible for Martin's death. The truce was a temporary one though. It would remain quiet long enough for both gangs to recover their losses and plan the next strategy of attack. Antonio knew this because Pscyho had told him so.

"You ever read a book they call *The Art of War* by Sun Tzu, Smart Man?" Psycho had asked him one day.

"No."

"Neither me. But ah hear in that book they talk about how to attack yuh enemy. And one way to attack yuh enemy is to surprise them when they least expect. That is what we going to do for these panty men up in Arima. And when we do, it go be pressure. They will know who I am."

He had smiled when he said that. He was planning something. He should have asked Antonio if he could read first. If he had, Antonio would have lied and said yes, but perhaps it would have made him think about school in a context other than what school had become to him now.

School was just a place to go when he wanted to get laid. He had a favourite girl he liked there but he told all the girls, they were his favourites. He had not been back in at least a month because the last time he was there, two of his favourites began fighting each other outside the school gates for him. He thought it best to stay away from his old school for a while after that. So now his jaunts were limited to Psycho's apartment, Frankie's pool hall and bar on the Eastern Main Road, and Fung Ki Chi's casino where he would sometimes help out as a bouncer. He still did his regular mongoose work and with time the items to be hid became bigger and bigger. From a gun or two that needed to be out of circulation to kilos of marijuana or cocaine. Pscyho knew he could be trusted with all these items but he was not so sure about his ability to kill a man in cold blood. He was still young in the business and he had done well so far. He was good at beating up a man, good at theft, good at hiding things and not getting caught. So one day in October when he gave Antonio a large, red, plastic pig bucket straight out of his freezer, Antonio could not possibly have known that by agreeing to hide that bucket he was signing his own death warrant.

"But this thing heavy boy, Psycho."

"Put it straight in your car and put it straight in the freezer. Ain't yuh have a deep freeze down by you?"

"Yeah, but it have all kinda ting in it."

"Well take out all them ting and make sure it stay cold."

"What in it boss?" he asked as he held the red plastic bucket, which had been secured all the way around the lid with grey duct tape.

"Just some pig leg and ting."

"I never know pig leg so heavy boss."

"Just put it in your car and straight in the freezer. My fridge full. It cyah take nuttin more."

"Anything else?"

"Nah. Just make sure that reach where it supposed to reach. I will need it by next week Wednesday so."

Antonio didn't think anything of it. After everything he had hidden for Psycho, why was he to doubt that there was anything other than pigs' legs in that bucket? Pigs' legs were a big improvement from some of the other things he had been asked to keep safe. He put the heavy bucket in the trunk of the white Nissan Almera that was his for working and decided to make a stop by a woman named Kesta who combed his hair down in Fifth Avenue in Barataria.

Kesta was a small islander. Antonio did not know what island she was from but most of Mr. Fung Ki Chi's men who had plaits went there for Kesta to comb their hair. She was older than Antonio, mid-twenties, slim with olive coloured skin, wavy Dougla hair and thick lips that seemed too big for her face. She wore multiple gold chains and had her ears pierced all the way around on both sides. Each ear lobe was adorned with large gold jewellery, which she often boasted she had acquired while working in Guyana, although she never went on to specify the nature of her work there. Antonio liked her a lot, not in a romantic way though. True she was easy on the eyes, with her firm, swaying thighs and buttocks like a balloon about to pop; but it was the stories she told and her spunk that Antonio liked best. Although she was of recent acquaintance, Antonio liked to go there sometimes just to hang out. This time he needed his hair combed though. It was still short but he wanted it re-twisted so the plaits could lie flat like tiny spongy caterpillars.

Kesta was busy as usual chatting up her clientele, while her hands worked magic to corn-row the hair of a young man. It was evening time and the rush hour traffic on the Eastern Main Road was still crawling at snail's pace. The sun had not yet set but as it made its way down the ladder of the sky, it cast off pink and orange hues in a majestic array around it. There were at least three people waiting to get their hair combed, so Antonio would have to wait. He didn't mind. While he waited and listened to the conversations of the young men around him, he couldn't help but reflect on how quickly his life had changed in just a few short months. He felt as though he had become a real man; not the kind of man his father Chester was. He knew he didn't want to become a man like that. He saw himself as a man who could demand respect, a man who people were afraid of, a man with a gun. He didn't know if his mother was coming back to Trinidad but even if she did, he was never going back to school. He was going to be his own man, make his own money and have his own women.

By the time Kesta got around to Antonio, the shop had closed and he was the last customer. It was night and he had had his fill of jokes and conversation in Kesta's shop. He would get his hair combed, drop off the pigs' legs and head out again later to Frankie's pool hall not far from where Psycho lived. Antonio was glad to be alone with Kesta; not because he wanted to be alone with her in a physical way but because she had a worldly wisdom and street smarts that he found attractive. He imagined that if he had to pick a sister in the criminal world she would be it.

"So you like what you doing wid dem boys an dem?" she asked as she tugged as gently as she could on the uncombed tufts of hair.

"Why yuh say dat? What yuh think I does be doin wid dem boys and dem.?"

"Steups! I wasn' born yesterday yuh know. How yuh think I manage to survive out here so long? Is not from being stupid yuh know."

"I know. I know yuh could handle yuh stories."

"Ah glad yuh know." She smiled, and for a moment there was silence in the shop. It was a silence eerie and calm, disturbed only by the faint sounds of dub music coming from the radio. She had reduced the volume on the radio once she realized she was on her last customer. She was tired of the noise. "Enough Rastafari Selassie I for one day," she had said.

"Well jus be careful eh. It have all kinda men out dere. Men dat looking nice and smelling nice and talking nice but dey not nice at all. Dey stink ah telling you and dey heartless."

Antonio felt a few drops of spittle land on his forearm as she stressed the word stink. He thought she was about to embark on her usual negative monologue about men and how terrible, evil and vile they were and about how God made a mistake when he made Adam first and tried to correct it by making Eve; and that it was Eve's rib that should have been used to make Adam instead of the other way around. But Kesta said none of those things.

"You does never know what in a man heart yuh know, Tonio. If is one thing I learn in this life is dat yuh does never know what in a man heart till he show it to you. And when he show you, he doesn always show you when yuh want or when you think is best or even how yuh want. Sometimes he doesn even plan to show yuh what in he heart at all but den de mark does buss . . . . Yuh ketch what ah sayin nah."

"Ah ketch yuh," said Antonio, not sure why she was speaking as she was.

"Yuh is a young fella Antonio. Yuh looking big like a big man and yuh moving like dem big boys and dem but yuh ain't able wid dem men and dem. Trust me. Dem men too ignorant. Dem doesn cater for yuh life. Dey doesn care bout you. Dey only out to use. I know, cause I see it already. I combing hair since I turn fifteen. Dem days ah used to work wid a gyul dey call Suzy. Reeaaaaaalll nice gyul. She end up getting shoot up. Something dey get she to do for dem. She was real nice."

"Dey kill she?"

"Yeah. She ketch two bullets on she chest. Steups! Nice gyul yuh know, pretty gyul . . . gone jus so."

"Hmmm."

Another moment of silence ensued.

"Jus be careful, horse. Yuh young in de dance and yuh small in de dance but yuh not too small for yuh shot to call."

There was something ominous about her warning. She had never warned Antonio before about anything. He thought about his cousin Martin and how swiftly and suddenly death had welcomed him to its courts. Antonio did not think he would die. He did not even imagine that he would get shot at. He had not stepped up to the plate in the way that Psycho had wanted him to and the killings had seemed to subside. Around 8.30 p.m., when Kesta had finished twisting his hair and Antonio was satisfied that he looked the way he wanted to, Kesta asked Antonio for a ride to the Croisée. He didn't mind. He didn't really like anybody in the car when he was transporting any goods but she was going a short distance and it was just pork in his trunk. He helped Kesta close the windows and turn off all the lights. She was grateful. As they made their way down the wooden staircase outside her shop, Antonio wondered if he could be brave enough to try to get with Kesta in a romantic way. He had enjoyed their conversation and even though he knew she was older than him, he could not deny that there was some attraction there. As they approached the car, Antonio looked around as he usually did. He did that routinely whenever he approached his car. The road was not too busy. There were only a few parked cars around. It was full moon and the night air was crisp and fresh. A timid wind blew sweet and cool on his face. He put the key into the driver's door and looked across at Kesta standing on the passenger's side, waiting to open the door. She really was a pretty girl he thought. He could get used to having a woman like that in his car. She had been talking all the way down the stairs and she was still saying something to him only he wasn't really hearing her. He was thinking about so many other things.... his mother, Andrea, school, Chester, Martin, Psycho. It was all a blur. She turned her head southward as she opened the car door. A car was coming up the street at a moderate speed. The music was blaring and the headlamps were on.

"*Who the cap fits . . . let them wear it.*"

The popular Bob Marley tune grew louder as the car approached. Antonio thought it was a taxi, someone probably working PH. He felt everything in his chest vibrating with the music from the loud speakers. The car was almost alongside them but he was not unduly alarmed. Kesta was still on her feet speaking about something he wasn't paying attention to, when suddenly she fell. He didn't hear the first bullet only the battery of bullets that followed. It was an assault on his ears. He did not have time to smell the sickening burnt smell of metal on metal or to see the faces of the men behind the guns. He ducked his head low and began running behind the building that he had only left a few minutes earlier. The bullets followed him. He jumped over a broken chain link fence and kept running and running and running. Antonio found himself in someone's backyard, brushing past men's jockey shorts and bed sheets. It was chaos. Dogs were barking. His heart was racing as he scaled a red brick wall and jumped over a drain on to an empty lot of land with tall uncut grass. His steps were too quick. He tripped and fell on something in that tall bush. Something hurt as his chest hit the ground. He was panting loudly. Each breath a deep gasp. He did not know where he was or how far he had run but there were no more bullets flying around him.

It was dark and the grass shielded him from sight. He lay there still, like an animal in hiding and for the first time in a long time he felt truly afraid. Someone had tried to kill him. Maybe the same men who had killed his cousin. He could hear his breathing loudly and closed his mouth so he could breathe through his nose. He felt a searing pain surging up his right shoulder. He was soaking wet. His hands groped around in the dark beneath his chest where he felt pain. He had fallen on the shards of a discarded beer bottle. It had not done as much damage as it could have, because there was a layer of cloth between his skin and that bottle. Still it hurt. He touched his shoulder where he felt the pain getting worse. The skin on his shoulder felt stiff and sore not like his own. It was wet. Something was oozing out of him. Something smelt fresh. Blood. He reached his left arm up to his right shoulder and tried to touch the spot where he felt the pain. It was wet and he grimaced in pain as he touched it. He could feel a hole in his flesh. Antonio had been shot.

Chapter Twenty-Three

A Matter of Perspective

"What yuh say?"

"Like yuh not hearing good ah what. I said is two weeks taking care of one person so you can't get a full month's salary for that."

Sandra's blood was beginning to boil. She would not restrain herself. She refused to be taken advantage of again by Ms. Goodridge. Not this time.

"Lady, like yuh feel I stupid ah what. Yuh feel like I born yesterday. Like it have a sign mark jackass on my head ah what. A contract is a contract. I am supposed to get pay by the week, not by the person. Yes, Ms. Olivia dead but while she was living I was working and just because she dead that not supposed to affect my pay. That is taking too much blasted advantage. Ah find . . ."

Before she could finish the sentence Ms. Goodridge interrupted her.

"Like you getting tie up. You really getting tie up. I thought you was brighter than Patsy but you like you more dhotish. You feel I cyah get nobody to do what you doing?

You feel that you doing something special? You feel as the white people like you that they wouldn't like nobody else? Well let me tell you something, it have about ten people waiting to do what you doing for half the price and half the stress. Eeeeevery body want to come to America, like is this place where they giving out free money. It have nothing free up here, Sandra. It have people out here who ketch they tail for years before they make a dime; people who come up here and lose everything they leave behind for the sake of a chance to reach in America; people who wish they did never set foot in this country; people who thought they was coming to heaven and end up in hell. But I not surprised by you, yuh know. I watch you good, smiling and grinning like a fool. I know you thought was big money yuh come to make in a six months. I thought Patsy woulda tell you. I thought she woulda show yuh a form about how things does happen out here. Steups! I ain't hotting my head about you nah, Sandra. You feel I so wicked eh. It have plenty worse than me. You lucky is me yuh meet. The money here if you want it. Is one thousand dollars. If yuh don't want it no problem but I done with you. I ain't bound to deal with you when it have people slimmer and prettier than you, eh, talking nicer and more respectful than you, waiting to work. I done with you. Pack up yuh things and get out from there this weekend. I sending somebody else, man. I fed up ah this shit."

Ms. Goodridge hung up the phone before Sandra had a chance to respond. In an instant Sandra went from being a woman with righteous indignation to a woman without a job. It wasn't that she felt that she was wrong to have behaved the way she did; Sandra simply did not anticipate Ms. Goodridge's response. Yes, she wanted to work and she needed the money but it was the taking advantage part of it that she could not come to terms with. Now she was faced with the dilemma of being jobless and having to start hunting for a job all over again. She did not have much time left in Brooklyn before returning to Trinidad. It seemed pointless.

"What you telling me here, Sandra? You do what? You say what? Nah, nah, nah, nah, nah. You got to go back there and beg back for that job." Patsy told her in disbelief. Sandra had never seen Patsy's eyes open up as wide as they did or the veins on her neck bulge as much.

"Nah Patsy. I cyah do that. Wrong is wrong and right is right and that woman been doing me wrong from the beginning. I ain't care what she say. I not begging she fuh nuttin yuh hear! I go make my own way."

Patsy wiped the sweat from her forehead with a baby pink handkerchief. Even though it was cool outside and inside the apartment, the account that Sandra had given her of Ms. Goodridge's exchange with her had her quite agitated."

"Make it how? Sandra gyul, like you not understanding how life is out here ah what. Yuh feel me and Lenny get what we get from standing up for we rights? Listen to me Sandra! Look at me!" she tugged on Sandra's sleeve.

"This is America. The almighty America. Money talks and bullshit walks up here. If yuh don't know, I telling you so. Is all about the dollar. When you walk off the job now, is money in Goodridge pocket yuh know and some other body to fool. I know what I telling you. You got to go back and beg back for that job. Tell her yuh sorry. Tell her yuh wasn't thinking straight. Tell her something but get yuh job back. Yuh have one month left so yuh might as well stay there."

No matter what Patsy said, Sandra believed she was well within her rights to demand a full month's pay. Sandra refused to beg for her job and vowed that after she collected her pay from Ms. Goodridge, she would never set foot in her apartment again.

"Is only as I have money there I going back there but never again," she had said.

Patsy was not happy about these developments. Sandra with no job would mean Sandra at home during the day, eating her out of house and land, using up her soap, her toilet paper and everything else. She would not have that for an entire month.

"You could always go back to Trinidad early yuh know, Sandra," Patsy suggested.

"I will get something. You doh study nothing. I have a friend from Guyana. I supposed to see her tomorrow to give her back some money I borrow. I will ask her if she know anybody who need a little help out for a month or something; maybe somebody who need to go back to Trinidad for a short month or something. I will get something . . . . But I ain't going back by Goodridge . . . no way!"

Later that night, while talking to Lenny, she expressed some of her concerns.

"What yuh think bout Sandra, boy? I never know she woulda be so pig-headed. Imagine she tell off Ms. Goodridge and talking bout she ain't going back there. You know what that mean? That mean she sending up the electric bill and eating more food and yuh ain't see the size ah she? Steups. She real harden boy. She say she goin an get some job from some Guyanese lady tomorrow. She just have one month again and I ain't think she save no money at all at all."

Lenny, who had just finished brushing his dentures and the few remaining yellow-grey teeth that belonged to him, turned away from the mirror over the bathroom sink. He looked an odd sight with his teeth out like that. Without his dentures, he was a man much older than his age. He walked across the worn out grey carpet to put away his Daily Racing Form. He had lost money on one of his favourite horses named Morning Dew, at the off-track betting hall, and was determined that tomorrow he would make the money back.

"Well, it's not like we can throw her out, you know. She came up here with good intentions and it doesn't seem to be working out for her. America doesn't work out for everybody, you know. Remember my friend Jeffrey?"

"Who? The fella who used to do carpentry down in Fyzabad?"

"Yes. Remember how he came up here and paid that white woman to marry him. Remember that? She took all his money, and never filed for his papers. INS end up ketching up with him and they send him right back to Trinidad."

"I remember."

"I don't know Lenny. I think when you come up here you got to be prepared to put up with a lot of shit to make it in America. You got to be prepared to humble yuhself and do what you would be too shame to do in Trinidad."

"Well is not just that, you know. America is not for everybody. Look at that gyul. Ms. Mabel daughter. You remember how she had got her green card and eventually send for her children to come up here? How she put the big son in high school thinking that he will get a better education and go to college and all that. And what happen instead? The boy end up joining a gang."

Patsy who had just finished powdering her entire torso with baby powder was now slipping into her nightgown.

"Yes . . . . Ms. Mabel daughter . . . What was her name again? Rose . . . . Yes, I talk to Rose. She say how the boy say that in order to get into the gang he had to shoot somebody. He say he didn't think the man he shoot woulda dead. As if bullet make out of plastic or something. As if he didn't know bullet does kill people," said Patsy shaking her head as she fluffed her flattened worn out pillow.

"Is not that, yuh know. He didn't think they woulda ketch him. This is America. It have all kinda camera hiding all about to watch what yuh doing every second of the day. He didn't know the camera was hiding and it snap him. But like he really didn't think the man woulda dead neither."

"Is that." Patsy chimed in.

"The mother never recover after that. And the daughter name was Rosalee. After the brother went to jail like she just went wild and next thing is because she end up with some drugs man and they ketch she with some kokene in she belly down in Bahamas."

"Is not ko-kene, Lenny is cocaine."

"I ain't he father. I ain't name he. Ko-kene, cocaine, whatever ... drugs."

"It wasn't in she belly neither. It was up in between she legs .... high, high up."

"Well yuh see, look how you know more than me bout the story," Lenny laughed.

"Ain't dey lock she up too?" asked Patsy

"Yeah. Dey lock she up too. It wasn't nice for Ms. Mabel. She really wanted a better life for Rose and she grandchildren but people doesn't realize that America doesn equal better life. As a matter of fact, for some people America equal hell and worse."

"I wouldn say so, Lenny," Patsy retorted as she got ready to turn off the bedroom light. "It is just a matter of attitude and how yuh look at it when you reach up here."

"Well, I doh know how Sandra looking at it, but which ever way she looking at it she better change, cause like it not agreeing with her at all. The way things going for her, is like Corbeaux pee on she."

The following morning Sandra was up early. She was meeting Lindy at eight o'clock, in the train station where they had first met a few months prior. Lindy was eager to receive her payment and had seemed reticent in her tone, almost as if she had regretted the way she had spoken to Sandra over the phone before. Sandra for her part was glad to get out of Patsy's apartment. With the loss of her job, the tension between herself and Patsy had grown and seemed unlikely to resolve any time soon. She hoped and prayed that Lindy would be able to assist her with getting a job and a place to stay during the week. That morning she wore a pair of black skin-tight jeans and a green cardigan that hid the massiveness of her behind. She had eight hundred of the one thousand dollars she had received from Ms. Goodridge. It was the remnant of her final salary. She hoped it would be enough to appease Lindy for the time being. She needed to keep a few dollars for herself. Lindy would have to wait for the balance.

That morning she walked up Flatbush Avenue full of hope. She did not need help to make her way around Brooklyn. She had got used to taking the bus and the train and knew how to read the city map the tourists used to get around. She boarded the subway at Beverley Road and listened to the grunting of the train and its grinding on the tracks as it pulled off, first slowly, then at high speed. At one of the stops a white woman hunched over with age boarded the train. She wore a black dress and every footstep she made was slow and deliberate. She was alone and so she held on to the door as she entered and the back of each seat as she made her way to an available space on the train. Perhaps it was the way the woman was dressed, or the make up she wore on her wrinkly folding face that reminded Sandra of Ms. Joan. She had left Ms. Joan walking just like this lady was, with slow deliberate steps. She had met Ms. Joan lying in bed unable to stand up and walk for herself and she had left her walking. Ms. Goodridge had given her no credit for that. Sandra thought that perhaps it was not really because of her that Ms. Joan had walked. Maybe it was Olivia's death that had made the old lady find the strength inside herself, to let go of that bed that was her safe zone and make those few brave steps across the bedroom to hold her sister one last time. However, it was Ms. Joan's parting words to Sandra that made her think that maybe, just maybe she had played a role. Sandra remembered the day vividly as she stared unaware at the little old lady on the train hunched over, frowning as though the world and the weight of her life had made her bend that way.

"You aren't bad for a Caribbean girl you know, Sandra. You aren't too smart but you aren't bad."

"Hmm. Well, Ms. Joan I don't know what kind of compliment is that but I will take it nonetheless."

"You are too good for that old Ms. Goodridge. I wish I could keep you but it isn't up to me. Ms. Goodridge calls the shots and my nieces agree with whatever she does, not because it's right but because it's cheap. They never visited Olivia and me, the wretches. They think that by keeping us alive, they are doing something noble, something that will assuage their consciences and help them sleep better at night. But you, Sandra, you have done more for me than all the other caregivers that money-grabbing witch has sent here. You listened to me, even when I was talking rubbish you listened to me."

Ms. Joan's eyes were glassy looking and Sandra could see a tear getting ready to break free. Sandra wanted to cry too. She felt as though she had failed, as though all her efforts to do her job well and to make her life and those of her children better had been in vain.

"Here Sandra, take this. I like to wear it, but I'm an old lady and some other caregiver will probably steal it off my neck while I'm sleeping." Ms. Joan took Sandra's fat brown hand and placed something in her palm.

"What's this?"

"Look inside."

Sandra opened her hand to see a light-weight gold chain with a golden locket for a pendant.

"Open the locket."

"Who is this?"

"Me and Olivia when we were kids. My father gave it to me before he died. He told me that no matter where I was, Olivia was my responsibility. He said I had to look out for her and make sure she was alright no matter what. She's alright now. So I want you to have it."

Sandra was moved by Ms. Joan's words and the depth of emotion that accompanied them. She opened the locket and looked at the picture. It was a small black and white photo of two little white girls, one with dark hair. They were smiling and happy.

"I dunno what to say Ms. Joan. Ah will really miss you."

She hugged the old woman, and kissed her soft freckled face. For all the trouble Ms. Joan had given her, it was the kindest and most sincere gesture Sandra had received since arriving in America. She kept the locket and chain with her wherever she went after that day, believing that it would somehow bring her good luck. If it didn't, she was going to keep the picture and sell the chain. It was fourteen carat gold and would fetch a decent price at any pawnshop in Brooklyn.

CHAPTER TWENTY-FOUR

Breaking The Cycle

He had never come so close to death before. He had never felt so afraid. The night of Antonio's attempted assassination was the most terrifying of his life. It all seemed like a nightmare; a nightmare that should have belonged to someone else, except it belonged to him. After lying in that mosquito infested, garbage riddled, unkempt lot of land for almost half an hour, Antonio got up and called for help. In those few minutes, which seemed like an eternity, he saw his entire life flash before him. He didn't know who the men in the car were. He had not seen their faces in the violent shower of bullets they had rained on him and Kesta. Kesta. O Lord! When he thought of Kesta he knew he had to go back. She had fallen, he had seen her fall. What if she was dead? She was an innocent victim. Those men wanted him. He knew that much. But why did they want to kill him? He had nothing on himself or in the car; no weed, no coke; only that bucket of pigs' legs in the trunk. It would have thawed out by now. He had to call Psycho. He had to call someone. He was alive but he was hurt. He could feel the pain in his shoulder radiating down his arm like needles of electricity. He reached in his pocket with his free arm for his cell phone and called for help.

Within an hour help came but not from the quarter he had expected. Psycho had not answered his phone and he had called him frantically at least twenty times. He knew that a crowd would have gathered outside Kesta's shop by now and that that gathering would not leave the scene until every sequence of events witnessed and imagined, had been recalled and repeated several times in an incredible way in true Trini style. But if Kesta was dead, that would mean police and if he returned bleeding in that sea of onlookers that could mean trouble for him. He hoped she wasn't dead. He needed her to be alive. He wanted to go back but could not risk it. Desperate he called a partner who worked with Psycho; a man they called Stones. He was not sure why they called him Stones, but he knew that if Psycho could not help him Stones could. Stones was tall and burly, with skin so dark and smooth that the white of his eyes and his teeth were a noticeable contrast. Stones did a lot of jobs for Psycho. He was not too smart and was in his mid-thirties. In fact Antonio was not sure Stones could even read or write. But Psycho had said he was loyal and in the underworld, loyalty was worth more than gold or money in the bank.

After three rings, Stones answered the phone.

"Yeah?"

"Stones, horse. Ah geh shoot." Antonio was panting with each word.

"WHAT? WHAT? WHERE?"

"Dey shoot Kesta too, dred. Ah geh shoot, boy. Ah geh shoot." Antonio kept repeating it almost as if he did not believe the words he was saying; the events of that evening were too shocking, too unimaginable for him."

"Where de car? Where de bucket?" Stones asked. His tone was hurried. Antonio could not understand why Stones seemed to care more about the car and its contents.

"Yuh eh hear what ah say dred. AH GEH SHOOT!"

Antonio said it louder, and as he shouted it into the phone, he could feel the tears welling up inside him. He wanted Stones to care about HIM, not the car or the bucket of pigs' feet, but how could he expect that from a man whose only loyalty was to Psycho and the money he made.

"Where yuh ketch de bullet?"

"In meh shoulder. It bleeding real plenty, horse. It real hurting plenty." Antonio thought that those words would be enough to burst open the damn of concern, but he was wrong. Men like Stones and Psycho knew how to detach themselves from feelings and events. They were immune to cries for help. Tears made no impression on them. This is how they were able to do the work they did with callous indifference.

"Where yuh?"

"Barataria. Ah close to the main road. Ah seeing de gas station it looking like. De one before Morvant Junction."

"Where de car?"

"It by Kesta. I doh know." His voice trembled.

"Alright I in de area. I go meet yuh by the gas station."

Antonio could not hold back the tears. He was in a great deal of pain. He started walking, slowly towards the noise of the cars and the streetlights. It was dark but a few passersby had pointed at him and whispered. One brave man tried to assist.

"Soldier. Yuh bleeding real plenty. Yuh need to go to the hospital," the man had said but Antonio pushed past him. Before Antonio could reach the gas station Stones had met up with him. Still bleeding, Antonio got in the black Nissan X-Trail and sat down.

"Yuh ha to go hospital, dred. Yuh real bleeding. Bes you go by Mt. Hope."

Antonio wanted to go to the hospital. He was crying the way men cry when they allow themselves to be human but don't want the world to see them being so.

"Dis ha to be one ah dem boys from East Dry River, dred. Dis is a real f—king disrespect, horse. Dey f—king disrespecting we, dred. Steups! Wheeeey!"

Antonio was not hearing all that Stones was saying. He didn't care about the disrespect. His head was spinning and he believed he was going to die. His thoughts turned to Sandra. He wondered if he would see her one last time before he died. He wondered if she missed him. He felt his heart racing. A sudden weakness came over him. He did not see the traffic lights that Stones broke. He didn't even know how or when Stones put him out of the vehicle. He heard voices all around him. He felt his body moving, being placed on something. He was being poked and prodded everywhere. He tried to open his eyes but they felt heavy. Something plastic was placed over his nose. He felt himself drifting. Someone was tapping him, asking him his name. He felt a surge of pain and then suddenly everything went silent.

When he awoke, Antonio was on a bed surrounded by doctors. They were mostly Indian and young looking.

"Sir, Sir, you alright?"

"What's your name?"

"Antonio," he whispered.

His throat hurt but he was not sure why.

"What yuh say?"

The tall black haired doctor leaned in closer to hear what he had to say.

"Antonio," he said as loudly as he could.

"Antonio, how yuh feeling?"

He thought for a moment. He wasn't feeling pain anymore. He wanted to sit up. He tried to.

"No. No. No. Don't try to get up. Just relax."

"Ah get shoot," he whispered.

"Yes. Do you know who did this?"

Antonio shook his head. The oxygen mask on his face made him very uncomfortable.

"Well you are very lucky, Antonio. You were not doing so well when you came in and we had to put a tube in your chest to help you breathe better but you doing alright for now."

Antonio looked to his right and saw a tube coming out of his chest connected to a bottle on the floor.

"You going to have to stay with us for a little while but hopefully not too long. Lucky for you, the bullet didn't do too much damage."

He didn't understand all that they were saying. He didn't understand it all. A brown-skinned nurse with a large bottom was moving around him fixing things. There were circular dots stuck on to his chest and he heard beeping noises above his head. He looked around for Stones. He was not there. No one was there. He heard the doctors mumbling something under their breath. They were talking about him.

"He is only sixteen yuh know! Imagine getting shot at sixteen! He should be in school."

"When yuh see that, he must be in a gang," another female doctor said.

Antonio knew they were judging him and he did not like their tone. He wanted to tell them that he did go to school. He wanted to tell them that he wasn't in a gang that he only did work for Psycho sometimes. He wanted to tell them that his mother was in America working and that his grandmother had died. He wanted to tell them that he had a father and that he lived on Evans Street. He wanted to tell them so many things but they had already turned their backs and walked away and now he was left with this big bottom, brown skinned nurse who looked at him with a certain amount of disdain. As soon as the doctors left, she began her assault.

"Hmm. Young boy like you. How this happen to you? You should be in school. You only sixteen. Hmmm. Nice looking boy like you taking bullet already. Who you living with?"

Antonio wanted to say he was living with his mother or his father or his grandmother even but that single question caused him to think. He realized for the first time that he was truly very much alone in the world. He was not living with his mother or father or anyone. He was not even living with Psycho. He was alone. He was in the world alone and in the hospital alone and there was no Psycho or Stones, no mother or grandmother to hold his hand and tell him that he was going to be alright.

"Meh mother in America," he said softly. He felt drowsy.

"In America?" she scoffed in disbelief.

"What she doing there?"

"Work."

She pulled roughly at his arm to fix his blood pressure cuff.

"She is an American?"

"No." Antonio was becoming irritated by her questioning.

"Hmm. Illegal nah. And where yuh father?"

Antonio didn't feel like answering anymore questions. He had not seen his father in months and he hated him. All the while his eyes opened and closed intermittently. He remained silent.

"Steups! I dunno what to say bout allyuh young people nah. Young, nice looking black boy like you done getting shoot up already. Steups!"

Antonio could feel the tears welling up again. The big bottom nurse was getting ready to move away from his bedside in her tight-fitting white pants and he was glad to see her go. She had made him feel as though no one cared about him and in light of everything that he had gone through that day it was a little too much to bear. He was not sure what time it was but he was glad for sleep to come.

His hospital stay was short. He was not sure how word got to Chester but Chester appeared at hospital the following day to visit him, looking as sheepish as he usually did. Ms. Barbara came too the following day with Andrea in tow. Andrea was not allowed on the ward because she was too young and watched sadly through the glass louvres on a corridor outside the ward. He missed her. He wondered how she was making out with Ms. Barbara. He never liked Ms. Barbara and he knew his mother did not like her much either.

"Yuh tell Mommy ah get shoot?" he asked Ms. Barbara

"What she say?"

"She not happy, Antonio. How you expect her to feel? She not happy you liming with all dis bad company you pick up and not going to school. Yuh poor grandmother must be turning in she grave all now to see how you going."

"She coming down?"

"No, son. I ain't think she coming down yet."

"Mommy say when she coming back?"

"No she ain't say." Ms. Barbara could hear the disappointment in his voice and wanted to give him some hope.

"She want your phone number to call you. I tell she yuh have phone but ah does hardly see you."

"Tell she to call me nah."

Antonio gave Ms. Barbara his cell phone number and asked for that of his mother's but she did not have it on her or so she said.

"She say don't call her she will call. She say it will run up the bill when people call she nah. Things different in America."

Antonio looked at Andrea watching silently and waving from outside the ward window. She looked sad. He felt sorry for her.

"Yuh got to go back to school, Antonio. Yuh got to get outta dis life yuh living or yuh will end up dead. Why yuh doh come and stay with me?"

Antonio knew Ms. Barbara was right and that he would end up like Martin if he didn't break free from Psycho's claws but he was not about to be bossed around by her the way Andrea was. In all the time that he was in hospital he had no visits from Psycho or Stones or anyone of his partners that worked for Mr. Fung Ki Chi. Psycho had sent him a text saying that he would deal with the men who had done this to him. He promised revenge and so on and so forth but whenever Antonio called Psycho, the calls went straight to voice mail. Stones spoke to him though. He was glad that he was alright but his conversations with Stones were short and truncated. He hoped to see his mother. He was sure she would come. He was sure once she heard that he had been shot that she would hop on the first plane to Trinidad. He imagined that he would just open his eyes one morning and wake up to see her there sitting at his bedside. But she never came. The police came though. They took his statement and asked him many questions. They were intimidating in their grey starch-stiffed shirts and dark pants. He had never had to be so close to the police before and he did not like it. They were the ones who told him that Kesta was killed. They were looking for the vehicle that he drove. They had said it was not there when they arrived on the scene. They wanted to know who it was registered to. He did not know but was smart enough not to implicate Psycho or Stones in anyway. He wondered what had happened to the car and the bucket in the trunk. He imagined that someone had come and removed it before the police came.

One day he received a call from a man with a gruff voice, who did not identify himself and promised that he would finish 'clip his wings'. Antonio knew his life was in danger. He had to get out of hospital fast and was glad when the doctors removed his chest tube and discharged him to come back for a follow up visit. He never made it to that follow up visit though. While Antonio lay on his back in that hospital surrounded by sick men with all manner of ailments, he had reflected on his young life and devised a plan to escape the hold men like Psycho had on him. In those few days, the man who he had risked his life for on more than one occasion; his brethren; his horse, had totally abandoned him. It was bad enough being abandoned by those who were supposed to take care of him but when he reflected on how close he had come to death and all the pain he had had to endure since the shooting, he determined that his career as a mongoose in Mr. Fung Ki Chi's world had to end. Months later, when he learnt that Kesta had been murdered for becoming a police informant, he would read the news about the decomposing head of a man found in the Claxton Bay dump in a red plastic bucket and know that he had made the right decision.

CHAPTER TWENTY-FIVE

Life-changing Decisions

Sandra had never experienced winter before but she imagined that if it were anything like autumn she would not enjoy it at all. As autumn swept through the streets of Brooklyn filling it with its assortment of scents, dried leaves and chilly winds, the friendly familiarity of summer disappeared and like the winds, stone-faced New Yorkers and Brooklyn folk began to practise unknowingly the expressions of winter. It was not because winter had already come but weathermen and women had predicted the winter that year to be one of the worst ever. When the cold bite of winter winds struck, squeezing blood and warmth from noses, hands and cheeks, it would be hard to smile. When ice and water mixed with mud greeted pedestrians hustling to work, it would be easier to frown. Sandra had got used to the fact that, unlike in Trinidad, people did not say good morning when they passed each other in the street. When she had first arrived in Brooklyn she would say 'good morning' or 'good evening' every time she boarded the bus. Sometimes the bus drivers would answer her, other times it was just as if she had said nothing at all. Rarely a commuter would reply with an under-the-breath "Good day". Sandra always imagined the ones who responded to be West Indian. She wanted to believe that all West Indians had manners; that they were somehow kinder, friendlier, more compassionate than Americans but then she would think about Ms. Goodridge and she would know this to be untrue.

Her meeting with Lindy had been a productive one. She had repaid the Guyanese woman eight hundred of the one thousand dollars she owed, and although she was the poorer for it, Sandra felt a huge weight lifted from her shoulders. Lindy smiled so much when she received the green notes in her hand that morning in the train station that Sandra noticed for the first time, that Lindy's teeth were riddled with cavities. She was still an attractive Indian woman though, with her straight, long, black hair falling at her waist. Sandra promised Lindy that she would get the remaining two hundred dollars owed in two weeks and Lindy seemed comfortable with that arrangement. She had not forgotten that she needed work and once the business with Lindy had been settled, she asked Lindy if she knew anyone who could provide her with short-term employment.

"When you got to go back to Trinidad?" Lindy asked.

"Middle of next month."

"Hmm well that goin be sorta tough. I know somebody who need somebody to work for them but they want something more long-term if you know what I mean."

"I really need the work, Lindy. I ain't make nothing much out here really. I want to take something back home for meh children. You could help me out? Please?"

Sandra was desperate. Lindy could see it in her eyes. She knew that look well. She had seen it before. It was the look that led many West Indians to do things that they ordinarily would not do, even in their home countries. She looked at Sandra from head to toe. She had gained weight since they first met and the folds of fat around her waist appeared to have increased in size. Sandra was not an unattractive woman but she was a little more than "thick" and the gold-capped tooth in her mouth did nothing to improve her appearance. Lindy had work all right. She even had workers but they didn't look anything like Sandra.

"Where yuh going now?"

"Nowhere in particular."

"Yuh want to come and have lunch with me?"

"Well I ain't have no money to contribute, you know," said a wary Sandra.

"That's alright. It's on me. I think I have a job you could do yuh know but is more long-term. That is the problem."

Lindy had looked thoughtfully again at Sandra when she said those words with a facial expression that Sandra could not understand. They took the bus back to Brooklyn and stopped off on Dorchester Avenue. All the while they travelled, Sandra spoke of her children, of her mother who had died, about her cousin Patsy, about Mr. Bell, Ms. Joan and Ms. Olivia. She was talking so much that she didn't realize that Lindy had barely said a word. At the corner of Dorchester and Springfield Avenue, the Haitian restaurant Veni Vous welcomed them. The doors that marked the restaurant entrance were painted a bright gold and blue with fronds of palm leaves pressed against them. The lighting inside the restaurant was poor and the sweet smell of incense seemed to overpower the smell of the food being served. Haitian music blared through loud speakers and although Sandra did not understand a word that was being sung, there was a liveliness to the beat of the music that spoke to her.

"I like this kind of music you know. Even though I don't know what the hell they singing," said Lindy as they moved towards the food counter where an array of native Haitian delicacies greeted them, as well as the nauseating smell of fried pork fat. The menu board was written in Kwéyol but the drinks menu was in English.

"I will have the rice and beans, Riz et Pois, with poule and she will have the same," said Lindy to the sullen faced woman behind the food counter as she pointed to Sandra.

Sandra had hoped she would have had the opportunity to order her own meal. She did not like what Lindy had ordered and Lindy sensing her discontent attempted to soften the insult.

"You have to eat their Riz et Pois, it's no point coming to a restaurant like this and eating anything else. They sell everything here so expensive like you paying for the food to come over the seas to New York."

The woman who had taken their order shouted something in Kwéyol to another woman in the kitchen behind her.

When the food and drinks arrived, Lindy picked out a table at the darkest corner of the establishment and led Sandra to it.

"I don't know any Haitians. I never met one before."

"They are nice people. Very expressive, very friendly, most of them work hard but some are tricksters." Lindy chuckled.

"All I know it's a poor country, Haiti."

"There's a lot of poverty but there is wealth too, in the hands of a few people. Politicians are corrupt. They promise to make things better for poor people but when they get in power, they take all the money for their friends and family. It's pretty much the same everywhere. Except that most other places have more wealth than Haiti. Look at Guyana where I come from. I sure you ain't here no good thing bout Guyana or Guyanese people. But it's not a bad place. Problem is the race. Politicians keep using it to keep the people divided. One group thinking the other group is the cause of all the problems and the country never getting anywhere. Trinidad is no different." Lindy paused as she attempted to pull a piece of chicken bone out of her mouth with her hands. Sandra had barely touched her food. As she expected it was not as tasty as Lindy had described it.

"Well Trinidad is not like Guyana. I think we get along a lot better than you all. It have all kinda races in Trinidad, black, white, Indian, Chinee, Syrian, Indian from India, Chinee from China and Nigerian from Nigeria. We even have Venezuelan and Colombian and all. And we does get along. Even though they saying we is Third World, we developed plenty more than Guyana," Sandra retorted. She was delighted to be having this conversation with Lindy. She was beginning to feel like an intellectual and secretly hoped that at the end of all this talk a job would be forthcoming.

"Third World. Ha!" Lindy scoffed.

"That's just a word. Ah sure you don't even know what it means. For all the wealth that Guyana has, we still lack so many basic things. Trinidad too. While all the other countries in Europe are coming together to form trade blocks, we in the Caribbean can't even agree on the Caribbean Court of Justice. A simple thing like that. We still hanging on to the Privy Council in England. Trinidad so rich and still when politicians get sick, they flying out to other countries to do surgery because they don't want to go in any hospital in Trinidad. And no matter what government we get in Guyana is the same corruption all the time. Same for you all too. But you know what is the worst part, while we arguing over all kinda stupidness, the world moving on and we staying stuck.

That is why they could call us Third World. We thinking too small. Too myopic."

Sandra could see that Lindy had become very passionate about what she was saying and was impressed by this. Most of what Lindy had said had gone over her head though. She did not know the meaning of the word myopic or what the Caribbean Court of Justice or the Privy Council was about but she was happy that Lindy had got so excited about it and hoped to steer her back to the more pressing matter at hand—her current lack of employment. There was silence for a while as Sandra picked at the tasteless brown rice on her plate and Lindy chewed on the marrow of her chicken bones. Sandra enjoyed the strong base of the music that was playing. The rhythms were sweet.

"So yuh think I could get a job somewhere for a month?"

"For you?"

"I not sure. Not unless . . . ."

"Unless what?" asked Sandra impatiently.

"Well not unless you overstay your time."

"Overstay my time? Overstay my time?" Sandra asked the question twice with her mouth wide open and a look of disbelief on her face. She could not conceive what Lindy was suggesting to her especially when she recalled that for non-payment of her debt, the same Lindy had threatened to report her to immigration. Thoughts exploded like fireworks in her brain as she tried to imagine what overstaying her time would mean for herself and her children.

"Is not so bad as all that, yuh know. I know plenty people who overstay their time already. It not sooooo bad as all that and eventually when they settle down they get a lawyer and get regularize. It does just be rough for the first few years. But if you get something steady, you will be alright."

Sandra had not heard a word Lindy had said to her. Where would she stay if she overstayed her time? What would she do? How long would it be before she could go back to Trinidad and see her children? No. She could not overstay her time. It was not practical. Not possible. Patsy had told her of people who had overstayed their time. Some of them got deported and could never return. She was not going to be one of them.

"Listen, is not as bad as you might think. There is a job I have right now. Eight hundred dollars a week."

"Eight hundred a week?"

"Yes. That is three thousand two hundred a month. Tax free dollars. A old white man living out in upstate New York. One day off every two weeks, living-in work. Now, if you get something like that and hold it down for a two years, yuh know how much yuh could make and send home with that?"

Sandra could not help but wonder if this perhaps was her lucky break. Still overstaying her time would mean not being able to see her children again for a long time and she knew that they needed her, especially Antonio.

"You could overstay your time and sort out your papers in two years you know. Then in five years time you could be back in Trinidad. Only thing you will have to work for me and me alone cause I am the only one who could get you the kind of jobs that paying that kind of money. And especially as you don't have no social security or nothing you will have to be real careful. But this job good for the money. No hard work at all. Just taking care of a old man. He could walk but not so good. He little horny and thing but he old. He cyah do nothing with what he got between he legs anyway." Lindy had finished eating now and was giving Sandra her full attention. She wiped the grease from her lips slowly and deliberately and looked straight at Sandra, eyes fixed.

"I dunno. Dem children and dem need me," Sandra argued weakly.

"Yes, but they need things too; things like shoes and books, clothes, lessons for school. Things yuh know yuh cyah give them if yuh go back now and start back working for seven dollars a hour in Trinidad. This is a chance to give them something, a betterment, a better life, better than what you get."

Sandra knew Lindy was right. She had been ketching her tail in Trinidad long enough and no matter how hard she worked or how long, the money never seemed to be enough. Andrea was getting older; soon she would be a teenager wanting clothes and shoes and things that Sandra knew she would never be able to give her; things a man would promise her as soon as her breasts began to rise and her hips started to sway in that womanly way that entices a man. She did not want Andrea to be beholden to men like Chester. She wanted her to get an education, to maybe even go to university like Mr. Singh's son would when he finished A-levels. She wanted the same for Antonio too. Although news of him not going to school had upset her tremendously, Sandra felt that if she could just talk to him, she would be able to get him to see reason and take up a trade at least. She had not yet learnt of his shooting, since no one had told her.

"This job is a good one. Easy money, no set of stress. Yuh could get it for the whole year. The whooooole year. No hassle, no fuss."

"But what if ah have to go home for an emergency or something."

"Yuh could go."

"But what about immigration? If I overstay my time I can't just go back to Trinidad just like that!"

"Yuh could go. Yuh just cyah come back."

Lindy knew Sandra was conflicted but she wanted Sandra to believe that staying in America was a good idea. She needed her to believe in the American dream but she knew the decision was not going to be an easy one. Sandra had responsibilities back in Trinidad. She was a mother and Lindy knew only too well that if she pushed too hard, Sandra would change her mind.

"You think about it. Don't rush but you have to give a decision by tomorrow. I need to know because the girl who working with him going back to Guyana next week and she want to send up a next girl from Guyana for me. But as you here already on spot it better. So you going to have to call me and let me know so I can know what to tell him." Lindy lied. There was no girl from Guyana going or coming. There was just a job.

"I will call yuh. I want the work. Is the overstaying part I doh like."

After the meal, Sandra who was still hungry since she had barely touched her food, bid farewell to Lindy and decided to head to Prospect Park.

She liked walking in that park. It was supposed to be a rough area; that's what Patsy had told her, but she couldn't see how a park that was as serene as that could be compared to any rough neighbourhood she had known in Trinidad. She had never gone there alone. Lenny had taken her there with him on two occasions when he went to exercise. Those times he would start walking and five minutes later would walk some distance off to answer his cell phone. That would usually be the end of the exercise, since the rest of his park experience would be spent laughing and chatting on the phone with someone other than Patsy. Sandra suspected that the Prospect Park excursions were clever excuses to entertain conversations with his outside woman. She would proceed to walk alone for the most part and after a couple laps, when Lenny had had his full of jokes, he would return to walk a few yards with Sandra before complaining of feeling tired and getting chest pains. Sandra had been around men long enough to know the game that Lenny was playing but she chose not to mention these phone calls to Patsy since as her cousin had painfully reminded her, she was only "begging a lodging." But today she would go to Prospect Park alone. She needed to clear her head. She wanted to think about what Lindy had told her. She wished Maye were still alive to advise her, tell her what to do. Her mother was good at that. She missed her wisdom and those telling words of admonition she would often hear. She looked up at the blue-grey sky and wondered if Granny Maye was somewhere up there. She marvelled at daylight in America. She was amazed by the seeming invisibility of the sun in a brilliant sky. In Trinidad you could always see the sun and feel the heat. It was chilly now but soon it would be winter. Patsy had told her that the first Christmas she spent in America she cried because she could not go to parang from door to door the way she used to in Trinidad. In fact, she had told Sandra that the whole concept of going outside in the wintertime like that, singing songs, was a novel one that nobody participated in for practical reasons. It was simply too cold. As each leaf crunched under her feet Sandra thought of Antonio. She could not leave him. She had to speak to him before making a decision like that.

The park was not deserted. In fact there were the usual joggers, cyclists and the odd couple making out on a park bench. She remembered that the last time she had been there she had seen two women kissing each other on the mouth. It had shocked her to see that so openly but Lenny had told her that was the norm in America and that she should not be alarmed because men were just as open about being gay as women. The park was quiet today. An occasional wind caused the huge poplar trees to perform a gentle swaying dance. The walls of the apartment buildings around the park were a dismal grey. In fact, in her time in Brooklyn, and even in Long Island she had not seen houses painted the bright colours that adorned the walls of homes in Trinidad. America was strange she thought to herself. Like a nomad in the desert she walked aimlessly through the park, reflecting on all the persons she had met since she arrived in Brooklyn. Patsy was her cousin but she had changed. She was not the cousin she remembered. The cousin she remembered would not have taken eight hundred dollars from her salary for staying with her. Then there was Ms. Goodridge who, for her, was nothing more than a crook. Mr. Bell had seemed to care about her. He had even professed to love her. Now she didn't even know where he was and wondered if anything he had told her about himself was true. The jury was still out on Lindy, who had been helpful at first but had threatened to report her to immigration if she did not pay her debt. This same Lindy was now offering her a long-term job and encouraging her to overstay her time. It seemed quite paradoxical to her.

She had not enjoyed her job taking care of Ms. Olivia and Ms. Joan at first but in a strange and twisted way, she had grown to care for those two old ladies. She wondered how Ms. Joan was doing. She would have loved to go back for a visit but her funds were swiftly diminishing and she had already pawned the locket she had received from Ms. Joan for a meagre twenty dollars. She presumed that Mrs. Foo Ming Choo had taken over the care of Ms. Joan and knew in that event Ms. Joan would be alright. She had walked almost two-thirds the way around the park, when the weather began to change. The sky became overcast. She looked up but could not see the sun, another thing she didn't like about America. There the sun played mysterious games of hide and seek in the sky with clouds. She didn't like having to be in search of the sun. In Trinidad if it was sunny, she could see the sun somewhere. She wanted to go home desperately but she remembered Lindy's words to her and wondered what she would be going home to if she could not give her children what they needed. She knew Ms. Barbara would take care of Andrea but who would look out for Antonio. He thought he was a man but in her eyes he was still a boy; her boy child; her first-born. She remembered the night of his birth when her water bag burst. How she had called out loudly to Chester who could not wake because he was too drunk and fast asleep.

It was Maye who took her to the hospital and waited for her outside till morning when the baby was born. She remembered the look of pride she felt holding that tiny baby in her arms. He had a full head of hair and even though she didn't have much milk in her breasts he had a good strong suck. She knew he was going to grow up to be strong and felt proud that this miracle had come out of her. It was the first good thing she felt she had created in the world and she was proud. Now that son, that boy she had carried in her arms with so much love was going astray. She needed to speak to him before making this decision. She could not stay if he was not okay. Overwhelmed by a sense of guilt, Sandra made an about face and quickened her steps. She would find a way to speak to Antonio today. Even if it meant spending the last few dollars she had in phone cards, she would hear her son's voice. Then and only then would she give Lindy a final answer.

CHAPTER TWENTY-SIX

A Long Way From Home

After Antonio's discharge from hospital, he disappeared. At least that is what Ms.Barbara thought until she heard from him a week later. She did not tell Sandra about his run in with the law for a number of reasons, all of them selfish. The truth was that although she grumbled to everyone she met about having the responsibility of taking care of Andrea at her age, she had begun to enjoy it much more than she had initially. She had never had a child; she was never a mother before. Now, God had smiled on her and thrust a child into her care. A child to love and cook for; a girl to admonish and teach about life's beauty and cruelty. She savoured every moment she had with Andrea. Even when she was scolding her she got a strange thrill. Andrea was hers, all hers. Sandra coming back to Trinidad, sooner than she needed to would spoil that. She had one more month before Sandra's return but it was a month she wanted to savour. Had she told Sandra about Antonio's shooting she might have wanted to return sooner and that would mean Andrea leaving. She did not want that.

Ms. Barbara had grown quite attached to the child, who for all intents and purposes was not as fond of Ms. Barbara as Ms. Barbara was of her. Andrea missed her mother. She missed her every morning when she awoke and every second of the day after that. It was acutely worse when Ms. Barbara scolded her. Her mother never scolded her so harshly. In the evenings when she came home from school Ms. Barbara would have some hot chocolate ready for her to drink. She didn't like the way Ms. Barbara made hot chocolate. She missed the snacks her mother would bring her in the afternoon and she missed rubbing her head on her mother's warm, soft belly. She missed Granny Maye too. The sight of her grandmother cold and stiff on her bed, remained etched in Andrea's memory forever. Once, on her way home she had seen her father walking with a woman and a baby in his arms on the main road. She had called out to him but with the noise of the traffic he did not hear. Often she cried herself to sleep at night. She would cry into her pillow because she did not want Ms. Barbara to hear her and fuss over her. She knew Ms. Barbara cared about her but Ms. Barbara was not her mother and Andrea was very clear about that. Andrea needed *her* mother as any girl her age. She hoped she would come back soon. She prayed for it. Antonio needed his mother too, but more importantly, he needed to be safe and it was not safe for him to continue to remain on Evans Street. The men who had tried to kill him would try again. The day he left the hospital, Psycho had been shot dead by police in Tacarigua. There was talk of returned gunfire and a shoot out but Antonio suspected it was a police hit. He was deathly afraid. He knew he needed to get far away from the men he had been associating with and decided that he would go to Moruga by his uncle Gerald and stay with him and his family for a while.

Gerald Denton was his mother's elder brother. He had left home at an early age and gone to Moruga where he worked as a fisherman. He had married a pretty Indian girl from the country. Her family had disowned her for marrying a black man and a fisherman at that. Leelawatee, or Baby as everyone called her, was devoted to her husband who she had known since she was seventeen years old. Antonio had spent holidays with them once. They had two sons; one much older than Antonio. They were douglas but one of them had hair as straight as Leelawatee's and did not appear mixed at all. That was the norm in Trinidad though. It was hard to tell who was African and who was Indian just from looking at a person's hair. Antonio remembered going to school with a boy whose last name was Singh but whose hair was just as tight and curly as his. He remembered some boys teasing him about it and saying he was adopted, but the boy's father, an Indian man, had come to the school and complained to the teacher and principal about it. The boy was only a little darker in complexion than his father but although his hair was like any African's hair he had got his father's nose.

Antonio liked Leelawatee. She was friendly. He liked how she had stayed with his Uncle Gerald. She had a simple way of doing things. She was used to poverty and although Uncle Gerald had elevated her standard of living only slightly, she did all the things that would have been expected of her had she been married to an Indian man. Uncle Gerald liked that. He boasted of her the way a fisherman would boast of a huge catch. She had straight, long hair that shone in the sunlight and ran all the way down to her waist. She mostly kept it up in a bun though, because that is how Uncle Gerald had told her he liked to see it. Even though she was as thin as a whip and plain faced, he would speak of her extraordinary beauty and would often remark that he would never get a woman as sweet as she was.

At Granny Maye's funeral Uncle Gerald had shook his hand briskly. He didn't say much, probably because he didn't have much to say. Antonio knew that if he went to Moruga, Uncle Gerald's doors would be as open to him as Leelawatee's arms. It made sense to go there. No one would look for him there. He could stay there for a while and figure out what to do next. He left for Moruga on the day of his hospital discharge. It was a long drive and he could not remember the way exactly but he knew how to ask a question and be discreet about it. He made his way to the sleepy village of Marac where his uncle lived. He passed the lone rum shop in the area with his head bowed, and said nothing to the men who were warming their insides with the fire their glasses contained. As he passed, their laughter and noise came to a sudden halt. He could feel them staring at him, their eyes following him around the corner leading up to his uncle's home. Once he made his way to Marac, the rest was easy. His uncle's house was the biggest in Marac and the only one made of concrete. There was no gate fencing around his uncle's house and the few pot-hounds that protected his home, did so well. They started up a raucous noise of barking and howling when Antonio entered the yard. There was a lighted flambeau outside the wooden door of his uncle's home. Leelawatee's son Pandu, short for Panduranga, answered the door. He was a fisherman too but he was not working that night.

Leelawatee had given her first-born that name. She had never asked much of Gerald except that she should be the one to give their first-born his name. Panduranga, she had told him, was a reincarnation of Lord Krishna. Gerald agreed, with the promise that he would name the second child.

Panduranga was born with thick, curly hair and anyone that saw him could tell that he was mixed. He was not that bright and although Leelawatee pushed him hard to do better in school, Gerald determined that he was better off learning a trade and took him out of school when he was fifteen to help him fish. His skin was bronze and burnt from the sun. His muscles were taut and his abdomen flat. He was indeed a handsome young man and many a girl in the village would have liked to be with Pandu. But Pandu was not interested in girls. He was not interested in anything except fishing. He loved the waves, the taste of salt in the air early in the morning before sunrise and the fresh smell of fish. Fishing was his life and he had been grateful to his father for removing him from school so that he could devote his life to the sea. His younger brother Jeremy was not like him though. Jeremy was the name his father gave him.

"This one is mine to name," Gerald had told Leelawatee when she tried to insist on giving him the name Ravendra.

Jeremy's hair was straight and his skin was paler than Pandu's. As a child his hair had been allowed to grow long but it was cut short when he started school. Jeremy did not looked mixed at all. In fact he looked more like Leelawatee's son than he did Gerald's. He was bright, quiet, and excelled at school. Leelawatee believed he would make it to university and she made sure that he never had too much house-work to do and was away from the burning sun and the sea. When Antonio arrived that night, they greeted him with open arms but were perplexed as to what he was doing there at that hour. It was already nine o'clock, and even in Moruga, it was not safe for someone to be travelling the road at night. There were dangers real and spiritual that lurked in every corner. Moruga was the home of superstition, a breeding ground for necromancy and practitioners of the dark arts.

"So, how come you manage to come out here so late?"

"Ah sorry to come so late. Ah just need a place to stay for a little while."

"Why yuh didn't send a message or call? Your uncle have a cell phone now yuh know. He out fishing tonight but he will come back in the morning."

Their home reminded him of the house he once called home on Evans Street. They pulled out a mattress from under Pandu's bed and laid it on the floor in a room at the back of the house, which Leelawatee used for ironing clothes. That night Antonio did not sleep. The mattress smelt of mould and squeaked every time he moved. He was safe in Moruga, better to be hounded by spirits than the kind of men who had killed Kesta. He wondered how long he would be able to stay there though. He hoped his mother would come back soon. He expected she would. Maybe he would be able to go back home eventually when things settled down. But things never settled down. The gang warfare had begun. There would be retribution for each killing and the blood of young men, mostly of African descent would flow through the land, soaking the earth. The cries of their mothers would be heard every night on television.

"He was a good boy. He never do nobody nothing."

Yes, a lot of "good boys" who never did anything would lose their lives for doing that nothing that they did so well. Many innocent people would lose their lives too, because they were either at the wrong place at the wrong time, or hanging out with the wrong type of 'pardners'. So, while 'good boys' died, boys like Jeremy stayed in school so they could get scholarships to go to university abroad. Fathers like Gerald worked hard to make sure that boys like Jeremy didn't have friends like Antonio to lime with. Mothers like Leelawatee made sure that their sons wanted for nothing that would catapult them on the road to success. For Leelawatee, Jeremy was the great family hope. He would be the first doctor. He would make her proud and the family she had forsaken for the love of Gerald Denton would have to acknowledge that something good and noble had come out of her marriage. She had lost Pandu to the sea but Jeremy would soar high above the sea. He would be her star.

By the time Sandra resolved to get in touch with Antonio, he had already spent one week in Moruga. He had left Evans Street without so much as a word to Ms. Barbara. However he saw Andrea one last time. He went to her school as if to deliver a message. She seemed excited to see him. She was playing as girls her age do during lunch. She had new yellow ribbons in her hair and they had become loose. She ran up to him and wrapped her arms around his waist not wanting to let go. She had not been able to do that in a long time. He hugged her back and instantly began to feel the groundswell of emotions.

"How yuh going little miss?"

"When yuh coming home?" was her response.

Andrea was convinced that if Antonio came home and stayed and went back to school she would be able to leave Ms. Barbara and stay with him.

"I going by Uncle Gerald for a while. Till mommy come back."

Her face changed.

"Is just a short while."

"Ms. Barbara saying all kinda things about you. How you getting into trouble and all kinda thing."

"You talk to Mommy?" he asked

"No. Ms. Barbara does do most of the talking."

"If yuh talk to her tell her I gone by Uncle Gerald, okay?"

Antonio wanted to be on his way. Speaking to Andrea only prolonged his anguish further. He had been so caught up in his own life and criminal affairs that he had not had the time to be a true big brother to her. He could only imagine how awful it must be for her living with Ms. Barbara, watching the place she knew as home empty and abandoned. Now he was leaving her and not sure when he was coming back.

"Ah have something for you. A snack."

He handed her a packet of Ripple's Crispy Cream chocolate bars.

She opened it ravenously like a girl who had not eaten.

"When you coming back?" she asked again.

"Next week, maybe week after. Tell Ms. Barbara to tell Mommy for me nah."

And with those few words he bade Andrea farewell. He wanted to tell her that he loved her but it was not something he was accustomed to saying. Instead he turned and walked away, head bowed. It would be two years before he saw his sister again.

Sandra had called Ms. Barbara one week later and was told that he was staying with his Uncle Gerald in Moruga. She was relieved. She knew that with Uncle Gerald he would at least have a roof over his head and food on his table. She wanted him to go back to school though and longed to hear his voice. It was the first good news she had heard about him since her departure. Ms. Barbara did not give any other information except to say that, that is what he had told the little girl, which was how she referred to Andrea. She had not made any mention of his hospital stay or the fact that he had asked after her. It was not because she did not think Sandra would find out somehow eventually. Trinidad was too small a place to hide news like that for long. Everybody knew somebody, who knew somebody who knew somebody, that somebody thought nobody knew. Ms. Barbara just did not wish to be the one to tell Sandra. She was taking care of Andrea and as much as she enjoyed having the little girl around, she was not being compensated for that and felt that she should be. No compensation seemed forthcoming and from the looks of things, the most she expected when Sandra returned for Andrea would be a "thank you very much". So she did not tell Sandra that Antonio had been shot or that she had seen him in the hospital. She could not have been expected to be responsible for both of Sandra's children.

When Sandra learnt Antonio was with her brother, she looked in her address book and got the number of her younger sister, Sonya. Sonya was not really her sister by blood but she had grown up in the Denton household and that was enough qualification to be considered a sibling. Sonya lived in Marabella on the old train line. She had had a hard life after leaving Granny Maye's doors but she never forgot the kindness that had been shown to her on Evans Street. She had become a lady of the night in Marabella but she loved Sandra because, despite her lifestyle, Sandra never judged her or looked down on her. She was always just Sonya, her sister, not step-sister or half-sister, just sister. Sonya kept in touch with Gerald because he was the only brother who could help her out of a financial jam if she got into one and Moruga was a good place to hide if she needed to get away from anyone she owed money to. Sonya was twenty-nine but looked like forty-five. When Sandra called her she was pleasantly surprised.

"Sandra. Dat is you girl?"

"Yes is me."

"You in Trinidad? Ah thought yuh was in America?"

"I in America. Ah still dere."

"But what trouble is dis? How yuh going gyul?"

"I dere. I alright."

"Oh gosh I so glad to hear from you girl. If yuh know how I wanted to get in touch wid you. How come yuh didn' come in Mammy funeral?"

"Gyul, I couldn come. It was a kinda complicated kinda situation."

Sonya waited to hear more. She thought Sandra would have gone on to tell her what the complicated situation was that prevented her from coming to Granny Maye's funeral. However Sandra said nothing and got straight to the point of the phone call before Sonya had a chance to ask her to bring anything back to Trinidad for her.

"Ms. Barbara say how Tony down in Moruga down by Gerald. De las time I check Gerald didn't have no cell phone. How yuh does get in touch wid him?"

"He get cell phone now yes, gyul," she laughed loudly.

"De boy getting wid de times. But how come Antonio reach down by he? He not supposed to be in school?"

"Gyul, he drop out from school it look like." Sandra said it almost as if she did not believe it to be true or rather wished it were not so.

"What trouble is dis! Dese children nowadays is something else. Steups! Now what he gone and do that for?" Sandra thought it ironic that Sonya would say that since she had left school at around the same age and run off with an old Indian man from Couva who had told her he had a lot of money.

"When last yuh talk to Gerald?"

"Is a while now. But ah could give yuh he number dey."

Sandra was glad to get the number from her sister. However, before the conversation ended, she knew that

Sonya would be asking her for some change, a sort of payment for being able to give Sandra something that she needed. Sonya was always like that. She knew how to be quick to get something from someone, usually it was money for services rendered. She wanted Sandra to send some clothes for her, jeans and tops she said. She said her clothes were getting old and she knew that everything was cheaper in America. Sandra promised she would bring something back for her although she knew she would not. She wanted to tell her of the predicament she had found herself in but she was too ashamed. She would get a hold of Gerald by telephone later that evening, while he was pulling in his seines. He had three pirogues he used to fish and four sets of seines. Gerald and Pandu used the two newer pirogues but the oldest one was worked by a young man called Chenet.

Chenet was twenty-four years old. He was hearing impaired and speech impaired but in Marac he was known as Chenet 'the deaf and dumb fella'. Sometimes they would call him Chenet other times they would simply call him "deaf and dumb fella." The villagers of Marac were not very kind to Chenet. They thought they were though. They imagined that a young man like Chenet would not have been able to accomplish what he had outside of the village. And what had he accomplished? Gerald had taught him how to fish and so he had a trade. Although he had worked with Gerald from the age of fourteen, when his mother left him in Marac to go to work in Princes Town, he would never be called Chenet the fisherman only "deaf and dumb fella." Chenet was an Indian man. His mother came to Marac years before, belly swollen with child, looking for a place to stay. She found refuge in the home of Mr. Smith an eighty-nine year old pensioner who lived alone and had no one to take care of him. Maybe he had invited her to stay there. Maybe she had just realized that he was too feeble and defenceless to put her out if she took up residence. Either way she stayed at Mr. Smith's home right up to the time of Chenet's birth. Neighbours had said she was hiding from someone or running away from someone and that is why she had come to Marac. In a small, close knit community like Marac it was difficult to keep business quiet.

Leelawatee had tried to reach out to Chenet's mother when she had first come to the village. Her name was Kavita. She was an Indian too and there were few Indian women in Marac. However Leelawatee soon discovered that there was not much she had in common with Chenet's mother and after Chenet was born, Kavita all but abandoned him into the arms of any mother between Marac and Cachipe who would hold him for a few minutes to comment on how cute he was. Kavita loved to drink and get drunk; rum drinking was her only passion. So Chenet was raised by some of everybody in the village but especially by Leelawatee. Kavita would leave Chenet with Leelawatee for weeks, then come and take him back, only to disappear for months at a time. It was Leelawatee who first recognized that Chenet could not hear well or speak well. He would make all sorts of noises with his mouth but none of them were intelligible and he could hear sounds but not very well at all. Chenet was a loving boy but as he grew older the instability of his environment and the ridicule he received for not being able to speak, caused him to become more and more introverted. And because Moruga was the place that it was known to be, full of superstition and all kinds of folklore, the rumour was that Chenet was like that because his mother had eaten too much chenet while pregnant with him. Others said that somebody had worked obeah on Kavita and that is why he was born that way.

It was not known whether Kavita had other children but when Chenet was thirteen, she left him to go to Princes Town to work and never returned. By this time Chenet and his mother were squatting on a small piece of land at the back of Mr. Smith's house. When Mr. Smith died, his children were quick to evict her from the house and fence around the lot of land on which he lived. Although in his old age they had seldom visited him and had left him to die alone, they knew the value of land. So Chenet the deaf and dumb boy, alone in the world by the age of fourteen, continued to live in the shack one of his mother's boyfriends had built for them. He lived in squalour and it was Leelawatee who persuaded Gerald to take him out to sea to help him to learn a trade. Gerald was not keen on the idea but Leelawatee had pleaded with him so much and it was hard for him to say no to her since she demanded nothing from him. Chenet learnt the ways of the sea and helped Gerald for many years before Panduranga joined them. Chenet and Pandu were like brothers. Although Chenet could not speak, he understood when Pandu talked to him and Pandu likewise understood Chenet. In fact he often felt closer to Chenet than he did to his own brother Jeremy who his mother pampered incessantly. Gerald was adamant that Chenet not live with them.

"I dunno who child he is. How I will have him living here wid we like he is one of we!" he had told Leelawatee when she begged to have him come stay with them. It was more than that though. Gerald had been teased enough about his wife when he had married her. His friends, mostly Creole had told him that before long he would be worshipping Ganesh and after his first son was named Panduranga, they saw him as being less of a man in his own house. He loved Leelawatee though and there was nothing he would not have done to make her happy but to take another man's child in his home, a deaf and dumb one at that, was going a little too far for him. So Chenet remained in that little shack and became a man there. The men of the village would still tease him but once he started working with Gerald their taunts were less and less. When he was seventeen, they brought a woman from Grand Chemin to have sex with him as a favour. This was considered live entertainment in the sleepy little town of Marac, where the men were mostly farmers and fishermen. When Leelawatee heard of what had happened she was extremely upset but Gerald had laughed it off.

"Who else a boy like Chenet will get to go with eh? The boy cyah talk. He cyah court nobody. Let de boy get a little happiness in life," he had told her.

Leelawatee did not see it that way but in a village like Marac, she had very little power. She was Gerald's wife, or 'the Indian woman that married to Gerald' and this was how she was known in the village. She was proud of her Hindu traditions and of her family even though they were poor, but the moment she had decided to marry Gerald her family cut her off and in a village like Marac none of these traditions mattered anymore.

It was almost six o'clock when Sandra got on to Gerald. He was with Chenet, Pandu and Antonio sitting on a piece of driftwood. The tide was coming in. Small waves crashed on to the beach and the white foamy waters ran timidly up and down the shore, encroaching further and further with each successive moan of the tide. A gentle breeze blew and the coconut trees that demarcated the dirt pitch road from the sand swayed to and fro. Gerald had taken Antonio out to sea for the first time and had allowed him to put down his own nets. The sun was setting and he was talking to them all. Antonio listened intently as though he were in a classroom.

The subject being taught was one that interested him. The ring of the cell phone interrupted the lecture.

"Sandra gyul, that is you? But ay ay! I say yuh still in America."

Antonio's heart skipped a beat. He wondered what she had heard and how much she knew.

"Yuh still dere? Oh ho. Yes, yuh boy here wid me. He right here yuh know. Yuh could talk to him." Gerald passed the phone to Antonio at once, quickly ending his conversation with Sandra. He was glad to hear from her but he was not fond of cell phones or talking on them for long periods.

"Mommy?"

"Praise God. Thank yuh, Jesus!" Emotion overwhelmed her as she heard her son's voice on the other end of the phone.

"Boy, yuh know how I worrying about you. Yuh know long I want to talk to you. I hearing all kinda thing bout you. How yuh drop out of school and yuh keeping bad company. What you doing down by Uncle Gerald? How come yuh not going back to school?"

Antonio got up from where he was seated on the sand and walked a little distance away from the group.

"I alright mommy. I alright."

"So what yuh doing dere? Why yuh not in school?"

"How come yuh didn't call me?"

"How yuh mean? Every time I ask Ms. Barbara for you she say yuh not home."

"She didn't give yuh meh cell number?"

"No. Yuh have cell number?"

There was a moment of silence.

"She didn't tell yuh I was in hospital?"

"Hospital! WHAT!! What yuh telling me here boy?"

"Doh worry, ma. Doh worry moms. I alright. I alright now."

"Some fellas shoot me an ting but de doctor say de bullet didn't hit no major organs or nuttin."

Sandra was cold sweating. The thought of her child being shot and hospitalized was too overwhelming.

"Lord Father! Jesus have mercy!" She began to cry. It was not only because of what she had just heard. The weight of everything she had gone through in Brooklyn came down on her like an unexpected thunderstorm in that instant. She sobbed, not only because her child had almost died and she had not been there but because she knew that it was her decision to go up to America that had indirectly contributed to the course of recent events in Antonio's life. Now, her decision to overstay her time would alter the course of his destiny forever.

"Doh cry, moms is alright. I alright. The doctor say ah lucky to be alive." He wanted to console her but he wanted to shout at her to scream even; to ask her why she had not come back when Granny Maye died; to tell her that he needed her to be there if he was to stay in school. There were so many things he wanted to tell her but all he could say were the same words over and over again while she cried on the other end of the phone.

"Ah sorry, mom. Ah sorry. Ah alright."

When she had managed to regain her composure, he asked her when she was coming back home. It was not a question she could answer truthfully and so she lied not because she wanted to but because it was too hard for her to tell Antonio the truth.

"Listen, Antonio. I want yuh to go back to school. You could stay in the house and Andrea could stay with Ms.

Barbara till I come back. Or you could stay with Ms. Barbara. I sure she would be glad."

"Moms, I cyah stay wid dat lady. She too bossy. She too dred. If yuh see how she does be bossing up Andrea. Yuh know what she tell me when I ask she for yuh number, she say she doh have it. She say doh call yuh. She say yuh will call me and look at how she didn't even give yuh meh phone number self."

"Doh mind that. Why yuh cyah go back home?"

"Nah moms . . . some fellas looking for me on dat side. De same fellas dat shoot me nah. I goin to stay here with Uncle Gerald for a little while till things settle down. By the time yuh come back home I will come back up."

But Sandra never came back home. Knowing Antonio was with Uncle Gerald gave her some small comfort. He would be safe there and Uncle Gerald was a strict disciplinarian. She called Antonio every week for the following six weeks and then her calls to him became less and less frequent. He knew she was not coming back home soon. She had abandoned him and it was something that he would never be able to forgive her for. In time Antonio grew to love the sea just like Pandu and Chenet. Country life was a quiet life, different from the life of the city. Marac had a rhythm all its own; from the rising of the sun, to its setting and everything that happened in between, there was a melody sweet and unspoken, like the waves coming in at high tide. In Marac, Antonio found his place in the world. He would no longer be the mongoose. Instead of hiding guns he would be catching fish.

CHAPTER TWENTY-SEVEN

Not What Was Expected

When Sandra decided to overstay her time, she did not think she would be staying for very long. Three to five years Lindy had told her. Antonio would be twenty or twenty-two and Andrea thirteen, fifteen maybe. She knew perhaps it would be too late for Antonio but she could still catch Andrea in time. It would not be too late to help her become a woman, a lady. She would still have time to teach her the things that Granny Maye tried to teach her. She would explain to her the ways of the world and more importantly the ways of men in the world. She would prevent her from becoming a "clothespin head" girl. The kind of girl who would open her legs for a man on the promises of a few sweet nothings. For the time being though, both her children were safe. Andrea was with Ms. Barbara, Antonio was with Gerald.

It was with this knowledge that she told Lindy she would take the job out in upstate New York. Going there would be a whole new set of buses and trains to learn but she didn't mind. The money was good. Where in Trinidad could she work for as much as eight hundred US dollars a week. She didn't even think that Granny Maye ever worked for that kind of money her entire lifetime. If she held on to that job, she knew she would be able to finish the repairs on the Denton property. She already had in mind exactly what she would do. She wanted to break down the sections of the house that were still wooden and put a proper concrete structure. She would break down the rusting barbed wire fence and put up a solid wall of brick. She would cover that wall with vine. The kind that grew and covered the wall like a carpet. She would make sure there was hot and cold water in every bathroom and then she would landscape the yard, dig up all the uneven segments, level the earth and put down a lawn like the kind that Ms. Barbara had in her yard. She wanted to build a dog kennel in the back for Buster too. She did not know that Buster had died. Sandra had many plans for the house and for her children. She believed in her heart that she had indeed made the best decision for them and their future.

It was this knowledge that kept her going through the long winter months year after year, that knowledge that consoled her the first time the old gentleman she went to work for pinched her on her thighs. Lindy had said he was old and horny but that he was impotent. She had said he could not do anything with what was between his legs. What Lindy had not told her was that he would greet her every morning by exposing what was between his legs to her and contrary to what Lindy had said he was not at all impotent. Mr. Fringer liked to expose himself all the time and every chance he got. He was not senile, neither did he have Alzheimer's Disease. Perhaps if he did, Sandra would have had an excuse to explain away why he did what he did. But there was no excusing Mr. Fringer. His actions were deliberate and his intent clear. He was determined to molest her however and whenever he could. This made it somewhat difficult to care for him since Sandra often felt that she was perpetually in defense mode whenever she had to do anything for him. At first she pleaded with him to desist, then she scolded him, then she shouted at him but it made no difference. When she protested to Lindy regarding the conduct of the bearded old white man, Lindy had told her to ignore him. She had said that if Sandra was lucky and she managed to stay a year with him and keep him happy, he would marry her and she would get her green card. Sandra wanted a green card. She did not know if the colour of the card was actually green but she did know that that card which everyone spoke about so longingly, was her ticket back to Trinidad.

It would be another two months till she could send down her barrel of clothes, shoes and cereal for Andrea and Antonio. She was thrilled to be able to finally send something home. When the barrel was collected, Ms. Barbara riffled through it, opening each bag carefully labelled Andrea and Antonio scribbled in black permanent marker. She helped herself to whatever she wanted or whatever she felt Antonio or Andrea did not need. Over the years Sandra sent many things in those barrels; clothes, shoes, cereal, books, a DVD player, video games, dolls, hair supplies and anything else she imagined her growing children would need. She tried to send a barrel or two once every three months at first but as the years dragged out, the time intervals between the arrival of each barrel grew longer and longer. Her telephone calls like the barrels would diminish in frequency too. At first she called Andrea once a week; then once every two weeks; then once a month; then once in a while. It was the same for Antonio. She tried to encourage him to try to get into a school in Moruga but he loathed the idea of putting on a uniform once more and becoming like his cousin Jeremy. He didn't think he could be that way or study those long hours.

As a fisherman he could be his own man and he imagined that in years to come he could even take a woman to be his woman. His mother could not possibly understand.

In time he would gain the respect of his uncle and his cousins, especially Pandu. Even though there were men in the village who did night farming in marijuana fields for well known drug barons, among other criminal activities, Antonio had decided that there was no profit in living that kind of life and his near brush with death had taught him this. Whenever Sandra sent a barrel, she would call to ask him if he had got this or that or if he had gone up to see Ms. Barbara. She had hoped as well if he returned to Evans Street, he would remember his days of going to school and long to return but she was wrong. It would be five years before he would return to Evans Street. He returned for Ms. Barbara's funeral. His uncle had told him he should. For Andrea's sake he had said.

He returned to find Andrea pregnant with her first child. She had grown quickly into a woman and although Ms. Barbara tried to control her there was very little she could do to contain her teenage rebellion. She became the prey of a man more than ten years her senior, a predator who had a penchant for teenage girls. She did not feel like prey though, nor did she act as though she had been preyed upon. Like Antonio, she was her own little woman. In some sick sort of way she was relieved when Ms. Barbara died. Her dying marked the end of an era that had begun when her mother went to America for six months. And so winter came then summer then autumn then winter again with all the changes of nature that delight. With each season, Sandra grew more and more estranged from her children. Her conversations with them grew increasingly awkward. They had become distant. They were growing up without parents to shield them from the harshness of life or teach them how to navigate the world. Other persons would take on this role, persons other than Sandra and Chester who had brought them into the world.

After five years, Sandra's relationship with Mr. Fringer had not advanced further. She would not have minded having sex with him but he smelt funny, even after he had had a shower. After one year of Mr. Fringer's relentless sexual advances, Sandra found a herbalist in Brooklyn who supplied her with a herb to reduce sexual drive. She did not know that such a herb existed but once she began to use it in his tea, she noticed the results almost instantly. Mr. Fringer could no longer keep his private parts hard and so his daily expositions became fewer until he stopped altogether. A depression came over him and it was this depression that allowed Sandra to take better care of him and come within arm's reach without his incessant fondling of her body. She did not like that he was depressed, but she was glad that he had stopped trying to interfere with her. It made her feel dirty. Perhaps if he were a little more attractive and a little younger, more virile like Mr. Bell was. But he was old and wrinkly with yellow, tobacco-stained teeth. She could never imagine herself lying with him, not in a million years. It would be a long while before she lay with anybody again. She never saw Mr. Bell again and with one day off every two weeks it was almost impossible to meet anyone she could have a meaningful relationship with. She did have one romantic interest though. He was from Grenada. She had met him at one of those West Indian back in time parties that Patsy would invite her to from time to time. He was sixty but looked like fifty. He was not as handsome as Mr. Bell but he was strong and tall with a good build. He did not have a hard time getting her into bed. She was lonely enough and she longed for intimacy with someone. She had grown tired of seeing Mr. Fringer naked, and wanted a different view to erase that image that had been etched in her brain. But the Grenadian was interested in only one thing and since her working schedule did not allow her much free time, their relationship soon fizzled.

She moved into Mr. Fringer's home and only visited Patsy and Lenny off and on. She was glad to be out from under them. She had one day off every two weeks and very often, by the time she arrived in Brooklyn, there was too little time to do much of anything else. Patsy and Lenny had not been happy about her decision to overstay her time.

"Sandra gyul, what stupidness yuh talking? Why yuh will do a thing like that? What about yuh children back home?" Patsy had told her.

"I will go back once ah get meh papers fix. It will be better so. They need things. I will be able to work and send things for them. I cyah work for this kinda money in Trinidad, Patsy. You know that."

"But Sandra yuh children need you. Is YOU they need. They don't need no barrel. Barrel doesn't raise children. When Andrea reach teenage and boys start to harass her for sex, is you she need to watch her and advise her. And look at what happen to Antonio. He drop out of school, he get shoot. That boy is a bright boy he could reach university even. How yuh think he will end up if he stay with Gerald and them? He wouldn't go nowhere. He will stay there and fish maybe, but he could end back up in trouble too. Moruga have drugs too yuh know!"

But Sandra would not budge.

"At least he will learn a trade. He was never going to no university. He not academically inclined." Sandra retorted.

There was very little that Patsy or Lenny could say to her to change her mind and so in a way, they were happy when she decided to take all her belongings to Mr. Fringer's house where she had her own private bedroom and bathroom. To them Sandra had lost her way completely and would eventually live to regret the decisions she had made.

In the ten years she remained in New York, Sandra often thought about going home. She had even discussed the possibility with Lindy who had promised she would get her papers sorted out soon. But soon did not come soon. It was only after Lindy was arrested for running an illegal escort service that Sandra began to pursue her return to Trinidad as a matter of urgency. Lindy had been running an illegal escort service in Brooklyn for at least a decade. When one of her girls was found stabbed to death in a hotel room by a client, Lindy's establishment came into the limelight, as did Lindy who was subsequently arrested and charged with running an illegal prostitution ring using illegal immigrants. The girls working for Lindy's escort service had been held and were being deported and those who had not been held had fled to other states. Lindy's sister Meera, who had renamed herself Mora, hired attorneys to ensure that the state did not have access to all Lindy's business dealings and operations. So while the legal wrangling proceeded, Mora tried to mobilize Lindy's employees and legalize those she could. For those who wanted to stay in America, Mora ensured that they received hush money and purchased tickets for them to leave the state. For those like Sandra who wanted to go home, she obtained new passports with immigration stamps that were dated a month or two prior. This would allow them to return to their respective islands, since according to their new passports they were well within their six months limitation.

Mora was well connected with the underworld. She had tentacles everywhere the same way Lindy did; hers were just a little dirtier than Lindy's.

This was how Sandra came to return to Trinidad. Her return was conditional. In exchange for her passport, she had to forfeit two months' salary. Sandra agreed and signed documents to this end. All she wanted was to set foot in Trinidad. This legal business with Lindy had scared her. She had heard of West Indians being deported and had read of their horrible ordeals at the hands of immigration officers. But more than that she wanted to go home. She had made money in America and saved most of it in Scotiabank in Trinidad, but she was lonely and unhappy. Her children had grown into adulthood and she had missed it all. She was almost fifty when she went back home. Ten years of chasing the American dream had not brought her the happiness she expected it would.

CHAPTER TWENTY-EIGHT

Along Came Papa Chunks

While Antonio was starting a new life for himself as a fisherman in Marac, Andrea was a girl growing up without a mother. Ms. Barbara was making sure she had food to eat and a place to sleep at night but because of Mr. Perkins being so sick all the time, Ms. Barbara was kept busy. Andrea's grades in school gradually fell. So it was no surprise that when Common Entrance came around, she passed for the Sangre Government Secondary School. It was not a bad school but by the time she started Form One, Andrea's hormone levels were at their highest. Being placed in a school with boys who were equally as hormonally charged, only made things worse. It did not help either, that she had grown used to travelling to school in the red band maxi owned and driven by a man called Papa Chunks.

Papa Chunks was a maxi-taxi driver, who had a penchant for young girls in uniform. He had named his maxi the Chunksmobile and had the words painted in bold red on the tinted front windshield. He was in his mid-thirties, handsome looking, mixed up with some of every race that had come to Trinidad, or at least that is what he told the girls he chose. He was very selective in his choosing. He liked girls with small breasts, intelligent girls, shy girls, from difficult home situations; girls who needed refuge. He could sniff out these kind of girls even if they were seated at the back of his maxi-taxi. Those were the girls he could easily woo. He was good at the chase too. He would buy flowers and food for the girl and her friends. Physical contact at first would be minimal. He would speak a lot about respect, marriage, waiting for sex. He would offer to meet the girl's parents knowing full well, in most instances, that it would never occur. He would tease and then gradually, slowly encircle his prey, until she willingly and unreservedly offered herself to him in love. Once he had achieved his objective there would be little else to sustain his interest. As soon as the chase was over, he resumed the hunt all over again with another girl. Maybe even from another school. Papa Chunks saw Andrea one day, with her small breasts and shy smile, hair unprocessed by chemicals—since Ms. Barbara had told her that she did not believe in that hair relaxing thing—and chose her.

He saw an opportunity for a hunt and he hunted. Before long, she was eating out of his hands. She was only fourteen when she met Papa Chunks and she had never had a boyfriend or known a man before he came along. He would encourage her to skip school so they could be together and take her for drives in the Chunksmobile down to Salybia, other times Chaguaramas. Andrea's friends teased her often about her relationship with Papa Chunks. One day while she was waiting on the maxi-taxi stand, a girl from an older class surrounded her with a posse of girls and beat her up badly. The girl accused her of stealing her man and cursed her up. This made Papa Chunks mad. He did not like girls fighting over him. Andrea had taken a good beating too.

She had been pushed to the ground, kicked, slapped and roughed up. When she returned home that day, Ms. Barbara was distraught at the sight of her and went into the school to complain to the principal. The girls were suspended from school for a week and Papa Chunks vowed to protect Andrea from these jealous girls and ensure her safety. He did this by picking her up from school every day and keeping her in the front seat of the maxi-taxi with him.

After drawing her in for a few months, gradually increasing the nature and intensity of his advances, Papa Chunks began a sexual relationship with Andrea. She was just turning fifteen when she got pregnant for him. He told her that a pregnancy would prevent her from getting an education and ruin her future. He did not want to ruin her future he said. He encouraged her to have an abortion and took her to a woman in Port-of-Spain, who gave her some tablets to swallow and pushed some more tablets up inside her. When she started to bleed, the woman dropped her off at the Port-of-Spain General Hospital and left her there. Papa Chunks was not there with her. She had tried to call him on her cell phone but he did not answer.

At the hospital, doctors spoke to her and asked her many questions. She was reluctant to say anything. She felt alone and afraid. She wished Papa Chunks was there with her. He had promised to never leave her alone. She wondered what her mother would think if she knew what was happening to her. She wondered if she would come back to Trinidad if she called her and told her that she needed her. Maybe if she told her how alone she was, how afraid, her mother would come. But Andrea knew better. She had not heard from Sandra in three months. It was unlikely that her unplanned pregnancy and impending abortion would be enough to get her to return home. Her abortion should have been straightforward. She should have aborted easily and quickly but the doctors examined her and told her that her cervix was closed. She was not sure what that meant.

"We will have to do an ultrasound in the morning," the young Indian doctor had said. It was awkward having a man look at her private parts—a man other than Papa Chunks. She wanted to cry but the tears did not come. That night while she lay in the hospital bed, she wondered what the ultrasound would show. She had never had an ultrasound before and she did not know if it would hurt or not. She kept trying to reach Papa Chunks to no avail.

"So where yuh chile-fadder?" a girl in a pink silk night gown asked.

Andrea did not answer and turned away from the girl who looked only a few years older than she was.

"Steups! Well suit yuhself. All ah we in the same boat yuh know. All ah we in the same boat. I doh want dis chile so ah take something. You looking like a school girl so you must be didn't want your chile neither."

Andrea did not think she was in the same boat as this nosy patient. Papa Chunks loved her, he had told her so. He had wanted to marry her but he also wanted her to finish school and that was why he insisted she get the abortion. The doctors had told her that there was a small chance that the baby was still alive inside her. If the baby was still alive, Andrea decided that night that she would talk to Papa Chunks about keeping the baby. She was not keen on finishing school. She would rather have a life with him than continue living with Ms. Barbara. She had concealed her pregnancy from Ms. Barbara who disapproved of her relationship with Papa Chunks. But Ms. Barbara was ageing and all efforts to forbid her from seeing the maxi-taxi driver served only to push her further into his arms. Exasperated, Ms. Barbara made a police report in the hope that the police would arrest, or at least warn Papa Chunks about his conduct. But the police had no time to be bothered with such complaints, not when the nation's murder rate was spiraling out of control.

When the ultrasound results came back confirming pregnancy, Andrea took this as a sign that she was supposed to bring forth the life that was inside her. She was discharged the following day with an appointment for review by the doctors in their clinic. On the day of her discharge she went to visit Papa Chunks at his home in Arouca. She had not heard from him and was worried that perhaps something had happened to him. She had been to his home a few times before but had never stayed long enough to become too familiar. It was mid-afternoon and he was not expecting her, so she was glad when she arrived to find his maxi-taxi parked outside. She pushed open the rusty iron gate that was never locked and knocked hard on the front door. Papa Chunks did not answer.

"Kevin. Kevin." She knocked the door harder as she called him by the name she had grown fond of; his real name. She heard a shuffle of feet. Then the door opened. Papa Chunks emerged with reddened eyes and a sheet around his waist. He was bareback and sweating.

"Andrea. What yuh doing here? I thought yuh was in hospital."

"I was there but they discharge me this morning."

"They take out the baby?"

"No . . . no . . . but . . . Ah could come inside?"

Andrea had just realized that although he had opened the door, he had not opened it fully so that she could enter, neither had he invited her inside.

"Well . . . hmm . . . . not right now. I now getting ready to go back out on the bus route."

"Is alright. Ah will wait for yuh. I could come inside?" She put her hand on the door to push it open and felt some resistance pushing it back. She sensed that he was hesitating but she was not sure why. He seemed to not want her to enter the house.

"Now is not a good time. Yuh know I doesn't like it when yuh come just so."

"Ah sorry. But ah just come out from the hospital and ah wanted to tell yuh that . . . ."

"Kevin. Ah thought you done wid she!"

The female voice shouted. Andrea recognized the voice. Papa Chunks face changed. All at once he was silent, morose. He looked at the person speaking to him from behind the door and she in turn, as if being prompted, pulled the door wide open so that Andrea could see her.

Andrea felt a coldness coming over her. It was the same girl who had put a good cut tail on her some months before. Her name was Keisha. Andrea remembered her face in between the blows that she had dealt. She was wearing only a tee-shirt and Andrea could see that she did not have on a bra. She did not know what to say, think or feel in the awkwardness of that moment which seemed like an eternity. Kevin was sleeping with this girl who had given her a blue and black eye and had shamed her in public, thrown her down into a drain on the Eastern Main Road, cursed her in the foulest language. There she was triumphant inside the home of Papa Chunks, the man she loved, while she stood outside the door, pregnant with his child. Suddenly her desire to discuss anything with him left her. She did not shout or scream or curse. Andrea simply turned and walked away.

"Andrea. Baby . . . ."

She heard the words but they were like painful daggers as she walked out the front yard and walked towards the priority bus route. It did not matter what he had to say to her. He had betrayed her. All that he had told her, all the words he spoke were just lies. Now, she was pregnant with his child, which had not been aborted as he had carefully planned. Suddenly keeping his baby did not seem like a good idea to her.

Papa Chunks did not try to contact Andrea after that. She had tried several times to reach him by phone but he did not answer or return her calls. While in hospital she had met another woman much older than her who was having her fifth threatened miscarriage. Threatened, the woman had told her was the word the doctors used when they were not sure what was going on. She had been to the hospital on previous occasions and spoke with an air of authority. But that air was a thin mask, for the fear and anxiety she felt at the prospect of having a miscarriage for yet another time. The woman was married and wanted desperately to have a child. The following morning, she entered the small bus that came to take patients over to the ultrasound department full of hope. She was hoping that for once, her baby would "keep". Those were the words she used. While most of the women on the bus were hoping that their babies would not "keep". She was hoping that hers would. Andrea remembered how bitterly the woman wept when she realized that her baby did not "keep". She wished she could have given the woman her baby. As she listened to the wailing of this woman, she wondered if one day, she too would be crying that way if her baby did not keep. She thought about the circumstances surrounding her own birth. Her mother had told her that she nearly died, that she too almost did not "keep" and that she had been born premature. Sandra had told her that she was only a little bigger than the size of her hand and that doctors were not sure that she would have survived. Every time Sandra told her that story she would smile and remind Andrea of how strong she was. Andrea did not feel so strong that morning on her way home from the hospital but she believed that the child growing inside her was. He or she was strong; fighting for life despite attempts to eliminate that life. This baby was just like her—strong. She wanted to give him or her a chance to be born, no matter what.

Her decision to bring forth this life at the age of fifteen was not one that was received well by Ms. Barbara. In fact, she often wondered if she had not contributed in some small way to her death by the distressing news of her pregnancy.

"So after all yuh mudder do and after all I do, dis is what you gone and do?" Ms. Barbara had said it almost as if her getting pregnant was some sort of malicious, intentional act.

"Ah didn't mean to Ms. Barbara. It happen all of a sudden."

"Steups! Like you feel I born yesterday ah what. So all of a sudden yuh panty start to drop right. And all of a sudden a magic wand wave and all of a sudden yuh get pregnant. Well gyul I doh know what to tell you. You ain't wake up and see what going on in life? You ain't see what life saying to you chile? Yuh mudder gone. Yuh fadder gone. Yuh brudder gone. Is only me yuh have. And instead yuh study to study yuh book, to get some education in yuh head, yuh decide to run down man and open up yuh leg and now look at. Steups!"

Andrea did not like the way Ms. Barbara was speaking to her. She wanted to tell her that she did not run down Papa Chunks and that it was he who had pursued her. She wanted to say that her mother had not gone and that Sandra was going to send for her to come to America. She wanted to say that her brother had not gone; that he was only living in Moruga with her uncle; that her father had not gone, he was just busy. But instead she said nothing. It was no point arguing with a woman like Ms. Barbara. Ms. Barbara was always right even when she was wrong. Arguing with her only served to make things worse.

When Andrea's school skirt could no longer conceal her pregnant belly, she stopped going to school. The guidance officer had told her that she could still come to class but she was too conscious of herself and too ashamed. Her friends did not help either and the girl she had seen with Papa Chunks the day of her hospital discharge, was determined to taunt her and make her school life miserable. With the help of Ms. Barbara she attended her prenatal clinic and got all her checkups. She was determined to have a healthy child. Barbara was somewhat excited about the child's birth, although she tried not to show it. Perhaps it was because of this excitement, that she did not hear Mr. Perkins rattling cough or observe his worsening diarrhea. By the time she did, he had pneumonia and a fever. There was very little the doctors at the Sangre Grande hospital could do for him. When his body could no longer fight the infection, he gave up his spirit and went peacefully to his maker.

Ms. Barbara's grief consumed her. His death did not come as a surprise but death no matter how expected or anticipated, is not often welcome, especially by those left behind. Ms. Barbara died shortly after Mr. Perkins. She was not that old but according to the neighbours, 'it was the grief that kill her'. It was only when Ms. Barbara died that Andrea realized just how truly alone in the world she was. So when Papa Chunks maxi tout Gregos, began to pay interest in Andrea, with her nine month pregnant belly, it was only a matter of time before she started a relationship with him.

"Ah coulda tell yuh Papa Chunks was no good. Ah coulda show yuh dat form. Yuh was too good for he. Fellas like he does just use and abuse. Take what ah telling you. Yuh plenty better off without him."

Gregos was tall and thin with small eyes. He said he had Chinese in him and that was why his eyes were so small. Andrea was not so sure whether she was better off with Gregos but at least he was there for her. He came to see her in the hospital after the baby was born and he moved into Ms. Barbara's house after she got discharged from the hospital. Andrea had a healthy baby boy. She named him Kwesi. It was the name the woman she had met in the hospital was going to name her son had he lived.

CHAPTER TWENTY-NINE

Home Sweet Home

The morning that Sandra arrived in Piarco International Airport, there was no one waiting to receive her. The airport she met was quite different from the one she had left so many years ago. It was bigger and air-conditioned. As she walked down the corridor towards the baggage claim area, she was filled with excitement. There were brightly coloured advertisements on every wall, with signs bearing taut bodies of beautiful women in carnival costumes welcoming people to Trinidad and Tobago. She returned to Trinidad one April. Spring had begun in New York. Summer was too hot, winter too cold, autumn too depressing, but spring was just right. It was her favourite season and she wished she could have stayed in Brooklyn to see one last spring.

Much in Trinidad had changed both from a political, economic and social perspective. The PNM government had been ousted two years prior when the Prime Minster called a snap general election. The new government had come in on a wave of popularity. It was a coalition government, the first of its kind in Trinidad and Tobago, led by a woman of East

Indian descent who had promised to bring change to the old politics of the former government. Two years into office however, there was much discontent in the land. There were many who still supported the UNC-led coalition government, but many others who felt that the policies and practices of the new administration mirrored to a large extent those of its predecessor. Some analysts believed that this coalition government would suffer a similar fate at the next general elections. There was talk of race by politicians on either side. There were protests by trade unions demanding better wages and communities protesting for better roads, running water and basic amenities. The general population however, lived harmoniously but yearned for a better Trinidad and Tobago; one where crime was not so rampant; where health care and education was on par with those of developed countries and where there was integrity in public life. There were many changes to the city of Port-of-Spain. In fact on her first revisit to the capital, she was overwhelmed by the infrastructural changes that had been made. There was the waterfront development, the National Academy for the Performing Arts and the highway interchange at the intersection of the Churchill Roosevelt and Uriah Butler Highways. But there were some things that had not changed. There were still many vagrants roaming the capital, people still littered the streets and downtown Port-of-Spain still flooded, despite the tall impressive buildings.

Sandra was glad to be home. Her return to Evans Street had been a traumatic one. The Denton house had been vandalized over the years. It did not take long for sprangers in the area to realize that the house had been abandoned. The theft was at first gradual, beginning with items from the shed. Once the shed had been cleared, it was not difficult to gain entry to the house. Buster having died from starvation and malnutrition was not around to raise an alarm and so, the property over the years, became a shell of what it was. By the time Sandra returned, the property was uninhabitable and overrun by rodents. The galvanize sheets that made the roof were all gone. The yard was overgrown with bush and there was not a single piece of furniture or a fixture attached to a wall that vandals had not carted off. It was the home of a vagrant named Skippy who would spend a few nights there, then be gone for months at a time. He was called Skippy because whenever he was high on drugs, he would skip as he walked down the street. Skippy was harmless, although he had been one of the sprangers in the vanguard of the vandalisation of the Denton property.

When Sandra saw the house that she had called home, that had once been a place of happiness and laughter she wept bitterly. In fact she was inconsolable. It was not that she could not fix it over and restore it to a form even better than the way she had left it. That house represented something to her that had been lost when she went to America. That house was her home, it was where her family was. That was where she went when she had no place else to go. Now it was in ruins as if nobody significant had ever lived there. But she had lived there, her mother lived there, her children too. It hurt her terribly to see the house in that way and she was overcome with a sense of guilt. She blamed herself for not trying to repair the house but how could she have? She could not come home and until Mora came on the scene she had no idea whether she would see Trinidad again.

The neighbourhood had changed a lot too. Many of her old neighbours had moved out of the area. The S & S grocery store was still there and some of the older families were still there too. Mr. Singh and his wife were still there. His son had graduated from medical school and was working at the Eric

Williams Medical Sciences Complex. Chester had moved to Chaguanas with his wife and children, Andrea had told her. She didn't care to know. He had never been a good father or husband anyway and meant nothing to her now. Sandra stayed for a while with Andrea and the father of Andrea's second child who had taken up residence in Ms. Barbara's home. Ms. Barbara had no children of her own and had been an only child. There was no one to claim her estate and so Andrea inherited her house by default; she and her new man.

Andrea was now twenty-one years old with a worldly experience similar to that of Sandra's sister Sonya. She was a beautiful woman, with brown even-toned skin and a shapely physique. Although she had two children, she had not allowed her body to become out of shape but there was a certain hardness about her facial features. She smoked cigarettes every day, a habit that Sandra abhorred especially since she would smoke inside the house with the children around. Andrea had not been elated to see her mother return. How could she be? She resented Sandra for every year that she prayed her mother would come back for her and didn't. Yes, over the years, she had shoes and clothes, but it was hard growing up without a mother and although Ms. Barbara did her best to be a substitute mother to her, she never grew to love her the way a daughter should.

Sometimes she would see her father with his children and this would grieve her tremendously. She wanted to matter to him. She wanted him to look at her with love the way he looked at his children with his new common-law wife. He was a father after all. She wondered why he did not love her, or care about what happened to her. She felt abandoned by everyone, even Antonio. She had begged him often to come visit her but he never did. It was only when Ms. Barbara died that he had come to see her. She was pregnant then with her first child Kwesi. She wanted him to come back to Sangre Grande but he seemed settled and happy in Moruga. Soon after Ms. Barbara's funeral, Kwesi was born. He was a difficult baby and cried often. Being a mother was not as enjoyable as the women in the prenatal clinic had told her it would be. Her freedom to move and do as she pleased ended. Sandra returned shortly after the birth of her second child and with her return Andrea got a new lease on life. Often she left Sandra to babysit while she went out to party. She had a lot of partying to make up for and Sandra owed her this much for all the times she had not been around.

Sandra loved her grandchildren but there was very little she could say to Andrea without an argument ensuing.

"I was like you, yuh know, Andrea. I was just like you. But life is not all about party and drinking and man. At some point you will have to settle down and see about your children. When you and Tony was small I had to give up plenty things, you know. You think I didn't want to party too but when you have kids it's a different story." Sandra had said this to her one night when she had outfitted herself in a fluorescent orange cat-suit to go to a party in a nearby nightclub.

"You could tell me anything! You cyah tell me nothing. Where yuh was all dis time? You leave me when I was ten years old with Ms. Barbara and yuh never look back. Yuh think I didn't need meh mudder? Yuh think it was easy? I ketch my tail. I ain't get half of what yuh was sending in dem barrels cause Ms. Barbara used to tief what she want for she self and sell out half. Steups! You cyah talk to me about mothering. You wasn't no good mudder at all. What kinda mudder does do what you do me and Tony!"

Andrea said this and things in a similar vein to Sandra often enough. She did not say them in an emotional way.

She was devoid of emotion. She had shed too many tears for Sandra. Sandra was dead to her.

Antonio however was not as belligerent. He was now twenty-six years old and had taken a woman who had given him a son. He named his son Anthony after himself. He had become a respected young man in Marac and had become a part of his uncle's family. When he met the woman he would take as his common-law wife, he took the little money he had saved and bought some wood and galvanize. With the help of Pandu and Chenet he built a shack for them to live in not far from the coastline. Eventually he would own his own boat and nets and stop working for his uncle. He never went back to school despite Leelawatee's encouragement and Sandra's pleading. His life was the sea and the sea was his life. When Jeremy won a national scholarship to go to university, Leelawatee and Gerald were overjoyed. They threw a big party in their backyard with endless fry fish, curry duck and roti. There were drinks galore too. Jeremy would be the first person in the Denton family to go to medical school. He had erased Leelawatee's shame.

When Sandra returned, she tried to get in touch with Antonio. She begged him to come see her. He promised he would but he was too busy with the demands of work and family to make the long journey up to Sangre Grande. After one month in Trinidad with Andrea, Sandra decided to hire a car to take her to Marac. She had not seen her son in years and she longed to see him very much.

She arrived in the tiny sea village of Marac after a long drive on almost impassable roads. She was exhausted and was glad to be received by Leelawatee and Gerald.

"Oh gosh, sis. Is how long I ain't see you for? Is years ent? How much years bout six ent?"

"Nah nah, is more than that."

They embraced each other. Uncle Gerald smelt of fish.

"Thanks so much for looking out for Antonio over these years eh? I real appreciate it."

"Tony is a big man yuh know. He is a good fella. As he get this little wife and child now he settle down even more. And how Andrea going? Ah hear she have baby and thing?"

"Yes she have two. A boy and a girl. She working nights now in a casino down in Valsayn."

Sandra was eager to see Antonio and so after getting the updates about family members from her brother, inquired as to whether Gerald could take her to see where he lived. Gerald obliged, although he suggested that perhaps because of the time of the day, Tony might not be home. It was about three in the afternoon and Gerald knew that Tony liked to go out to sea around that time. When they arrived at Antonio's shack Sandra was horrified by the size of the one-room structure.

"Is here my son living?" she remarked.

"Yes and yuh know he build it himself!" Gerald said proudly.

The shack was exactly that—a shack. There was an outdoor smaller shed adjacent to it and this Sandra assumed to be the outhouse. There was a tiny lock on the one door that led into it and the roof was made of rusty galvanize. The smell of the sea and its salty winds enveloped her. Sandra could hear the crashing of the waves on the seashore. The sound soothed her spirit which was aggrieved to see Antonio living in a structure that was half the size of his room on Evans Street.

"Like he not here now. You want to wait and check him later?"

"Well, I guess I don't have too much choice really."

As they began to walk out of the narrow dirt track that had led to Antonio's humble abode, sounds of laughter could be heard.

"That laugh sounding like my child own," Sandra said immediately.

"A mother never forgets."

She was right. As she turned the dirt track corner, a tall young man accompanied by a woman and child approached. Sandra did not know how to feel at that instant. She was nervous. She had not seen her son in so many years. Perhaps like Andrea he too was resentful of her.

Gerald sensing her anxiety, called out in a loud voice to his nephew.

"Tony boy, look yuh mudder reach all de way down Marac to see yuh, boy. Ent ah tell yuh she woulda come down."

Antonio's face changed. His heart raced. Here was his mother standing before him. The mother he had loved and hated and loved over the years was a few feet away from him. How often he had wished that she were just a few feet away. He could see her plainly now standing there in a pair of khaki pants and a sleeveless yellow shirt that covered her hips. She had aged. He walked right up to her and embraced her tightly. He stood there on that track and held his mother. As the tears rolled down his face he remembered all the nights he had cried for her and prayed that he would see her again. He feared that he never would have. Sandra too, overwhelmed with emotion sobbed loudly. She could feel his strong arms around her. He was her son, her only son and she was glad that unlike Andrea, he at least seemed happy to see her. But what Sandra would soon discover was that the damage had already been done; and the joy Antonio felt on seeing his mother again would not be enough to erase ten years of hurt and resentment.

Chapter Thirty

Is America She Gone?

It would be a whole year before Sandra would see Antonio again. During her visit to Marac she had spoken to him about many things. She wanted to know what his plans were and if he would stay in Marac. She had tried to convince him to come back to the house on Evans Street. She said she had money that he could use to build it back. She had given him five hundred US dollars on that visit in the hope that he would come to visit her.

"The house gone right down, Antonio. I want to fix it but I can't do it myself. I am not as young as I was before. You could come up there and fix up the place. You have a young wife. You should put her in a proper place."

"We good just here. What I will do if I go back there. I have a family now. I have to put food on the table for them."

But Sandra pressed him further.

"Tony boy, you could do better than this. You could do much better than this." It was the tone in her voice when she said this that upset him.

"Better than what, Mommy? Better than being a fisherman. You have any idea what I coulda be? Well leh me tell yuh. I coulda be dead. Dead and cold jus like that. Ah wonder if yuh woulda come back to Trinidad for my funeral? Ah wonder. Yuh mighta do me just like Granny eh?"

She could see the look of hurt in his eyes as he spoke.

"You don't understand how it was, Antonio. It wasn't easy. You think I didn't want to come back home? You think I didn't want to see you all? Is you and Andrea I was studying why I stay up there so long. You don't think I wanted to come home? It was me alone. Your father never give me nothing to help me mind you all. I wanted to give you something better, plenty better than what I got. I wanted you to stay in school and get an education not end up doing this kinda work that don't require no brain. It don't require no brain to fish, Tony. Where you will go in life with fishing?"

Antonio did not mean to raise his voice at his mother. He did not mean to curse her, but it angered him that she did not seem to comprehend how her departure from his life had changed its entire course.

"At least I have a life to go somewhere with. When dem fellas shoot me where yuh was eh mommy? Tell me where yuh was? I was in hospital for days. Yuh never call, yuh never come. Is meh life I was trying to save how I reach down here by Uncle Gerald. If Uncle Gerald didn't take me in, yuh know where I woulda end up? I was hanging with big men, dangerous men; men dat does kill other men easy, easy, just so. Yuh doh think dat bullet coulda kill me dead! I coulda dead! De gyul dat was with me, I watch she drop down and dead. It had blood all about. When I reach in hospital I nearly dead. I pass out. I didn't even know yuh number to call yuh. I was dere by mehself and I didn't have nobody. Nobody to bring meh a little soup self. I coulda end up dead like Martin,

Mommy. What yuh woulda do then? Now you want to tell me bout what I doing here! Ah working dat is what ah doing! I working hard every day and I taking care of meh family. And yuh see dat boy dere, I not going to leave him to go nowhere. Dat is my child. I not going to leave him for nobody else to mind. You is *my* mother and yuh leave me just so. Yuh leave me, Mommy. You leave me to fend for mehself. Meh father had leave we long time, Mommy but is YOU who was to stay with we. We was still small, Mommy. I was just a boy, Mommy. I was just a boy. You just went and yuh leave me, Mommy. How you coulda leave me just so? I did need yuh. I did need yuh, Mommy . . . ." Antonio's voice began to tremble as he spoke. He was fighting hard to hold back the tears. He was sitting on Uncle Gerald's porch in a wicker rocking chair when he began to speak but now he stood up, almost as if standing would help him to keep calm.

"Ah sorry, Tony. Ah so sorry."

"I sorry too, Mommy. I sorry I didn't just forget bout you. Cause you is not no kinda mother at all. I ain't see you in ten years and now you coming to tell me bout what I coulda be doing with my brain? I coulda be dead. I coulda dead."

Sandra did not know what to say. How could she make him understand that everything she had done was for him? How could she make him know that she loved him more than life itself—he and Andrea, both. All the barrels she had sent, all the clothes he never got—it was all for him, for them; so that they would have the things that she didn't have as a child growing up.

"Look, bes I go yes. Bes I go."

"Wait, Tony." Her eyes pleaded with him as she rose from the chair in which she had been sitting.

"Wait for what Mommy. More lies, more promises, more excuses. Is too late now Moms. Marac is my home. Dis is my family. I not going from here. I happy here. I happy ketching fish. If yuh wanted me to be something different yuh shoulda stick around. Maybe if you or Daddy was helping me I woulda be something better but I happy being what I is. Cause what I is is better than what I coulda be and at least I ain't dead."

Sandra tried to embrace her son as he turned to leave but he shrugged her off. The son who as a child loved to embrace her when she came home from a hard day's work, rejected her affection. Somehow his rejection of her hurt more than Andrea's. Maybe because she had felt less guilty about leaving Andrea in Ms. Barbara's care. Antonio would never try to visit her after that exchange. The drive back home to Evans Street that night was long and difficult, not only because there were no street lights on many of the roads leading out of Moruga but the roads were bad and full of potholes. Sandra left Marac with a heavy heart and would never return there again.

For months after, Sandra toyed with the idea of fixing over the Denton property. She got estimates from contractors that varied in amounts but she was apprehensive about taking on the project without the help of a man. Antonio would not help her and Andrea was too caught up with her man to have the vision to see the possibilities. She needed to move though. Living with Andrea was difficult. There was never any quiet. The radio was always on, blaring some kind of loud music she couldn't comprehend. The children were always crying and Andrea was always shouting at them. Not to mention the smoking. Everything smelt of cigarette smoke. The scent had seeped into Ms. Barbara's living room upholstery and everything that was not solid. Sandra wondered how Ms.

Barbara would have felt about the way things had turned out. She imagined that she would be turning in her grave to see her yard littered with cigarette butts.

Sandra was grateful to Ms. Barbara for taking care of Andrea. She had sent her many money orders. She had asked her to open bank accounts for Andrea and Antonio so that they could have something when they got older. Ms. Barbara never did. She loved money and she deposited each money order Sandra sent into her own bank account. It was sad that she had done this instead of giving it to the poor or using it to help Andrea and Antonio, because seven years after her death all that she had saved would belong to the Government of Trinidad and Tobago and end up in the nation's treasury. Sandra had returned to Trinidad in the hope of building a home for her family. She had the money to do it now but she knew her children would not come to live with her. After six months of living with Andrea and receiving steady abuse from her, Sandra decided to find an apartment to rent. She put the Denton property up for sale and hoped that she could use the money from the sale of the land, together with what she had saved over the years, to buy herself an apartment in a gated community in Tunapuna.

As much as Andrea despised her, she was grateful for the help Sandra gave her with the children. Sandra loved her grandchildren. They seemed to be the only ones who were always happy to have her around. After she moved, Andrea would call her often and ask her to keep them for a weekend or a day. Sandra did not mind. She enjoyed combing their hair and taking them for walks. Her relationship with Andrea, though strained, had relaxed into an awkward sort of unspoken agreement. Sandra could never regain her affection as a daughter but she could compensate for her actions by helping Andrea take care of her own children. This is what she did.

She eventually bought an apartment off the Eastern Main Road in Tunapuna and got a job as a caregiver with the Ministry of Social Development. The job kept her busy. She didn't earn much but she was in her mid-forties and wanted to be employed. She was done with America. It had not proved to be the paradise people had made it out to be. New York was the 'Big Apple' but it was rotten to the core as far as she was concerned. Sandra settled into a routine sort of life in Tunapuna. It was not the one she had imagined for herself but in time she made new friends, reconnected with old ones and joined the nearby Church of God Pentecostal Church where she became an active member. She prayed for healing for herself and her children, especially Andrea who it seemed was doomed to repeat the same mistakes she had made.

They didn't speak for very long even when they spoke, but one Saturday night when Andrea came to pick up her two children, now five and three years-old respectively, she asked to speak with Sandra about her time in America.

"So Moms, when you went up there, how much money yuh was making so?"

"I wasn't making no set of money really. When I went up the first six months I didn't really make nothing at all."

"But I mean eventually yuh make some money right?"

"Why you asking me all this?"

Andrea looked away hesitantly.

"Ah met a lady today who tell me she could hook me up with a six months job in America. She say is good money and she only charging me five hundred TT dollars. She say ah could get a job working for five hundred US dollars a week. That is true?"

Sandra was deeply disturbed.

"Listen, they did tell me that too. But it have plenty other things they doesn't tell you about that place they call America.

Everybody doesn't go there and get rich. Look, I thought I woulda have endless money when I come back. And look, I couldn even buy this house cash without selling the place on Evans Street. Is not what people say it is. Things different up there, Andrea. Take what I telling you. You have two small children. Stay and mind your children."

"I fed up ah dis job what I doing, Moms. Is one setta work and dey paying yuh next to nothing and if yuh call in sick any day yuh cyah even get pay for that."

"I know, chile. Life not easy. It not easy as a single mother out here. And you start off young. You didn't get a chance to finish school and get a good education so you could do some other kinda bigger work than what you doing now, but take what I telling you, America not easy. It not easy at all and is not for everybody."

"But look you went up and look you didn't do so bad for yuhself. I feel I could go up there and make a decent change for mehself. Is just to find somebody to leave the children with."

"Don't leave your children to go up in that place, Andrea. I know what I'm telling you. It have nothing up there for you. You could stay here and go back to school. Look it have night school and so much of courses you could take now. So much government programmes to help you learn. Better you do that, Andrea. This lady who telling you about this job she have. She tell you what kind of work you have to do? She tell you what contract you have to sign? Don't do it, Andrea. You too young for that place and your children too young for that place. Look at me. I leave allyuh when you was ten and Tony was sixteen. You all pass through so much of things in life and I wasn't here to help you make better choices. Maybe if I was here you and Antonio would be in university all now. I don't know. All I know is that if I had to do it all over again I woulda never set foot in that place. I was just lucky to get out how I got out but take what I'm telling you, don't study that woman with that job talk."

Sandra could see the look in Andrea's eyes. She knew Andrea would not let the idea rest. The following day Andrea returned and pummeled her with questions about her time in Brooklyn and about how much she was able to save. Sandra could sense that she was becoming more and more frustrated with her job and was afraid that the woman's job offer would be too good to refuse. Either way, she expected Andrea to tell her if she decided to leave. Sandra had become a big part of her grandchildren's lives but she did not wish for them to become her full time responsibility.

One night, two weeks after that discussion, when Andrea came to collect Kwesi and Tishani, she would speak to Sandra one last time on the subject.

"Ah really thinking bout going to America, Moms. Ah have a friend who just went up there. She say it real nice. You could get everything yuh want cheap, cheap and she say is best to come up when yuh young so yuh could work and thing."

"Your friend have children?"

"No but she say how . . ."

"You have children, Andrea. You can't leave your children behind. Not for six months, not for no time at all. By the time you gone and come back, you know how much could happen. A mother is not supposed to leave her children for nobody to mind . . . excepting is the father, but even then. It have things only a mother could do for a child. Love only a mother could show."

"So why you leave we then, Moms. You leave me and Tony and you went up. So it was alright for you to go but is not alright for me?"

"No, baby is not that. You could make it here. I know what I telling you. Trinidad not so bad as all that that you cannot make a life for yourself here. A good life, a decent life."

"If it was so, why you went then? If it was so easy to make a good life why you went America?"

There was a moment of silence. In that silence, Sandra heard the crickets chirping in the yard loudly. She wished she could recruit them to argue her case. She wanted Andrea to see that life in America was full of snares and snakes. She thought of all her experiences with Patsy and Lenny, Ms. Goodridge, Mr. Bell, Lindy, Mr. Fringer. She reflected on how much despair she had felt after Lindy's arrest when she imagined that she would be stuck in the US indefinitely. She remembered how relieved she was when Mora contacted her and arranged to send her home. Now her only daughter was getting ready to make the same mistake she had made and she felt powerless to stop her.

"Think about it, Andrea. Don't rush and go. You have some time. Think about it. Don't believe everything you hear. Is not as this woman saying it is."

"I will think about it, Moms. Ah wouldn go just so hurry, hurry."

"You promise me?"

"Yeah man. Ah will think about it."

That night Sandra did not sleep soundly. There was something about Andrea's tone that unsettled her. She did not believe her. She did not believe she would think about it. She knew Andrea had already made up her mind and was determined to go. What she did not anticipate was the way in which Andrea would leave.

In the days before Andrea's sudden departure, Sandra reflected on Antonio and the man he had become. As hurt as she was by his rejection of her offer to fix the Denton property, she realized that he was happy. Money was not everything. With every murder she read of in the daily newspapers, she began to see that Antonio really was lucky to be alive. Most of the killings reported were gang related and the men, mostly black, were usually under the age of thirty. Antonio was not living the life she had hoped he would but at least he was alive. He had found his place in the world as a fisherman. He had given her a grandson and she decided that in the coming year, she would try to establish a better relationship with him.

On the morning of Andrea's departure there was nothing different in her routine, nothing to suggest what she had planned. She dropped off the children on her way to work, as she usually did when she went to work the night shift but the following morning she did not return for them. Sandra called her cell phone but the calls went straight to voice mail. Andrea's boyfriend had not seen her either. A police report was made. Andrea was considered a missing person. Sandra had her suspicions. It was only when she went to check the mail two days later, that her worst fears were confirmed. There in the mailbox was a letter from Andrea, scribbled on a page that was neatly stapled together. When Sandra opened the letter, she could barely withhold the tears. It read:

Dear Moms,

I think about all what you said and I think I want to go to America anyway. I feel I will get a good break up there and I know that I will be able to make money. I going to work for a lady in

Brooklyn. Please take care of Tishani and Kwesi for me till I come back. I not going to stay more than six months. I just going to work for six months and come back so don't worry. I am glad you here to help me take care of them. It real hard for me alone and I real struggling with that small pay job. Thanks Moms. I real glad for the help out. I will call you when I reach up.

Love
Andrea

Sandra held on to that letter for hours, reading it over and over again. She lay it under her pillow that night and every night for the next six months. In six months, Kwesi and Tishani had grown but it was a challenge caring for two small children at that age. Tishani's father Gregos visited intermittently and on the odd occasion gave Sandra one hundred dollars. It was not enough to take care of one child but it was better than what she got from Kwesi's father which was nothing at all. Sandra often wondered if the agony she felt when Andrea left was similar to what Maye had experienced when she had left that fateful summer. Eight months later when Andrea called to say that she had got a better job making more money, Sandra knew that her grandchildren would be with her for much longer than she anticipated.

They missed their mother but they were still very young. On afternoons, she would take them for a walk in a nearby park. On one such occasion, she encountered her old neighbour from Evans Street, Ms. Janice. She had not seen her in a long time. The two embraced and Sandra proudly showed her grandchildren to her old neighbour.

"So where their mother is? She still up on Evans Street."
"No Janice, girl," she replied sadly.
"Is America she gone. Is America she gone."

THE END

Glossary Of Terms

Word	*Meaning*
Ah	I, of, a - depending on the usage. E.g. Ah get ah hand ah fig (I got a hand of fig)
Ain't	Is not, isn't it so?, am not
Allyuh	All of you
AIDS	Acquired Immune Deficiency Syndrome
BIG C	Cancer
Begging a lodging	Term used to refer to a person who is being accommodated in someone else's home for an extended period of time
Betterment	Better quality of life, improvement
Bling	Wear flashy jewellery
Braps	All of a sudden
Baddam	Just like that, all of a sudden
Buss a lime	The act of hanging out and having fun with friends
Bounce	Greeting which involves the bouncing of closed fists
Breaking Biche	Skipping school

Cattle horn never too heavy	Responsibility, usually that of parenting is never too great
Chile	Child
Chile-mudder	Mother of a child
Chile-fadder	Father of a child
Chinee	Chinese person or anyone with mixed Chinese heritage
Coo Coo	Popular dish made with cornmeal and ochroes
Cut Arse	Beating up
Creole	Term used to describe people of African, European, or mixed Afro-European descent. Usage varies
Cyah	Cannot
Deep- Freeze	Another word for freezer
Doh dig ah horrors	Never mind that/Not to worry
Dong	Down
De mark buss	Expression used when something that was previously hidden becomes discovered
Doubles	Popular East Indian delicacy made with curried chick peas and commonly eaten at any time of day
Dougla	Person of mixed East Indian and African heritage
Dred	Another term for friend
Dutty	Dirty
Eh	Huh or What? Used at the end of a threat or request. May also be used in place of ent

Fire the work (wuk)	To quit a job
Fix your face	Change your facial expression
Ghetto-ish	Of or belonging to the ghetto
Handle yuh stories	Take care of business
Have sugar	Expression used to describe diabetes
Have pressure	Expression used to describe hypertension
Hot my head	To allow oneself to become agitated or upset
Horse	Liming partner
INS	United States Immigration and Naturalization Service
Jus	Just
JFK	John F. Kennedy
Ketch	Catch
Ketch tail	To see experience difficulty in life, usually financial in nature
Knock-knee	A person with a valgus deformity of the lower limbs
Kwéyol	Haitian dialect
Kokene	Cocaine
Lime	To hang out with friends
Mt. Hope	Word used to refer to the Eric Williams Medical Sciences Complex located in Mt. Hope Trinidad
Mama Man	Man who is too dependent on his mother
Mash	Get Away (term used to chase dogs away)
Money Kong	Person who is always concerned about money making

NALIS	National Library and Information System Authority of Trinidad and Tobago
Neck pop	Murder
Nuttin	Nothing
Normel	Normal
Obeah	Caribbean version of witchcraft with roots in African sorcery and rites
Pass water	Pass urine
Playing whé	Card game which was previously illegal, now legalized by the National Lotteries Control Board
Pardner	Partner
Pelau	Popular rice dish made with pigeon peas and chicken or beef
Picong	Teasing between friends
Piper	Term used to describe a drug addict
Pong	Pound
Playing de arse	Behaving silly, clowning around
Riding Out	Leaving a place, usually after a party
Soucouyant	Character in Trinidad folklore who turns into a vampiric fireball at night. Term used to refer to persons who are deemed parasitic, either by their behaviour or actions
Obeah woman –	Woman who deals in obeah
Small in de dance	An insignificant player
Sorf	Soft
Shot call	Order of a hit/murder by a gang member
Show a form	To explain something to someone or to enlighten someone

Steups	Noise made when one sucks one's teeth. Used as an expression of anger, disappointment or unhappiness
Sweet Talk	Use charming words to win a woman's heart
Spranger	Person who is known to be a substance abuse and who sells stolen goods to obtain money for drugs
Tout	Person who solicits business or employment in a persistent and annoying manner
Tomorrow please God	Local expression to mean God's willing
Tief	Thief (noun) or Steal (verb)
Tie up	Confused or the act of confusing someone
Whaz de scene	What's up?
Went off	To become crazy or insane
Whappen	What happen?
Whey	Where or that, depending on the usage
Working PH	The use of a privately owned vehicle car as a taxi for hire. This is commonly practised in Trinidad and Tobago
Yampee	Term used to describe the mucus that appears around the corners of the eyes after sleep

About the Author

Beverley-Ann Scott is a medical doctor and author of the novel *The Stolen Cascadura*, which was selected by the Trinidad and Tobago National Library and Information System Authority (NALIS), for the 2012 One Book One CommunityProject.

Dr. Scott holds a BSc in Information Systems and Management from the University of London and a Doctor of Medicine degree from Our Lady of Fatima University, Manila, Philippines.

She spent many years in the business and banking sector before deciding to pursue a career in medicine. She is one of the youngest authors of West Indian fiction from the island of Trinidad and Tobago where she currently lives and works.